Every Rule UNDONE

a novel by

Nancy SM Waldman

Book Cover Art and Design by Nancy SM Waldman | Additional image credits: Moroccan door, https ://unsplash.com/@jmagrippison, Unsplash | Interior illustrations by Nancy SM Waldman

First edition 2024 | Every Rule Undone, Book 1 - The Last Magic City, By and By Press, Nancy SM Waldman, https://nancysmwaldman.com

ISBN 978-1-7776202-4-0 (print)

ISBN 978-1-7776202-5-7 (ebook)

to

Cadi, Jonah, Benny, Zakai

Contents

Prologue — 1

Part One: City

1. Bad Advantages — 7
2. A Dirty Little Game — 13
3. Warm Hands, Cold Heart — 17
4. Pills and Pies — 23
5. Cross-Cursed — 33
6. To What End? — 43
7. Situated — 49
8. Casting Doubts — 59
9. A Bit of Talent — 71
10. Heavy Loads — 87
11. The Wardrobe — 95
12. Undone — 109
13. Found and Lost — 119
14. The Witch's Lair — 127
15. A New Name — 135

Part Two: Country

16. Womb — 147

17. Encounters   155

18. Caught   165

19. End Game   175

20. The Two Most Unbelievable Things   185

Part Three: Cathedral

21. Turning and Returning   199

22. Hot Water   211

23. Unguarded   221

24. The Best Time for Romance   229

25. The Connection   241

26. Hand and Glove   253

27. Helpers   263

28. A Fantasy Come True   269

29. Consequences   277

30. Tolled   289

31. The Lockbox   297

32. Adapting to Change   311

33. Accountable   319

Epilogue   329

Acknowledgements   331

About the Author   333

Also By & Coming Soon   335

MARIPESA
COLVARA
Gerland & Ness
NOPTVA
Country House
LUFTVA
Village
The Farm
The Wardrobe
The Villa
GEN
The Tapinak
The Komeh
The Round House
BESIN
PURAPLES
KRUIK
The Pavillion

PROLOGUE

AFTER A BUSY DAY of cleaning for the family, thirteen-year-old Aza Gen walked through pleasing late-afternoon sunshine. She was on her way to the library on the second-floor mezzanine and the light angled dramatically from the wall of clerestory windows in the Komeh's grand entrance hall below.

Aza had many unfulfilled wishes: attention from her father, answers to all her questions about life in Maripesa, companionship—*at least one real friend, please.* For the moment, however, her needs were simpler. She wanted several uninterrupted hours with no more curses to clean for the rest of the day.

She heard voices, looked over her shoulder, and saw Mam Sior's eldest sons come up the wide staircase and turn in her direction. Backing against the paneled wainscoting to let them pass, she idly searched for faces in the veined marble beneath her feet. Sunlight warmed the toes of her slippers that peeked out from under a robin's-egg blue skirt.

Then Hasip, the younger brother, stopped and turned toward her.

Bats and rats! More work?

"Good day, Gen."

Aza gaped.

He placed a hand on the wall next to her and leaned in. "It's time we got to know each other. We *have* lived in the same house all these years." His thumb touched her upper arm.

On purpose?

"Eww," his older brother Ferjival said in a high-pitched voice, which then deepened as he continued. "What the *Maripes* are you doing? She's a servant. Get away from her."

"After all, Aza, you are growing up."

This was unprecedented. She had been the official Gen Clan cleaner of curses here in the headquarters and home of the Puraples Clan since she was eight. Ferjival and Hasip, her elders by five or six years, had always been in the house, too. But they only spoke to her when they wanted some Kruik-cursed object cleaned. She had no clue how to respond—or if she should.

Doors opened at the end of the hall to Aza's right. Mam Sior Puraples, ruler of the city-state of Maripesa, filled the double doorway with her wide, black, floor-length skirt, overweight frame and overbearing presence. Taking in the scene, she strode forward as Hasip pulled back.

In an intense whisper that seemed to Aza to hold more force than all Sior's usual bellowing, the matriarch said to her son, "This young woman is, as all of our household help, unavailable to you!" She sent a baleful glance toward Ferjival to include him in this statement as well. Swiveling her head back to Hasip, Sior said, "Tell me why."

Hasip gave a tiny nod. A bead of sweat ran down his temple into his patchy sideburn. "Clans do not mix, uh, intimately, on pain of death."

"Because?"

"It...it might, uh, *would* dilute each clan's Talent. And...or, well, mingle them."

"And that would..."

"Undermine our rightful place in Maripesian society."

"Do not ever approach her in this way again. Is that clear?"

"Yes, Mother. Perfectly." He nodded, skirted around her, and walked toward the council chambers. Ferjival, smirking audibly, followed.

Aza kept her eyes on the floor, aware of Sior's bulk blocking her sunshine, her toes growing cold.

"Stay away from my boys. All of them. And anyone else who isn't...of your clan."

Aza pulled at her skirt and curtseyed. "Yes, Mam."

After Sior disappeared behind closed doors, Aza remained against the wall. Of course people were put to death for breeding outside their clans, but that fact had never impinged on *her* life. Even more: Hasip noticed her? She could still feel the spot on her upper arm where his thumb had been. An involuntary movement somewhere between a shiver and a shudder went down her spine even though the sun shone on her once again.

Aza's wish for a calm few hours in the library wasn't going to happen. Her insides felt like jelly and her heart still thumped. She walked down the servants' hallway to an anteroom off the council chambers. The small space held a spindly chair, a sideboard for serving dishes, and a Gen cleaning table.

Aza lightly tamped down her skirt with gloved hands to keep her petticoats from rustling, bent at the hips and peeked through the ornate iron keyhole.

Mam Sior, at the head of the long table, leaned forward on her elbows. A sharp ray of sun reached the back of her head, its hard edge contrasting with and lighting up Sior's fluffy top-knot of greying hair.

Like a tarnished halo.

Aza felt at home in this room. Her breathing calmed.

In the council chambers, Ferjival and Hasip bickered over some detail of a Kruik Clan curse the council had been discussing before Aza arrived. Mam Sior cut in. "Enough! The Kruks have pushed me too far. If we let them befoul a seed, soon the whole orchard will rot."

Mam Sior used the common slur "Kruk" for the Kruik Clan; the Puraples were often referred to as the "Purples." Aza knew that neither clan appreciated the nicknames. They were considered rude. She also knew the Puraples matriarch wasn't talking about growing fruit. *Though a Kruik-cursed orchard would be a ruin. I'd hate to be charged with that cleanup.*

"Council Leader Droht, I want you to hit Kruik Leader Rodjo and—oh, I don't care—one of their other senior councilmen." She tapped a fingernail on the table, thinking. "Use lichlia. Time it for late night to increase the chance of prolonged discomfort. Make sure they know it's a present from me."

The Puraples' lichlia—one of various malady curses in their arsenal—produced an almost immediate painful, spreading rash lasting until the unlucky target could get to a Besin Clan healer for treatment.

Aza didn't know the soon-to-be uncomfortable Rodjo, or any other Kruik. She only knew their curses. They were not the maladies of the Puraples, but flux curses that manifested a variety of disgusting, disabling, gooey, sticky, sometimes smelly, spreading substances.

Their women wear pants, not skirts. Does that mean they are more like men? Are the Kruik people spoiled and rude like the Puraples I live with? Do they curse so often because they are awful or because the Puraples deserve to be cursed? Or both?

There were too many holes in what library books, news pages, and snippets of spied information could tell her. She wanted to take all the bits of overheard conversations and scraps of written notes she "happened" to find and piece them into an overview of where and how everything and everyone fit here in Maripesa. She wanted to understand.

Aza's belly heaved suddenly and seemed to flip-flop. Apparently, she hadn't recovered from what happened with Hasip after all. Dizziness followed. She put a hand on the door and breathed deeply, willing the discomfort to pass.

When it did, Aza could see from two perspectives.

She still saw Mam Sior through the keyhole, but she could also see herself in profile looking through it. This new envisioner leaned in close and Aza marveled at how transparently amber her brown iris appeared with light pouring into it.

She stood up abruptly, jerking her head around.

And: She saw herself doing this.

What is happening?

When it was clear that nothing stranger could possibly happen, something did: this other, invisible self, passed through the wall into the council chambers. Aza—no longer peeking through the keyhole—could see the whole room. At the far end, elderly Councilman Kalijal was saying, "...buying as much wheat as we can..." Other council members nodded or commented.

With another wave of nausea, Aza's viewpoint returned to normal.

A headache blossomed above her left eye and she felt sticky, hot moisture on her inner thigh.

Her first menses.

Part One

City

I

BAD ADVANTAGES

Thirteen Years Later

THE SUMMONING BELL RANG for Mam Sior's office.

"Spellfire! Again?" Aza said. "How many is that today?"

She and Maleka Gen were working in the cleaning room tucked between offices on the mezzanine level, trying to catch up with the day's onslaught of Kruik curses. A substantial pile of cleaned objects, waiting to be returned to their owners, sat on the floor.

"I've lost count," Maleka said. She sighed as she worked on a befouled lady's handbag. "The beading on this thing is making me crazy. I'm going to run out of fresh niltehs if it doesn't stop soon. Is it always like this on an execution day?"

"No. It's because one of the condemned is a Kruik."

"O-oh. I can see they are definitely not happy about that."

Maleka Gen had been working at the Komeh for three years now and Aza thanked *Maripes* for her several times a day, every day.

"Now, Aza!" Mam Sior shouted down the hallway, since the bell hadn't gotten her there fast enough.

Maleka crossed her large, hazel eyes and grimaced so comically that Aza laughed out loud before rushing to the matriarch's office.

Sior was back at her desk. Without looking up, she said, "This," indicating, with a flip of her wrist, what might be a map lying on the desk, though it was impossible to be sure because it teemed with renyers.

Renyers were the most common of the Kruik flux curses. They were tiny, grey, elongated ovals that looked like bugs. This insect illusion was reinforced by rapid multiplication which caused them to shift and move. Visually creepy, but not "alive," they would continue to spread on the cursed target—making it disgusting and unusable—until Gen magic removed every one.

Aza, her hands always covered by thin, supple leather while working, picked it up and walked to the Gen cleaning table while admiring her new gloves—mint green, embossed with a blue and silver design.

"Blighted Kruks," Sior mumbled.

"Indeed," said Aza as she draped her voluminous, white voile apron over the table and placed the map on it. She tilted her head back and dropped her nilteh—a sheer, embroidered handkerchief—over her face while chanting. *Betifini-bri-dati-ons-olnate-bri-datis...* The nilteh lifted as the spell imbued woven strands with the magic to remove this type of Kruik curse.

She plucked the cloth from her face, wrapped a corner section around her index finger and pushed firmly against the map's vellum at the upper lefthand corner. She twisted her finger upward while chanting subvocally and the renyers she touched vanished.

How fun that it's a map. Aza couldn't begin to estimate how many filthy boots and dainty slippers she'd been called to attend to over the years. This job was fascinating compared to most.

She heard Sior leave.

What must it be like to go out on a lovely afternoon and kill two people in front of a crowd?

Minutes later, Maleka came in. "I'm done. Do you need help?"

Aza looked up, grateful. *Here she is. The sister I never had.* They didn't look much like sisters. Maleka was lanky, like most Gens, with thick, wavy auburn hair and flawless light sienna skin. Aza's skin tone was similar, but she had inherited her father's freckles. She was also more curvy—short of stature and thick of waist—with wild curls of the darkest brown.

"No thanks. We'd just be in each other's way. I thought you might have left," Aza said.

"I was waiting for the weekend Gens to arrive. I'm not feeling well, though. My flow started."

"Of course it would on a day like today. Why don't we have a Besin cure for menstrual pain?"

Maleka had walked to the wall-length windows behind Sior's desk to gaze across the expansive grounds. She scoffed. "Menstrual pain is a curse all right, but not the kind the Besin cure. Mother will give me willow tea when I get home. It helps."

"Wish I had a clever mother who would take care of me—or even a stupid mother."

Maleka laughed and said with an old fisherman's brogue, "Nay, one should ne'er wish for that which might make one's life more burdened."

Aza grinned.

"I've forgotten what you told me," Maleka said. "Your mother died of—?"

"Of a horse. Or...the ground? A horse-riding accident."

"How are you so matter of fact? Isn't there a sense of loss in there somewhere?"

Aza stopped working and looked up, staring at nothing on the wall. After a moment, she shrugged and went back to cleaning. "I've never known anything else. I don't remember her. I do miss having a parent who treats me the way your mother cares for you. My sense of loss is that my father isn't more...engaged in my life."

"I'll bring you some willow bark tea for your next period."

"Thank you. That would be great. I, um, have been wondering..." Aza paused, unsure about whether to bring this up or not. She didn't know if anyone else had her ability to slip out of their body to see an alternate viewpoint, but she had noticed that while she could summon up Zaz—the nickname she'd given her other self—anytime, it was more likely to happen involuntarily during her monthly period. She took a breath and said, "Have you ever had something odd happen during your flow?"

"Odd like what?"

"Maybe an...increased...propensity to magic?'

"Propensity? What are you talking about? My only magic is cleaning up Kruk fluxes."

Well, I tried.

"That, and charms. You have magic I don't know about?"

Aza trusted Maleka with most of her secrets, but she was too insecure to tell this one. *What if my ability goes away once I speak of it?*

"It's just a feeling I get sometimes," she said. "I've read old books that mention women's magic."

"Literally, old wives' tales."

"I know."

But do I?

Impulsively, she split, letting Zaz drift toward Mam Sior's desk to do some snooping. Having a secret assistant made her feel special. "Are you going to see that fellow this weekend? The one you have been hinting at but not actually telling me about?"

Maleka looked around the room, shivered, and hugged herself. "Maybe, if I feel better."

Aza thought a boyfriend might be nice but could not relate to Maleka's rush to find her one true love. It was as if Aza's usually active imagination didn't reach far enough to think of marriage and a family, even though she was old enough.

Maleka walked to the cleaning table and unclasped a charm from her loaded bracelet. "Hope your weekend at home is restful. Here...so you'll be less lonely." She held it in front of her mouth, blessed it, and slipped it into Aza's apron pocket. "May your heart feel full of friendship when you rub this charm."

Maleka left, Zaz reintegrated, and Aza bent to her work.

Before long, Garnia Dal came to the door with a mop and bucket. "May I come in?"

"Of course. We can work in the same room."

The map was clean enough now that she could commit to memory street names and wonder at the meaning of various red X's and arrows she'd uncovered. "Garnia, do you know the area called Noptva?"

The maid leaned on her mop, breathing heavily for a moment, and then approached the cleaning table. "Indeed. It is the neighborhood of my mother's family."

"Is this a fair rendering?" Aza picked up the map.

Garnia reared back, her dark eyes almost closing as she winced. "Don't force those cursed renyers in my face!"

Aza stifled a snort at the woman's reaction. It wasn't her fault that she was afraid of what couldn't hurt her. "Sorry. I have cleaned it. Just doing a few last swipes."

The housekeeper peered over Aza's shoulder. "Can't make front nor back of that anyway. A map's pure gibberish to me."

Aza named some of the intersections.

Garnia nodded. "Yes. That's Noptva. Haven't you been there?"

"No time or freedom for wandering, I'm afraid."

"I'm surprised. You, with all your curiosity. I've seen you at the keyholes. Sneaking books out of the library. I would take wagers on your new knowledge of Noptva and its byways."

"I never knew I was being watched."

"Precious few advantages we Dal Clan have, dearie. Got to make do with what we see, hear, smell, and taste." Garnia walked back to her mop. "Aye, we all get caught in our own misery from time to time, don't we? But there are good advantages and bad advantages in all lives."

Aza smiled to herself.

"Sure," the housekeeper continued, "I'm Dal Clan, but I could be cleaning slop in the Butchery with the Undones. Instead, I work in the grandest house in Maripesa."

"That's a wonderful perspective, Garnia."

Speaking of perspective, Zaz is my good advantage.

On the bad advantage side, Aza felt awash in what she didn't know about the world. *How do I go about learning what I don't know I need to know? Get out of this house, for one thing.* She vowed to explore Noptva soon and try to decipher what those red arrows pointed to.

Aza dropped the cleaned map on Mam Sior's desk. "Oh," she said, "the execution."

Both women crossed to the window. Sun slashed through tall trees still full with early-autumn leaves, so they couldn't see much other than people streaming in for the event.

Aza stood there long after Garnia left, sober at what was happening beyond the beauty of those trees while also intensely preoccupied with the mystery of Zaz.

2

~

A Dirty Little Game

Dirty, angry, and late, Ferjival Puraples arrived at the Execution Grounds. He'd taken a fall from his horse during a polo game his team lost.

Executions always put him in a bad mood. *Why not do the deed and publicize it in print afterward?* But as long as his mother was in charge, the old ways would continue. Of course, sex between clans happened, but this condemned couple had been stupid. They weren't careful or circumspect. She got pregnant. People found out. The child they'd made had been stillborn, but nevertheless it caused a massive scandal for both clans. It was the law.

His mother would prefer he sit on the dais. But she would most definitely not prefer him arriving late in a dirty polo uniform, so he walked deep into the crowd and found a spot next to a young Gen woman who looked familiar. *That new one. Maleka. The pretty one. She is three or four years my junior? All right, more like six.* She'd cleaned many of his cursed objects over the last few years.

Ferjival, pulling at his goatee, turned to the Gen and whispered, "How are you today?"

Her cheeks colored sweetly. "Well, sir," she said, swallowing hard, "it *is* an execution."

"So it is." Her words made him feel foolish. *Thanks, Mother.*

The ensuing silence felt extremely awkward, like those formal parties where it seemed everyone else had someone to talk to except him. He was not good at chatting up women, but he knew he was supposed to ask the other person questions about their life.

"I'm curious," he said. "Do you have a room at the Komeh?"

Her dark, arched eyebrows rose at the question. "No, sir. I live with my family and go home every evening. I've never been quite sure why Aza Gen stays there most of the time."

"Oh. Well she's been there all her life as far as I know. Part of the household."

"Yes, sir."

"Do you see yourself staying on in this role?"

"I expect to marry soon and have my own family, so no, I won't be working here much longer."

"Oh! Good, good. Who's the lucky man?"

She turned to look him. Her eyes were large, amber-green with long lashes. "Oh sir, I can't say. He hasn't asked me yet."

They shared a smile that was immediately taken away by the action on the dais.

Sior stood, a black monolith. The crowd grew silent.

Next to her in a voluminous robe was a person of the Tchuvari Clan—the Keepers of the Magic. Only they had the power to execute.

"Maripesa thrives because our clans are interdependent," Sior intoned. "None of us contrived to make it so. The Gods themselves decreed our hierarchy. How else could one explain the exact matching, the elegant design of the genetically determined Talents that keep our society in perfect balance? For this reason alone, mating outside one's clan is forbidden. Those foolish enough to reproduce a mixed-clan child will be found out and put to death. As it is. As it always will be. As an example to all. Rest in peace."

Mam Sior nodded to the Tchuvari elder who cast the execution curse. It caused the lungs to fill with dead cells—fast-acting, but not immediate.

There wasn't much to see, which was one reason Ferjival hated these performances. Puraples didn't need it reinforced to the populace that they were the most powerful of the clans. It seemed like an overreach; as if Mam Sior didn't quite trust it herself.

Before the Kruik man choked his last breath, he reached out and took the hand of his Besin girlfriend, already gone. Ferjival looked on with a disgust targeted more at his mother than the foolish, romantic idiots.

He turned away just in time to catch Maleka as she fainted.

When the young woman recovered, Ferjival saw to it that she got a private coach home. Twenty minutes later, he strode through the front door of the Komeh.

The Grand Hall ran the width of the mansion with a triptych of two-story clerestory windows at the other end. Ferjival took in the golden last-light that splayed in elongated trapezoids over the lustrous stone floor. This room had always made him feel small. And lonely. He should be over that by now, but it lingered.

The floor space was interrupted only by four massive sideboards spaced two-by-two along each wall with massive fireplaces in between. In the middle near the front doors sat a hexagonal table which always had a huge vase of flowers on it. A dark, mulhao wood staircase, wider than most people's homes, led off the right wall, circling out of sight until it met with a mezzanine landing that ran around and open to the hall below.

He slapped his glove across a thigh harder than was necessary in order to dust it off—a little pain to go along with the irritation he felt at the vicissitudes of the day. He called for a servant.

She appeared almost immediately, curtsied and bowed her head. Ferjival thrust his hat and gloves into her hands, both filthy from the fall he'd taken off Rik, his bay mare. "See that these are cleaned," he said. "Where is my mother?"

"I am not privy to that information, sir. Would you like me to inquire?"

"No."

He took the marble stairs three at a time, hoping to get to his quarters on the third level without being seen by anyone, but Hasip emerged from his chambers.

His younger brother was the only sibling he had any relationship with, but that didn't mean they liked each other. They were the oldest of Mam Sior's eight...*or was it nine? Who could keep track?* The woman seemed to be continually pregnant for years, all made more confusing since some miscarried, or died soon after birth. Thank *Maripes* she was too old for all that now.

Along with Hasip, there had been another sister and brother from their father and four younger ones from the second husband. *Eight, then.* "The brood," as he called the half-siblings, were like a different family. And while he and Hasip outgrew their habit of casting reciprocal *drobes*—a mild, fleeting clumsiness curse used by Puraples children—they still quarreled like boys.

"You wore *that* to the execution?" Hasip said.

"Shut up. It's been a long day for everyone. Did you get cursed?"

"Twice."

Ferjival couldn't keep a small smile off his face. "My, my. You've got to be more aggressive on a day like today, little brother. I had none because I acted first."

Hasip ignored the comment and said, "Mother's on a rampage."

"What is it now?"

"It seems the execution is having a different effect on the Kruks than Mother bargained for. A warehouse full of our goods, bought and paid for, is freshly cursed."

Ferjival backed up a step, literally recoiling at the thought. "Why would they go to those lengths?"

Hasip glared at him but said nothing.

"Don't look at me! It was our dear Mother's decision to execute one of them. Anyway, it's all so pointless. It'll be war, and the Kruiks will lose as they always do."

Hasip folded his arms across his chest, crossed one ankle over the other, and leaned a hip against the wall. "Not always. You never were too swift on history lessons, were you?"

"*Bosh*, we have more power in our first level spells than the Kruks have, period. Yes, sure, renyers take time to clean, but that's what we have Gen for. There aren't enough Besin in the city to control our maladies if it comes to that." He stroked his trimmed mustache. "How'd a Kruk get into our warehouse?"

Hasip gave a large shrug. "As if Mother would tell me the details of a major crisis. I only know because I happened to be passing by her office when Droht came in with the news."

Ferjival scoffed. "Passing by, my horse's ass. Get out of my way. I'm going to clean up."

"Looks like you took a spill."

"It's nothing. Just a dirty little game."

3

WARM HANDS, COLD HEART

AZA PACKED A FEW things for the weekend and, in the fading light, walked to the street and flagged a coach for her ride home. As she climbed in through the steam that rose from the idling vehicle, she thought miserably of the two people who had to die on what had been a beautiful day.

The cabin smelled of raw onions and human sweat.

After telling the driver her destination, she settled in a front-facing seat on the driver's side. A Salizan or Dal woman sat across from her, dozing. Her head dipped forward slowly and then jerked up suddenly, only to settle again.

Aza wondered if Garnia would be unable to stay awake on her journey home each night. Would she even be able to afford a coach? Maybe she would have to go on the trolleys. Aza's rides were paid for by the presentation of a card to the drivers. The houseman Reth gave her a new card periodically with actual payment changing hands by some mysterious process her gloved hands never touched and, until now, never wondered about.

Garnia's right. Being set aside to do tedious work in the grandest home in all of Maripesa isn't the worst fate.

She cracked the window to let in some air, removed her gloves, took out her sketchbook and graphite stylus, and quickly became lost to her immediate surroundings while sketching the streets, intersections, waterfront, landmarks, and even those red X's and arrows that had been on the map of Noptva, Burg 29, Maripesa.

The coach stopped repeatedly, with people getting on and off, but she stayed focused. Only when she had drawn everything she could remember did she look up, blinking in the twilight gloom. Both benches were full.

A man wearing gloves sat next to her. Zaz separated and showed her that he was good-looking, about her age, and fastidiously dressed head to toe in expensive clothes in varying shades of grey. A Gen gentleman.

She glanced up at him.

He was looking right at her.

As Zaz reintegrated, Aza looked away, blushing.

"You are talented with a stylus, Miss Aza."

"Oh! Do I know you?" Her words tumbled out before her brain engaged enough to stop them.

He laughed. "I believe we do know one another, though not since we were children. You are the daughter of Leo, leader of our Gen Council."

"I apologize not to have recognized you as I'm sure you are, um...someone's son who I must know. It's only that I—"

Smiling broadly, he held up both hands to stop her. Then, putting an open hand over his heart, he said, "I am Duma, son of Palter. Our fathers are friends." He removed the glove from his right hand and held it toward her.

"Ahh. Yes, of course. Palter is a frequent visitor. Thank you for introducing yourself. We probably did play together as young children. You, I assume, have changed considerably from then."

She offered her hand—worrying that it might be dirty with graphite. This thought immediately dissipated as his much larger hand enveloped hers.

Zaz separated, this time seeming to flow from her body instead of the more usual light pop of splitting. She viewed Duma's face closely without him knowing as Aza fully experienced his touch. It was warm, soft and surprisingly gentle. His smile seemed genuine and warm.

"I should hope I have changed," he said. "I was usually covered in grime."

"As was I! It seems long ago that I had time to be thoughtlessly dirty," Aza responded, reluctantly ending the overly long handshake. "I used to love to hunt salamanders after the rain. That's the kind of girl I was."

His grin widened.

"What?" asked Aza.

"I'm crushed that you don't remember, as I am the very one who helped you break your record for the greatest number of salamanders ever captured in one rainy evening."

Aza gasped, and then laughed. "You? Oh, I can't believe it. That's one of my favorite memories. It's wonderful to have met you again! Where are you headed?"

"Well, that's the thing. It's possible I wouldn't have recognized you either—you have changed a great deal too, though, uh, your curls and freckles are the same and very distinctive. In the best possible way! I, uh...oh, I hope that isn't rude. Both are lovely. My point is that your family is on my mind tonight as I'm scheduled to meet with your father."

"You are going to my house?"

He nodded.

Her floaty mood became stodgy at the thought of Father once again scheduling business meetings late on a day of her homecoming. On the other hand, this handsome man, a childhood friend, seemed happy to see her and was extremely engaging. She would not let her father's stiff personality intrude this time.

"Very nice, then," she said. "A lovely coincidence."

❧

As they entered the courtyard of the large house everyone called the Villa, Aza was laughing, happily aghast at Duma's anecdote. "I don't believe it! Reth actually lost his temper?" she said between giggles.

"Oh yes! He pulled me up by the collar until my feet dangled."

"What did he say?"

"I was so traumatized, I can't remember. But he scared me. I stayed out of his way after that." Duma looked around, his story forgotten. He turned in a slow circle, taking in the space.

The courtyard, longer than it was wide, had a partial ceiling around the edges and near the doors to her father's office and the Gen Council room to the right of the wrought iron entry. Perpendicular to that was the entry to the rest of the house. Otherwise, it was open to the heavens. Plants as tall as trees lined the walls while flowering shrubs filled three oval beds set in green and white tile. An elaborate, tiered fountain splashed. Magenta bougainvillea vines grew around the roof opening, trailing profusely.

"I know I have been here before, but I did not appreciate it as a six-year-old. This is stunning."

Leo came out to greet them. As soon as the pleasantries were over, he dismissed Aza. He literally waved his hand in her direction as he ushered Duma into his office and closed the door.

You could, at the least, look at me. Address me. Acknowledge me. He never saw her, it seemed. She was an occasionally useful household component, not a loved and known human being. He wasn't mean, never cruel, but he noticed his easy chair or pipe more than his only child.

Pulse rushing in her ears, Aza sat on the bench just outside his office and took out her sketchbook to pretend to be busy. She split with a fleeting rush that left her feeling slightly empty. Her body had adjusted to Zaz's comings and goings over the years. Aza simply got out of the way and let Zaz go. There were limits. Staying split for too long caused overwhelming fatigue and headache or vertigo if she tried to send her too far away. She thought briefly of the unusual floaty feeling she'd had when Zaz left her body in the carriage.

It had been almost...*sensuous.*

Zaz showed her Leo and Duma sitting face-to-face before the unlit fireplace. Father rested back in his chair, while Duma leaned forward, elbows on knees. He was talking about his business. His mother and father. Small talk.

"It's time for me to take a wife, Leo, and father immediately thought of you...and your daughter."

In the courtyard, Aza gasped.

Leo paused, unlit pipe in hand. "I...uh."

"I'm sorry to spring this on you, sir, but I knew of no other way than to just come out with it. Aza is of age and we knew each other—"

"You have been seeing each other, then?"

"Recently?"

Leo nodded.

Duma looked down and brushed at his trouser leg. "No. Not until the coach ride today, which was happenstance. I meant that we knew and liked each other as children."

"Might it not be wise to get to know her first? I'm all for strategic alliances, but I wonder if marriage isn't a bit more complicated even than politics."

He laughed awkwardly. "Certainly. Of course. Father thought that it might be better—I don't know what to call it—perhaps, better manners to talk to you first. About my intentions."

Leo took time to light his pipe and take a first draft. His face showed mild amusement. "I do not stand on formality, Duma. Aza is strong-willed and intelligent. I suggest you two work this out as you are able. If it's my blessing you have come for, then, of course, you have it. As long as Aza is happy."

Duma stood and Aza was about to bring Zaz back so she could quickly leave the courtyard before they came out, but she heard Duma say, "She's talented with renderings and maps, no?"

"What do you mean?"

"In the coach tonight, she drew a detailed map of Noptva, of all places."

"Why?"

"I didn't ask."

"Can't imagine she's ever been to Noptva. If she has, I need to know why. It's a battleground for the ruling families at the moment."

"I've heard rumors of that. But my comment was more to her artistic skills."

"She's clever in many ways," he said, his voice grown rough, "like her mother."

Aza rose, reintegrating. Feeling off-kilter, she entered the main house proper, climbed the flights of stairs to her room, and collapsed on the bed.

This virtual stranger comes to Father instead of mentioning his little life plan to me first?

Her whole body heated up. She struggled out of the tangle of her shawl, anger growing. The warmth she'd experienced from Duma on the ride home now showed itself to be phony, a ploy, and a bad one at that. *A "strategic choice?" Her? A curse cleaner? Short and freckled? Her? Ridiculous! She, whose only claim to success was gathering a record number of salamanders when she was six! And her father saying she was strong-willed? Even he can't recommend me?*

Too many conflicting emotions had washed through her in the last hour. Excitement and pleasure at having a man's attention. Anger that this same man would presume to claim her without so much as a please or thank you *to her*. And the all-too-familiar despair at her father's dismissiveness.

She untied the sash of her sheer, white apron and then remembered the silver charm Maleka had given her earlier. She took it out of the pocket and examined it. A butterfly, with intricate detailing.

Charms had never become a common practice for Aza the way they were for Maleka. Some considered them to be mere superstitions. *But why not believe in small blessings when malicious curses are real?* She rubbed her thumb over it, opening herself up to the thoughtfulness of her friend.

It helped. Her breathing relaxed and her mind drifted. She felt less confused, less alone.

Aza rolled over to lie face down across the bed, still trying to sort out what had happened since she got on that coach to come home. Duma, elegantly dressed and so self-assured, did not seem like someone who would be attracted to her.

Well, Aza, he isn't. He's looking for a strategic match, not...romance. His touch, though. *Just a stupid handshake, for* Maripes *sake, you ninny.* But a ninny she was, because she began to wonder what that gentle hand would feel like if it were to touch her somewhere more intimate. Say...if it were slipping a strap of her underblouse off her shoulder. *Stop it. You are angry with him.* But in her imagination, both of his hands were touching her all over and *she would not stop it.* Because this was pleasurable and all that other folderol was most definitely not.

Perhaps it was the magic of the blessed charm. Perhaps that little bit of undivided attention from a man was the opening she needed. She touched herself, imagining it was Duma, and felt the release she sorely needed and had rarely attained.

❦

The dinner bell woke her.

Aza had just enough sleep to be groggy and irritable, but she was starving, so she rallied and began to freshen up.

She came home every other weekend and holidays and it was always nice to see Reth. Her "mother." This thought made her laugh. Hardly anyone's idea of a mother. Maybe she'd tell him Duma's story about him losing his temper. Yes, she could face another meal with her uncommunicative father now, thanks to Maleka's charm and Duma's other kind of charm, and she would do her best to let go of the maddening conversation she wasn't supposed to have heard.

One phrase, however, caught in her mind. Leo's offering to a virtual stranger what he had never said to her: She's "like her mother."

4

PILLS AND PIES

A WOMAN PARTED THE curtain and peeked into Vijo Besin's stall at the mid-week clinic.

"You're back again?" he said. His hand went to his lips, embarrassed that this unprofessional comment had escaped his mouth, but then remembered it was Benelek Kruik. *She* never stood on protocol.

"I told you," she said, unfazed, as she came into the room, "that I've taken a personal vow to needle Purples whenever I find an opportunity. So, yeah, I'm cursed again. But this time, I don't actually recognize what the blighter's done to me."

She had visited the Besin clinic so often in the last two months that Vijo had begun to think of her as a friend instead of a client. Statuesque with dark skin and black hair common among the Kruiks and less typical vivid green eyes, she was strikingly attractive. Vijo, pale, blue-eyed, with a short mop of blond curls, felt he might just be her exact physical opposite except for the fact that he matched her in height.

"Symptoms?" he said, patting the chair next to his apothecary—a large portable case that opened in a tiered fashion so the contents were all visible and accessible.

Her short jacket and wrapped leather pants squeaked against the chair as she sat. She rubbed the back of her neck. "I'm exhausted."

"That's your symptom?"

"First symptom. Insomnia."

"That's no curse. It's an irritating, but normal human challenge."

"No. My sleeplessness started after this yah-yah got into a scrum with me on the field during a game." She paused, her eyebrows raised even higher than their usual dramatic arch. "It was supposed to be a friendly game of kuab."

"Except, there's nothing friendly in your attitudes toward the Puraples."

"Ah, see? You do know me. Anyway, it was a bit of an illegal hit that I gave him, but no curses were flying! *Maripes!* Can you imagine sport if we all cursed each other? That's not a game; that's war."

"Indeed. Do you remember what he said when he cursed you?"

"Hmm. Some of it. My knowledge of Puraples curses has gotten quite good. Of course, that document that...someone I know stole from their archives helped a great deal. I'm a quick study."

"I have no doubt. Is there a similar type of 'document' for Kruik curses?"

She looked at him sharply and then grinned. "Aren't you cheeky? Why? Are you collecting curses?"

He pursed his lips and tilted his head back and forth. "In a way."

"Of course. Lots. Volumes. We have to write these things down so they aren't subject to too much, uh, drift. You know? Aren't Besin cures written down?"

"They are."

"And considered 'Top Secret'?"

"Yes."

"So I'm afraid you'll just have to gather information the same way I do, by being in proximity when a curse is delivered, having a keen ear, and a cool head."

"That, or thievery?"

But she was not going to give him the satisfaction of rising to his insult. She simply smiled like an angel. *How does she manage it?*

"What did the curse sound like?"

Benelek reeled off a series of rhythmic words while Vijo jotted them down as best he could. Not all Besin healers did this as part of their treatment, but he had always wanted to understand more about magic. When off duty, he researched as much as he could about the curses he was entrusted to undo.

"Thanks. Now. Do you have other symptoms?"

"Lichlia."

"Really," he said dryly, not quite believing any of this. "Let's take a look."

She sat up and shook off her jacket while Vijo rose and closed the curtains. By the time he turned around, Benelek had removed her blouse.

"*Zlo!*"

Her neck, upper chest, shoulders and arms were covered in a uniform bright red rash.

"Hurts like hell."

"But Bek, this doesn't follow the pattern of lichlia." He sat and started pulling out vials from his chest. "Questions, questions. When did this happen?"

"The curse? Three days ago. The rash, not till yesterday."

"Oh. Uh-uh. No. Lichlia shows up almost immediately. Your curse is katiri. Did the rash come first?"

"No. I told you, it started as insomnia. I know what normal insomnia feels like. This is different. My eyelids feel cursed." At his gaping look, she nodded and said, "As if someone inserted a stiff ring around my eyeball. I can't close my eyes properly, no matter how sleepy. Help me!"

Vijo recorded her comments and then poured a teaspoonful of a coppery powder and a dozen drops of liquid from a narrow green bottle into a ceramic bowl. He chanted in a whisper as he mixed them with the tilia, a disposable tool made from strips of the tree of that name, until it resembled a small mound of dough. He scraped that onto his mixing board and, working rapidly, used the flat side of the tool to roll the remedy into a neat oblong cylinder. He reached into a bowl on his workspace pulled out a pinch of white powder, sprinkled it over the roll and said, "*Bavtuya*."

"That's one I haven't heard."

"I believe you have a 'new' condition. Whether on purpose or because of that drift you referred to, I don't know. It's new to you and me, at any rate. I'm treating you both for what I'm going to call an uooleh—the insomnia—*and* katiri. Anything else I should know?"

"Pain. I'm in pain."

"Right. I'll prepare that cure in a moment." He turned back to the compound he'd made, took a scalpel and made vertical cuts in the now hardened cylinder until he had six identical, round tablets. "Did you bring your receiving pouch?"

"Always...these days." Benelek reached for her jacket on the chair behind her and pulled it from the pocket.

Using his tilia, Vijo brushed the pills he'd just compounded into a small glass bottle called a temblir. He corked it, and with the bottle secured between thumb and index finger, extended his arm and began chanting energetically.

Bek loosened her pouch's drawstring and held it open.

Vijo widened the distance between his finger and thumb. The bottle stayed, suspended in mid-air. It rotated, quickly gathering momentum as a continuous spiral of words fell from Vijo's mouth, soon reaching a spin so rapid that it seemed to disappear except for a dull glow.

After a few minutes, the spinning slowed to a lazy rotation and then stopped.

"Ready?" Vijo said as he uncorked the bottle. He spilled the pills into her pouch without touching them. "One now, please," he said, pouring her a glass of water.

She plucked one out and swallowed it.

"One more tonight, and then once a day afterward. I might have to do another dose. Depends on how ingrained that spell is. It has been three days." He gave her a sharp look, but as usual, she was unbothered.

"This takes time, Besin. I come when I come. But yes, this curse is more bothersome than most. I'll be good. Now, where's that pain removal spell?"

Once she had been treated for pain, she left without a spoken thank you, but with, Vijo knew, gratitude.

He reviewed his notes of Bek's symptoms in his log. A combination curse of a subset of uooleh—the insomnia—with a slow-growing katiri—the rash. The pain was probably part of the katiri with a large side-order of sleep deprivation, but he made note of it just in case there was a pain-inducing curse he hadn't noted before.

Being a Besin practitioner suited Vijo, but it could be lonely. He spent more time with Kruiks than anyone else and they usually treated him as a servant. So however strange Benelek's vendetta with the Puraples was, he was fine with her behavior. She was a wealth of information, a breath of fresh air, and maybe, a friend.

Aza stepped out of the coach at the intersection of North Eznik and Geno. It was mid-day, so she was one of many out and about. Even though the temperature was warm for late fall, she clutched her cloak, feeling self-conscious and out of place. On the other hand, referencing the map in her memory, she immediately knew where she was.

Her father had called it a battleground.

Noptva seemed an unlikely place to begin either a war or a plan to change one's life, but Aza, who wanted to do the latter—*please not the former, thank you very much*—would start here.

Two weeks and a day had passed since the evening Duma visited. That night had changed her. She had no intention of sitting passively while others decided her life's trajectory.

The warren of streets, some serviced by steam trolleys, were lined with warehouses, manufacturing plants, and small businesses—often with apartments above. *Maybe Garnia's mother grew up in one of those.* Aza envisioned the map she'd memorized and walked toward the closest of the red X's.

Facing west, a few blocks ahead of her, lay the Strait of Jeka, the waterway that narrowly parted the city-island of Maripesa from its much smaller and less populated sister island, Luftva. To the north on her right, the strait widened as the coastline wound northwesterly to the surrounding sea of Mediterranea. To her left, or south, the borough of Noptva ended at Avenue Granocia, a major thoroughfare that crossed the Holba Bridge connecting Maripesa to Luftva.

Aza's plan was to use her natural curiosity as her primary means for change. She would be an expert on the Puraples and whatever they were planning on doing to the Kruiks or vice versa, if possible, though she didn't believe she had ever spoken to a Kruik in her life. What she would do with the intelligence she gained was, as yet, unclear but knowledge was good in its own right, and someday the knowledge she held would make her father look at her. Really see her. If he ended up valuing her, so much the better. One step at a time.

The X on the map had been on the right side in what looked to be an alleyway between two buildings. Of course, from a map, she couldn't tell the height of a building, but she knew it was some kind of narrow space. After a block and a half, she spotted it. She had to hand to to the cartographers, they certainly did their job well. She wondered what clan was responsible for that kind of work.

What if I could decide to be a map maker? Or something else I haven't ever considered before? How many Gen spend their days cleaning curses? Father doesn't. Of course he is the Leader, but what about Duma? She couldn't envision him wiping renyers off maps. *Soon, Aza, soon you must come right out and ask your father that kind of question.* She had to keep giving herself these pep talks because she dreaded trying to pull anything out of him. He intimidated her so.

She took a step into what was, in fact, an alley about ten strides wide. *This doesn't look promising...or interesting.* Turning back toward the street, she saw a sign hanging over a door to her right that said, *Cozy 'n Good—Meat Pies.* On her other side was the tall, plain stone building she'd walked past. There was no door, windows or signage.

A warehouse, then. The map indicated that it's part of a "war zone." How strange.

A Kruik woman swept past her on the sidewalk. Aza followed her passing. This tall, dark, confident woman—Aza could tell by her posture, her upturned chin, and her nonchalant gait—wore pants of deep blue leather with a short jacket of lighter blue. She entered the café.

Aza stepped back onto the sidewalk. She hadn't eaten. *A person, any person, might just go into a place to get a bite to eat.* Aza had never done this outside her own neighborhood. She felt conspicuous. Everything in her wanted to retreat, to run, to stop this feeling of awkward self-consciousness.

A mental image of Garnia standing, mop in hand, came to her unbidden. *Come on, Curious Soul, let's snoop.*

The restaurant was deep and narrow and smelled of freshly baked pastry and roasted meats. To the right was a counter, painted deep red, behind which stood a young woman around her age. Her face was flushed, probably from standing in front of an oven. To Aza's left, were tables set in booths with high partitions between them. The three customers that she could see all looked up at her before going back to their meals.

She immediately sent Zaz out to peer into each stall. Zaz always made her feel bolder. In the last booth, there were two young Kruiks, obvious because of the tone-on-tone patterned, dark-leather jackets they favored. One of them was the woman she'd seen on the street.

"What have ya then?" the countergirl asked.

Aza reassembled and cleared her throat. "I, um— What is that delightful smell?"

The woman smiled, obviously appreciating the compliment. This was unexpected and heartwarming. Aza relaxed a little.

"Meat and veg handpies just outta the oven. Might be a little hot yet, but you know they're fresh."

Aza ordered two spiced lamb and onion pies. She paid for them with pocket money she'd found in her dresser drawer at home. She walked to the second from the last stall which she already knew was empty and sat facing the door. Behind her were the two Kruiks, deep in conversation.

She broke open both her pies. The steam that rose from them filled her nose with tantalizing aromas that caused her mouth to water. Luckily, her favorite pastime—eavesdropping—awaited her while she waited for them to become cool enough to eat.

"The whole shipment's cursed, I tell you. No amount of Gen magic could get rid of the blighted mess. It'd take dozens of them working for years!"

Aza split Zaz off again and saw the woman from the street, her long black hair pulled back tightly and flowing over one shoulder, listening to a male Kruik about the same age.

"It's stupid. Our people need that shipment as much as the blighted Purples do. The warehouse was enough," she said. "That was only a loss for the Purples. But this...this is going to hurt the whole city and the Kruik's most of all because the Purples are going to come after us. And with the pitiful, do-nothing Kruik Council we have now..." Her voice faded away.

"Any rumors on who's gone rogue?"

"I have my suspicions. But you can hardly call it going rogue when there's no leadership at the top telling people what they should or shouldn't do. Honestly, I doubt we'll ever get our place back as rightful rulers of Maripesa." The woman sighed deeply. "I'm going."

"You're not going to order?"

"No. My stomach's turned by the thought of that ruined ship. I'll be in touch. Keep an ear out. Tell your pals to do the same. I have a feeling anyone with the right answer to this one could get paid from both sides."

Zaz came back to her and Aza sat, her pies cool enough to eat, watching her first Kruik in the wild walk away.

"Father, would you have a moment to speak with me?" Aza asked as soon as she got home that evening.

Leo, pipe in hand, looked up from his reading. He looked comfortable sitting in front of the fire wearing a faded, grey-blue afterhours jacket that showed signs of wear at the elbows and cuffs. Smoke, the color of his hair, streamed from his mouth. He only nodded as she entered the room and sat across from him in the chair Duma had used.

"I want to speak with you about something."

Father's left eyebrow lowered. He clasped the bowl of the pipe, lifted it from his lips and put it onto its holder. "About Duma?"

Three distinct feelings of dread washed through her simultaneously. One, that she'd somehow been caught listening in on that conversation. Two, that her secret ability to split wasn't special or unique or even secret. Three, that he was going to order her to marry. She hadn't even begun and they were already off subject.

"No, Father. It's not about Duma." But what to say next? If she hadn't overheard the conversation, then she would be confused by his question and ask why he might think she wanted to talk about Duma. But she didn't want to talk about Duma, or any possible future marriage partner, and she certainly didn't want to know what he thought of Duma's suggestion.

Her hesitation made things worse.

"I see that it's hard for you to talk about. He's been in touch with you since coming here?"

"Ah...no. No." She took a gulp of air and said, "Why would he?"

It took her father a while to answer.

Aza's spirit lightened a little because it was becoming obvious that he didn't know she'd overheard what Duma had proposed. But, in the meantime, her question hung in the air between them.

"He, ah, he...well, you know, dear..."

Leo never called her "dear."

"...perhaps it's a mistake on my part. You two came in together the other evening. I somehow got the impression that wasn't accidental. I thought maybe you had been seeing each other...you know, romantically."

The word sounded so artificial coming out of his mouth that each of them looked away from the other. The room had grown too hot. She threw off her shawl. He pulled at his collar.

"I see," Aza said. "No. It was, as far as I know, a coincidence that we were on the same coach. I have no relationship with Duma." She lifted her eyes to meet his. His were blue, an icy pale so unlike her own. *I look like my mother,* she thought, though this was only a presumption. *Except for the freckles.* She took a breath and started. "Father, I overheard something today and wanted to bring it to you in case it might be of interest. Working in the headquarters of the Purples—"

"Aza, do not call them that. It's a child's nickname and will get you in trouble."

Her emotions shifted again, this time toward anger. "I've spent more time in their home than I have in my own. I do not fear them."

"Fear them. Fear all the ruling families and while you're at it, fear the low-clans as well. We are both lucky and ill-favored to be in the middle."

She looked at her hands, still in gloves. Today's were lavender with green leaves stained into the leather. *Immediately, he lectures me on my place in society. He can't imagine that I'd be of any help.*

She pulled on her gloved thumb and then the other fingers of her right hand. "Do you want to know what I came to tell you?"

He seemed flustered, which made her feel a tiny bit more powerful than she had seconds ago. Her gloves off and in her lap, she said, "I heard about a shipment. I don't know what was in it, but I know that it was paid for by the Puraples and was a ship full of something that is necessary for the city. Its entire contents had been cursed with renyers. The people I overheard were Kruik, but they did not know who had done this. They talked about it being some lone person perhaps acting out a personal grudge." She placed her gloves in her apron pocket and looked up.

Her father regarded her blankly.

She could not conjure one guess about what he might be thinking. She stood. "That's it." She turned to go.

"Wait."

"Yes?"

"Who said this?"

"I didn't know the people. I've never seen them before."

"Where did you overhear it?"

"Is it important?"

"I'm curious as to where you were, that's all."

"I *meant,* is the information important to you?"

"I knew about the ship. The Synod Chair contacted me this morning. They want an unprecedented number of Gens to clean the mess. I've spent my day working on it. I'm stunned to hear about it from my daughter, however."

"I see." *Of course he knew. He's the clan leader.* She felt foolish to have thought she could bring him information he wouldn't know about. Exactly the opposite of what she was trying to accomplish. "Sorry to have taken you from your work. How was I to know that it's common knowledge?" She walked to the doorway.

"It isn't."

She turned.

"It isn't common knowledge. How often do you overhear...conversations?"

Aza clasped her hands and breathed shallowly. Her answer had to be at least part lie, but she wanted him to know that she could be useful. "More often than you might think. The Puraples aren't particularly careful around me because they do not *see* me unless they need my services. I'm like the walls or the furniture. Almost invisible." *Just as I am at home.*

He rose and walked to her, taking her hand in his. "I doubt that. I am worried for your safety. What is true, is that these people do not value your life. They kill, if and when they want. They answer to no one."

Outright anger flashed through her. She pulled her hand from his. "Then *you* need to answer as to why you placed me among these dangerous people when I was eight years old! Why would you only now think about how unsafe it is? Don't start being concerned about me now!"

"Aza..." He reached for her arm, but she bolted out.

Upstairs and out of breath, she locked her bedroom door. She needn't have bothered. He never came up here.

She paced, back and forth and in circles, while she thought about the conversation.

All her life, she'd seen people come into her father's office where he would talk with them about whatever matter was on their mind. He served as a judge in people's dealings with others, he solved problems, he told people what to do, gave them advice or simply issued orders. The essence of his leadership, however, was always and above all, as a gatherer of information.

But not from her. He completely missed the fact that she was another useful person, someone in a position to provide some of the puzzle pieces that helped the Gen Clan negotiate the culture they lived in. An image of a little girl's bread and jam sandwich came to her. She saw all her words, her knowledge, her potential pressed into the sticky middle, muted and infantilized. She plopped down in a chair by the window, blood pumping hard and fast in her veins, hearing its *whoosh-whoosh* in her ears, as she wondered how—or if—it was possible to change one's life.

5

CROSS-CURSED

IT DIDN'T MATTER TO Ferjival whether a woman from another clan was un-available to him, attractive was attractive and there was no law against appreci-ating beauty. The woman across from him in the coach was a beautiful human specimen. Even if she was a Kruk.

Her name was Benelek, though she was often called by a shorter nickname he couldn't recall. He knew her slightly from sporting events and socials at the Wardrobe. But either she hadn't noticed him when he entered the coach or she was pretending not to see him.

He hated the way the young Kruik women dressed like men. That part was not attractive, but he had to admit, on her long legs, the tightly wrapped pants looked good. *She's taller than you are, Ferjival.* Her black hair was pulled back tightly and the tail of it hung over one shoulder atop her right breast which, though hidden underneath her heavy jacket, he knew from having seen her at the Wardrobe, was large. She hadn't looked up—being absorbed in some reading material—but he thought he remembered that her eyes were blue. Yes, she was a fine specimen and should make some Kruik fellow quite happy.

The coach stopped and everyone but the two of them gathered their belong-ings and climbed out.

She looked straight at him as the others left. Her eyes were not blue but vivid green. She glared at him for a long moment and then said, "Ferjival. May I help you?"

"Whatever do you mean? Of course you may not help me." He blared this out in a deeper, louder-than-normal tone, trying to cover the fact that she'd caught him ogling.

"Then stop staring at me."

"My eyes have to be somewhere."

"No. They do not. Close them and give the rest of us some privacy."

"Everyone else has gone, as you see."

"More's the pity."

"You should not talk to me in that tone."

She stared fiercely, but at the same time lifted one shoulder in a dismissive gesture.

He stared back. Usually, because he was Mam Sior's eldest and everyone thought he had power and sway, people didn't make eye contact with him. Unless of course, it was some *sweet* female trying to attract him. So far, he'd been able to avoid becoming permanently latched to one, though his mother nagged him often enough to choose someone off her suitables list.

Benelek Kruik, though, was still staring, and he had another ten minutes on this ride. He wasn't going to give her the satisfaction of thinking that she'd scared him off.

Benelek kept her stare steady. Inside, she shimmered with glee, thrilled to have found herself alone in the back of a coach with Ferjival. She'd always known she had arrived under a lucky star, but this was too wonderful.

"Stop looking at me as if I've somehow violated you. I haven't." Ferjival said in his whining, eight-year-old voice. It wasn't, she admitted, actually a child's voice. His was an unusually deep bass, but the edge it got when he was upset—which was often, she had gathered—was positively infantile.

"Bully for you," she said. "Yes. Bully. That's the appropriate word, isn't it?"

"Why are you speaking to me like this?"

"Oh, it's not just you. I hate all Purples."

"What a surprise coming from a Kruk. But no matter how well-honed your provocation is, I won't give you the pleasure of reacting. Pleasing to the eyes you may be, but your attractiveness is draining away by the second. What a royal blue bitch you are."

"Exactly."

"Benelek, isn't it?"

She sighed and shook her head. "You know very well who I am. Going to report me to your mommy?" She took her eyes off him for the first time and reached in her jacket pocket. "Here, let me help you."

She extended her arm toward him, her calling card held between the tips of her fingers. But before he could take it, she spread her fingers and cast a renyer curse over him. The card drifted to the floor.

He squealed, his eight-year-old fully loosed as he reared back and away from her in a failed attempt to keep the vermin-to-follow off the bulk of his clothes and belongings.

In the next instant, he stood—as best he could in the moving vehicle—turned to face her and theatrically threw a curse over her. At that moment, the coach swerved and the spellcast went wide.

This seemed to infuriate the man even more.

He steadied himself, reared back and cursed her solidly. "Driver!" he yelled. "Stop the coach!"

The vehicle pulled to the right and halted so abruptly that Ferjival lost his balance, falling back onto the seat. "Have fun in the clinic tonight. I won't forget your insolence and aggression toward me. I never forget."

"And I never forgive," Benelek said to his back.

As he marched away, the coach driver told her in no uncertain terms to leave his coach at once. She exited with a big smile and a hefty tip for his trouble.

Aza and Maleka sat together in the small sunroom at the rear of the main floor where they took their meals while at the Komeh. When Aza had come to live at the mansion, the staff knew it wasn't proper for a Gen to have meals with the family, but also felt it wasn't proper for her to eat with the staff, so they'd made the room hers. When Garnia told her about it, she was trying to make her feel special, but at the time, Aza saw it only as another example of having been set aside. Isolated.

Over the years, however, the room had become her retreat—a private, sunny place with plants to care for, a comfy reading chair, and a view of the sky. Since Maleka had come, it had become theirs: a place to share meals, secrets and snide remarks about the family in residence.

They had just eaten their midday meal. Maleka was talking nonstop about what she'd overheard that morning. "I think they just forgot I was in the room or something, because Hasip was gossiping away with Jetal, not even being a little bit wary. They mentioned several Kruik names I don't remember, but the gist of it is that the Kruks are going to curse a Gen business!"

Aza shook her head in disbelief. "I've never heard of such a thing. Why? What business?"

"I don't know. I mean, it's not like they gave me an outline of the plan or something. The Kruiks—some of them anyway—think of us Gens as their enemy because we work with the Purples!"

"But we have no choice. Just like the Besin work with the Kruiks. It doesn't mean the Besin are our enemies."

"Of course it doesn't, but you can't expect the two upper clans to be as sensible as we are, can you?" Maleka picked up her teacup and took a sip.

"If I knew what business, I could warn Father. Do you know where it's located?"

"Yes!" she said brightly, clanking the cup down on the saucer. "One of the streets off Avenue Granocia. Do you know it?"

"I know the street, but that hardly narrows it down. It's a major avenue."

"They mentioned that it's a block or so from the the strait. We should go." She said the last sentence conspiratorially.

Maleka, her eyes wide, looked eagerly earnest to Aza. *That's usually my role.* "Did he say when this attack was going to happen?"

"Tomorrow. That's why we must go today."

"How can we get away at the same time?" Aza asked. "We're supposed to cover for each other."

"We don't ask. We just go. You know that mid-to-late afternoon lull, the family's all out, or napping, or hunting, or getting ready for their fancy parties, or whatever it is that they do."

"Some of them are out getting fluxed at sporting events or at the shopping arcade," Aza said wryly. Of course Aza wasn't and couldn't have been there at the ready for every single curse. The family had their Gen backups not far away. They would manage. She sighed, realizing how utterly fed up with the Purples she was. "On the other hand, what are they going to do, take our jobs away?"

They laughed.

"All right. I'm in."

"Excellent. We leave at four."

⚜

An empty coach sat at Aza and Maleka's usual stop as if waiting for them. They were about to climb in when in the driver opened the separator window and yelled, "Misses! Stop!"

At the same time, Maleka glanced inside and said, "You have renyers!"

"Apologies. Apologies." The driver, a tidy, uniformed man in his forties or so, got out and came around to the back. "I was trying to warn you. I only just pulled over because there was a bit of a to-do back there."

Aza saw the corner of one seat teeming with the shiny, charcoal-grey specks. "Sir, as Gens we are not at all worried about catching the curse, but you can't be in business with this mess back here."

"I know," he moaned. "It only just happened. My last fares—a young Kruik and a Purple—were being unfriendly. I heard it escalate, but what was I to do? The curses started flying. *Maripes* knows what kind of disease the Purple threw around before I ejected them from my cab."

"I don't know about that, but the Kruik missed their mark and got it on your cab instead of the passenger. Or maybe both." Aza looked at Maleka. "Shall we?"

"Sure. If the curse just happened, it won't take that long."

"Would you? Oh Misses, I would be in your debt! If I have to join the queue to get my coach cleaned, it's at least a half-day's fares gone. My kiddies'll go hungry."

Aza had no clue if that was an exaggeration or not. She made a mental note to find out what ordinary people had to go through to get their possessions cleaned of curses. Add it to the long list of things she had never considered before.

Maleka was already reaching for her nilteh as she said, "We can do it on our way. Drive us to Avenue Granocia, please. Near the bridge."

"Yes, Miss. Thank you, Miss."

"And no sharp turns, my good man," said Maleka, with a smile on her face.

As they went, they chanted into their niltehs and started working. It was weirdly fun. Aza cleaned while being absorbed by the newish experience of having a friend who could, it seemed, make a party out of any situation.

The work was done by the time they arrived. The driver jumped out, opened the door and examined their work. "Excellent. Wonderful. No charge of course." He stood aside so they could get out, bowing like a gentleman from times of old. "Please, whenever you need a coach, here's my card, just send word. All the dispatchers know me."

Aza looked at the card while Maleka put on an imperious expression and said, "We shall take you up on that, my good man," in a voice that sounded just like Mam Sior when she was lording her power over someone. Which was always.

Aza laughed and turned to the driver. "Thank you, Gerland. You will definitely be hearing from us." She offered her calling card to him, while Maleka fumbled in her pouch for hers, finally bringing up a wrinkled one.

Gerland took them and put them in his breast pocket, nodding and smiling. "Do you need a drive home from here?"

The women looked at each other.

Aza said, "Yes, I guess we do. Give us an hour?" She glanced at Maleka who nodded vigorously. "Does that work for you?"

"Certainly. In your debt." He bowed again.

After he'd driven off, Aza and Maleka looked at each other and giggled.

"All right, my friend. This is your show. Which way?" Aza asked, looking around.

Instead of answering, Maleka walked over, put her arms around Aza and squeezed her tightly.

"What's that for?" Aza asked, barely able to breathe.

Maleka let her go and pulled back. Her face was serious. "Nothing, really. Just happy you came with me and that we're out of that damned house. Honestly, I don't know how you've stood it all these years." She took Aza's arm and pulled it slightly until Aza started walking next to her. "We're going to find a pinkish building with a black and white...I don't know, awning or sign, or mural, or...something."

Aza laughed. "Glad you have all the details pinned down."

They set off at a brisk pace, keeping a close eye on the commercial buildings on either side of the street. "It's not likely any of these," Maleka said. "Jetal said *near* Avenue Granocia. Let's walk to the water and make our way back on the next street over."

It was three blocks to the Strait of Jeka where Avenue Granocia continued onto the bridge to Luftva, the smaller island. Aza had never been there, but knew it was rural with a small population, farmland, and lots of sheep. She watched an almost empty trolley steam past in that direction. The bridge also held a two-lane road for coach traffic, and a footpath.

At the strait, they turned left. Across the street were a couple of large shipping piers and many docks with a few mid-sized and a lot of small boats. There was some activity, but it looked like end-of-the-day closing down and tidying up. Beyond was open water, choppy today, with a strong wind— noisy and penetrating. She couldn't make out the island from this vantage point.

Even though this outing was Maleka's idea, Aza was happy to get here. She knew from her spying that the Puraples council was buying up properties in this part of the city.

"It's cold!" Maleka said, sounding like a little girl. She repeated this complaint twice more until they took a left. Happily, this street wound a bit and soon the blast of wind from the strait was cut off by the three- or four-story buildings between them and the open water. The women looked at each other, grinned, and began pulling their outer shawls off their heads where they'd wrapped them for protection.

"Oh, that's better," Aza said, wiping her eyes which had been watering the whole time.

By the look of this block, the Puraples might be buying rundown properties as opposed to the more commercially vibrant ones on Granocia proper. These would likely be inexpensive, but being so near to a bustling commercial part of the city, they would certainly rise in value. *The Purples do have a knack for business.*

They searched each side of the street for a "pinkish" building that might hold a Gen business but there was nothing. The buildings here were either abandoned or, evidently, so unimportant that they needed no signage. Stopping at the end, Aza said, "Which way?"

"Let's keep going straight."

The next block had more signs of life and was more cared-for. Toward the end, on the left, they found it. A three-story rectangular building built of pink stone blocks, the color of Maripesa's beautiful cathedral. The double doorway was arched and slightly recessed with glass doors. Over the door it read, "Objita Fabrics." The archway and entry were made of black and white mosaic tiles.

Maleka seemed a little stunned. "That's it."

Aza grinned. "Excellent work, girl. Now what?"

"Um, well, what do you mean?"

"What's the plan? Are we going to warn them or what?"

"Oh, hah. Yeah. I guess I don't know. I never really thought I'd find it."

"You could've fooled me," Aza said.

"How can we be sure?"

"I don't know if it matters. Let's just go talk to the people. We'll tell them what we know."

"But...what if...I'm wrong and then—"

"You're overthinking this." Aza stepped into the doorway and pulled on the latch. "Rats and bats, it's locked."

"Oh. It is getting late."

"I supposed we should have thought of that," Aza said, giving the handle another useless jiggle.

"Could you? I don't know... could you maybe warn your dad about this?"

Aza said, "I probably should. I'm not due to go there, but we can stop at a Messagery on the way back and send a note. He'll probably dismiss it as nothing."

"Oh stop. He'll be happy you told him."

"If he is, *you* will get the credit, my friend."

"We should get back," she said and started walking. "We don't want to miss Gerland."

"We could always get a different coach."

"Not one 'indebted' to us," Maleka shot back over her shoulder.

Aza broadened her stride to catch up. "This has been fun. Hopefully we'll both be up for more snooping excursions when the opportunity comes up."

Maleka gave her a tight grin.

"Are you all right?"

"Of course. Just, you know, I'll get in trouble with my parents if I'm late without a good reason."

Aza shrugged this off. *Who could predict the mercurial moods of Maleka?*

❧

Vijo watched a Salizan coach driver limp into his stall at the downtown Besin clinic not far from the sprawling grounds of the Tapinak, Maripesa's cathedral.

"Your name, sir, and tell me what's troubling you?"

"I'm Gerland. Two Uppers had it out in my coach. I seem to have gotten caught in their little spat." The man turned and pulled down the collar of his uniform jacket.

"Please, sit." Once he did, Vijo took a look. Angry red welts the size of Sunday biscuits dotted his neck. One was spreading to his jaw and another down his spine.

"Hurt?"

"Wha' you think, boy?" the driver said, and immediately looked contrite. "Sorry, I might be a bit out of sorts about this."

"No offense taken. We are trained not to take bad moods personally. No one likes to be cursed." Vijo ran his fingers through curls that had fallen over his forehead as he bent to look at the man's condition. "I know, too, that it sounds like a stupid question, but we are also trained to not make assumptions. Have them anywhere else?"

"No, sir. Not that I can feel anyway. As I said, it just happened. I picked up the fare of two kind Gen misses who agreed to clean the coach of renyers. I thought it had been my lucky day with that. But then I realized—" Gerland pointed to his neck. "How long will it take? I have to return to get the Gen ladies soon."

"*Lichlia*. Won't take long. Good thing you came right in. By morning your body would have been one angry, painful welt, particularly along your spine." Vijo turned to his apothecary and rummaged for the ingredients he needed, talking to himself as he gathered bottles and vials.

"I have to take medicine? Isn't there a spell you can do?"

"You've never had a curse-induced malady?"

"Surprising, isn't it? Me being around so many of the ruling clans."

"Hmm," Vijo said, as he measured and mixed his remedy. "Yes, you have to take medicine, just like for a normal disease. Except it isn't 'normal' medicine. It's Besin magic."

"Knew that."

"And it's not so surprising that you've never been hit. The ruling families aren't common thugs who go around slinging spells at each other on the streets."

"Coulda fooled me."

Vijo thought of Bek and said, "We *are* seeing more of this kind of randomly acquired disease. Innocent bystanders struck with uooleh or gwavera. Even heard of a couple of cases of giarmial."

"What's that, then?" Gerland asked.

"The worst. It's the only malady that's contagious. Spreads to anyone. Even the Puraples can catch it."

Gerland said, "I think it's from having too many children. Oh, don't get me wrong. I'm all for children. I have ten of them myself. But we—Ness and I—we keep 'em busy. Give them useful work to do. It's the idleness that's the problem. I have to drive those ruling clans. Coming home in the wee hours, so out of their minds they can't speak words properly. What else do the rich have to do but get into mischief?"

Vijo nodded as he finished his preparation. Once he had the medicine in the temblir, he began vigorous chanting.

Gerland's eyes widened as the small bottle defied gravity and spun so fast that it seemed to disappear.

The chanting and the spinning slowed. Without taking his eyes from the bottle, Vijo reached in the commodious pocket in the front of his apron and pulled out a small, hooped net with a long handle. He positioned it under the bottle and stopped chanting, whereupon the bottle fell out of the air into his net.

Vijo turned to the driver.

"Is it done?" Gerland said.

"Yes. But it's hot after all that spinning."

"Ahh, I see. The net."

"Yes, for one thing." As he waited for it to cool, Vijo instructed Gerland on how to take his medicine. Then, he brought the net within reach and said, "Retrieve it, please."

"It's still hot?"

"No. It's cool enough. The net serves a second purpose. Our cures only work for the person who first touches it after it's done."

"Oh right. I've heard that."

"That's why we can't just open up a shop that carries cures for all the maladies."

"Tosh, that'd be a lot easier."

"True, my good man. But magic doesn't always work the way we want."

Maleka glanced over her shoulder several times as they headed back to the pull-off where Gerland was to meet them.

"What are you looking for?" Aza asked after the third time.

"Nothing. I don't know. It feels strange to be here so late in the day. All the working people have gone home. It's a bit creepy. What would my mother say?"

"We are grown women."

"This, from you? Seems like I'm always trying to get you to step outside your own lines, not the other way around."

Seems like you are even moodier than usual.

As they arrived back at the coach stop on Avenue Granocia, Aza said, "See? He's not here yet."

Maleka walked to the curb, craning her neck this way and that. Traffic was light.

Aza heard a screech of wheels. She turned toward the strait and saw a black car careen around the nearest corner.

"Watch out!" Aza shouted at Maleka, afraid the car might hit her.

Instead, it stopped, the brakes squealing. Two men jumped out of the back seat and grabbed Maleka, under her arms, literally lifting her off the ground and moving toward the private car.

"Stop!" Aza screamed finding her voice and her feet at the same moment. She lunged forward, eyes darting around, looking for help. There were no pedestrians nearby. Even the road traffic was at a lull. "Help!" she shouted, getting close to the vehicle. Maleka had already been pushed into the back seat by one man while the second went to the other side and got in. The driver took off before the back door was fully closed.

Aza was left in the coach lane, taking in the smell and taste of burning rubber and acrid steam. In the small, back window of the speeding car, Maleka's head turned, her face appearing vaguely, her eyes wide, her mouth in a grim line.

"Help!" Aza screamed again, her voice small and lost. The wind whipped off the strait as twilight overtook the city. Arc lights came on. The cool day transformed into a chilly night, and a thin wail came from Aza's throat as she turned in a slow, useless circle, her face wet and cold.

6

TO WHAT END?

THE PART OF AZA that was conscious of anything but the fact that Maleka had been abducted was aware that—in a scene eerily similar to the one she'd just witnessed with her friend—their previously scheduled driver was putting her into the back of his coach.

Did Maleka even have time to struggle?

She sat on the back seat, shivering uncontrollably. Her face felt frozen with all the tears she'd shed while standing in the wind.

The driver brought her a lap blanket and put it over her shoulders. "I'm Gerland, Miss. Remember? Now, calm down and take some slow breaths so's you can tell me what's happened."

"My friend is gone."

"What? Where did she go?"

"Men came and put her in their vehicle."

"Do you know them?"

Aza took in a long, ragged breath and settled back into the corner of the seat, wrapping the blanket around her shoulders more tightly. "No. Oh, I have to report this! She's been abducted!" Her words became increasingly fast and shrill.

Gerland pulled a flask from his coat pocket. "Have a sip. I'm going to get you help. Just drink one or two swallows. It will warm you. Slowly, now."

Aza put the bottle to her lips. She winced as the spirits hit her throat, and handed it back to the driver, who retreated, closed the door, and got behind the steering wheel.

At some point, she realized he was driving her home. *How does he know where I live?* But immediately, she forgot to care as she—again and again—relived those last moments with Maleka.

Gerland stopped near the front door of the Villa. Aza gathered up her shawl and her satchel, which had fallen off the seat onto the floor. Looking around to see if anything had slipped out, she picked up a calling card and a stylus and put them in her apron pocket as she got out of the cab.

"Are you better, Miss?"

"I don't know. I'm a mess." She looked up at him. His gray-blue eyes showed genuine concern. "You have been more than kind. What do I owe you?"

Just then, Reth opened the iron gate. "Miss Aza," he said, "are you due here today?"

"I need to see father immediately," she responded, brushing past him into the courtyard. "Please pay the driver."

"Father!" she called. "Father!"

Leo emerged from his study. He looked past her.

Aza turned to see that Gerland stood just inside the black iron gates, as Reth passively impeded him from coming any farther into the room.

"Sir, if I may be so bold," Gerland said, derby in hand, "it may be wise for me to come in and speak with you about what happened today."

Father bowed his head and motioned for Reth to let the man enter.

"Maleka's been abducted," Aza said.

"What?" Father's calm cracked.

Aza explained—her body, her voice reacting again to what had happened.

Leo turned to the driver. "Were you there?"

"No, sir. I picked up Miss Aza on the street just after."

He turned back to her. "What street?"

"Avenue Granocia, near the Holba Bridge."

Gerland said, "Sir, I took them there. They asked me to return in an hour. I wouldn't have dropped them if it seemed unsafe. The misses had helped me earlier."

Leo rubbed his forehead and then turned, motioning them to come into his office. He sat at his desk and took out pen and paper. "Tell me the details. Where you were. What time it was. A description of the men and the car."

Aza told her part, her voice growing weaker with every detail. Her throat felt like it was going to close up entirely. Gerland added what little he could.

Leo wrote a message, sealed it, and rang for Reth. "A missing person report. Urgent. The information is in the note."

Reth nodded and left the room.

Leo rose and went to Gerland. Aza stood. Her father put his arm around the driver's shoulder and held out his other hand for a shake. Gerland responded as Leo led him from the room and out the front gates.

Aza sat in the nearest chair with a thud. Gravity pinned her as she felt the full impact of what had happened. Then Father returned and pinned her with his glare. "I'm sorry this happened to you. I know you are extremely upset, but what the spellfire is going on?"

"Maleka overheard that a Gen business will be fluxed tomorrow. We went to find it. You have to warn them."

"Why did *you* have to go there?"

"Because when you overhear things, you don't get the whole story. We didn't know the name of the business. We just—oh, it's not important anymore! We have to find Maleka!"

"You're right." He sat down and got his voice under control. "The rest isn't important for now. I have to talk to her family. Is there anything else I should know?"

"The car zipped in. Two young men—kind of young, though older than I am, I think—rushed toward her." She had already told him all this, but the words tumbled out anyway. "Dressed all in black, so I don't know their clan."

"How far from her were you?"

"From the sidewalk to the curb."

"Why didn't they take you?"

"I don't know. They ignored me, even when I screamed for help."

"Did she scream?"

"No. No. Father, it was as if she'd turned into a statue."

Aza slept poorly.

The next morning, she sat up in bed and thought about the difference between waking in the bedroom of her home, as compared to the sparely furnished, tiny room at the Komeh. Here, she had a beautiful, spacious third-story room with two windows high above the treetops, where she could, in winter, glimpse the sun glistening on the Strait of Jeka.

The strait.

She rose, shivering at the cold floor under her bare feet and the memory of the blast of wind that came off the water as she and Maleka walked near it. She opened the curtains to a sunny day. Dust motes glimmered.

A sunny day...to what end? Maleka is gone. Aza got back in bed and let the seemingly endless tears come freely. *Where is she? Who took her? What condition might she be in?*

There was a rap at the door. "Miss?"

"Yes, Reth," she said, her voice thick after all the bawling.

"Breakfast, Miss." He came in with a tray. "After the night you've had, I thought you might need both sustenance and privacy."

Aza was momentarily speechless. She'd rarely had food served to her in bed. "That is so thoughtful. Thank you."

He waited while she arranged pillows and propped herself up. He then placed the tray on her lap. "How are you doing?"

She immediately teared up again at his tender tone. She gestured toward her face with one hand and shrugged.

"Yes, I understand. We are all stunned. Your father is out. He's meeting with Maleka's family and there will be a Synod meeting later."

"Of course. Thank you. I should be at the Komeh, so I will have to pull myself together quickly."

"Yes, Miss." Reth turned to leave and then stopped, making a quarter-turn back before saying, "I...I wonder if you might not send a message of regret to the Komeh today?"

"Regret?"

"Yes. Letting them know that you are...indisposed and can't be there today."

"I can do that?"

"I could send the message for you, if you like. I don't mean to overstep, Miss. If you wish to go—"

"I don't. I don't wish to go. Yes, please."

"Very well, Miss. Let me know if you need anything." He gave his tiny bow and left the room, closing the door behind him.

Why have I never in my life thought to stay here instead of going to work one day?

The rules were all set when she was a child! Before she knew to question anything. But her own lack of independence frustrated her. She didn't consider herself a particularly obedient person. Her father told Duma that she was...*what had he said?* Strong-willed!

Still...going to work at such a young age might tend to make one believe that you have no choice in the matter. She sighed. Sitting around this mausoleum of a house with no one to play with and nothing to do would not have been a great childhood, either.

Am I an employee? If so, are the wages paid to my father? What about my education?

Other children went to clan-run schools, but Leo hadn't cared enough to see that she knew more than the basics. "Sleep on your own shoulder," Leo had told her many times. Teach yourself...do for yourself...by yourself. He also told Duma she was intelligent. *Well, that's not the same thing as educated!* It had always been left up to her to learn, or not. She had, as much as possible, but there were so many holes in her "education."

Finally, Aza ate, and felt better for it.

She went to her wardrobe. There wasn't much there. A few changes of underclothes, a spare apron, and several dresses for holidays or socials. Her normal day clothes were at the Komeh. She put on fresh underpants, a pink undershirt, and yesterday's white cotton under-blouse with a tiny pink-and-green print. Over that went a worse-for-the-wear, pale green blouse. She slipped on her petticoat—noticing grime at the hem from walking on the streets of Maripesa—and then donned a thinner, pale pink petticoat and an overskirt, in a delicately striped fabric that brought all the colors together. She made sure the neck edges of her two undershirts showed evenly and wrapped the overblouse's long tails around back and to the front again where she tied a square knot and tucked the ends neatly.

Aza studied the apron she'd unceremoniously dumped on the chair the night before. Gens took as much pride in their aprons as they did their gloves. Hers was a wrinkled mess. She had the spare, but wondered if Reth might have time to launder this one today since she wasn't going to work. *You could do it, Aza. Reth might be up to his ears in responsibilities.*

She reached into the pocket of the dirty apron to remove her nilteh and rediscovered the items she'd picked up from the coach floor last night. A crushing weight filled her chest as the scene of Maleka being stuffed into the car came back to her full force. She sat down, wondering what kind of awful person she must be for letting so much time go by without thinking of Maleka's whereabouts. Eventually, she focused on her breathing until the worst of her chest pain passed.

The items in her hand hadn't spilled from her satchel after all. They didn't belong to her. Curiosity, as always, gave her a spark of life.

The calling card was a Kruik design, done in their clan flag colors—a dark blue border, medium blue center and a wavy line of light blue between. *Benelek Kruik, Assistant to the Provost.* Her address was below.

What's a provost? The address meant nothing to her, but she could search for it. This was just another snippet of information like the hundreds of others she'd gathered and researched for most of her twenty-six years—mostly to no avail.

The other object, however, was more fascinating and unique. In her rush and misery last night, she had thought it was a pen or stylus. But it wasn't. It was the shape of a pen, but heavier and slightly longer. There was no pointed end with which to write, no matter how she tried to open, push, click, or twist it. It was white enamel with three chevrons in magenta, gold, and purple. They were expertly painted about a third of the way down the shaft. These colors weren't traditional for any of the clans, but purple always meant Puraples. Plus, it looked expensively made.

I should get in touch with Gerland about it. I wouldn't want him blamed for its disappearance.

This fascinating item went into the inner pocket of Aza's satchel, its function a mystery...for now.

7

SITUATED

A FORTNIGHT PASSED WITH no word, no clue, no ransom note, no Maleka. Nothing.

The Gens continued to look for her. Mam Sior's resources had also been put behind finding the young woman. Maleka had, after all, been employed in her household. The effort, Aza was certain, came more from Sior's sense of control over her own rather than concern or affection. However, even the ruling family's resources had found no clues.

The pain of losing her only friend, and her accompanying guilt—no matter how illogical—were a double-pronged misery. She exerted strict mind control to keep herself in motion, counting it as a personal victory when she went a whole workday without tears breaking through her defenses. But it bled through in unguarded moments—the midday meal, a coach ride home, when she thought of something she wanted to tell Maleka, and every night when her pillow grew damp with tears.

On a Friday afternoon, she arrived at the street to find Gerland's coach waiting to take her home. He was her regular driver now. Since Maleka's abduction, she spent every weekend at the Villa. This change—what to Aza had seemed a monumental declaration of independence—had been met with no objection, not even a comment from her employer.

"Good day, Miss."

"Good to see you," Aza said as she climbed in. It was, but this coach and his presence brought up that evening on Avenue Granocia. This immediately dissolved the barriers she'd kept raised throughout her day. She rubbed her eyes to dull the sudden stinging and to keep the tears at bay.

"Miss Aza. I was hoping we might take a side trip, unless you're in a hurry to get home. There's someone I'd like you to meet. Are you interested?"

"Who is it?"

"Her name is Rimna. She's rumored to have unusual Talent."

"For..."

"Finding things, Miss. Finding people, perhaps."

Her heart leaped and then immediately sank. She didn't believe in that kind of Talent and didn't need more disappointment. Also, she had to consider her father and Reth. Might they worry if she was late? On the other hand, Gerland was looking so hopeful and it might be pleasant to take a drive with him.

As if reading her mind, he said, "We could stop at the Messagery first, to let your father know."

"Oh, of course then, that would be splendid. I would be happy to go with you. Where should I tell my father we're going?"

"Gosh," Gerland said as he pulled into the Messagery. He looked down, rubbing his jaw. "I know where Rimna's house is, but not the address. We're headed to Colvara, Miss. My neighborhood."

"Your address, then?" she asked as they both got out and walked into the office.

"I have a better idea. Tell him, in case of emergency, to check in at the Besin clinic in Colvara." He gave her the street names. "Prominent corner. Can't miss it. Ask for my favorite healer, Vijo."

Aza felt a little lost, but jotted down: *Father, Driver Gerland Salizan is taking me to meet a friend. All is well, but just in case, if I do not arrive by the after-dinner hour, send Reth to the Besin clinic at the corner of Dwami and Springflower Roads in Colvara and ask for information from a healer named Vijo. Again, all is well. —Aza*

With Aza sitting up front, they drove through busy streets, up over the Little River bridge and past the imposing pink Tapinak, through an industrial section of warehouses and factories and into a residential area. The houses and lots were significantly smaller than in Aza's. It was after work for most of the city, and the beginning of the weekend. The weather was not too chilly, so people were about—doing yard work, chatting on the walkways. Children played in the many small green spaces or, occasionally, in the streets.

"I have stayed in such a miniscule part of this huge city! What is wrong with me? Going back and forth between the Komeh to home? It's exciting to see more of Maripesa. Thank you."

"That's a bit hard for me to understand, Miss, being from a driving family. I was brought up in this coach, usually sittin' in that seat right there."

"With your father?"

"Yes. The old buggy is showing its age, but I replace parts and tinker with it to make sure it keeps going. Now, I have a nephew who's a wiz at it. He's manufactured new thrusters for my steamdrive. It's purring like a kitten again."

At the clinic, Gerland parked in front of the expansive one-story building. "We need to confirm that Vijo is here and tell him about the message—just in case."

"Why Vijo?"

"For my money, he's the best healer in the city. And young...like you."

Aza didn't know whether to grin or grimace at this now obvious attempt to broaden her horizons beyond seeing the city's byways. Gerland wanted her to meet this fellow. Since she counted not one Besin among her acquaintances, she could hardly object.

He opened the door for her. "Miss," he said with a courtly bow.

She laughed and held out her hand. He took it and pretended to kiss the tips of her fingers.

"Kind sir," she said, curtsying.

Laughing, they walked into the clinic, where Gerland asked for Vijo. In a few minutes, a young man came around the corner. Sure enough, he looked to be about Aza's age. He was slim and tall with a complexion on the fair end of skin tones and had gorgeous, sky-blue eyes.

"Gerland, are you fluxed again?"

"Nay, my good man," he said, continuing the role playing, "my companion and I are free of all curses. We have a small, non-magical favor to ask. First, let me introduce you to the Great and Talented, Illustrious and Notorious, Aza Gen."

Aza blushed deeply, but she also laughed because it was clear that Vijo caught Gerland's playful spirit. He, dressed in simple Besin white with bright blue ribbon trim as his only decorative element, bowed deeply and said, "My Lady."

"My friend Gerland has a flair for the dramatic. I apologize if we are taking you away from a busy schedule."

"Not at all. We are enjoying a lull. How may I help you?"

Gerland launched into an explanation. "Aza has within the past weeks undergone a traumatic event—"

Vijo's eyes locked onto Aza's. Embarrassed, she wanted to look away but managed to hold his gaze while Gerland continued.

"I'm taking her to a person who might be able to help solve this situation. We have no specific address for this person and so Miss Gen has messaged her father to let him know that if she does not arrive home safe and sound within the next couple of hours, he should check in here for any word. Your name and this address were sent to him." He paused, and then said, "My apologies if I am out of line. Here are our cards. Miss Aza's father's name is on the back."

Somehow, this barrage of words summed things up in more reasonable way than Aza had had any hope of.

The healer, still studying her, took the cards from Gerland.

Aza bowed her head, carefully considering the scuffed but clean, blue and white checkerboard floor. She felt on-the-spot and silly to have taken this precaution. Aza looked up at those serious blue eyes and said, "My friend was abducted in front of me. We've had no word of her since. All this probably seems unnecessary, but it's left me feeling vulnerable."

"I see. I am so sorry. Do you trust Master Gerland?"

"Oh, yes. Utterly."

"Good then. I'm happy to help, though I trust you won't need it at all."

After evermore narrow and winding lanes, Gerland finally pulled up in front of one of the tiniest houses Aza had ever seen. It sat slightly apart from the others on the street because of a wide circle of green space all around that encompassed a garden. It took Aza's breath away.

Trees, vines, flowers, vegetables, fruits and herbs, all grew in higgledy-piggledy profusion. She couldn't breathe in the aromas often or deeply enough on the short path to the front door.

A bell tinkled when Rimna opened her bright green, round-topped door.

She was rounded too. A rotund woman dressed in layers of colorful print fabrics in varying lengths. Over her head was an inglethe, the scarf/shawl that Dal women frequently wear.

"Oh," Aza said. She immediately covered her mouth with her hand in an attempt to cover her involuntary exclamation, but the woman had heard.

"You didn't know you were visiting one of the lowest clans, dearie? Well, come in, come in." Rimna turned and walked into the tiny room, much of which she filled with her girth. She sat in the middle of a settee covered in the same kinds of fabric she wore on her body, thereby rendering herself almost invisible except for her hands and face. Nodding at Gerland, she said, "Please, both of you, sit."

Aza did. "I'm Aza Gen. Thank you for inviting us in."

"That you are Gen is obvious, dearie. No need to add a last name when you wear it so proudly. Yours is an important family within your clan, I take it?"

Why was it so obvious? "My father is Leo, Clan Leader."

She felt something against her leg and glanced down to see a large black cat smelling her shoes and the hem of her dress.

"That's Trilst," Rimna said. The cat leapt into Aza's lap at the sound of his name.

Gerland said, "Auntie, we are here about a missing person. We're hoping you can help."

She nodded again, her hands in her lap, knees splayed, ankles crossed. She closed her eyes and began to hum softly.

Aza looked over to Gerland, who gave her a reassuring nod.

Dals have Talents? She'd been taught that they did not. *Oh, for* Maripes *sake, you ninny! This is nothing more than common superstition—what people make up if they have no magic of their own.* A surge of disappointment ran through her.

Aza realized she was holding her breath and made herself relax, focusing on the fact that this couldn't hurt and might be entertaining. The woman was fascinating and seemed kind, if a little bit brusque. Gerland's presence, as always, comforted her.

After a few minutes, Rimna opened her eyes. They were dark and small and reminded Aza of someone.

"I have situated myself," she said. "Tell me what I need to know."

"My...my best friend, Maleka Gen, was taken off a street near the Strait of Jeka on Avenue Granocia weeks ago. There's been no sign of her since and—"

"This, I know. What do you want from me?"

Irritation rose up in her. "I want to find her. What do you mean you know these things? How could you?"

Rimna regarded her sternly. "I see that you don't understand. I will explain, but I expect a modicum of respect from the people I help. Can you give me that?"

Aza's face burned. Two factions vied within her. Gen pride, first. Who was this witch, with her supposed Talent, to lecture her, a woman of the mid-clan with verifiable Talents? The second was pure and utter embarrassment at having been a discourteous brat in front of someone who seemed to be willing to help—whether she actually could or not. Embarrassment won, quickly settling into shame.

"Rimna, I am sorry. Please accept my apology. This is all new to me and I am somewhat...skeptical, but that's no excuse to be disrespectful. I needed reminding that I'm no better than anyone else in this world."

Rimna's face stayed firm, but she said, "Of course you are better than some people. Some people are horrors. But—" she raised an index finger—"you are no better than many others. Take each one as they come to you. You'll be better off for it."

Aza bent her head for a moment and then lifted her face and said, "Thank you. I very much need your help and if you're still willing, I'll be grateful for any assistance you can give me."

"To answer your question, I know about Maleka because I can 'hear' what is in the front of people's minds. I also catch people's emotions when they are strong, but that's no great Talent, is it?" She waved her hands dismissively and then went on. "I could hear your thoughts about a missing friend. When I 'situate,' it means that I put myself into your inner situation so that I catch the flow of it."

"Respectfully, Rimna, if your Talent is to hear what's on people's minds, how does that help you find someone? I don't know where she is, or I wouldn't need help."

Instead of answering or being offended that Aza was questioning her skills, Rimna reached out and took Aza's hand. Hers were plush, soft and warm. "You know her very well, eh?"

Aza nodded, tearing up.

"Think of her. Put her and all that you know of her into the front of your brain."

Aza wanted to ask how one managed to place something in a certain part of one's brain, but didn't.

She thought of Maleka.

How she looked when she first came to work at the Komeh, with her thick, bouncy, dark hair and shining skin. Her frequent laughter, and willing, playful spirit. Her small acts of kindness, silly crossed eyes, jangling charms, fits of sudden anger that went away as fast as they came. Aza thought of her romantic nature and expressed need to find her one true love in life. Maleka, on the day she was taken. How she had urged Aza to come with her on the outing. Her whining about the cold wind. How much laughter there was when they warmed up. The excitement about finding the pink building with the black and white tile. And then, after...she showed tension about getting back to meet Gerland on time, about being late and worrying her parents. *That moment just before the sound of squealing tires. Maleka seemed more than tense. Worried...maybe. Almost as if she knew something was about to happen. Could Maleka have a Talent for premonition?*

She didn't fight or scream. It wouldn't have made any difference, but why not yell out? She thought of Maleka's squeal—which she used often, and often over the silliest of things. A salamander on the lawn, a beetle in the house, a stain on her gloves, and yet, *when she was being kidnapped, no sound came from her mouth.*

Aza stopped thinking. Her head was bowed and her eyes closed, but she sensed it was enough. When she was ready, she opened her eyes and looked into Rimna's.

Garnia. That's who she reminds me of. The housekeeper at Mam Sior's has the same reflective dark eyes.

"Rimna, why do I feel calmer?"

"Because you shared some of your most troubling concerns with me. I have some information for you, but don't expect it will make you content ...even as it is, objectively, good news."

"What do you mean? What?"

"The message I get is that Maleka does not want to be found."

Aza stared, her mind blank.

"It does not feel as if she is in any current danger."

Still, Aza had no words.

"It feels instead that, for now, she is where she wants to be."

By the time Aza entered the Villa that evening, she had draped herself in her now familiar numbing cloak. Her evening with Gerland had been exhilarating, distracting, and at times, fun, but she was hungry, exhausted, and had no clue how to process what the Dal woman had told her. She walked into the courtyard and realized that her father was holding a meeting.

Reth came in. "Oh Miss Aza, we received your message. Your father was grateful that you sent it. Are you all right?"

"Very tired, but yes, fine."

He looked worried. "I'm sorry to tell you this when you're worn out, by the look of it, but the Gen Advisory Council is meeting and your father would like you to attend."

"What?"

He nodded once.

Aza's eyes burned with fatigue, but suddenly her mind felt sharper. "Am I in trouble?"

"I shouldn't think so, Miss. I believe he simply wants you to understand what's going on. Perhaps they are discussing Miss Maleka, which of course concerns you. Shall I bring you a plate of food? I'm sure no one would mind."

"Yes," she said, drifting toward the sound of her father's voice at the end of the plant-filled corridor. "That would be lovely."

All eyes looked toward her as she walked into the chamber—a long, narrow, table-filled room.

Leo finished his sentence. "...increase in these incidents, particularly in the northern burgs of Maripesa."

The room was full. She knew most of the attendees by sight. They were matriarchs or, more often, patriarchs of each of the branches of their clan—Willa, a woman around her father's age whom Aza, as a child, pretended was her secret mother. Miervaldis, advisor and closest friend of Leo's. Jea, Maleka's father. Duma's father, Palter. The eldest, whom she had always called Old Lekt.

Several nodded as she slipped in and found a seat against the wall.

After the briefest of pauses, Father continued. "The contents of the ship that was ruined, and before that, the warehouse full of cursed containers, were bad enough, but we now know of three Gen organizations fluxed by the Kruiks and several incidents of malady curses given to innocent bystanders."

Aza thought of that big red X on the map. *The warehouse, a battleground.*

A man in the back whom Aza didn't recognize said, "Palter, how is your business faring?"

Duma's father spoke, his bass voice compelling. "We are recovered...from the curses. Not from the loss of revenue. They hit us with fidova *and* dahke."

"Fidova? *Maripes.*" Aza had rarely seen this slimy curse. "What a mess that must have made."

"It took five, cleaning for almost a week. Business is down overall. So is our reputation! *We* all know that an object cleaned of a flux curse is not damaged and no danger to anyone, but who wants a once-befouled cloth for their new dress if they can go buy the fabric somewhere else? Our business is struggling for the first time."

What? The pink building was Palter's business? No, it can't be. They had warning; it would have been prevented. Surely the tip from her and Maleka must have been about different business. Did Father not provide warning to Palter? She threw a look at her father, but he was focused on the conversation.

Palter was still speaking. "It's a curse for a curse out there, though it's more like three curses for a curse. There's a splurge of maladies cropping up in pockets of the city. There are even reports of giarmial. So far, the Besin seem to have contained it."

"The Puraples aren't known for their restraint," said Jea.

Leo nodded. "True. Though I want you all to know that I've spoken at length with Mam Sior about all of this. She fears escalation and is trying to hold the line. She is formidable, as we know. But the clan is so large, with many headstrong youngsters spoiling for a fight. There are those who mistake their own youth and boredom for activism."

Father is in council with Mam Sior? Aza had never seen him at the Komeh. They must meet at the Council of Clans building.

"I don't know if the younger among you are familiar with giarmial," Father said. "We haven't seen it much in over a generation. But it is *the* weapon that put the Puraples on top. Without it, they wouldn't stand a chance against the Kruiks."

"Why's that?" someone in the back asked.

"Because most maladies are specific to the person who is cursed, just as the fluxes only grow on the target of the curse. But giarmial passes from person to person like a normal, contagious disease."

"Of course," the voice in the back said, "I knew that."

"But you weren't born the last time we had a ruling family power struggle, so you haven't seen it. We're at a tipping point. Kruiks are tired of being second class. We don't know yet if this is a concerted effort with the Leader Rodjo's tacit blessing or a few rogues. But we don't want to wait around to find out."

"What happened to the ship that was fouled?" Aza asked.

"It's at the bottom of the Strait of Jeka. The Synod, with Puraples' consent, set fire to it."

"It couldn't be cleaned?"

Maleka's father spoke, "By the time it was discovered, it was too late. We were already stretched thin by cleaning the warehouse and our own targeted businesses. Burning that ship was the only viable option. Luckily, everyone agreed."

Just then, Reth opened the door and slipped a plate to her. Bread, cold fish, cheese and fruit. She nodded a thank you.

"...still have dozens of Gen in the warehouse. I can only hope that we've seen the worst of it."

"And what of Maleka?" Willa asked. "Is there any news at all?"

Aza felt stinging pain around the rims of her eyes and thought of what Rimna had said. She looked at her plate of food, certain she would not be able to eat anything.

A short silence followed.

Jea cleared his throat and said, "No. Nothing yet."

Father took up the topic and asked the council to round up new volunteers to go door-to-door in selected neighborhoods, looking for leads.

As they discussed how to organize this, Aza glanced around, feeling that no one dared look in her direction. *The last person to see Maleka. And I don't belong here. Everyone else is the head of a major branch of the clan. Who am I? The Leader's daughter, but so what?*

She stayed in her chair when the meeting adjourned. As if she were being fed by someone else, small bites were in her mouth and therefore had to be chewed. Aza felt light-headed and a moment later realized that she could not only see her plate but also a scrum of Gen standing outside waiting for their coaches. Zaz sometimes had a mind of her own.

"Do you think she knows something she's not telling us?" Palter asked Jea.

"Who knows the mind of a young woman?" he answered. "They could have had a pact or something."

"She looked guilty, if you ask me."

Jea shrugged. "I've implored Leo to get the truth out of her, but he's certain that she's as worried about Maleka as anyone. He saw her right after Maleka disappeared and is convinced that there was no acting or lying on her part."

"What was she doing at the council tonight?" Palter asked.

Jea shrugged again. "Because of Maleka? Or because he has no sons?"

Palter scoffed. "So what? It's not like it's a hereditary leadership. Even if he did have sons, they'd have to earn their leader role same as anyone else. Next time, I think I'll bring Duma and see what Leo thinks of that."

Aza slowly rose, leaving the empty plate on her chair. She reintegrated Zaz and ascended the stairs to her room. She went to the window, admiring the twinkly lights and pink glow that came from the Tapinak's spire. But even if her eyes were pleased, her thoughts were bitter.

Men! Why are they always so sure of themselves? It's not as if they're doing a great job of running Maripesa. Maybe I will become Gen Council Leader, just to show them how it can be done.

8

·ᶜᵏᵉ·

CASTING DOUBTS

FERJIVAL'S YOUNGEST SISTER PASSED by him in the hallway without a glance.

He stopped, turned, and called to her. "Dusia!" He had little contact with his mother's "other family," and seeing her, unexpectedly, made him realize how grown up she'd become.

She turned. There was a softness about her that wasn't a part of the rest of them.

Eight of us. Mam had certainly done her part to grow the Puraples' population. When Ferjival was born, she hadn't been running Maripesa. The job had been done by her brother. He died young and the leadership passed ineffectually through that portion of the clan until, in a coup that was, thirty years later, still talked about in hushed tones, Mam Sior, not yet thirty years of age, took over. And then she bore three or four more children.

His sister was looking at him but hadn't walked over. "Yes?" she said, finally.

"Oh. I, yes, I was just wondering something."

"What?"

He, realizing that she wasn't going to come to him, took the strides to be within conversational distance.

"How old are you now?"

"Nineteen."

"Nineteen..." *No wonder Dusia was the last. Mother was over forty when she was pregnant with this one.*

"How old are you?" she asked him.

"What? Oh, no, it doesn't matter how old I am. Old as the hills."

"Hmm." She waited, her delicate hands clasped lightly, her shoulders and jaw relaxed. It wasn't often that he talked to someone so utterly without tension.

She had a long line of golden charms pinned to the sleeve of her dark brown dress. The dress was trimmed with gold in a pattern that brought to mind a military uniform.

"I am thirty-two. And now you're all grown up."

She laughed a little and shrugged. "I should go."

"Where are you off to?"

"Lunch with friends."

"Good, then. Oh, and Dusia, be careful who you associate with. There's a lot of wild cursing going on these days. So...no Kruiks, nay?"

"I have no Kruik friends! How extremely scandalous, brother." She laughed—more to herself than with him—turned smartly and walked away, her taffeta dress swooshing with each step.

Was I ever so young? To believe that associating with Kruiks was a scandal? Innocence. Or was she mocking him and what she thought of as his old-fashioned views? It pained him that he didn't know.

Of course, the clans mixed socially. You couldn't help it. Kruiks and Gen—the more upper-crust of them—and even the occasional Besin were part of his sports competitions and the drinking afterward.

He watched her go and came down on the side of innocence. Under his breath, he said, "Good. Good that you were taught properly. We should all get back to our own. I'll make that a priority when I take over Maripesa."

He was on his way to see his mother; perhaps that's why he'd talked to Dusia. He wasn't looking forward to the audience with Mam Sior. In fact, his heart was firing rapidly and his mouth felt dry as a new wick.

She kept him waiting for ten minutes. His anxiety had turned to irritation by the time he was let in, so he wasted no time. He walked to her desk and said, "I have a proposal, Mother."

"What is it? I'm busy, you know, so don't beat around the bush."

He cleared his throat, thinking that beating around the bush was the opposite of what he had done. He held back a sigh and said, "I've been thinking about what you said, what you've said many times, in fact. That I'm not using my time to the benefit of the city. I do spend too much time in sport. I thought it might please you and do me some good, if I took more interest in the—*ahem*—details, well, some of the details of keeping the city running properly."

During this introduction, which he'd practiced a lot more than the rest of what he was going to suggest, his mother stopped poring over her papers, took off her glasses and leaned back in her chair. Her expression was hard to read.

"Go on."

"As you know, we are seeing so many attacks by the Kruiks. Large ones like the warehouse and the cargo ship, but also small ones. Gen businesses and the like. Vermin being tossed at the kuab tournament, for *Maripes* sake. At first I thought it was just a spate of bratty behavior, but it's—I don't know—as if it's taken hold as a thing that they take pride in doing."

"What would you like to do about it?"

"I would like to head a...a committee, let's call it. A committee of sons of the most prominent Puraples houses." He, while saying this, had been looking at the carpet under his feet and part of his brain mulled over the intricate blue and purple design, even while attempting to sell a concept that he'd never spoken out loud to anyone. He looked up at his mother's wrinkled face.

"You. Heading a...committee."

"We would, ah, figure out a way to tackle this, this flurry of curses. To punish the Kruiks responsible, or at least counter them. It doesn't do, Mother, simply to respond tit-for-tat. We must let them know that we aren't taking this lightly and that we will not sit idly by and let them get away with attacking us for no good reason. Well, they've always done that, but not in such a concerted way!"

"'Idly by?'"

Her words, as they so often did, entered him, not in the ears, but somewhere near his heart. She was going to mock him. His bypassed ears grew hot.

"You think that's what our policy is? To be idle? To be ineffectual? To be uncoordinated? What do you think I do as leader of this city?"

"Mother. I—"

"I am in charge."

"Of course you are! I know that. Everyone knows that! I wasn't saying that you or anyone wasn't doing a good job, only that I'd so like to be a part of the solutions that are being undertaken."

"What do you think the Puraples Council does?"

"I—I know."

She shook her head and ticked her tongue against her lower teeth. "No. You don't. Because you have chosen not to attend."

"I—" It was true. He'd stopped attending several years ago. Tired to the bone of his mother's nastiness.

"I understand. The meetings were boring. Right? Well, your seat, which you had a right to, given the accident of your birth, has long since been given away. It's too late."

"No. It isn't. I demand a role! You can't complain that I do nothing useful and then refuse to give me a path to becoming useful!"

She had leaned forward again. Her elbows reddened on the desk. One hand held her glasses, the other tapped its shiny surface. "I'll think about what you could do. But no 'committee.' It's the most ridiculous thing I've ever heard you say. And that's a long list."

"Why do you hate me so?"

She gazed at him a long time. "I do not. I don't care about you at all. You've disappointed me too many times. All my children disappoint me. I think that's what they are here for. To keep me humble. With so many of you, that's a lot of humility."

"*Holy spellfire,*" he said under his breath.

"What?" she said sharply.

"I don't think of you as a humble person, Mother."

"No? Well, you should have seen me before you all wore me down. I'll assign you some job. Is that what you want? A job? So you can be useful? That's how most people do it, you know. They work. Sure. But don't come whining to me when it is 'boring' or 'tedious.' Oh, just leave. I don't know why I'm wasting my breath. I have actual work to do. Get out."

Ferjival walked slowly across the room, not because he wanted to take a long time to leave, but because his legs were wobbly with rage. They felt like they might falter, his body sprawling on the intricate swirls of blue and purple.

Or instead, he might turn, grab the nearest...what? *Oh, there. A bronze statuette on the library table, only two strides away.* He might veer slightly, pick it up, turn, and hurl it with all his fury, smashing his mother in the face, knocking out all her teeth, ruining her power of speech, maybe even killing her. He walked slowly, deliberately, to reach the door, push the latch and leave her presence without, in fact, killing her violently.

Once in the hallway with a solid door between them, he walked briskly. When he reached his study, sweaty and slightly nauseated, he went to a window and concentrated on taking a few deep breaths.

The fallow gardens of the Komeh lay below and, past that, the stand of bare-limbed trees that provided a buffer before the the Execution Grounds. Beyond, the city sprawled to an unseen horizon. To his left, a bright spot of sunlight reflected off the Strait of Jeka.

What if I left? Maybe with enough of a pay-off, he could get work on a cargo ship. Go to the Eastern Isles. He was a capable person. He could blend in somewhere else; no one would know he was from this banished city. It would be worth it never to have to lay eyes on his mother ever again. Better than being executed for her murder.

He heard a knock at the open door.

"Yes?"

"Sir Ferjival. A message for you."

A strong and confident young man, tall with broad shoulders and flat belly, came into his study. *His confidence comes from being so typically handsome.* Ferjival wasn't. He was overly thin, gangly, with his father's sharp visage and a receding hairline that no one else in the family seemed to have. He did his best with what he'd been provided, always dressing appropriately and representing his family well. But this nobody, no-Talent, low-clan lad could just stand there and *look* like a lord.

"From whom?"

"Mam Sior, sir."

"I don't want it."

"Sir?"

He strode forward with all the fury in his heart and grabbed the lackey's perfectly tucked cravat. "Can you not hear?" he roared.

The messenger's eyes reflected shock and repulsion, but not fear. He took hold of Ferjival's hand and put pressure on it, while pushing himself away with the other.

Ferjival let go. "Get out!"

"Sir," the young man said. He didn't bow or even nod, didn't click his heels, did not turn away. The boy walked backwards toward the door and, just before leaving the room, laid the crumpled message on the side table.

"Wait!" Ferjival walked over, ripped open the message and read: *Congratulations on your new job. Your title is Assistant to the Deputy Director of the on-going renyers remediation. Report to the Noptva warehouse this afternoon.*

His lips thinned out, his face grew red, his lungs ceased working. He looked at the messenger, who had no hint of subservience.

"Is there a response, sir?"

Ferjival spoke in a whisper. "I do not know who I hate more at this moment."

The man's perfect eyebrows rose in question over his dark blue eyes, but he said nothing.

"You, or my mother."

"Ah," the man said, taking a step backwards. "I am sorry if it is bad news. Such is our fate—we, the messengers—to deliver what may not be welcomed. My apologies. May I go?"

Ferjival glared. *Such fucking impudence. Such a downfall of standards that this nobody thinks he can talk to the eldest son of the ruler of Maripesa as an equal.*

"Go."

The man nodded once, turned and started down the hallway.

Ferjival followed quietly, keeping pace as his arm rose. He spread his fingers toward the man and chanted sub-vocally. He chanted his rage at his mother, his impotence, his extreme displeasure at the way he'd always been treated. He cast giarmial.

The boy never knew what hit him.

It would be a day or two before the symptoms showed themselves, but he would figure out where it had come from. "Let it be a lesson to that impudent upstart to never underestimate the power of the ruling family ever again."

❧

Aza felt a trickle of sweat between her breasts as she prepared to meet Duma, already waiting downstairs. She'd gone to seasonal parties before, but the last had been with a group of Gen Councilmen's offspring she barely knew. Hardly a fun evening. This would be her first dance with an actual date.

Aza wore a traditional Gen gown. Tonight's colors were hues of lilac, peach, and green, in typically Gen pastel shades. A corset came first, along with a cotton underskirt and voluminous, net petticoat. She donned a form-fitting, low-cut, off-white blouse layered at the neckline with thin, padded rows of a half dozen different silk fabrics—small floral prints, a swirly diagonal stripe and a couple of solids. Next came an ankle-length, satin skirt, richly embroidered down the right side and around the hem. A wide sash of coordinated but unique satins went around her waist, tied in an elaborate knot in front. Her dancing shoes were grass-green brocade.

Her unruly hair required much attention. She managed an upsweep by straightening it and parting it into four sections. Aza back-combed each section, smoothed the outer layer, and then entwined the ends from each section, pinning as she went until the strands had twisted into a complex knot which looked loose but was firmly pinned in place. It was a skill she had practiced on Maleka in their idle hours. Maleka had thick, manageable hair, and Aza had loved experimenting with it. Doing it on herself was more challenging, but taking one last look in the mirror, she was pleased.

She pinched her cheeks, put on coral teardrop earrings—a gift from her father—and left the room.

After all these weeks, Aza felt more curious than angry with Duma. He had, almost a month from his meeting with Leo, sent a calling card and a charming note, asking if she would accompany him to the Winter Dance tonight. Curiosity, and the possibility of a waltz or two, won out.

If Father's warning about her being clever and strong-willed had put him off, then so be it. She felt no distress at having those words attributed to her personality. If Duma didn't feel comfortable approaching her, perhaps that was to his credit. Better a shy man than one who thinks he can waltz in—*waltzing, wouldn't that be a lovely attribute in a man?*—and get a marriage partner without even talking to or courting her.

She reached the bottom of the lower staircase, straightened her posture, took a deep breath and walked into the rarely used receiving room.

Reth was there, as was her father, and Duma, looking very good in formal wear: a medium grey knee-length coat over a blue and white small-print, silk tunic wrapped tightly around his torso and belted with a wide matching blue satin sash and white ribbon. Darker gray pants and highly polished shoes of midnight blue finished the look. In his left hand, he held a top hat that matched his trousers. His signature dove-grey gloves were in it. His chestnut hair, several shades darker than his skin, was swept back off his forehead—except for one gravity-defying tress that bobbed, oh so winningly, over one thickly arched eyebrow.

"Ah, Aza," her father said, turning to her.

She looked at Duma and could tell that he was pleased at how she'd turned herself out. She might not be as tall and slim as most Gen women, but she felt pretty as she witnessed his smile spread. After a few too many seconds, and as if suddenly remembering that he must say something, he dipped his head and said, "Miss Aza."

"Duma."

"You look...divine."

Aza walked over and he took her hand, gloved in ivory leather over-worked with embossed peach blossoms and tiny pearl beads. She dipped slightly at the knees and said, "You as well, sir."

Father, in an expansive mood, began talking about asking Reth to bring wine, but to her relief, Duma diplomatically refused for them both, saying that his coach was waiting and that they should be off.

Reth helped Aza into her lilac, down-lined silk stole, and Duma held the door for her. She turned back to her father. "Good night."

He took two steps forward and kissed her cheek.

"Have fun, Aza."

The party was in full swing.

A dance was held each season at the Hexhoreh on the cathedral grounds. The six-sided building had a magnificent round room at the center of four ballrooms—one each for the Puraples, Kruik, Gen, and Besin clans. The other two sides held the grand entrance, and directly opposite that, administrative offices and smaller social rooms.

Aza and Duma entered the center room and stopped, admiring it for a moment.

An expansive chandelier, with tiny twinkling, infinitely reflective lights hung over a commodious hexagonal table full of all the good things to eat that the city of Maripesa had to offer.

They swept forward to the table.

There were intricate and creative bite-sized canapes and savory treats in the shape of hats and gloves and angel wings. Suckling pigs and grilled fowls, smoked fish terrines. Frozen creams and creamy puddings, toasted fruit-filled meringues, and the finest cocoan sweets. A huge sculpture made of molded and spun sugar in the form of a white crane—the city's symbol—stood in the middle.

Two sets of musicians sat on opposite sides of the room. They alternated, playing rounds of traditional Maripesian dance music, rousing and energetic, as dancers spun out of the main room and back to their clan's dance floor. As divided as the society was, they all enjoyed the same music.

They meandered into the Gen ballroom.

"It's a little overwhelming," Aza said. Everyone was so decked out that she was beginning to feel self-conscious. Was her outfit up to this level?

Then Duma leaned over and whispered just the right thing. "Shall we dance?"

She nodded enthusiastically.

He held her raised hand and they walked onto the dancing floor, which was less packed than the verges, though plenty of people drifted in a circle around the space. The song now being played was one of the slower ones and Duma, she was happy to find out, did know how to waltz. He was, in fact, a better dancer than she was.

She told him that.

"Oh, not at all," he said with a warm smile. "I think we're quite well matched."

After four songs, they made their way back into the center room where the air was cooler, but the crowd, flowing in from all four dances, was thick around the table. "Looks like we're out of luck for food for now," Duma said as they found a spot not too far from the front entrance where the night air came in every time someone entered.

"That's fine. But we need drinks!"

Duma snagged a couple of stems off the tray of a passing waiter.

After taking several gulps of the mildly alcoholic punch, Aza brought out the first topic of several she'd come up with in an attempt to get to know this man, but even more, to avoid dreaded silences. "How do you spend your days?"

"I work for the family business. Businesses. We're in textiles. We operate the largest silk farm on the island. Plus wools and linens. Over the last few years, we've negotiated the right to import from select places who have, um, willingness to do business with Maripesa."

"Oh, Duma, of course I know of your father's business. I, um, know about the flux curse you recently had to deal with. But I had no idea that you worked there."

"Yes, that was a trial. I found myself in the position of having to clean curses, something I hadn't done since I learned the chants in school."

Aza opened her mouth but closed it again when she could not decide what response she should have to that. It didn't matter because Duma continued.

"I don't usually work in that building. I'm more on the acquisition side of the business. We have an office near the Tapinak. It's quieter there."

"I see. I assume you know what I do with my days."

He nodded. "I understand that you are on the front lines, serving our beloved ruling family."

Aza, surprised by this, grinned. "You do not know how accurate a description that is."

He did an exaggerated shudder and said, "Your clan and your city are indebted to you."

This is interesting. He is teasing me, but he *knows it isn't a job most Gens would want to do.* Aza was only now seeing that broader perspective. It was a lowly job, and not a service to anyone but the Purples. *So what does it mean that Father signed me up for it?*

She must have been silent for too long because he said, "I'm sorry. I've offended you. I was trying to be light about it, but I mean it. It is an honorable job that you do."

"Thank you," she said. "I'm not offended. Just a bit confused."

He downed the rest of his drink, put his glass on a waiter's tray and grabbed two more full ones. "How so?"

Aza finished her drink, trying to decide how much of herself to share with this man. "I am afraid that I have done almost nothing with my life except clean flux curses. I know so little. I never thought of myself as a stupid person, but as I have begun to branch out, I realize that I just might be."

"Oh no. I have it directly from your father that you are exceedingly clever."

She eyed him for perhaps longer than was comfortable for either of them. Finally, she said, "How kind of him. However, he did not see to my education."

"Well, how much education does one need, really?"

"How much did you have?"

"Me? Oh, well, I'm not typical. In fact, I'm still in the process." He looked at her almost apologetically.

"What are you studying?"

"Just some advanced accounting. Things I'll need to run a business."

She looked at the throng. The clans mostly stayed with their own, but there was some mixing. "How many of these people, do you guess, have had no formal education?"

"Oh, I should think most of them went to their clan schools. This is the cream of the upper and middle clans, so...most of them."

"This is my point. Not me. My father sent me to work at age eight. I learned to read and do basic sums first, but that was it. Whatever else I know was gleaned by keeping my eyes and ears open while being in the Komeh and by reading books in my time off."

His eyes narrowed. "I had no idea. Now I really have offended you."

"No need to apologize. We are simply getting to know each other. But you see, we may not be as good a match as you might have thought, you being an educated man and me being...you know...stupid." Aza had intended lightness, but failed to pull it off.

Duma took the empty glass from her and gave her a full one.

"Have a sip or two, please."

He didn't need to ask her twice. She swallowed a reasonable-sized gulp as he moved from her side to stand in front of her. He put one gloved hand on each of her shoulders and, to her great surprise, shook her—twice. "Stop calling yourself stupid."

Aza laughed, more at the surprise than the comment. She wriggled a little, but his hands stayed put. "What should I call myself?"

"Undereducated? But 'stupid' girls don't get to sit in on meetings of the Gen Council."

"That surprised me as much as it did everyone else. I'm sure your father and many of the others took issue with me being there."

This made him pause.

He's trying to think of something diplomatic or charming to say. She could have let him off the hook but wanted to hear what he'd come up with. She *was* trying to get to know him, after all.

After rubbing his jaw while looking down, he raised his head and said, "Some of them were unhappy. But your father doesn't feel the need to explain his decisions."

Aza let out a scoffing laugh.

"Palter asked if I wanted to attend the next one and I doubt I'll be the only offspring to be there."

She grinned. "Let the curses fall where they may, right?"

"Want to see if we can get close to that food?" he asked.

And, of course, she did.

Once replete, they danced and drank and danced some more, with no more serious conversation. Duma knew a lot about fabrics and fashion, so they spent much of the evening critiquing and admiring various outfits—what worked, what didn't, and why. They awarded a pretend grand prize winner of the best outfits in each clan for a man and a woman.

As the evening waned, Aza excused herself.

As she entered the commodious Ladies' Room, she enjoyed seeing a knot of Kruik women gossiping in their dramatic tone-on-tone outfits. So far tonight, Aza was most impressed with these women. They gave off an air of confidence that she admired. *It's the pants. What would it be like to wear them?* Tonight, their pants were not the leather or sturdy fabrics of day wear, but sheer or shiny silks, satins and often brocades, some embellished with reflective mirrors and faceted stones.

A group of Puraples women in elaborate satin and taffeta dresses with hoop skirts stood chatting and laughing in front of full-length mirrors. They turned to leave and Aza recognized Dusia and Kalah, Mam Sior's two youngest.

Kalah's hair is frizzing like her mother's.

She went into a stall and let Zaz go.

The Kruiks spoke quietly, but Aza heard them clearly.

"We can't stand by while they execute one of ours, when theirs—and at the highest level—are doing the same but being protected. I hear Hasip is positively thriving."

"But surely he must be in hiding?"

Hasip?

"The point is, *he's* still alive and living his life free and clear. Maybe Kruiks would have let this go in the past, but not now. The Purples actually believe we'll let them break taboos after they've executed our kind as an example in an attempt to keep the lower classes in line. But they are wrong."

"They've held all the power for too long, Bek."

"Right. So, we hit them hard, relentlessly and below the belt until they change their beliefs."

"No...that isn't our goal. Our goal is to become the ruling party again. We will oust them."

Zaz moved in close on this last speaker. Her dark skin glowed plummy-brown in the gaslight. Rosy lips set off her complexion while a gold dusting on her eyelids reflected the yellow specks in her green irises. Her long black braids were intricately nested in an up-do that added to her already impressive stature. And Aza had seen her before. *Noptva!*

Three Puraples women entered, their skirts so expansive that they took up most of the space. Aza didn't recognize any of them and called Zaz back.

As she washed her hands in one of the basins, she had to repress a gasp at seeing in the mirror the green-eyed woman throw a curse toward the hem of the nearest Puraples. *She's not wasting any time getting started with her warfare. Curses at a dance?* No one except her saw it happen. In less than an hour, the woman's sumptuous violet gown would be teeming with some nasty flux. *Should I tell her? Clean it for her?*

Instead, Aza dried her hands, skirted around the full skirts, and followed the Kruiks out of the washroom.

Gen responsibilities be damned. She had a fellow waiting for her, and she was going to be kissed before the night was over.

9

A BIT OF TALENT

AZA ASCENDED THE BROAD front steps of the Tapinak, Maripesa's cathedral and home of the Tchuvari Clan. Her heart pounded, not from climbing stairs, but from the majesty of the building. She stopped midway to admire her view and commit it to memory so she could draw it later. Constructed of stones of varying shades of pink, the cathedral was massive. Some of the blocks had been carved in intricate geometric designs.

The day after the dance, when Aza still felt as if she was waltzing through life, Reth came to her in the downstairs library in the Villa, and said, "Your father has set up an appointment for you at the Tapinak." He handed her a card with the date and time and the name, Oscera.

Aza let out a noisy, frustrated breath. "I just shared a meal with him, for *Maripes* sake. Why didn't he tell me?"

Reth's expression didn't change but he shifted his feet, minutely.

"Out with it."

"I won't be able to tell you what your father is thinking, Miss. Based on long years of exposure to his habits, I would suggest that he allows me to deliver the message so that he doesn't have to answer any of those many questions you tend to have."

Aza laughed. "Oh, you *do* know him well. And me. Of course." But her mirth dissipated quickly as she once again pondered the mysteries of Leo. She got up, passed through the courtyard—having a flash of remembrance of the scent of Duma's cologne—to her father's office. The door was open for once.

"Father," she said, waving the card Reth had given her. "What is this about visiting the cathedral?"

He cleared his throat and said, "Oscera is an old friend of mine. From long ago. She—uh, excuse me, *they* would like to meet you. That's all."

"Oh. She is of the Tchuvari Clan?"

"Yes. I believe you will like each other."

"As simple as that, Aza," she whispered to herself as she crossed the threshold into the enormous Grand Nave of the cathedral. "Let us see what awaits you in the cathedral of the Keepers of the Magic."

Her eyes rose to the glowing, carved, inlaid, intricate, colorful, domed ceiling far above. She'd been in this space before, but only for yearly rites, and that, years ago. The citizenry was supposed to come periodically to reaffirm their commitment to Maripesa—a city where magic is so cherished that they choose to be isolated from the rest of the world. During the rituals, the room was full of benches and people. Today, it was empty. She stood in the middle of all that silence, space and solitude, gawking.

Opposite the immense doors she'd just entered was a kind of stage with curved, honeywood staircases symmetrically placed on both sides. Its backdrop was a lacy, gold and mother-of-pearl reredos, at least six times her height.

Aza heard no footsteps but saw, from across the expanse, a person coming toward her. The person bowed and said, "Welcome, friend. How may we help you today?"

"I, um. Sorry. Did I come in the wrong entrance? I did, didn't I? I'm sorry. I, I have an appointment. I am Aza."

"Do not fret. You've done nothing wrong, and you are expected. Come with me. How familiar are you with our clan?"

"Not at all."

"We, the Keepers, refer to ourselves in the plural. It can cause some confusion, so we like to tell everyone. Our name is Freja."

I should try to enjoy the drama and magic of this place.

Even Freja's robe was a work of art. Made of silk, painted in a bold abstract pattern in deep jewel-tones, but with body, as if it might be layered with down. It seemed to flow over their shoulders and onto the floor in back. An amazing crane clasp, the size of her hand, held it together at Freja's sternum.

They climbed three flights of ornately carved stairs. The stairwells seemed to glow from within, went down a long mulhao wood–paneled hallway, taking several turns. Aza began to feel as if she were going back in time. They entered a small oval room with a high ceiling and five carved wooden doors, all shut. Her guide rapped lightly on the second one to the right, using a bronze knocker in the shape of a hawk. They pushed the latch to open the door and stood back to let Aza enter.

Sunlight filled this room through two floor-to-ceiling windows in the curved wall made of marble, pink with white and gray streaks. Some of the bricks were highly polished, others left in their raw quarried state. It wasn't a large room, but the ceilings and windows were so high that it didn't fail to impress.

Behind a simple but elegant table stood a woman, quite a bit older and a little taller than Aza. Their hair—pulled tightly back from their face and disappearing under the hood of their robe—was pure white, giving the impression of age. But their face had only the hint of wrinkles and gravitational softening. Their eyes were deep green-blue, their skin creamy brown. Their large, graceful hands were clasped in front of their upper chest, fingers interwoven in greeting. They smiled and bent their head once.

Aza paid respects by bowing formally. She rose, clasped her hands in front of her skirt and waited, feeling her face flush from the neck up. Other than a sense of being on the spot, her mind was quiet, waiting.

"Aza Gen," the Tchuvari said, their voice mellow and layered. Their robe was similar in shape to her guide's but rendered in softer colors. "We expect you are full of wonderment at what you are doing here."

"Yes. Wonder is the exact word I would use, madam. Please forgive me if I am not using the proper honorific. I have not actually been prepared for an audience with the Tchuvari."

They laughed lightly. "Not a problem, dear. Our official name is Oscera, Faj sect, the Keepers, Tchuvari Clan. Call us Oscera. People often assume that we are big on hierarchy and ceremony, but it is not true. We have comfortable, simple lives."

"I suppose it's the" —Aza looked all around— "magnificent cathedral that you live in that gives that impression."

They laughed again. "No doubt." Coming around the table, Oscera touched Aza on the shoulder briefly. "Your dress is lovely. We were raised a Gen and are still partial to pastels. Let's walk while we talk. We will show you some interesting and beautiful things."

"Thank you. I would love to see it all."

"It is vast. You will have to make many return visits to accomplish that."

They began retracing the route Aza had taken to get there, at some point veering off to a new staircase, where they went up.

"It is all so elaborate."

Oscera smiled. "Not all of it. We will show you some of the more mundane parts as well as the more sacred. We're headed to the Archives Museum. Oh, we should have asked. Are you interested, or did you see it often enough with your clan class?"

Aza flushed. "I...yes. That would be great. I, I did not attend clan school. This is all new to me."

Oscera turned to look at her, brow furrowing. hey reached out, took her forearm and said, "Good, then. It will be our pleasure to show you."

High in the building, they arrived at a small, round room with white plastered walls facing an arched doorway. The entry led into a wide corridor that veered right. Gas-lit alcoves, with artifacts from Maripesian history, lined both sides. They showed jewelry, paintings, fragments of sculpture, pottery, and clothing. There were weapons and tools, riggings of various types. Mechanized parts with diagrams. Household items. Ledgers and personal diaries. All the while, the corridor curved to the right as if the archives were winding them tighter and tighter.

"Once upon a time, Maripesa was one of the most active trading ports in the world. Because of this, our citizens' ancestors come from many cultures."

Oscera stopped in front of another lit booth and Aza could see that the right-hand spiral ended here. Beyond, the corridor took a sharp turn to the left. The way out. In front of her, displayed in a semicircle on white satin, were seven items and one obvious vacant spot.

Aza studied them for a moment, a fluttering anxiety building inside. "What are these?" She kept her voice mild, but her heart started to pound and sweat formed on the back of her neck because she knew what they were. No, that wasn't true. She had no hint of what their function was, but these seven thin cylinders—each one decorated differently—were other examples of the mysterious device she had found in Gerland's coach.

"Soltecs. Personal devices for warding curses. They were used in the early days of Maripesa."

"Soltecs?" Aza repeated, her mouth grown dry.

"These are the only known soltecs in existence, except for one. It went missing many, many years ago. The archivists chose to keep a vacant space for it because of their belief that it will be found some day."

I am in deep trouble. This has to be why I was summoned here. Someone, somehow, knew she had the soltec and had told the Tchuvari. *How?* She'd kept it safely hidden in her bag since she'd found it. Yes, she meant to tell Gerland, but she...hadn't. *Should I confess?*

Before she could say a word, Oscera said, "It seems a bit silly, but their logic is that because it's magical, whoever took it—and that person would be long dead by now—would have treasured it. It has to be somewhere. Perhaps one of the ruling families is holding onto it for greedy reasons. Whether it ever makes it back to this display case is another question entirely, but," they paused and laughed quietly, "our historians have nothing if not long memories. It is their belief that it will find its way back."

Oscera turned and started walking left, out of the archival labyrinth. "They were no longer needed when the Hierarchy of Talents was firmly instituted. Part of the plan, dear. Part of the overall plan."

Maybe Oscera couldn't show her the entirety of the Tapinak, but the tour seemed to go on and on. But this was a good advantage, because it took forever for Aza's heart rate to settle. She could think of little else except the need to return that soltec as soon as possible—*anonymously.*

They had gone down many flights of stairs when Oscera said, "We promised you mundane. For example, these are the city's registry offices. Here, Maripesians register all the rites of passage."

A Tchuvari Keeper in a solid green robe of the same design as Oscera's and Freja's sat behind a desk that took up a doorway. Behind them were rows of filing cabinets with hundreds of small drawers. "Our name registry."

"Every person's name is here?" Aza asked.

Oscera nodded. "It's an alphabetical file of first names with a date of birth. Upon someone's death, that card is labeled with date of death and is placed in a different file. Expectant parents must come here and consult with our clerk here before naming their child. Once the child has been born and has a unique first name, the parents return and get their Official Name Registration card that has the child's information printed on it—clan, gender, name, and so on."

"So my little name is in that huge file at the end of all the As?" Aza said, managing a shaky grin.

"Yes, and no one else can legally use it. Well, until you die."

On that cheery note, they went down another flight to the kitchens, laundry, three dining areas, and the children's living area and school.

"A school?"

"We do have children in our clan," Oscera said, "even though the Tchuvari do not produce offspring. We take in orphaned and abandoned children. Also, adults." Oscera brought a hand to their chest. "We came into the order as a twenty-three-year-old. It had been our lifelong dream."

"But...why? I mean...you said you were born Gen."

"Ah, yes. Long story. The Gen people I come from live in the slums of Maripesa. We were the poor cousins."

Aza was stunned. She thought of Garnia telling her how protected she'd been. "I never knew."

"Our need to escape wasn't so much being poor, but more that our father died young and Mother had mouths to feed. We always looked for something we could do to lift at least one burden off her shoulders. It took us a lot longer to get here than we hoped. But that's a story for another day."

"I always thought the Tchuvari were...chosen."

"In a way, but the Keepers have to become aware of us before we can be selected. There is an apprenticeship to make sure we are compatible."

"Are the kitchen workers from outside your clan? I mean, is it like the Komeh where Dals and Salizans come in to do the work?"

"No. The Tchuvari do their own work. We all serve in our own way."

Aza felt her eyebrows rise. "So...what do you do? Do *you* have duties? Chores?"

Oscera gazed off into the distance as they thought over an answer. "We have all of the above. It's a highly structured clan. But most of what we do involves ordinary things, not spiritual ones."

"Like keeping those marble floors shiny and spotless?"

"Yes, and food, clothing, filing documents. All the things that go on in any large communal building. Also, organizing. Someone must see that we have enough people to tend the gardens and keep the trails clear and the building in good maintenance. There is a whole department concerned with who does what and when."

"And you?"

"Admittedly, our role is mainly a spiritual one, but not as you might think. Some of us are contemplatives who never leave the grounds. Others live simple lives within the city. They provide information and insights that no one else here could know. The sect we belong to, the Faj, is somewhere in between those two. We have contact with the outside world, but also spend time in contemplation. Often, we work with those from different Tchuvari sects. The Historians, truly the Keepers of the city's past, might come from several sects. Same with the Futurists, of which we are part. Our attitudes, the ones that made us seek you out and want you to feel welcome here, partly come from what the Futurists believe is happening. Did you know that the original Tchuvari Clan was made up of people who were each proficient in multiple Talents?"

"How?"

"That was before the days of the Hierarchy of Talents. Some people had a natural gift for magic of all kinds. The original, overall mission, of course, was to keep our city from degrading into interpersonal, daily warfare, and chaos that once was our downfall. It was thought that those with experience in all kinds of magic could best be trusted with finding that solution. Which is...ironic considering the strategy they implemented." Oscera sighed. "Did you know that the word 'maripes' has come to mean 'chaos' throughout most of the rest of the globe?"

"No." She might not be properly educated, but even Aza knew that the city had once floundered because of their unrestrained use of magic curses and spells. And, that the Tchuvari, by developing strict rules and organizing the society around clan-specific magic, had brought about order. "I've wondered," Aza said, "how other places dealt with this."

"They outlawed magic eons ago."

"How can you outlaw magic?"

"Deny it. Punish those who use it. Ridicule believers. Destroy the written word of it. If it is talked about at all, it is given the same credence as we think of women's magic. It was minimized. Talked about as superstition. Fantasy. No one believed in it anymore, so it had no power. It died."

Aza's mind reeled. She wanted to ask more about "women's magic," but was too preoccupied with the concept of a world where no one had to worry about being cursed. "I— I don't understand how that's possible."

"Burn the books, the papers. Don't allow them to be taught. Root them out."

"If you take away our knowledge of how to do our magic, it simply ceases to exist? Wouldn't people figure it out again, the way they once must have?"

"It took many generations and much sustained effort for it to die out, just as it took a similar amount of time for us to use magic to our advantage. We simply took a different tack and devised ways to limit the chaos by keeping magic pure inside each clan. Because of that, we are isolated. No one out there wants their world contaminated by our Talents."

They arrived into an arched mezzanine that overlooked the Grand Nave. Stopping at the almost chest-high railing, they rested their elbows on it, looking at the room below. Light radiated from the walls in addition to the daylight that came from the domed ceiling that projected random rainbows throughout the capacious space.

As Aza admired the view, she was troubled by much of what she'd seen and heard. On her mind was the lower level where people did the mundane chores of daily living. *Those might be Tchuvari, but they're doing servants' work. A hierarchy within a hierarchy.* And this cathedral was spookily empty. *All this space and beauty, with so few people to enjoy it.*

As if reading her mind, Oscera said, "Our home has outgrown our clan, Aza. It should be used more by all the people." They stopped talking for a while and then, still looking off toward the far wall, said, "We knew your father long ago. He showed great integrity and fortitude as a young man. We wanted you to know, for he'd never tell you."

"Oh. He told me you had been friends. Thank you. You're right that he isn't one to talk about himself. Even in council meeting, he lets others do most of the talking."

"You've attended council meetings?"

"I—uh. Well, really just one...at his request. Recently." That, since the age of thirteen, she'd often split herself and sent Zaz to eavesdrop on what was going on in the Gen world, wasn't something she could add. Perhaps someday she could ask Oscera about "women's magic." But not today.

"We Futurists want our councils to reflect, to represent, our whole population more than just the men of your father's generation. They populate most of them at the present."

"A woman rules Maripesa."

Oscera nodded their head slowly. "Yes, though any particular woman may not be the answer to any specific problem. Women can be just as spellbound as men. The Futurists are in favor of more variety. More voices. More flexibility."

Aza didn't have a response to this, so she nodded her head and waited.

Oscera touched Aza's forearm and turned to go down the wide staircase behind the golden altarpiece. They walked down to the main floor.

It's over.

To emphasize this, Freja appeared and handed Aza her coat before disappearing again.

At the massive open doors, Aza said, "Oscera, why am I here?"

"We wanted to meet you. Your father and we were close."

"Wait," Aza said sharply, her fingers suddenly cold.

"What is it?"

"Are you my mother?" The words came out harshly. Inexplicably. What was she talking about? Her mother was dead.

Oscera gasped and put their hand to their mouth. The answer was almost whispered. "No. No."

"I— I don't know why I said that," Aza said.

"Oh, sweet child, we are sorry. No. It never entered our mind that you might think that. No. Of course—."

"My mother died in a horse-riding accident. I was not even three years old. I've always known this. I—"

Zaz left her body to view Oscera from the back.

Oscera took Aza's hand. They seemed at a loss for words for a moment, but then said, "It's all right. Some things—like missing mothers—go very deep. Perhaps...we are not sure...but perhaps you have some early memory that we somehow stirred up. But we were not *that* kind of close with your father."

A shimmery feeling slithered down Aza's spine as an unheralded headache arrived, the pain settling emphatically behind her left eye. "But...you knew my mother. You must have," Aza said with a desperation that shocked her.

Zaz saw Oscera's shoulders square and spine tense as they said, "We are not going to talk about that."

Aza's shimmer changed to dizziness and she felt like she was going to throw up from the pain. Oscera let go of her hand and Aza's fingers went to the spot over her eye, kneading it in circles. "A sudden headache. I have to leave."

"Wait." Oscera's voice was soft again. "The Tchuvari are ready for change, but we don't want to repeat past mistakes. Those on the outside, those at the vanguard must use us, get our advice. We are here to help you. Any time. Come back when you are ready."

"I don't know why you're telling me this. I don't know anything. I'm not important."

Once again, Zaz saw their shoulders level out as they emphasized each word. "You are more than you know."

"I'm sorry to leave so abruptly."

"Go. There is nothing to apologize for. Give Leo our most sincere regards."

Aza reintegrated and dashed outdoors. Even before she reached the last of the steps, her headache had lessened. Her stomach, though still unsettled, was no longer threatening to bring up lunch. She slowed, put on her coat and began to walk through the cathedral's park space. The cool air was bracing.

She veered off the paved walkway onto a dirt path through tall trees and happened on a secluded spot with a stone bench and a tiny pond that had a frog fountain in it. The splashing water, along with the back-and-forth *tweeling* of two unseen thrushes in the gathering evening, calmed her body even while her mind was reviewing what had just happened with Oscera.

Aza's brain felt fuzzy every time she tried to focus on the details, but out of that unnatural blur, six words rose up in high relief and sharp focus: *You are more than you know.*

Gerland dropped Aza off in the heart of Charaton where the uppercrust Kruiks lived.

"So Miss, I should pick you up here in two hours?" Gerland asked.

"Yes, please. And don't let me disrupt your day. Look, there are benches nearby. I can sit comfortably and sketch if I need to wait for you."

The man, still anxious for her well-being, had peppered her with questions as they drove here. He desperately wanted to know what she was doing, but Aza lightly prevaricated, seeing no benefit in drawing him further into her spying.

It was enough that she'd taken those items from his coach. She fully intended to return the soltec to the Tapinak soon. But, Aza reasoned, the treasured artifact was closer to being "found" now that she had it than in all the many years before, so the occasional stab of guilt was bearable. She needed to find out who dropped it in the coach and her first and only suspect at the moment was Benelek Kruik, the woman whose calling card she held in her hand. Also, if Aza's instincts were correct, she was the curse-thrower from the dance.

The tree-lined street she stood on was lined with solid, stately, stone homes of three stories with small front yards, ostentatious front doors, and wide bay windows.

Gerland had told her that there were urban sections of Maripesa like Rosunda and Falkrum, where many younger Kruiks and Puraples lived. "The elders," he said, "assume they'll come back to the 'proper' clan neighborhoods, eventually. You know, the ruling clans grow up more slowly than the rest of Maripesa."

Aza could not identify with a parent who might pressure her to stay home.

She walked down the sidewalk, trying to look casual. While the homes all had imposing facades and entries, quite a few boasted fantastical statuary in their small front gardens. Aza didn't have to fake an interest in these.

Number 43, the address on the calling card, was built from deep red-brown, rough stone bricks and had wide steps to double wooden doors made from jacnut, a rosewood. All very *de rigueur* for this street, but the statuary in this front yard would have caught Aza's eye, regardless.

She marveled at the skill it must have taken to carve this tableau: a gnarly tree trunk, taller than Aza. At the bottom, in amongst bare roots tangled in a mound of boulders and small plants, were animals. She immediately saw a fox, goose, and cat. On closer inspection she found a squirrel and spotted salamander. They were all either in earnest pursuit of or playfully chasing one another—the artistry was happily ambiguous.

As she leaned on the short, scrolled-iron fence to admire it, another part of her brain became aware of two people talking inside the house. Aza split, and Zaz easily slipped the short distance into Benelek Kruik's parlor.

A man and woman argued. They looked to be in their late thirties. The man was dressed in Puraples daywear: short-tailed jacket, black with a white herringbone weave, off-white vest and blouse with black trousers. The woman wore Kruik pants of dark blue and a blouse of embossed, pale blue linen.

Yes, the curser from the dance. And the café in Noptva!

"Keep your curses under wraps!" the Puraples man said.

"No."

"We have the power to execute anyone. You must know this. You've become a pest at the highest levels of my clan. This is your friendly warning."

Anything but friendly.

Benelek turned away insouciantly.

It heightened his anger. He put a hand on her shoulder and jerked her around roughly.

She matched his height. Looking him in the eyes, she said, "Never touch me again."

"You wouldn't put one of your puny curses on me. You have too much to lose. Our friendship still counts for something, doesn't it, Bek? I'm trying to help. You could lose your life if you don't back off."

Bek. That's what her friends called her in the ladies' room at the Hexorah.

"What is my one life, Jetal? Is mine more important than those two you killed last fall? Or ones who are simply taken out without the benefit of a crowd of watchers? Do know know how many people hate your clan? Especially Mam Sior and her brood of half-wits."

"That's enough! I could take you out with one curse right now."

"Going to cast giarmial? Continue to spread the malady that's already careening out of control?" Benelek paused, her arms crossed, fingers tapping her irritation. "Yes. I know about that. I have friends in all clans and I talk to the Besin because I'm so often Purple-cursed! You and I have been friends and, yes, that means something to me. But instead of warning me, you should warn your people. I am only the leading edge of what will soon become a city-wide war against your clan."

Jetal's face reddened. His body taut, he took two shaky steps backward, raised his arm and closed his eyes.

Aza rang the doorbell.

Pulled into movement by the unfolding drama, Aza, without a plan, waited for it to open. Zaz reintegrated. Nothing happened. She rang again and then saw movement behind the leaded glass doors. The woman answered. Her face showed the turmoil she was immersed in, but she was, even in this state, stunningly beautiful.

Bek, adrenaline running high, yanked opened the door to a stranger.

"Benelek Kruik?" the young Gen woman said too loudly. "I'm here for our appointment."

"What?"

Jetal brushed past brusquely, also pushing past the woman on her doorstep without saying a word. Both women's eyes followed as he marched to the end of the block and turned the corner.

"My apologies," the stranger said in a more normal voice. "We don't know each other and, of course, I don't have an appointment. I, um, happened to be on the sidewalk admiring your sculpture, and I overheard a heated argument. It was impulsive of me to be sure, but it seemed as if an interruption might be helpful. I apologize if it was a bad decision."

Bek let out a long, noisy exhalation and shook her head slowly back and forth. "I can't say that I'm sorry, but how extremely odd. Uh, thank you?"

"You're welcome."

The Gen stood her ground, an anticipatory look on her bright, young face.

She's cute. Petite. Freckled nose. Curly dark hair, very thick, and tied off her face with a pale yellow scarf.

"Did he curse you?" she asked.

"No. You saved me from that. Um, would you like to come in...for tea?" The Gen seemed to have some agenda, so she might as well see where it led. *What a strange day.*

"Thank you."

She came in and sat down on the settee that faced the bay window.

Bek ordered tea and then sat opposite the visitor, pinning her with a stare. "Who are you? You know my name, so your 'admiration of our statuary story' doesn't fool me."

The woman caught her breath and then something happened that Bek couldn't quite fathom. At the same moment, the Gen seemed released of her tentativeness and tension. She leaned forward, held out her gloved hand, and said, "I'm Aza. I'm a snoop."

Benelek did not shake her hand. "No kidding. A snoop? More like a rat, I'd guess."

"Oh, that's not a nice assumption. Why do you say that?"

"You work for our enemy."

A maid came in with a tray, placed it on the table between them and poured two cups. After she left, Aza spoke more boldly. "Full disclosure, then: I clean curses at the Komeh."

At least six different emotions came and went, leaving Bek momentarily speechless.

"I've worked there practically my whole life cleaning the messes you Kruiks make. But I don't think of you as the enemy. It's clear that the Purples—as least the ones I know—aren't kind or good people. They want to retain all the power. So the Kruiks have to do what they can to hold the Puraples in check. In the same way, we Gen do what we have the skills for. We aren't rats any more than you are. Or any more than the Besin are for curing maladies." She paused and then added, "I may be inexperienced, but do not mistake that for ignorance."

How amusing she is.

"I saw you in the ladies' room at the Winter Dance," Aza said.

Bek held up her hands in a helpless gesture. "What does that have to do with anything and why would you remember me from a ladies' room?"

"I was eavesdropping—snooping, you might say—and you were doing a lot of talking. Plus, you must know that you're kind of unforgettable."

"Hmm," Bek said. "Thanks."

"Then, you cast a curse at the hem of a Purples' lovely orchid dress."

"Yes. That did happen." Bek's eyes narrowed. "What does that have to do with you coming here?"

"Nothing, except that I was surprised, when you opened the door, that the person I noticed at the dance is the same as the name on this calling card." She reached in her pocket and showed Bek a rumpled card. "Let me explain. I'm searching for information about my friend who was taken from a street near the Holba Bridge four months ago. Abducted by two men in unclanned clothing, right in front of my eyes. I am trying to find her."

"She's Gen?" Benelek asked.

"Yes."

"But what does this have to do with me?"

"That same day, I found your card on the floor of the coach that took me home."

"I'm sorry about your friend, but I don't know anything about her. Was she taken out of that coach? Even if she was, it hardly means that I had anything to do with or know anything about her disappearance."

"I know. I'm certainly not accusing you of anything. But I have no other leads and these two things that happened back to back. She disappeared. I found your name. I'm sorry if it doesn't make sense, but I'm going to ask questions until I find her."

"I get that. As I said, I'm not sorry you showed up when you did, but I'm afraid I can't help you with your friend."

"Well, what about this? You must know a lot of people. Will you keep your ears open? Her name is Maleka."

"Sure, I can do that." She picked up her cup and drank the cooling tea. She found the taste insipid. "Hey, did you somehow know that Jetal would be here today?" After saying this, Bek looked over her left shoulder and then her right.

What is going on here? What else *is going on here?*

"No."

Benelek looked around again. "There's something very odd about you. I can't put my finger on it, but it's as if you aren't quite as present as you should be. Or maybe it's that you're more present than you should be. Well...that sounded crazy."

Aza's gold-brown eyes widened, and Bek experienced that shift in the atmosphere again.

"What just happened?"

"I'm sure I don't have a clue what you're talking about."

Benelek's eyes narrowed. "I'm sure you do. Your speech gets all formalized when you are avoiding telling the truth. I felt magic. I don't know what kind or anything else about it, but now that I think of it, I was feeling it even before you rang my doorbell."

The Gen sat speechless, lips tightly closed, avoiding her gaze.

Bek waited.

"I—" Aza started, and then cleared her throat. She took a sip of tea and said, "It may be the first time I've practiced this bit of Talent while in the same room with someone. I had no idea it was detectable."

"Maybe I'm more sensitive than most people. And what do you mean, 'a bit of talent'?"

"I have always kept it a secret. I had no reason to tell anyone and assumed that others wouldn't believe me or would call me crazy." Another long silence extended. She pulled the shawl from around her shoulders and tugged at the back neckline of her blouse.

Benelek waited.

Aza let out a noisy sigh and said, "I have the ability to split myself. It's an out-of-body experience where I can see the world from two vantage points at the same time. Quite handy when one has trouble controlling one's curiosity. I let my other self loose when we started talking, not because there's much going on that she might view, but because you intimidate me. I needed to feel stronger in order to get through this."

Benelek was very pleased that she had pressed for information. This strange day was getting more intriguing by the minute.

Aza said quietly, "How could you tell?"

Bek shrugged. "I felt the passage...the presence of magic. No one else ever noticed?"

"Not that I know of. I mainly use it at work when I want to overhear something. The walls are pretty thick around there, but not for Zaz. That's what I call my other self. She slides right through them."

"How exceedingly handy, and at the Komeh, no less."

"Yes. I, um, I listened in on your argument with Jetal. Sorry." She fidgeted with her pale pink gloves and then looked up and said, "What do you think?"

"It makes me wonder about magic."

"Me too! I can't be the only one who has this ability! Have you ever heard of it?"

"No. Though I have heard of other kinds of—well, let's call them talents with a small t. They are magical, but not about casting curses or healing spells."

Aza said, "Right. They don't fit anywhere. What kind do you know of?"

"The more I think about it the more ridiculous it is to consider curses and healing magic, but leave out the magic of charms and all the little spells we use without thinking—like every adolescent learns the hangover cure spell, right?" Bek thought this over for a moment. "But this is the strangest I've come across. I know a Kruik gal who seems to have the ability to push people to make the decision she wants them to make."

"What?"

"I know. It doesn't sound real, but I've witnessed it. She's a cousin and not a persuasive person. I mean, Cvita's not charismatic or particularly charming. Just a normal girl who, from time to time, will turn on this ability. I was with her and her housekeeper one day when Cvita wanted to gain access to something in the house that was under lock and key. We were teenagers. It was alcohol. No big crime, but this housekeeper was a stickler! Cvita...loosed this talent on her. She only had to say one normal sentence, no chanting or magic words, but the housekeeper took the keys out of her apron pocket and unlocked the door to the wine cellar."

"That's quite a bit more useful than my talent," Aza said, grinning.

"No kidding. But," she sighed, "it turns out that Cvita grew up to be a scared little slither of a person and won't use it anymore—for good or evil."

"You've tried, I assume."

"You already know me so well? Anyway, when you— What'd you call it? Split? It felt the same. I could sense magic, but it was subtle and could be easily ignored or dismissed."

"Do you know when this talent first became available to Cvita? Because mine happened for the first time the day I started menstruating."

"Whoa. That's interesting. Could be a coincidence."

"Maybe. I don't have enough information. But it could have something to do with 'becoming a woman.' I know a Tchuvari who spoke in passing about 'women's magic.'"

"Well, that's fascinating. You didn't ask your mom about it?"

"I don't have a mother."

"Oh. Sorry."

"No need to apologize. There were only men in my house. I went to work at the Komeh long before this happened. Maleka is really my only female friend and I haven't even known her for that long. You don't know anyone else who has this particular type of talent that I have?"

Bek shook her head slowly. "Nope. But...I think we both need to do some snooping. Don't you?"

Aza grinned. "My specialty."

IO

HEAVY LOADS

FERJIVAL PERSPIRED EVEN THOUGH the room was cold. The room was cold even though a fierce fire burned in the council chambers not five strides from him. A shiver zig-zagged along his spine as his cheeks flushed warm.

Around the table were leaders of the major Puraples families, with his mother, of course, at the head. She had reconsidered her hard line after their argument and readmitted him to the council.

Perhaps this happened because he'd actually taken seriously the job she'd given him in spite of the fact that he'd wanted, that day, to shove his mother's assignment down her throat. Perhaps guilt over having given the messenger giarmial had played into his decision to become a proper Assistant Deputy. He must have done it well enough because here he was, one of the inner circle again.

Hasip isn't available, so she had no other choice. The confidence he'd just found vanished. The doubts about his competence, planted and nurtured by his mother, would never die. Speaking of dying, the councilors were discussing the epidemic. They weren't sure where it had started, which was...good. Of course, he didn't know either. No one could be sure.

They shared anecdotes of "indiscriminate" casting. Spats between clans that had resulted in "excessive cursing." The blame returned over and over to the Kruiks and their major acts of war—cursed imported cargo and warehouse stores. No one at this table was sorry for the Kruks. But giarmial didn't hit only their enemy. *That* was a problem.

His mother was talking. "...though the outbreak can affect anyone, it can only be blamed on us. This undermines our every effort to rule the citizenry fairly. It must be contained. What are each of you doing to get the Besin on top of this?"

Silence followed. No one wanted to point out the obvious. Finally, Kalijal, the elder, took on the job. "We've mobilized clinics in each of our home areas, but we don't have a Besin network the way the Kruiks do. Of course, the Besin are duty-bound to cure those affected by giarmial, but they do not...*answer* to us."

"Spellfire!" Mam Sior shouted. "Everyone answers to us. We have to pull together to fight this thing."

Ferjival put a hand on each of his upper arms and rubbed, trying to stave off the cold that his body seemed to have soaked up. Cursing a busy messenger with a communicable disease might not have been the best decision he'd ever made. But there were no witnesses. No one would ever know.

Late morning on a Sunday, Aza greeted Duma at the wrought-iron gate of the Villa an hour after a message had come from him saying that he needed to see her before she went back to the Komeh. There had been short messages between them and a couple of planned but missed meetings. But they hadn't been together since the dance three weeks ago. Aza had no idea where their relationship stood or if they even had one, so the greeting was awkward. He too seemed uncertain, but his charm rose to the surface quickly.

He gave her a winning smile and said, "I'm so glad to see you. You look wonderful. May I?"

Without waiting for a definitive answer, he leaned in and gave her a kiss on the cheek. Aza turned toward him, returning the kiss and their cheeks—his cool, hers warm—pressed together long enough that they ended in an almost embrace.

That helps.

Aza led him into the seldom-used drawing room of the Villa. Reth had left tea and a plate of pastries. They sat at a small round table near the bay window that looked out onto the sloping, grassy back garden.

After Aza had served him tea, he looked around and said, "It's a beautiful room."

"Yes, the house is lovely. Too bad it hasn't had more life in it over the years. But let's not talk about that. You seemed eager to see me."

"I was. I am. I simply couldn't let another weekend go by without telling you how sorry I am that I haven't been able to take you out for another evening. Many evenings! I had such a good time with you at the dance."

"We've tried," Aza said with a half-hearted laugh.

"My life has been unusually disrupted lately. You know about the business situation."

"I do. Is it picking up? No more curses, I hope."

He took a gulp of tea and put the cup down. "I'm afraid there was."

"Oh, no."

"Yes, middle of last week. We don't know who. We're very careful if a Kruik customer comes in. We can't afford to lose their business, but we follow them closely. You can imagine how well that goes over. Even so, late on Wednesday, we found fidova on several bolts. Very difficult to notice, being invisible. Father had to call in a group of Undones he knows or we'd never have discovered it all. The Kruks cursed them randomly, so we pretty much had to inspect all our inventory."

"That's horrible. I'm so sorry. Your mother and father must be at wit's end."

"Yes. Honestly, Aza, my time has not been my own. I'm so sorry."

"I don't blame you. You've stayed in touch when you've been able. I get it. It feels as if the whole city is under siege with so many people coming down with giarmial."

"I know. Many of the Besin healers had never treated even one case of it, much less dozens a day. While they scrambled to catch up, it got worse."

"Have you heard how many have died?"

Duma scoffed. "No. I doubt anyone is keeping track, considering our head of government is the clan who loosed this death on the city. But it must be high because everyone, it seems, knows someone who knows someone who has succumbed to it."

He reached out and took her hand. "How are you?"

She sighed. "No illness, so I must be fine, right? Before I got your message, I was planning to sit down and write a letter to Mam Sior letting her know that I'll no longer be living in the Komeh."

"Oh Aza! That's wonderful."

"I haven't even spoken with father about this. But everything that has happened—Maleka's disappearance being at the top—has, well, brought me to an overdue realization that staying in the childhood servant quarters is absurd. I belong here."

"I am delighted. I'm sure Leo will be as well."

Duma's visit didn't last long, but it ended with several sweet kisses and a warm, lengthy embrace.

Aza fairly floated back to the sitting room, sprawled on the not particularly comfortable settee, and thought about the need to get that letter to Sior written. Instead of writing, however, she gazed out the window into the back garden. There had been an unusual late-winter snow during the night and a dusting of pristine white changed everything.\

Maybe cold weather will slow down some of the chaos.

Benelek sowed that chaos as much as anyone, with her determination to overthrow the Purples. Now it was spreading even to the Gen—like Palter's business. *Duma said a "group of Undones" helped them clean?*

She sat up, alert. *What does that mean?* The Undones—those of no clan—were talked about in whispers. Aza thought they'd been made up to scare young children. How would it be possible to be clanless? Everyone had to be part of some family, didn't they? Otherwise, they were put to death. If they cleaned Kruik curses, that meant they had to be at least part Gen. And people like Palter knew about them?

"*Zlo*, the more I learn about this city, the more confused I get."

She flopped back down on the small couch, too beset by all these disruptions to think about writing that letter to Sior.

Bek knew everything and everyone, it seemed. She could answer Aza's questions. *She talked as if we were to be friends. But how am I to see her again, when every day Maripesa becomes more dangerous and more thoroughly under siege?* Aza shivered. *Would the Kruiks be any better if they ruled?* Aza couldn't imagine that they could be any worse.

Vijo and Eltah returned to the Colvara clinic after supper at a nearby eatery. "Back to work," Vijo said wearily.

"The line is half again as long as when we left," Eltah said.

"We'll get on top of this."

"You think so?"

"I have to."

But he didn't know how. A lack of experienced Besin had slowed them down and then, when an adequate level of proficiency had been gained by the working healers, the numbers needing a cure had doubled. They were training more of their clan who normally did other work—business, the arts, raising the children—but so far, the cursed multiplied faster than the healers.

"If we could always cure it with just one treatment, we might have a chance, but there are so many relapses. We're going to lose some people," Eltah said, staring at nothing.

They were standing in the waiting area, chaos swirling around them.

Vijo took his older sister by the shoulders. "It's the fatigue talking. We have no choice but to be optimistic. Look," he said. He grasped her hand, reached into his apron pocket with the other, pulled something out, placed it in her palm and rubbed it. "Given to me this morning by a lovely Salizan woman."

"Ah," said Eltah when she could see it. "A cat charm."

Vijo brought it close to his mouth, charmed it, and gave it to his sister. "Rub its belly and you'll feel as does the cat lounging in a pool of sunshine."

Eltah smiled. "Very sweet of her...and you. Serenity to you as well, brother."

He managed a thin smile as they both went back to work.

❦

Benelek ran her fingers over her face in frustration. She sat at her desk in the Office of the Provost, facing her Uncle Berker, The Provost of the Kruik Institute of Higher Learning.

"I'm a glorified secretary and you know it. And you also know that I'm made for more important things in life."

He looked genuinely hurt at this pronouncement, which, in turn, hurt her. She almost always said whatever she wanted without much thought to other people's feelings. Most of the time, this worked for her, but not with her elders. *It shouldn't be that difficult to remember, Bek.* It was just that her uncle, who had stopped by her desk on his way home for the day, happened to get caught in her foul mood.

"I'm sorry. You did me a favor by getting me this position. It has more status—and pay—than I deserve. But..."

"But you are meant for more."

"Am I a fool for believing that of myself?"

His face changed. His eyes almost disappeared under wrinkled eye folds as he laughed gently, though not without with some lingering bitterness. "Not in the least. We've always known it. We—your parents, your family, your clan—have been wondering when it would occur to you."

"But—but there's been nothing but criticism of me for as long as I can remember."

"Well deserved."

She twisted her mouth, looking at him steadily. "Yes...well. I am a handful. Headstrong. Mouthy. Rebellious."

"Stubborn. Inflexible."

"So...give me some sage advice. What can I do? It feels like the right time for me to step up, step into some role that can propel us to our rightful place as ruling clan."

"Go. Please. You're a lousy secretary."

Her head jerked up, her eyes widening, then softening. She laughed. "We agree on this at least. No sage advice?"

"That was my advice." He laughed gently and then grew quiet. "Do you want power?"

"Oh. That is a loaded question."

"You seem to."

"I want to make this happen. Or be a part of those who do. I want to use this horrible epidemic to change Maripesa! I want to capitalize on what the Purples have unleashed on its citizens. I want to crush them!"

He gathered his coat, gloves and scarf, then turned to her and said, "I became the provost of a school, Bek. I don't know how to be the person you're talking about. But I don't doubt that you do. I wasn't kidding. My sage advice is for you to clear your desk, walk out the door and make who you are into who you want to be. You're the most charismatic, persuasive Kruik I know. My only request is that you use these plain talents for the good, not only for our clan but also for our city."

She swallowed hard, thinking of Aza's small "t" talent. Maybe not so small. When she spoke, it wasn't to say thanks, even though she was overcome by his openness and generosity. It wasn't to guarantee him that she even knew the difference between good and evil. Instead, as usual, she said what was at the forefront of her mind.

"Even the Purples?"

He nodded, but Bek wasn't so sure she agreed.

⛩

Three in the morning.

Aza sat in her father's bedroom watching his breathing, waiting for the help that had to come soon. Reth had awakened her around midnight with the news that Leo was ill. She'd come down and nursed him with cool rags and clear broth, while Reth went in search of a Besin. He'd been gone a long time.

Her father was fitful when she first came, but now he had slipped into a deep sleep that she scared her more. He no longer responded to the sound of her voice.

"Father," she whispered, "don't die. I don't even know you. I don't even know myself." Tears rolled down her cheeks. "What have we done with our lives? Why did you send me away? Why did you never talk to me about my mother? I don't understand anything about my life. I thought we had time. Is that the way it always happens? Did that happen with my mother? You thought you had time with her, but didn't?"

She rose with a sigh and went to the window. A clear night, moon almost full; the snow had melted and likely would not be back until next winter. Moonlight glistened on the metal arch of the Holba Bridge across the Jeka. Her eye moved to the city where she saw leafless tree canopies, the blocky tops of buildings and, overreaching them all, the towers and glowing spire of the Tapinak.

Where could Reth be? There was a Besin clinic not far. On the border of her neighborhood, Latigen, and the next over, Wallston. But they must be overrun with patients. *Should I try to take father there?* But no, it was too late. She had no way of getting him downstairs, much less into a coach.

She went back to her chair, and at some point, fell asleep.

Reth woke her.

"You're back! Did you—?" Through sleep-clouded eyes, she saw a young Besin woman on the other side of the bed arranging her kit to treat Leo. Dim light came in the window. "Thank *Maripes*. You've brought help."

"Yes, Miss," Reth said. He had deep circles under his eyes. "The clinic was overrun. It is only because your father is so important to the clan that I was able to get a healer to come. I simply had to wait until this young woman took pity on us."

"Thank you for coming," Aza said to her.

"I'm Eltah." She smiled as she continued to work, her fatigue evident in drooping shoulders and curved back.

"Is there anything you need? I am Aza."

"Nothing, thank you, Aza. I only need the focus to cast an effective spell."

"Would you like us to leave?"

"It might be a good idea." She stopped and looked over. "I don't mean to be rude. It's been a long night. My manners may be slightly lacking. But to heal your father, I shouldn't be interrupted."

"Of course. I'll be right outside if you need anything at all."

She and Reth left the room.

"Get some sleep," she told him. "You'll be ill too if you don't take care of yourself."

"Oh, I couldn't."

"You must. At least lie down. I insist."

He looked at her, his eyes showing moisture, whether tears or simple fatigue, she couldn't tell. She put a hand on his forearm and said, "You brought help. He'll be all right, now."

"Yes. Thank you. I will stretch out then. Please come and get me when she's ready to go. Will you?"

"Of course."

Aza sat on the bench in the hall and sent Zaz into Leo's bedroom. She'd never witnessed a Besin healing.

Father's eyes are open!

Eltah spoke to him softly as her fingers worked on pouring and mixing ingredients. She lifted a small vial full of the magic elements, started chanting and, as the spell began to take hold, lifted her thumb and forefinger off the bottle. It hovered in mid-air and began to spin. At that moment, Eltah's attention was drawn away. She started and looked back over her shoulder, directly at Zaz, who was, of course, invisible. The vial stopped its spin.

Eltah swore under her breath, looked all around the room again, told herself to focus and started the spell anew.

Aza reintegrated with a shiver, drew her legs onto the bench and reclined as best she could, pulling her shawl more tightly around her. *Eltah* knew. *She sensed Zaz the way Benelek had. Zaz has to be made of magic if others feel her.*

What is this Talent and others like it? Where did it come from? How is it categorized and why does no one acknowledge its existence? She vowed to get answers once this crisis passed.

Father, please don't die.

II

THE WARDROBE

Aza and Duma were making a day of it, starting with a late breakfast at a riverside eatery. Spring had begun and the fresh, not quite warm, but sunny weather gave Maripesa an air of hopefulness. Aza's personal belief in a hopeful future came from Leo's recovery. He'd regained most of his strength and returned to work—despite the healer's warnings about not overdoing.

After their meal, and a stroll through the weekend market, Aza watched Duma's polo game. Unfamiliar with the rules, she felt lost and, before it was over, bored. By early evening, he emerged from the fray, filthy and happy at his team's win.

He gave her a hearty kiss, smudging her face with dirt. She blushed to the roots of her hair to be so treated in public, but that didn't keep her from responding.

It was the first time they'd seen each other since having tea at the Villa. Duma continued to be immersed in keeping his father's business afloat... sometimes literally. Another cargo ship had been sabotaged, this one with a shipment of Palter's silk. They'd found it in time to save the contents—the Purples were on high alert now—but it had taken so much Gen labor to clean the mess that the boy who had replaced Maleka at the Komeh was called away to help. Consequently, Aza's workload increased, too. The Kruik barrage of annoyance curses continued unabated alongside their spectacular large-scale ones.

Aza wanted to talk to Benelek about it, but didn't know how. The more time that elapsed since they'd made their impulsive vow to be allies, the more Aza doubted her memory of the conversation. Even if it was accurate, she couldn't know if Benelek had been sincere.

When the flurry of congratulations following the match dissipated, Aza said, "What now? Are you taking me home?"

"No, there's a victory party. Of course you'll come, right? I thought we were spending the whole day together."

"I want to, but..." She grasped and spread her mud-spattered skirt. "I'm not fit for a party."

Walking to Duma's private car, Aza was distracted by a rumble of thunder in the distance.

"It's not fancy," he said. "Just the opposite. Everyone comes as they are. It'll be the usual bedraggled gang at the Wardrobe."

The wardrobe? Aza's lips tightened as an all too familiar feeling of bitterness overtook her.

Duma took her hand. "What's wrong?"

Taking a quick breath, she let it out and said, "What is the wardrobe?"

"Oh. Well, no reason why you would know, I suppose." His words slowed as the sentence went on, as if he'd suddenly realized he might offend her.

She squeezed his hand. "I want to know what I don't know."

"It's a warehouse that has, over time, turned into a space for young people. It's been divided—quite roughly—into a variety of spaces from tiny to large. We use it for impromptu parties, like tonight."

"I see."

*And, I just caught it: ward-drobe. Very cute. A double-magic name that sets a playful tone—*drobe *spells being mainly used by mischievous children.*

"A couple of floors are divided into rentable spaces."

"Rentable?"

They'd reached Duma's car. She leaned against it and turned to listen. She thought she saw an embarrassed flush come over him, but his voice didn't alter when he said, "A sort of home away from home."

Gerland's comment about young Kruiks and Puraples who had places to stay near downtown Maripesa came back to her. "Apartments?"

"Not that nice. They're tiny and shared by friends to help pay the monthly fees. People sleep there sometimes if they've been partying too hard and can't—or don't want to—go home for the night. Or they just visit or change clothes."

"You have a room there?"

"I...did. I gave it up since I've been working so much. No time to be there anyway. Plus, the place has gotten—"

"What?"

He sighed. "Let's go. We can talk while we steam up."

They sat in his two-person car—a luxury by anyone's standards. Duma talked over the sound of the pistons churning. "It'll seem bad, I'm afraid, that I'm taking you to the Wardrobe when it's less fun than it used to be, but you know how the city is now. Everything spoiled by the bratty behavior of a few

Uppers. But the mates I play polo with are all friendly—we have to be, or a sporting event wouldn't be sporting, would it?"

After getting them out into the busy, early evening traffic, he reached over and took her hand. "You're quiet. What's on your mind?"

She liked this about him. He really did seem to care what she thought.

"I'm angry. But kind of like steam inside an engine. It builds, has to escape periodically, and then dies down when the engine cools. My anger bubbles and dissipates, but it is always there."

"Because you've been so overprotected by your father?"

"I don't feel 'protected' by him. That's part of what's so maddening. In order to be protective, you have to worry about someone's well-being, their safety. I have no evidence that he is concerned about my welfare."

"He's your father; of course he cares."

"Now you're being naive. You think all parents are the same?"

"He acts as if he's so proud of you."

"Not to me. I've been isolated, not protected. Though I reside in the city like everyone else, I was fostered out to live with the Puraples, at the beck and call of Mam Sior herself. It happened when I was too young to question it. I assumed all Gens cleaned curses every day."

"You just didn't know."

"Right. I didn't know to question any of it, which explains why I never thought to choose to live at home instead of in a tiny, bare room in the basement of the Komeh."

"I still can't believe you were put in the servant's quarters! Gens aren't Dals! Our Talents provide skilled assistance and they're treating you as if you scrub floors? Why would your father allow it?"

She gulped hard, thinking of Garnia. "That's not what bothers me. The room was warm, and the bed was fine. At least I had the company of the other staff, though certainly, the Purples were never the least bit personable toward me. It's that my father never took an interest. I can't remember him ever visiting my room there. And there's something else I have been wondering about."

"What's that?"

"Payment. I never got any."

He turned to her sharply and then looked back at the road, having to brake sharply to avoid stopped traffic ahead. "That's crazy," he said, when he'd maneuvered into a right turn to get away from a street blocked with vehicles.

"Is it?"

"You've been working since you were eight, you're twenty-six now and you haven't received pay for your services?"

"I assume they pay my father. But I've never asked. And before you ask why, I'll remind you that it's only been in these last few months that I've known enough to question it. Reth gave me pocket money. The amount increased as I got older. I had credit with dressmakers and a few shops. I didn't *want* for anything. I've been given what I asked for. I just didn't know to ask for more."

Her voice grew quieter as she talked. She felt listless, with a slight headache. A party was the last thing she wanted. "Where is this place?" she asked, hearing involuntary irritation creep into her voice.

"We're close."

He pulled into a parking lot protected from the street by a short brick wall. When he shut off the engine, there was a soft *puff* sound and the coach settled into silence. More thunder boomed, quite close now.

"We should get in before the rain comes," he said. "How are you?"

She shrugged. "I need to have a serious talk with my father. I'm more aware of that since he was so ill. If he—if he died, I...I don't have one clue how I would function."

Duma leaned over and kissed her lightly on her cheek. He whispered, "I'm hoping you'll let me be there to help you with that and everything else."

More than a little overwhelmed, Aza said, "We'd better get inside."

But the rain arrived in a downpour as they ran the better part of a city block to the Wardrobe's nondescript entrance. Duma ushered her inside.

They stood, dripping, in an L-shaped space about the size of her room at the Komeh. The walls were marked and stained over layers of peeling paint. In front of them was a service elevator, its metal grate decorated with a painted vine so poorly done that it only heightened the overall ugliness.

"I'm soaked through."

"C'mon, you'll get cold standing here." He took her elbow, urging her into the elevator.

She didn't resist, but misery settled in. She wouldn't stay here and pretend to be having fun at a party full of strangers while in layers of drenched clothes. Not for long. She could almost feel her hair frizzing to half again its usual volume. Just as she opened her mouth to request that he take her home, the elevator stopped with a jerk and the grate screeched opened while emitting steam vapor.

Before them lay a large, dark room full of people, noise, and music. It was maybe a third as large as the Hexorah ballroom, though it was hard to tell because there were so few lights on. She had more of an impression of who was there and what might be going on than anything specific that her senses could accurately determine.

Duma put his hand at the small of her back and pressed forward. Once in the room, he took her hand and pulled her along, skirting the edges of the crowd. No one, as far as Aza could see, even glanced in their direction.

When they reached the back right corner, there was a little more floor space, lighting was better, and the noise wasn't as overwhelming. He stopped and turned to her. "Sorry. I had no idea there would be so many people here tonight. We should go upstairs where there'll be a smaller group. You up for it?"

"No," she said. "Look at me."

"But you can see. No one is dressed up."

"It's so dark, I can't tell, but that's not the problem. I'm wet and uncomfortable."

"We'll just get more drenched if we leave right now. I promise we'll leave when the rain stops."

She acquiesced.

Her eyes had finally adjusted to the low light. Knots of Purples and separate knots of Kruiks—but sometimes small integrated groups of both stood in the open space. She saw a handful of Gen, but no Besin. *Would they be here if they weren't all flat-out treating giarmial? How fair is that? The Purples socialize while others clean their messes. Not to mention those who actually died.*

Aza, you are in no mood to be here.

Then she realized there were a surprising number of people wearing unclanned clothing. *Some of the never-seen Undones?* She stopped in her tracks when she recognized Ferjival dressed in all black. She literally rubbed her eyes to make sure.

Why, it's just silly privileged people "dressing up" for a night.

But she still didn't understand why.

Duma touched her arm. "I'd gone on ahead. Didn't realize you weren't behind me. Are you all right?"

"Yeah," she lied, and turned to follow him.

They took the stairs up two levels and came out into a much smaller room. This one was about the size of a parlor in a grand house, except there was nothing fancy about it. The middle of the room was empty, but around its walls were mismatched couches, easy chairs, and gaming tables.

"Duma," someone yelled from across the room, "you old dog!"

They walked over.

"This is Aza," Duma said when he reached his friend, also a Gen.

"Hi, I'm Bartlet."

He didn't wait for a greeting from her, but turned to a table full of glasses, bottles and beverages. He turned back with a full glass in each hand. "Here!

Have what I'm drinking." He winked at Aza and said, "Not too strong, I promise."

"Thanks," she said, feeling like that eight-year-old on her first day at the Komeh. *Stop it. You're a grown woman and the daughter of the Leader of the Gen Council.* But that little pep talk fell short. Those weren't exactly accomplishments. Not that any of these people seemed to be looking for her resume.

She tried to relax. *They're just having a good time. They aren't even looking at you, much less judging you.*

As Duma and Bartlet discussed the afternoon's match, she sipped her drink. It didn't take five minutes for her legs and mental acuity to go wobbly at the same time. *Not strong, eh?* She put the glass on the table and tapped Duma on the shoulder. "Wash room?" she asked, noticing that his glass was empty. He pointed her in the right direction and said, "You'll be all right?"

"Thanks, but I'm going to the toilet; I think I can manage."

He looked mildly hurt at her tone, but she was in no mood to care. Maybe it was the liquor, or maybe it was that she'd said outright that she didn't want to be here. Her clothes were sticking to her in very uncomfortable ways.

She went to the stall first, peed, and then spent time at the mirror, trying to repair her appearance. She splashed water on her face to clean off mud spatters as well as clear the fog from the alcohol. Then, she went to work on her hair. Moisture—even a small amount—made it bigger and more unruly. She always carried a scarf, just in case, and had put it on as a headband while watching the match. Now the gravity-resistant bulk ballooned out from under it in all directions as if her head had exploded. She took off the long narrow scarf, finger-combed through her tangles and then pulled the length tightly together high on her head. She twisted it until it doubled back on itself. Holding the resultant coil, she put one end of the scarf between her teeth and wrapped the middle of it around the topknot three times. With the mass under wraps, she used both hands to tie the scarf and then circled it around her head, knotting it to one side at the nape of her neck and draping the scarf ends over one shoulder. A few curls sprouted out of the twisted length at the crown, as if her head had grown tendrils of ivy, but it at least looked intentional. She pulled out a few more strands at her temples, ears, and the nape of her neck.

When she came out of the washroom feeling better, most of the people were gone.

She heard raised, but muted voices. *From the stairwell?* She sent out Zaz. Sure enough, the stairs were full of shouting people, all headed down.

"Duma?" she called, reintegrating herself. The few people left in the room looked over at her. One said, "He probably went downstairs. They've started another war. Best stay here till it's over."

Aza walked over. "The third-floor space?"

"Yep."

"What happened?"

Her question was met with shrugs.

The same young woman who'd talked to her—a Kruik—said, "It happens every week now. The Purples—" She looked over at the Puraples man next to her. "Sorry. Some of the Purples..."

"*Puraples*...and some of the *Kruks*," he said, quite affably. He looked familiar to Aza.

"They're both to blame," the Kruik continued. "Taken to spoiling the fun for the rest of us by tossing about curses and spells instead of just the usual, um, *interactions* that go on at the Wardrobe. Right, Jetal?"

"That's one word for it," he said, and gave the woman a look of such pure lust that even Aza had no difficulty recognizing it. She felt her cheeks go red and turned away, saying, "If you see Duma tell him I went to his car. No. Tell him I took a coach home."

She rushed to the elevator and pushed the button. Could she even find a ride here at this time of night? In a rainstorm? *Doesn't matter. I'll sit in the car and wait for him if I have to.*

Why am I so embarrassed? I didn't do anything wrong. But it felt wrong to even be here. This place, those people, the disguises, the curse-wars—all of it—was a fireball of revelation, especially the sexual innuendos. She'd gotten hints of intermingling, but actual, out in the open, mating between clans? Kruiks and Purples? These traditional enemies?

For Maripes *sake, people are put to death for interbreeding!* It was the highest taboo. She really needed to talk to Duma. Were these people all just foolish brats, teasing themselves with this...this intimacy? Seeing how close they could come and then not going through with it? Or was it as it seemed? Open. Accepted.

The grate parted noisily, startling her out of her ruminations, and she was greeted by an empty elevator. She noted that she was on the fifth floor. The door clanged shut and started moving. Up.

"Aza, you idiot."

The thing stopped again on seven. Three Puraples women got on, took one look at her, and stopped talking. She was wedged into the back corner by their voluminous skirts as the lift crept upward. It stopped on twelve, the top floor. As the door opened, she saw another crowded party in full swing. All seemed jovial. The three got off without a glance and immediately started chatting again.

Aza jabbed the ground floor button, praying no one else would get on. On the third floor, it stopped again. She made herself as small as possible as the door opened and a good thing too, because so many people flooded in that she feared the lift would plummet all of them to their mangled deaths.

❦

Everyone was talking.

"Did you get hit?"

"What the crossfire is wrong with that toad?"

"...saw at least four different vermin cast."

"The Purples went batty!"

"Gods, more giarmial. This *is* war."

"Worst ever..."

"Never saw..."

"AHHHHH! I'm itching!"

"Lichlia!"

"Don't worry," someone giggled, "we gave as good as we got!"

The door opened. In the general scramble to leave or stay, a Kruik woman turned back to see if Aza wanted off.

"Hey!" she said.

"Benelek."

"What are you doing here? Were you there when it all happened? Oh, did you just get here? Your clothes are soaked. Hey!" She turned to the others and said, "Hold the door! I'm getting off." She grabbed Aza's arm and tugged. "*Zlo!* Hold on! We're coming. Look what I found in the back of the el."

"What we need is a Besin! Gieta's over here dying from welts and you found a Gen. She should go tend to the Purples."

"Oh shut up," Benelek said. "She's a friend. Not *a* Gen...*my* Gen." She turned around and grinned at Aza.

They were in a corridor lined with doorways on both sides.

"Benelek. I should go. I'm wet."

"Everyone calls me Bek. I have clothes. I'll give you something dry."

She's definitely under the influence of something. Dry clothes sounded wonderful, though. *Well, you have been wanting to talk to her and at least now you know you didn't dream that conversation.*

One of Bek's friends touched Aza's hair and said, "That's so cool. Can you do mine like that?"

Bek stopped at the fourth door on the left and unlocked it. "Come in," she said, and then yelled to the others. "Get thee to a clinic, Gieta and Ostiv!" Before closing the door, she stuck her head out and said, "Bring me my share when the food arrives!"

The room held a rumpled bed, a small table with two drawers, a worn couch, and one wooden chair. Along the corridor wall was an alcove, lined with shelves haphazardly laden with clothes, bottles, books, paper, glassware, and trash. It was shabby and messy and saved only by artwork pinned on the walls.

Aza flopped onto the couch, staring at the drawings and paintings. She sighed, even while drinking in the expressive talent on display. "I need to go home. I can't wear your clothes. You're heads taller than me. And skinnier. And Kruik. Did you do these? I love them."

Bek sat on the bed and gave her a drunken smile. "Nah. A stablemate. I've no artistic talent. True, we aren't the same size. But one of my spacers—that's what we call our co-renters—is shorter and broader in the hips. I think you'll fit into her clothes. Don't go yet. I've been meaning to get in touch with you, but...just hadn't. To see you here so unexpectedly is perfect. Don't you think we need to talk?"

Aza smiled but knew it didn't come close to the enthusiasm radiating from Bek. More than just layers of wet clothes weighed her down.

I should explain.

"I've been meaning to contact you too, but I'd begun to doubt my memories of that day, so I might have never reached out. It is great to see you. But...I'm so tired. I've been out all day and then we got soaked and haven't eaten for hours. I've lost track of Duma—my date—and don't know if I can get a coach from here at this time of night and—" She looked up. Benelek wasn't grinning anymore, but she still had a happy, if vague, expression on her face. "Sorry," Aza concluded. "Someone gave me a drink upstairs. It sapped my energy."

"I get it. But I heard it's still pouring. You *will* have trouble finding a hired ride, so leaving might not be the best idea, especially if you're tired and hungry. We've ordered a massive number of meat pies. I will feed you. Then we'll see how you feel."

Bek found a pair of dark green pants that fit despite being snug across the hips and a little too long. Aza was also given a blouse in burnished gold that wrapped and tied at the waist and a short, blue and green embossed jacket with gold buttons, the too-long sleeves of which she pushed up to her elbows.

Bek stood back to admire her work. "You could pass for Kruik! I mean, your skin's on the light end for our clan and that scarf is so...floral. But otherwise!"

"Hmm," Aza responded. "I don't know what to say. It hasn't exactly been a goal in my life to pass as a Kruik. No offense. It is a huge relief to be out of those wet clothes. Thanks. But I've never worn a pair of trousers. I can't go out in them."

"So we'll stay here."

Just then, the food arrived.

They ate with total concentration.

Afterward, Aza relaxed into the couch, let out a huge sigh and a little burp. "Those pies restored my faith in everything."

Bek, still chewing, nodded and said, "Eating is good."

"I never knew this place existed. I'm tired of feeling ignorant."

"There's no point putting yourself down," Bek said, wiping her mouth with a corner of the bedsheet.

"With the irony being that I eavesdropped on all those conversations and meetings."

"Ooh," Bek wriggled her shoulders, "Yes. I hadn't forgotten about that."

"It all meant nothing to me because I had no context."

"Now you're finding out, so good for you."

Maybe it was the trousers, or the growing intimacy in the room, but before she could think twice about it Aza said, "I have a burning question that I am afraid to ask."

"Why?"

"Because I don't want to be made fun of. Will you talk to your friends about how stupid I am?"

"Aza. Sometimes people tell me I'm a jerk, but I am not *that* kind of jerk. I promise. What's your burning question?" She pretended to take out a key and lock her lips.

"Are Kruiks and Purples having sex here?"

Bek burst out laughing.

Aza's face heated up. "Glad we could determine exactly what kind of jerk you are."

Bek, looking abashed, reached over and patted her on the knee. "So sorry! It just surprised me. I thought you were going to ask about some affairs of state between the ruling families and...well, I guess in a way, that is exactly what you asked. The answer is yes. Not just Kruiks and Purples."

"Why do they dare?"

"Because the rules are stupid."

"Stupid to risk death, I'd say. A couple was executed not that long ago!"

"That's a case of *them* being stupid. You're not supposed to get pregnant, for *Maripes* sake!"

Aza stared, her mouth agape. She wasn't about to voice any of the questions that crowded in.

"You know...don't you—?" Bek stopped and started again. "We have a spell that prevents pregnancy. Available to any clan. If we have sex, but don't use it or use it improperly, then we run the risk of getting pregnant. That's when we run the risk of being killed by the Purples so they can 'maintain the purity of the clan magic hierarchy'. See?"

"Yes." But the word came out as more of an exhalation than a word.

"If we use the magic properly, then we don't get pregnant. And if we don't get pregnant, then we can have sex with anyone we want, from any clan we want, and no one will care. How would anyone know? It's taboo...but only technically."

"Has it always been this way?"

Bek shrugged. "Our parents, our grandparents...? Can you imagine them breaking taboos like this? I can't. And don't want to." She laughed and obviously expected Aza to laugh with her. When that didn't happen, she said, "I've broken your brain. I can see that. Did your mother teach you anything about sex?"

"I never knew my mother."

"Oh, that's right."

"Maleka, my friend who was kidnapped, taught me the basics. As much as she knew." *But nothing about a contraception spell!* "As I told you, I've worked and lived in the Komeh with no social life until a few weeks ago."

"You quit?"

"Still work there; go home at night. I don't even think they know I'm not sleeping there anymore."

"What if you didn't come back?"

"Why would I do that?"

"Don't know. You tell me."

Aza stared off into space, while Bek waited for a response. But Aza didn't have one, so she rose and said, "Let's see what's going on."

Bek brightened. "Going out looking like that?"

"Why not? I should try to find Duma. Do you know him?"

Bek did. Of course she did.

They took the stairs to see what was left of the third-floor war.

The place was deserted.

"What now?" Aza asked.

"Hmm... Drinks!" She came back with two bottles of ale.

"There was a party on the top floor," Aza said. "Want to go there?"

"I do. It's often a Puraples stronghold, but everyone's drunk or spelljuiced by now, so let's give it a try."

They took the elevator to the fifth floor first, to look for Duma, but that room was deserted, too. Then, at Bek's suggestion, they rode to the eleventh floor, got off and walked the last flight. "The elevator's too much of a grand entrance. From the stair entry, we can slip in and see if we want to stay or not."

"I'll send Zaz out to see what's going on."

Bek beamed. "Oh, that *is* handy." She roped one arm around Aza's shoulders and gave her a rough little hug.

As Aza split herself, she held up a hand to signal Bek to be patient. After a moment, she said, "There are lots of people. A mix. No obvious arguments or spellcasting. Shall we?"

Bek drained her bottle. "Let's go."

Aza reassembled herself and followed Bek into the crowd. She felt a buzz from the ale—much more pleasant than her reaction to the earlier drink. Her mood had changed drastically. She felt contented, if not comfortable, to be with people her own age. Even when people talked to Bek while ignoring her, she was pleased to be among them instead of on the other side of a doorway, snooping. This absence of self-consciousness made her even happier.

The space wasn't a room at all, but the rooftop. A section near the elevator and stairwell was covered, which is why they could gather here when it was raining. But there was a bigger unroofed space on three sides, all surrounded by a brick half-wall. The floor was wet, but without standing water. Stars shone above.

She had forgotten about her Kruik attire until Ferjival arrived, greeting Bek with much more formality than everyone else had.

Bek, all cheek and daring, said, "Have you met my friend...Zaz?"

Aza was aghast, but the man was obviously under the influence of something because he extended an arm, bowed slightly and said, "I haven't had the pleasure until now."

Aza took his hand—the first time she'd touched him, or any Purple—and found her voice. "Nice to finally meet you."

As he turned back to Bek, she saw confusion in his face: his forehead wrinkling, one eyebrow dipping with a wince, as if part of his brain was trying to make sense of something about which the rest of his brain wasn't conscious. It passed and "Zaz" was forgotten.

Their banter had a nasty edge, however, and being in Ferjival's presence messed with Aza's happy loop, so she wandered away to find another ale. She had no coin or credit with her, but the fellow didn't ask. She stood in the open next to the outer wall, feeling contentedly invisible and let Zaz loose to do some snooping.

Many people talked about the incident on the third floor. The Skirmish seemed to be already enshrined as its official name.

Then Zaz focused on one conversation near the elevator.

"Maleka's going to...___...___" The last words were unintelligible, but Maleka's name came through loud and clear.

Zaz moved closer to the speaker's back. *Duma. He's changed clothes.*

He leaned toward a Puraples woman whose back was against the building, his palm flat on the wall next to her head. "Can you believe it?" the woman said. "Hasip's 'in love' with her? It's insane."

"Ferjival's told me Hasip is Mam Sior's favorite," Duma said. "The brother who can do no wrong and all that. I just can't believe a Gen would be so stupid. He may be safe, but she isn't!"

Aza reintegrated so rapidly that she staggered slightly. A Kruik walking by noticed and offered her a steadying hand. "Hey there, maybe it's time to stop drinking, doll," he said, obviously highly inebriated himself. Aza thanked him, put her bottle on the wall, and walked straight to Duma.

He looked at her for a long, confused moment, and then stood. "What are you—? They told me you'd left. I went to the car and looked for you, but— *Spellfire*, I'm sorry. I assumed you'd gotten a coach home! What are you—?" He spread his hands and looked her up and down, speechless.

"It's no big deal. We got separated. I left you a message that I was leaving, so I'm not offended that you took me at my word."

"I—"

"I'm wearing Kruik clothes. Mine were soaked, as you know. I see you've changed too."

"Yes. After I couldn't find you."

Aza glared.

"I told you that I have a place here," he said.

"You told me that you *used* to have a place here."

"Right. I'm in the process of letting it go."

"That is not what you said. What else haven't you told me?"

The Puraples woman excused herself.

Aza looked only at Duma, while his eyes followed the woman and then darted around to those nearby. "Let's look for a more private place to talk."

"No."

"What?"

"What else haven't you told me?"

He looked frantic for a moment and then found his defensiveness. "That's a broad question. You're obviously upset that I left when you were in the washroom. I apologize. I thought I'd only be gone for a few minutes."

"Apologizing for something that didn't bother me isn't helpful. Do you have information that I need to know?"

"Maleka," he said, breathing the word out.

"Yes. Maleka. My best friend for whom I've been grieving all these months. The one I've never stopped looking for."

"How...could you—? You overheard my conversation?"

"Is that the important thing? Not to me. Why didn't you tell me immediately when you heard something about her? Does Jea know? Leo? Why not me, the woman you're courting? Or is that all for Gen show? Is there someone here you're more interested in?"

"Stop it. How much have you had to drink? You're talking crazy." He took her by the hand and moved to the corner of the rooftop. "I am interested in *you*. You. I want to marry you. I have wanted to for a long time. I even talked to your father about it months ago. But I'm not good at saying these things."

"Batdung. You're the smoothest talker I know."

"Why are you so angry?"

"You kept news of Maleka from me."

"No, I—I only just found out."

"Where is she? How do I find her?"

"I don't know, and if I did, it wouldn't be *safe* for you to talk to her. She's..."

"*She* is my best friend."

"I don't know where she is. I only heard of her situation, uh, recently. Tonight."

He tacked on that last word, knowing she would ask more questions if he didn't. He was lying. He had known about Maleka before tonight and, for whatever reason, didn't tell her. He'd also lied about giving up his room here. For no reason.

Her once-happy loop twisted and tied into a tight, tangled knot, Aza turned away from him and went to find a ride home.

Duma didn't try to stop her.

12

UNDONE

"FATHER, HOLD ON. RETH has gone for Eltah. You'll be all right. Just hold on." Aza's voice was thick with fear.

Relapses were common, but Leo was so stoic that he collapsed at his desk before Aza or Reth knew he'd been having symptoms. Now awake and in pain, Leo stared at the ceiling as his head bobbed back and forth in tiny movements on the pillow. A tear track from the corner of his eye glistened in the flickering gaslight. "Sior..." he whispered.

"What about her?"

"Sior made me send you to work in her house."

Aza's heart sped up. "Made you?"

Leo grimaced, still not looking at her. "Our deal. She— I swore I'd never tell you... That's...not fair. Your mother..."

Her breath caught. She waited, but he struggled to find the words.

"What about my mother?"

"We couldn't be together because—" His head remained pointed toward the ceiling, while his eyes moved toward her. "You weren't ever supposed to find out."

"Because she died, right?" Aza tried to keep the frustration and desperation out of her voice, but when he didn't respond, she said, "You must tell me! I can take it. I *should* know."

He's going to die without telling me.

No, he's going to get better.

Once he's better, he won't feel the need to tell me.

How was it possible to be so sad, frightened, and bitter all at once?

Finally, pushing the words out, he said, "You aren't...fully Gen."

Aza gasped.

"Sorry!" The word sounded like a sheep's bleat. Tears spilled down the side of his face, into his ears, onto the pillow. "I loved your mother when we were young, foolish." His speech came a little faster. Aza rose and bent over him, so she wouldn't miss a word. "But the pregnancy..." He shook his head with more vigor than before. "That came later. I didn't know. We were not so young then. Then—" He choked on his tears. With effort, she shifted him onto his side. Leo coughed, each spasm taking a toll. When he could speak again, he said, "Sior had all the power by then."

Aza's thoughts stumbled around like drunken children. What came out of her mouth was, "My mother wasn't Gen? *I am* not Gen? Sior knew this? Why didn't she have us executed?"

Her father stared at her, freckles standing out boldly against ashy skin. "Our bargain. I did what I had to. You survived. Your mother—"

He was overcome with a coughing fit. It seemed like it would never stop. The raking, rattling sound filled the room.

When he could talk again his voice was weaker but his need seemed stronger. "Aza. Be careful."

Sior kept me alive. For what? Slave labor? Power over Leo? "This is why you warned me about the Puraples?"

He neither spoke nor moved.

Crushing weight pressed on Aza's chest. She coughed, trying to clear it. Why hadn't she ever cornered her father and demanded to know the whole story? But he just said it: he'd vowed never to tell her. *He kept me at arm's length.* All she could manage were short inhalations until the pain around her heart felt as if she were the one who might die. Her mother had not been a Gen. *I belong to no clan. I'm an Undone.* "Who else knows?"

His face seemed to come into focus, eyebrows rising. "No one who would breathe a word."

That's not no one, then. "Who else in the *Puraples Clan* knows?"

His face became even more distressed. "Sior promised not to tell. Our bargain."

Silence.

"What else was in this bargain?"

"My shame. My triumph. You live." Another coughing fit intervened. "Aza," he grasped her forearm, his fingers icy, "in the attic—"

His eyes closed.

"Father?"

He opened them with a start.

"In the attic?"

"Some things for you. Be safe, my Aza."

The rattle in his chest grew worse. His eyes closed, like a heavy curtain lowering slowly.

"Father? Stay with me. Father! Wake up!" She pestered him until her throat felt raw.

He said nothing else, though it took hours for him to succumb to the Puraples malady.

Aza sleepwalked through the funeral. Reth was in even worse shape. The Gen Council stepped up and made all the arrangements. She was told where to go, what to do, and how long to stay. She did all that she was asked, but no more. One of the only perks to being the closest relative of the dead person, she now knew, was not being expected to function.

No one had to know that she was grieving not only the loss of her only living relative, but also her identity.

She was expected to accept condolences after the service, which took place in a small chapel of the Tapinak. Aza stood on hard marble for over four hours, bowing her head at each person who passed by—people who occasionally stopped to talk, but who more often offered a quick touch, a compassionate smile, or a kind word that sought nothing in return.

Oscera, their eyes red, gave her a hug and whispered, "Come see us when the time is right."

Duma came, his eyes tender, but also guilty, though of what exactly Aza couldn't be sure. It didn't matter anymore.

And then, not bothering to wait in line, Mam Sior stood in front of her, a black monolith.

Aza's brain seized. She could barely breathe, much less think.

Dressed in richly embellished silk, all black, her grey hair tamed by a scalp-fitting feathered hat, she looked at Aza for a long moment before speaking. When she did, her words came out slowly as if she had to exert great effort. "You will have the week off, of course. Longer, if you need it. But I will personally check on your return. We can't do without you, you know."

"Yes," was all that came out of Aza's mouth. One word, with an avalanche of others waiting to bury this woman. Aza could wait. She needed more facts.

"We are sorry for your loss. He was too young." Instead of moving on, she lingered.

"How well did you know my father?" Aza didn't know that she would ask this question until it was there, hanging in the air between them.

Mam Sior's jaw unclenched, then quickly returned to its tightly held position. Her cheeks flushed.

She is wondering if Father told me or not.

"I know all the clan leaders, of course."

"My father wouldn't have died 'too young' if this malady hadn't been set loose." These words were another complete surprise to Aza. She had never spoken so boldly to anyone, much less her boss, the ruler of the city.

Sior's bodyguard moved forward slightly, but Mam Sior raised a queenly hand to stay him. "Those responsible will be brought under control and punished."

Aza glared.

Sior stared back and then, at last, moved on.

But as Aza dealt with the seemingly endless stream of mourners, she sucked on her rage at this person who not only kept her father bowing to her wishes, but also kept a whole state under her thumb while her family caused death and mayhem.

When she fell into bed that night, even her bones aching with fatigue, she didn't sleep. She rested her body, but her mind was active, thinking of ways she could bring Sior and her weasel-children down—for once and for all and forever.

❧

The day after the funeral, Aza went to the Komeh.

Anxiety arrived with her as she approached the servant's quarters. But she'd spent most of her life within these walls and she had to see it one more time in full knowledge of what her father had told her. Her need to take down this family was front of mind. But she had no actual plan. Not yet.

Aza wouldn't resign, wouldn't announce that she no longer worked for them. That could put her life in immediate danger. They'd figure it out soon enough, and by then she'd be somewhere else...someone else.

She went to her room, passing only two of the downstairs staff who would find it perfectly normal for her to be here. The room looked the same, as if no one had touched it, even though she hadn't slept here in weeks.

Propped against her pillow was a soft, once-pink bunny, whose nose and tail were long since worn away. She placed it in her satchel and then rifled through the small assortment of clothing, aprons, gloves, niltehs in her drawers. *I'll take the gloves.* A spasm of pain shot across her sternum. She was not a Gen. Not blood-pure enough to wear Gen gloves. She allowed herself a moment to recover and took them anyway. *I should leave most of these clothes here, so no one suspects that I'm never coming— What's this?* At the back, under a petticoat, was a sealed envelope. She had never seen it before.

She sat on the bed, unsealed the envelope and took out a folded note.

Dearest Aza,

I hope you find this soon. I had to hide it, so I fear you might not discover it right away. I have gone away of my own accord. No one kidnapped me, though we have planned it to look that way and in front of you because we know everyone will trust your eyewitness account. I am sorry to use you. But I must believe that in the fullness of time, you will forgive me. I have done this because my happiness requires it. I hope you support me in that pursuit. Thank you. The only reason for me to be sad is that I will miss you very much. Please take good care of yourself.

All my love~

No signature.

Aza's eyes stung with tears, but they came from an overflow of anger—not sadness. *Spellfire! So many secrets.* Were people who loved you supposed to keep you in the dark about such important things? How is that "love"?

Everyone had taken their own way, made their own rules, without regard to anyone else's feelings or consequences. Starting with her mother and father. Sure, she wouldn't exist without them having done what they did, but would that have been such a loss to the world? No. No. They were selfish and stupid and their actions led to her servitude, her father's shame—whatever that consisted of. It had also led to a lifelong estrangement between her and Leo.

Then there is Duma, who only wanted to marry her to keep his father happy, who cared so little that he couldn't be bothered to be truthful or open with her.

And now, Maleka. Foolish, impulsive Maleka. *She must be pregnant by Hasip.* A pregnancy was the only reason she could imagine that Maleka would choose to disappear. They staged her abduction, throwing Aza into worry and horror, grief and turmoil that lasted months. A strangled gasp came up from inside her.

Their poor hapless child! A product of idiocy, like me.

Aza stuffed Maleka's note into her pouch and, leaving it in the room, shut the door and took the back stairs to the second floor. She sent Zaz out ahead to scout, stayed in the servant hallways, and made her way to the servant entrance of the council chambers.

She sent Zaz in. The room was empty.

Disappointed, she looked around the small anteroom she stood in. Here in this very spot, with her eye glued to the keyhole, Zaz first split from her. *What was this ability? Was it from my mother's side?* She huffed in frustration. Her father hadn't even told her what clan her mother came from. *And you didn't ask!*

A sudden necessity to be anywhere else, doing anything else, struck Aza. Top on her list was finding a private place to look through what she'd gathered from the Villa's attic. It would be in those items that she'd learn about her mother, her other clan, where she'd come from, and what kind of combination of attributes had brought about her looks and her abilities. Maybe there would even be some clue about this Splitting Talent. She resolved to leave at once, say goodbye to Garnia and a few of the other staff and then move along into her uncertain future.

Instead of moving on, however, she stood, rooted to the spot, because Zaz had moved out of the council room into another space.

Where are we?

It was a small, darkly paneled space, poorly lit with only one old-fashioned gaslamp on the wall. Aza had never been in this room, and didn't know where it was in relation to the chambers.

Zaz turned and Aza saw Mam Sior on a chaise longue. An old metal lockbox lay open on the floor. Papers were strewn around her. Notes, documents, drawings, and letters. Some had fallen to the ground, others were tucked in the folds of her voluminous skirt and under her thighs. One was in her hand. Zaz, unbothered by solid walls, slipped behind the woman and peered over her shoulder.

It was in view, but difficult to read because Sior's body heaved repeatedly. Aza/Zaz had the time to be patient, however. It was short. *A love note, perhaps?* Hard to believe that someone like Mam Sior ever had a lover, but there *had* been two husbands and all those children.

Aza/Zaz read: deep feelings... kept apart... rules we live by...

Sior, crying, tossed the letter onto the chaise longue and blew her nose with the handkerchief she had been holding in the other hand. Zaz's eyes followed the paper as it fluttered to the edge of the couch and onto the carpeted floor.

It landed face up.

Zaz leaned over it, and Aza read the ending. "...and with our understanding always in mind. Yours In Gratitude, Leo."

"Mother!"

Sior snatched it up and then sat up stiffly, more letters falling to the floor.

Zaz slipped back into Aza as they heard Ferjival's voice on the other side of some wall calling again to his mother.

Silence followed. Aza sent Zaz out.

Mam Sior snapped to standing, gathered up the letter and documents and dropped them in the lockbox. Then, holding onto the small chest of drawers, she used one foot to flip closed the lid. She stood in front of the mirror, wiping her eyes. Aza saw emotions she'd never seen on that face. Indecision, regret, maybe even fear. But in an instant, all these were mastered. Her face once again wore a mask of imperiousness. Sior turned, looked down and, again with her foot, pushed the box under the chaise. Then she walked to the wall, touched something Zaz couldn't see, and the door slid open. She strode into the council chambers through the space between the buffet and the side of the gigantic fireplace. The door slid back into place.

Zaz followed her into the chambers.

Sior walked the length of the table and was almost to the other end of the room when Ferjival entered.

"Where were you? I just looked in here."

"What do you want?" she asked in a withering tone. "I'm on my way to lie down. I'm not feeling well."

"Mother. You're neglecting things. The epidemic's out of control. We must insist every available Besin is brought in to get on top of this thing."

"You have my permission to so order."

"What?"

"You heard me."

"I do not...I— You're giving me that authority?"

They left the room, as Zaz, at the end of her range, zipped back.

Whole again, Aza left, picked up her things from her room, and hurried to leave this hateful place—hopefully forever.

It had taken Ferjival ages to locate his mother. Of course, the Komeh had hidden rooms. He had one himself. As children, he and his siblings had found others, but he suspected his mother had kept at least one to herself. That was fine. He was usually happy not to have to see her, but in needing her today, he started wondering what would happen if she died and no one knew where she was; what if she started stinking up the place like some rat in the wall?

Once he'd found her, on his second look inside the council chambers, he was sorry. Her mood was even rattier than usual. She looked terrible. Maybe she would die.

But he persisted. "Mother, we have to talk. You're neglecting things. The epidemic's out of control. We must force every available Besin in to get on top of this thing."

An amazing thing happened.

"You have my permission to so order."

This had never happened before.

Of course, his follow-up attempt to pin down that statement pushed her into a tirade of insults and resentments about him and her other offspring.

But she didn't look good, so he took her by the elbow and said, "You aren't well. I'll walk you to your quarters and we'll get a Besin to examine you. Not even *we* are immune to giarmial."

Ferjival winced about what would pour forth from her mouth at that, but she said nothing. She *was* sick. On their way, he stopped a footman and sent him off with a note card on which he had jotted down a request for Trovo, the head of the Besin clan, to come immediately to evaluate Mam Sior.

When, at last, she lay on the chaise in her quarters, he rang the bell for servants. Soon, people scurried about, readying her bed, lighting a fire, serving tea for her to spurn.

"Mother, please try to be civil. I know you aren't feeling well, but—."

"Puraples do not get maladies!" Mam Sior said through gritted teeth.

Ferjival's knees went soft, and he felt that he might keel over. He found the nearest chair and sat, his arm on the side table, his hand over his eyes. "Mother, I don't believe you are suffering from giarmial, but of course we are capable of catching it. We must be certain, mustn't we? None of us saw this coming and..."

"The girl," she cut in. "The girl's father died."

"Who?" He sighed. Many people had died. "It's an epidemic," he said, too softly for her to hear. To his knowledge, mental lapses were not a symptom of their own curse. *Perhaps she is simply going demented all on her own with no magic curses involved.* "Who are you talking about?"

"Aza Gen."

"Aza? The...Gen. Yes. Hardly a girl anymore, but what about her? Yes, her father was the head of their council."

"She's half-clan. I want her executed."

Ferjival sat up. "What?"

"Immediately."

"Mother."

"DO IT!"

She must be going mad.

"If...if she were half-clan, why would she have been here all this time? Did you just find out? Who told you?"

"Doesn't matter. Bring her in. Immediately."

Maripes give me strength. "I will. But we'll have to convene a Synod meeting and things are in a bit of turmoil right now, what with so many people ill. Including you, evidently."

Her face grew redder.

"Mother? Calm down, please. I will go see what's keeping the Besin."

"No! Find Aza Gen and put her under detention until the execution can be scheduled."

He rose, looking at the servants who all knew Aza Gen. They were trying to act as if they had no ears. He turned to his mother, his arms outstretched by his sides, palms facing out. "Why do we want to execute her *now*? What is your proof that she isn't pure Gen? I need some help to move forward with this, especially now, in this time of heightened criticism of our rule."

"You useless sod. Get out."

"Mother."

Usually her first "get out" would be followed by increasingly loud repetitions, but this time she only whispered it twice more and then squeezed her eyes shut and turned her head away.

Ferjival left the room.

She could actually die.

This realization hit him harder than he could have predicted considering how often he *had* imagined just such an eventuality. He quickened his step. He had to get busy solidifying his hand on the reins of power. He would not let this slip through his fingers.

He would not.

13

FOUND AND LOST

ON THIS SUNNY DAY, the Wardrobe entrance looked even more forlorn than it had the first time she was here.

Aza stood at the doorway, unsure of herself. Of everything. She'd come to return Bek's clothes, but also had a glimmer of an idea to rent space here. It would be a roof over her head until she could figure out where to go. But considering her dry mouth and sweaty palms, she had to admit that this visit might be more about the hope of seeing Bek.

There were way too many complicated feelings about this person she'd only talked to twice. Those two meetings had in no way been typical 'getting to know you' encounters. The presence of Benelek Kruik was nothing to take lightly. The first, at her parents' house, was full of intimacies. Bek sensed Zaz and, *by the clan*, Aza revealed her biggest secret. *Well, the biggest at the time. Now I have a much bigger one.* But then, as she wondered if she would ever see her again, Bek appeared in the elevator of the Wardrobe—larger than life—and in front of all her actual friends, had treated Aza as if she were the most important one. Of course, Aza wanted to see her again. Of course, the thought of it was daunting...and irresistible.

She took the decrepit elevator to the fifth floor. At the fourth door on the left, she rapped twice. No answer. She tried the handle. It opened. *How like Bek to leave the door unlocked.*

Peeking into the relative darkness, Aza jumped back toward the corridor at the sight of two people asleep in the bed. Aza couldn't see either of their heads, only bare legs and feet amongst mounds of rumpled bedclothes. She was very sure, though, that one was Bek and that they both were women.

They didn't stir.

She could not wait to be gone. She quietly unbuckled her valise, pulled out the clothes, placed them on the arm of the couch, quietly closed the door, and left. Running to the stairwell, she careened down, one bag under her arm, the other bumping against her legs with every step. At the ground floor, she burst out onto the street, face flushed, chest needled with emotion. She dropped her bags, and leaned her back against the building.

Instead of calming down, her panic grew.

If only the ground would open and swallow me whole. No one would care. Or notice. She had nowhere to be. No home, family, fiance, best friend, job, clan. No plan. How could she have even considered staying at the Wardrobe? The place was rife with Uppers. She had to vanish, not only from the Purples, but also from those who knew her as Gen.

Aza adjusted the long strap of the valise more comfortably onto her shoulder, grabbed the carpetbag, and started walking.

The vision of Bek lying with a woman came back over and over. They hadn't looked like sisters in that bed. They had looked like lovers. This made her furious and she didn't know why. But anger felt better than embarrassment or jealousy. Her stride became stronger as she remembered the goodbye conversation with Garnia yesterday.

"What will they do without you, Aza?"

"Find someone else," she answered with a shrug. "Any Gen can do what I do. Just don't tell them you saw me. It should be a mystery."

"Like Maleka," Garnia said, shaking her head.

"Yeah," she answered, fury rising, "in a way."

Except it wasn't. Maleka chose to disappear because she wanted to "be happy." That seemed like the most childish of excuses for doing anything, over and above the fact that Maleka's actions wouldn't bring her happiness. *What if she's pregnant?*

With a half-clan...like me.

And hasn't that turned out well?

Aza stopped and looked around. Nothing looked familiar. *I've got to pay attention to street names. Maybe I can find a store where maps are sold.* Then, across the road, Aza spotted a different kind of store. Her heart leapt at this literal, small sign that providence might be with her, after all.

Painted on the window in black and gold scrolled lettering, it said, *Used Clothing.*

Aza took a trolley to Colvara, dressed in a rich yellow, ankle-length, shirtwaist dress with forest green buttons and trim. Underneath, she wore a simple cotton slip instead of petticoats. It surprised her, how freeing that alone felt. Her curls were held in place with a scarf the color of the dress with swirls of deep blue and burnt orange. These were bold colors compared to the Gen pastels she'd always worn. Other than purple, which was claimed by the Puraples, bright colors were considered a mark of the Dals and the Salizans. Aza couldn't see herself in red...yet, but the bright yellow felt like middle ground.

This outward change imparted an inward shift: a wave of rebellious energy for entering her new life. Before boarding the trolley, she'd stopped at a coach office, and putting on a big, friendly, pretend smile said, "Gerland Salizan was kind enough to accept less than the standard fare from me when I was short, so I need to pay him back. He wrote down his address in Colvara, but I'm afraid I've left it at home. I'm going there today anyway—there's a bakery that sells the very best dopi rolls in the city—and I thought I'd clean two curses with one spell and drop by to pay back what I owe him. Can you help me with his address?"

She made up the story on the spot and felt ridiculously pleased at her inventiveness. It had worked like a charm.

Now, the trolleyman signaled to her when they got close to the stop she had given him.

"You'll 'ave to walk a few blocks that-a-way." He motioned to her right. "Don't know from there which direction ye'll need."

The trolley steamed off. She stood on the deserted corner, thinking about Maleka.

Where do people go when they need to hide?

Where were the Undones? No one ever talked about that. Anyone could dress in another clan's style. Disguising oneself allowed an Undone—such as herself—to go about in the city as a member of any clan. But that was different from living somewhere with neighbors who would wonder, inquire, and notice that you had no clan connections. Then again, maybe there were whole burgs of Undones. *Just one of many things I suddenly, desperately, need to know.*

Bek would know. Will I ever see her again? Beautiful Bek, who has sex with men from other clans and also with women, it seems. Could I ever tell Bek my secret? Stop it. She's part of your past. Forget her. Forget everyone you knew. Except Reth. And Gerland—though he too might have to be forgotten at some point.

She walked slowly, taking in her surroundings. She'd been fascinated with the neighborhood when Gerland brought her to see Rimna. The homes were small, sometimes tiny, and close together, but they were mostly tidy, often painted bright colors, with flowers on windowsills and thriving gardens. The cooking smells coming from some of them right now made her salivate. There was an open, neighborly atmosphere here.

The homes on her street—the Villa's street—were sequestered behind walls and fences. She hadn't seen that many Puraples' homes, having been a resident of the largest in the city with acres of land surrounding it. The stately stone homes of the Kruiks in Benelek's area, which all faced the street openly, were not inviting but more imposing, by design. Homes meant to impress, not welcome.

But the folks who live here in Colvara, as Garnia and Gerland had taught her, no matter how approachable their homes, had struggles she knew nothing about.

She found Gerland's street and asked a woman out washing her front stoop if she knew the man.

"Aye, everyone knows Gerland. This time o' the day you might see his coach parked next to the house. It's down more 'an a block, on this side. Blue house, with kids falling out the windows and doors." She chuckled as she went back to work.

Aza found it easily. The house looked well-used. Not that tidy and a bit rundown. Three children chasing one another in some kind of adventure game almost ran into Aza as she approached the front door.

"Side door!" one shouted.

"No one uses the front one!" said another, as he disappeared around the corner.

She walked to the side where the porte-cochère held Gerland's familiar vehicle. Unbidden, the memory of cleaning its back seat with Maleka came to mind. The last time they'd done magic together.

"May I help you?"

The children must have alerted their mother. The woman—even shorter than Aza, with white-gold streaks in red hair and cheeks like peaches—stepped onto the stoop.

"Hello," Aza said, dipping her head. "Is this Gerland Salizan's house?"

"It is."

"He has driven for me several times. I'm Aza..." She hesitated. She had no right to call herself a Gen anymore. "He...well, he's been very kind to me and—"

"Aza Gen?"

"Yes." The word came out in an almost whisper.

"Why ever are you dressed like that? Of course he's told me about you. He was so distraught at the disappearance of your friend. He *is* here, but I can't let you see him. He's been ill."

"Oh no," Aza said, her heart speeding up. "Is it the malady?"

"I'm afraid so. He's on the mend, however. I've forbidden the children from being around him, but they miss him so. I'm constantly having to shoo them away from his room. Would you like to come in?"

"I shouldn't. You have your hands full."

She laughed as she motioned Aza up the steps. "That is an apt description of me at any time, Miss. Come in. You, at the least, must take time to tell me what brings you all the way out here."

As Aza entered, she felt her tightly controlled emotions threaten to escape. The overly warm kitchen smelled of fresh-made bread and a savory pot of goulash, or some-such, simmering on the back burner. It was enough to make even an untroubled person cry. Gerland's wife's attention was on one of the children—not one of the three who had been outside—so Aza walked to the far end of the narrow space, past the kitchen table and, facing the wall, tried to re-bundle her feelings.

"There you go. Sorry for the distraction. We'll have some tea and—hey. Hey there, are you all right?" She touched Aza's shoulder and then peeked around to look at her face. "I can see that you are not. Sit. Go on, sit. That's all right then. Oh, and so much for my manners, I haven't even introduced myself. I'm Ness."

Aza wished fervently that Ness could be her mother. "Thank you. I'm so sorry to be troubling you. It's just that your kitchen smells so good and—"

"And isn't that a proper reason to be crying and looking like the world was about to fall from the heavens?"

"Sometimes, it is," Aza said. "I've had a hard time lately."

"Oh?" Ness was busying herself getting tea prepared. When Aza said nothing, Ness glanced over her shoulder and said, "Tell me."

"I don't want to upset you."

"Your problems aren't mine, sweets. Not that I know of. And if they are, I should know about it. Let it all out."

I can't let it all out. That is the problem. Too late, she realized that she should have fabricated a reason to be outside her own world in non-Gen clothing. She had only been thinking of disappearing into the city; going where no one knew her. And she would do that. But right now, she had to talk to someone who knew that she was out of place.

"My father died of giarmial. I didn't want to mention it because...gods, Gerland is ill."

"Oh, you poor dear. Don't you worry. Gerland is better. He's been in the good hands of his favorite Besin. Someone who knows him well. That helps, you know."

"Vijo?"

Ness beamed. "Why yes! How lovely that you know him, too."

"Gerland introduced us. Are you sure?" Aza asked.

"Of what?" Ness was sitting next to her at the table now. She pushed a stack of drawings and crayons out of the way and put two cups and a teapot on the table.

"That he's going to recover fully. It can relapse."

"Aye," she said, looking into space. "That's exactly why he's still abed and as quarantined as I can manage. If it were up to him, he'd already be out driving! But we were warned, and by *Maripes*, I'll keep him bound with pigtail ribbons if I have to! He's going nowhere until completely out of danger."

"Oh," Aza said, breathing deeply, "that is good to hear."

"I'm so sorry to hear that you lost your father. Didn't Gerland tell me that he was head of the Gen Council?"

"Yes."

She made a *tsk*ing sound with her tongue as she prepared a sweet, milky cup of tea for Aza. "You'll stay for dinner. Gerland will be very happy even though I will not let you see him and still don't know what to tell him about why you've come."

"I will tell you. You're so very kind and generous. I'm not surprised, as Gerland is as well. I'm here because the houseman at my father's home may need to get in touch with me. I've...left home for reasons I can't go into. I'm sorry. Not trying to be dramatic, but anyway, I've no address yet that I can give Reth and was hoping I could give Gerland and you the information about where I'm staying, that is, once I've found some place, and then if Reth does inquire, you can let him know where to find me. I hope that won't be too much trouble."

"You've no place to stay?"

"Not yet. I just walked out the door this morning."

"But it's almost evening. Were you going to sleep in the bushes?"

Aza felt her cheeks redden as she stared at this woman who was so competent that she could not only take care of herself and a sick husband but also a seemingly uncountable number of other small human beings, while Aza NoClan couldn't even think things through clearly enough to start looking for lodging early so that she didn't end up on the street after dark.

She studied her hands, which felt rudely naked without gloves, and wished for everything to go back to the way it so recently was. Life hadn't been great, but this was so much worse. "I'm afraid that I'm overwhelmed. Not thinking straight. I haven't had to make decisions before about things like having a roof over my head. Is there—? Do you know if there's a cottage or a room somewhere that I might rent? Or do you know of someone I could ask? I have...at least, I will have...money. My father—"

"Child...stop. It's all right. Your life is in upheaval; I don't need to know all the reasons why. I'll let you sleep here, if needs be. But you won't be comfortable."

She took a sip of tea and looked off into space, her fingers tapping on the waxy surface of the tablecloth. "Leave it with me. I'll think of someone who can have you for the night at the least." She smiled reassuringly. "No questions asked. Go on now, drink your tea. It'll help."

After, Ness sat Aza in the tiny backyard with two of the younger children—a boy and a girl—for a board game called Sparks and Spells. The rules were basic, and in no time, Aza was busy, distracted, and under the spell of this charming pair.

When Ness returned, she told the kids to wash for dinner and handed Aza a note.

"What's this?"

"I talked it over with Gerland and he suggested Rimna, so I sent Ladner over with a request. This is her address. She'll be happy to have you. We only asked for the one night so neither of you would feel locked into something if it's not comfortable or convenient. Gerland said that you've met her."

"Yes, he was kind enough to take me there after Maleka disappeared. But I—"

"What?"

"I felt she didn't quite approve of me."

"Oh, I doubt that. She can be quite direct in her speech, but her heart is as big as the city."

"How can I ever thank you? You've taken care of me in every way."

"Posh, it's nothing. You've lifted Gerland's spirits by dropping by. Soon, you two will be able to talk things over. It's good for him to have that to look forward to."

"That's so kind. I look forward to it as well. Shall I go now?"

"Nay, we'll have dinner first. The rest of the kids are dying to meet you. I kept them away so as not to overwhelm you, but a wee warning: You'll be fair game at the meal."

Aza laughed, grateful to have something to feel lighthearted about.

Later, Ness walked with her to Rimna's. It was dark, but the evening stayed mild. New growth gave the air a rich loaminess that Aza decided might be the smell of optimism.

"I don't know how I'll ever repay your kindness."

"Posh."

"Seriously. I've had the best evening. The food was restorative. And I love your children. Each and every one is delightful. Unique. Clever. Hilarious."

Ness leaned over with a huge smile and squeezed Aza around the waist. "We are blessed times ten, for certain. Thank you."

"You're even walking me over!"

"Now that is purely selfish. I could've sent Ladner or Larch over with you, but no, this is a time apart from all my blessings. A relaxed walk and talk with an adult woman? That is precious to me, especially on such an evening as this."

Aza laughed. "I am happy to have been the excuse for a small escape."

They walked in silence for the last half block. Aza got the feeling that Ness would have loved it if she confided all to her, but she was a good enough person to wait. Aza was not ready. In fact, fatigue was overwhelming her again, and this made her ashamed, because what must Ness feel like at the end of every day?

She recognized Rimna's storybook house immediately. The green arched doorway had a gaslight above it, casting a swirly edged triangle onto the porch.

"I'll not stay," Ness said, as Aza turned onto the walkway. "Give Rimna my best. I'll talk to her soon. I must get home and put the little ones to bed." She opened her arms, and they shared a warm hug. "Let me hear from you soon. Stop by anytime. You know the way?"

Aza nodded. "I can find it."

"I mean it. You're no trouble, and Gerland will be pestering me about your welfare. Understand?"

"I do. Thank you for everything."

She walked away. Aza turned back to the house. She'd forgotten just how tiny it was. Where would Rimna find the room to put her? It didn't matter. She was so exhausted, she'd sleep on the floor, in the garden shed.

She had been taken in; the details didn't matter.

14

THE WITCH'S LAIR

A PATTERNED HAZE MET her eyes after a cloying, smoky smell woke her.

The haze came from three overlapping silk scarves draped across the doorway of the alcove she was given to sleep in. The smell? Incense, she decided, but the aroma was more complex. Something cooking? She didn't feel hungry at all. In fact, she was slightly nauseated.

Rimna's black cat, Trilst, walked across her legs and settled in against the crook of her knees.

You're in the lair of a witch, Aza.

Her arrival the night before felt like a dream.

After Ness's unconditional and motherly warmth, Rimna's response seemed as complicated as it had the first time they met. It wasn't unfriendly. She had, after all, welcomed her into her home on short notice. But there was a haughtiness that radiated from her, and Aza found it difficult not to take personally—as if she had offended the woman by her very Gen-ness.

Ironic, considering her utter lack of clan status.

They hadn't talked for long, because, as Rimna said, "It's obvious you need sleep more than anything else." Then she had asked, "Have you found Maleka?"

"No, but you were right. She disappeared on purpose."

Rimna nodded. "People shouldn't doubt me."

Now, lying in a bed with a roof over her head, Aza decided that was true. People shouldn't and she wouldn't ever again.

She didn't want to move. She didn't want to talk. Didn't want to feel guilty about feeling that way. The nausea continued. Plus, her knees and lower back ached, probably from traipsing all over creation with her bags.

I have plenty of reasons to feel lousy. Grief. Betrayal. Loneliness. Being a societal outcast who could legally be executed.

Stop being dramatic. You're fine.

But she wasn't.

She woke later at the insistence of her bladder. The house was quiet. The smells gone. She stumbled to the washroom to discover that she was menstruating. It was a relief to have an explanation for feeling so lousy.

Rimna was not in the house.

On the small, coarse wooden table in the kitchen, a plate of cold meats and cheese, alongside a teapot ready for hot water, awaited her. Aza nibbled at one piece of cheese and got a drink of water from the tap. She took it back to her room, grateful not to have to make conversation.

Sitting cross-legged on the bed, she thought about the things she'd taken from the attic at the Villa only yesterday morning. When she found them, she wanted to go through them all immediately. But the urge to leave her father's house was even more pointed. *Why, really? What was the rush?*

There's danger. She started. *Danger? Who said that?*

Zaz had split to the other end of the bed. She could see herself. But even so, she was the only one here. That the words seemed to come from Zaz was odd.

Aza looked pitiful. Paler than usual, eyes dominating her face, and her freckles standing out like pepper on a potato. Was she thinner? That made sense, because—notwithstanding the hearty bowl of stew and thick slice of bread she'd eaten at Ness's—she hadn't been eating regularly since her father had his relapse.

"All right," she said softly to both herselves, "I get it. The danger is that I haven't been taking care of myself. But I don't know how. I'm afraid to talk to people because I don't know who I am anymore. I'm incapable of finding a real place to live. I can't even use this time to focus on my mother's things." This was a truth she hadn't admitted before. She felt deep dread about what might be waiting for her in those keepsakes, and she did not have the reserves to deal with any more surprises or unpleasant news right now.

She curled onto her side and went back to sleep.

That evening, she and Rimna shared a meal.

"You've gone to the trouble of cooking and I'm afraid I don't have much of an appetite. I started my flow this morning."

Rimna grinned. "I'm so old that I sometimes forget about menstruation. Not everything about aging is bad."

Aza smiled back. "I'll remember that." Then she added, more softly, "If I have the chance to grow old."

"You seem very changed since last fall."

"Do I? I guess that's not surprising...considering everything that's happened."

Rimna tapped her chin and said, "You seem wiser."

Aza laughed. "No. Definitely not."

"Why? Because you're confused? Lost? Adrift?"

Such a witch.

"Yes."

"Out of these things wisdom arises. We don't know what lessons we're acquiring when we're in the middle of upheaval. Grief teaches us."

"I could do without that sort of wisdom."

"Tosh. You are more aware now."

"That's probably true. The young woman who came here last fall knew little about other people's lives."

"Why are you here?"

"I needed a place to stay."

"Why?"

Aza looked at her hands. Her cuticles were dry, reddened and cracking.

When Aza didn't answer, Rimna said, "All right. I won't push you. But you could have stayed in your father's house. Instead, you are here, homeless, without a plan, and dressed in clothing not of your clan. There's a story there and people will fill in the blanks for you if you don't give them an explanation."

She went to the stove and turned on the fire under the teakettle.

"I can't right now."

"Understood. I'm just trying to protect you from the gossip that will spread."

"I have a question for you."

The woman, in the process of getting milk and sugar, turned and nodded.

"I have this ability. And I don't know where it came from or if others have it and I've never had anyone I could ask. Well, I discussed it with a Kruik woman a while ago and she hadn't heard of it, but she knew someone who had a different kind of ability. We might call it a Talent, even though it has nothing to do with spells or curses. So, I thought of you, of course. You certainly have some kind of ability, but I don't know how to define it or—"

"If it's real?" Rimna said gruffly.

"I suppose."

Rimna gathered the tea things and brought them to the table. "What is your ability?"

"I can split myself to see and hear what is happening around me from a second point of view."

"Ah. I've heard of this."

"Really! Oh my. I never knew."

Aza described the talent that Bek's friend seemed to have.

"Never doubt that these are real Talents," said Rimna. "I have seen them, mine, and a few others. Never in men, in my experience, though perhaps they have their own that they don't share with us."

"But why aren't they considered 'real' magic?"

"You tell me."

"Because...because it doesn't fit the hierarchy?"

"Perhaps."

"Because the lower clans aren't 'supposed to' have magic?"

"Yes."

"Because women do these things and...oh. Women from every clan?"

"So it would seem, though I have no direct evidence of a Puraples with this kind of Talent."

"Do they not believe us?"

"That's likely part of it."

"I didn't believe in your Talent when Gerland brought me. I'd always heard that Dals have no magic. I've even had Dals tell me that. My friend Garnia said so."

Rimna leaned forward and whispered, "Our Talents aren't talked about. And yes, people see them as women's tales, superstition, 'poor folk remedies' that don't have a bit of magic. They *are* quite different."

"Right. They require no chants, no words. They're more part of who we are instead of something we do."

"Nicely put. What are you going to do about all this?"

Aza eyebrows raised. "Me? Nothing. I don't know. What should I do?"

Rimna finished her tea and rose to tidy the counter.

"I'll clean up," Aza said.

"Nay. It's no trouble. I want you to rest as much as you can. You need it more than you think."

"I feel guilty."

"Don't waste your energy on that." She turned around and leaned against the counter, her hands folded across her belly. "Do you remember how I described my Talent?"

"You can find things...but no...I've forgotten how you explained it."

"I sense what's in the front of people's consciousness."

"Oh yes. That must get tiring," Aza said dryly.

Rimna smirked. "It doesn't function all the time. I use it intentionally, the way I did with you that day."

Aza nodded. "I tell myself to split. I even named my other self, Zaz. But, with me, sometimes it just happens."

Rimna mirrored Aza's nodding. "Mine too. I wanted to mention it because it's happening involuntarily for me right now. Really, ever since you came. I need you to know that. It's awkward, since you haven't asked for help other than a bed to sleep in. I'm not *trying* to intrude on your privacy."

Aza hated that Rimna would be aware of secrets she was holding onto. But she had to admit that she had often invaded other people's privacy. She had no right to judge Rimna for doing it, especially if it was unintentional. She sighed, not knowing what to say. Finally, to fill the growing silence, she stammered, "I'm so confused. It might be instructive to know what you sense is at the forefront of my mind."

The woman inhaled slowly and let out a long breath. "That you don't belong. Anywhere. That's what I'm getting. I'm sorry. I can't discern the reasons behind it, but it must be very hard."

Aza's mouth dropped. She took a moment and then said, "That's a concise way of putting what is a complex situation. I'm not upset with you. I'm in your debt. In many ways."

"Nonsense. Now, I want to tell you something. I'm leaving tomorrow for a visit with my twin sister. I'll be gone a few days. She lives on a farm in Luftva. Do you know it?"

"Just seeing it across the water. I've never been out of the city."

"It's lovely there. Still technically part of Maripesa, but with fewer people, more animals and a lot more open, green space."

"Will it be all right if I leave in the morning?"

"No. No, no. I want you to stay. You need time alone. There's no reason to look for something else. Please use my home while I'm gone, We'll see how you're feeling when I return."

"I can't thank you enough."

She wagged a finger toward Aza. "Water my garden and feed Trilst. Deal?"

"Deal," Aza said, relief washing over her. "I thought you didn't like me, you know."

"Hmm, maybe you have some Talent for discernment, too. I didn't much at that first visit, but that's my fault. I'm getting more intolerant as I age. Don't like privileged people who come slumming. But I was a little hasty with you. Forgiven?"

"Oh, there's nothing to forgive. Everyone's allowed their opinions, I hope. I was sheltered. That's something I have to deal with every day. Oh, speaking of that..."

"Yes?"

"Um. I have an embarrassing question. You see, I had no mother to tell me about sex. I know the basics and it's the last thing I am considering at the moment with all that's happened, but I only just found out that there's a spell that prevents pregnancy. I should know it, don't you think?"

Rimna smiled, sat down and explained what Aza needed to know, just in case.

Aza hadn't been able to eat. She'd had no more than tea for the two days since Rimna left. Her mind felt fuzzy. She had also developed a weird, stinging rash around the cuticles of her fingers. She blamed it on not wearing gloves. But when it developed around her toes, explanations failed her. She knew that food might help, but an overriding apathy kept her from dealing with any of her current problems.

Sitting on the floor of her alcove with her back against the mattress, Aza removed Trilst from her lap for the umpteenth time. She was trying to get through her mother's keepsakes.

She fingered a delicately crocheted baby cap. It was tiny and sweet and brought tears to her eyes, but her feelings hardened when she realized she had no way of knowing if her mother made it or bought it, or indeed, if she had ever even placed it on her head. There were a few other baby items alongside a thin, bound journal, some sketches, decorative hair pins, a key, several sets of gloves, a letter opener, jewelry, and an ivory comb.

Aza had immediately put on a bracelet of colorful polished stones and a thin-chain necklace that held a tear-drop shaped pendant made of filigreed silver encapsulating an irregularly edged gem that shone with slender ribbons of fiery opalescence. She loved them both unconditionally.

The gloves confused her. If her mother was not a Gen, why were there gloves in her things? Had Leo tried to pass her off as Gen by dressing her so? Perhaps. She didn't even know how old she was when her mother died.

Her anger against both parents—for having a mixed clan child—had settled firmly onto her father for keeping all of this from her. For not telling her until it was too late. For not allowing her the time to ask all the questions she needed answers to. For dying. For making whatever deal he'd made to save his own skin. Hers too, of course. But how had Mam Sior found out? Well, she has spies, stooges everywhere. Did she know from the beginning, or after her mother's death?

The memory of seeing Mam Sior in obvious distress, reading a letter from Leo, formed a core of confused, fierce emotion in her gut.

This was *his* shame.

Had he loved her mother? So much that he could, would, never talk about her? Or so little?

"I don't even know what you looked like."

❦

Later, Aza found herself on the bed, tangled in sheets damp with sweat. The gaslight on the wall flickered. She looked at it for a long while, thinking that she needed to get up and fill it or it would go out. Her mouth was parched, so she rolled over to find the cup of tea she'd made earlier. It sat within arm's reach on the floor. She drained it, barely lifting her head. Lying back, she felt something hard underneath her shoulder. She pulled out the journal.

Rubbing her eyes to clear the sleep, she opened it for the first time.

A drawing filled the end pages. *My mother liked to draw.* Father told Duma I got my artistic ability from her. The now familiar sharp, quick surge of anger rose in her chest, and then receded.

The drawing was intricate, the marks spontaneous and free. It looked as if it had grown out of the sureness of an artist who trusted her hand. Done in a variety of colors of ink—predominantly dark blue—the left side showed straight-edged, geometric and patterned shapes interspersed with a few flowing lines that led to the right side. It was all fluid curves ending in spirals and squiggles. Aza lost herself in tracing individual lines. She turned the page.

"I am breaking rules," it began. "I do it voluntarily and with full knowledge of the consequences, but I do it with hope as well, and with some confidence that it is only when we as Maripesians freely live out our dreams that we shall become the people we have the capacity to be. For too long, we have been living blindly, insensate to what is obvious: magic should not be used to control..."

Aza's hazy focus became pin-point sharp. She read the finely printed pages, not to remember each word—she couldn't—but to inhale her mother's mind and spirit before it was too late. These precious pages held not only her mother's personal thoughts on upending the status quo, but also silly, squiggly, skilled sketches of people and places.

The back cover made Aza gasp. On it was a carefully penned name: Arja Salizan.

Arja. Arja is similar to Aza. I am Salizan? I belong to Gerland and Ness's clan?

I hate my father for keeping all this from me.

No. I am not Salizan. Neither Gen nor Salizan. I am Undone. I am nothing.

At some point, her eyes closed again.

When she woke, the gaslight had gone out, the room completely dark. A repeated, hard noise resounded, but she could find no connection with whatever was happening outside herself.

Sometime, maybe much later, maybe not, there was pounding. She visualized the green door with the rounded top, but drifted again, helpless. In a miasma of pain and fever, she was lost in sick-dreams of executions on a field of sharply drawn, patterned lines over which she kept tripping and losing her way amongst crowds of cartoonish people for whom she was invisible.

She couldn't respond to the calling voices. She couldn't rouse to tend to herself or the hungry Trilst who rubbed against her cheek, her shoulder, over and over.

"I don't even know what you looked like," she whispered, her mind cycling, her head pounding in cadence with the knocks at the door as she searched through drawn lines for a face she could call Mother.

15

A New Name

Benelek, up early and full of energy, was waiting in Vijo's clinic room when he arrived.

"Oh!" Vijo put his hand to his chest. He was even more pale than usual. "You startled me."

"I...um, slipped in."

"Are you ill?"

"Why don't you have a seat and catch your breath? Seems like you might be the one who needs fixing today."

He did, placing his apothecary on the table. "I'm all right. I just wasn't expecting anyone to be in the room. Please tell me you don't have symptoms of giarmial."

"I'm not sick. I wanted to talk to you and don't know how to find you outside of work."

"Spellfire, Bek, I don't even know what that is anymore. I work and sleep and sometimes find a moment to eat. It isn't easing up. Did you see the waiting room?"

"I did. I should have waited my turn, but we both know that's not my style." She waved a hand.

"What's so urgent?"

"Aza. Remember her? I told you about her when I was here...I don't know. The last time? Everything runs together. She showed up at my parents' house and somehow wormed her way into my life. Calls herself a snoop. The Gen?"

"Oh yes. What about her?"

"The Purples want to arrest her, but she left home with no forwarding address. Or that's the gossip. I thought she might have come down with giarmial since her father died of it, recently." She paused. "Honestly, Besin, I'm worried about you too."

He rubbed his eyes. "Look Bek, I'd love to have a long talk with you, but you saw the waiting room. I don't have time."

She stood abruptly. "I'm sorry."

"No. Wait. It's just that you're rambling. Come to the point. Aza Gen is missing and you think she might be sick. Do you know where she is?"

"No. I don't know how to find her. I ran into her at the Wardrobe one night. Then, she dropped off clothes that she'd borrowed. I was there, but I guess she just slipped in and left them while I was sleeping. Very put out about that..." Her words trailed off.

"The point. What do you want me to do?"

"Keep your eyes and ears open. Even if she's not sick, there's a warrant out for her arrest and I don't even know if she knows that."

"She probably *does* know if she's left home."

"True. I'll let you get to work. There's just another—" Benelek stopped, chewing on her upper lip.

"What?" Vijo asked

"I want you and yours to know: the Kruiks are going to strike back hard. I am worried but don't know if I can stop it."

"Why tell me?"

She let out a frustrated snort. "Do those lovely curls of yours make you dense? I like you. You're a great guy. The same way I like Aza, the Snoop. You're Vijo, the Fair. Friends. I like people, big deal. Especially now, Vij, we gotta stretch outside our boundaries because all cursing hell is about to shake loose."

"What exactly do you mean?"

"The Kruik Council's been supporting the development of a new combination curse. They're working on one that will spread from its original object to anyone or anything that touches it."

He stared at her.

Bek nodded slowly. "Yeah. That'll make a person speechless. If no one talks sense into their thick skulls—and believe me, I'm trying—we're not only going to have this out-of-control epidemic but also a city completely brought to a halt by crawling Kruik muck!"

"Why?"

"They think they have the Purples on the ropes, so that now is the time to 'show their might.'" Bek put a hand on his shoulder. "I should go. How are you doing?"

"Exhausted," he admitted, "and have more than a full day's work ahead."

"Poor Vijo." Bek put a hand on either side of his face, rubbing it and then pulling her fingers up into his curls and then down the back of his skull. By the time her hands got around to the back, she was giving him a scalp massage.

"You're gonna be all right. We'll get on top of this. I'm sorry I unloaded on you. Forget the Kruik weapon. We're working on the *ancient ones* on our council, trying to show them this isn't the way. In fact, I am lobbying to get on the council. It's just taking time."

She stood back. He looked better. *Sometimes touch with a small "t" helps as much as magic.* She gave him one of her best smiles. "I will literally get out of your hair now."

"Thanks. That was unbelievably great."

She went to the door, opened it, looked back and gave a little wave.

"And Bek," he said. "I'm glad to see you healthy. Stay that way, will you?"

She laughed, but her mood shifted the minute she was in the hallway. It was crowded with sick people. She pulled the neck of her jacket closer and got out with all due haste.

Ferjival couldn't *find* Aza Gen.

At first, he didn't care one way or the other. He intended to arrest her only to stop one of the many complaints from his mother, but he also assumed it would be easy. She worked in their home, for *Maripes'* sake.

He had *not* planned an execution. Putting to death the daughter of the Gen leader so soon after he died of a Puraples curse wasn't going to gain the Puraples any community approval. If, at the same time, it somehow leaked out that one of their own had recently impregnated a different Gen girl who wasn't put to death, then there could be a full-fledged revolution against them.

How like his mother to bring ruin on the whole clan—no, the whole state—when she was on the way out.

But Aza Gen never came back to work. The servants said they hadn't seen the woman since before her father died. They all seemed genuinely clueless, except Garnia. Something about the look in her darting eyes made him think she might have some information. He'd had her followed, but that proved to be a waste of time.

He'd staked out Aza's father's house, but she hadn't been seen there. Today, he'd ordered the houseman in for questioning. She didn't seem to have any other relatives. He wondered at that, but didn't have time to worry about ancient history.

The longer the Gen stayed gone, however, the more obviously guilty she seemed. He had politely asked his still-ailing mother if she might have tipped her hand to Aza. She, of course, bit his head off. Why, indeed, should this situation be any different from all the others?

His mother didn't have giarmial. Maybe she'd get better and maybe she wouldn't, but—despite this problem of the missing Aza Gen—Ferjival had been busy running the city in her absence. At last. He'd held two council meetings, had met with the Synod—the leaders of all the other clans, except Leo, of course. The Gen hadn't decided who would take over his role.

The epidemic was, in this one area, working to his advantage. Everyone was preoccupied with getting their family well and back to work. The Besin had come in for almost universal criticism for not doing a better job from the beginning. However it had happened, he had stepped into the void left by his mother's illness and had no intention of being set aside, whether she lived or died.

After knocking, his secretary entered and announced, "Reth Salizan, sir."

A tidy, thin man of short stature, well-dressed in the livery of a fine house, entered the room. He strode forward, about half-way across the room, stopped abruptly, all but clicking his heels, squared his shoulders, his arms clasped behind his back, and nodded once. "You asked to see me, sir?"

Ferjival looked at him for a long moment and then pretended to look at a report on his desk. He'd found it useful to make people wait. He had learned a thing or two from his mother about wielding power. When he looked up, Reth hadn't moved a muscle.

He's used to waiting. That's what servants do.

"Where is Leo Gen's daughter?"

"I do not know, sir."

"Is that unusual?"

"What do you mean, sir?"

"For her to leave without telling you where she's going? She's supposed to work here but hasn't been seen since before her father died. How long has that been?"

"Ah, fifteen days...or sixteen, depending on how you count it, sir."

"And?"

"Miss Gen did not tell me her plans. She explained that she was going away for a while."

"Aggrieved over her father's death?"

"I couldn't say, sir."

"One would assume."

"Yes, sir."

"What else do you know?"

"About...?"

He was about to lose patience, but he held his tongue, his hands feigning busyness with the folders on his desk. He was working on his temper. A leader couldn't go around cursing everyone. A leader had other people to do that for him. However, he felt his breath coming too rapidly and tried to slow it before he spoke.

Finally, he said, "Where might she be likely to go? Is there a relative? An aunt or cousin she visits?"

"Sir, to my knowledge, Miss Gen has no relatives. Her father was a single child, as she is."

"Are you not concerned for her? A sad little orphan? What about her mother's side of the family?"

"Sir?" The man's gullet rose and fell.

"Her mother?"

"From my understanding, her mother died when Miss Gen was a baby. I was not with Leader Leo at that time."

Ferjival cleared his throat. "What about her mother's family?" he snarled. *Bats, how* does *one learn to keep control of one's temper?*

"Sorry, sir. I am trying to answer all your questions fully. Leo and Miss Gen never had contact with her mother's family, to my knowledge. I do not know of any other blood relative. She's alone in the world except, as you might expect, the larger clan. And yes, sir, I do feel concerned about her."

This was a long speech and, in its bland, non-informative way, it gave Ferjival hope. The Gen *had* told this man something. Maybe not where she was, but how to get in touch with her if needed. He was certain of it. "You may go."

The servant turned sharply and started walking away.

Ferjival immediately put a security detail on Reth with instructions to tail him at all times and report in daily.

Vijo put his case on the bedside table.

The young woman's freckled medium-brown skin was chalky, stretched across high, round cheekbones. Her closed eyes sank deeply into the sockets. Her dirty hair lay in tightly curled tangles around her shoulders.

Aza, the snoop. Bek's friend, Gerland's friend. Though he hadn't put that together until today.

She'd been staying alone at Rimna Dal's house when she fell ill. There was indeed a story here, and he hoped to be around when it was told. Bek had been right about Aza being sick. He'd have to let her know when he got a moment—if he ever did.

He lifted Aza's hand, noting the telltale blisters around her nails. He felt her forehead and whistled at the heat it gave off.

"Aza?" he said softly.

Her eyelids fluttered.

Responsiveness to sound was a good sign.

"Don't worry about opening your eyes just yet. I'm Vijo. I'm going to make you feel better." As he talked, he opened his case and gathered the necessary ingredients. He began to mix, chanting softly while he worked.

Gerland had brought her in, reminding Vijo that he met her briefly, months ago. Vijo finally realized she was the Gen of Bek's stories. But there was another connection. His sister had treated Leo, Aza's father. Eltah still grieved that she hadn't been able to save him.

Healing was never just a simple matter of providing the right medicine. The Besin were taught that the most effective treatment happened when the practitioner held a mental focus of the person he or she was healing. So, as he worked, he never let it slip his mind that this medicine was for the health and well-being of this particular young woman. *Aza, the Snoop. Aza, Gerland's friend. Aza, whose friend was missing. Aza, grieving her father. Aza, being sought by the Puraples.* He wondered about that last one but couldn't be distracted by questions right now.

Vijo's preparations were almost done when he had a strange sense that someone else was in the room. He knew for certain that wasn't true. He had closed the door after entering. It was a small room. Only he and Aza were present, but he looked over his shoulder anyway.

Fatigue. That's all it is. Refocus.

He concentrated on the vial between his thumb and index finger. His vocalizations became louder and, at the right moment, he let go of the bottle. When it spun in mid-air as it was supposed to, he let out a small sigh. He'd been worried that the interruption in his focus might have spoiled the spell. However, all seemed fine, except for that nagging perception that a third person was watching. He wriggled his shoulders to shake off the feeling and reached out to Aza.

She needed to wake if the medicine was to work quickly. If she couldn't regain consciousness and "own" the cure, he'd have to administer it to her, and that would take longer. She might die before he could bring her along.

"Aza," he said firmly, "open your eyes now. Time to get your medicine." When he touched her, he felt a moment of vertigo, the weird sensation of being watched disappeared, and he suddenly stared into Aza's wide open, gold-brown eyes.

"I know you," she said.

"Right," Vijo said, pleased that she was so aware.

He held out his net, caught the medicine as it dropped in and explained to Aza how they were going to make her well.

"How long have I been here?" Aza asked.

The Dal woman, who came every day to bathe her and change the sheets when needed, shrugged and said, "Since I came to help five days ago, but I've no idea how long you were here before that. They tell me you were on death's lap, dolly. You waited too long for treatment and that's a fact. Giarmial is not something to ignore."

"What's your name?"

The woman, tall, with a flawless pale complexion, ridged cheek bones and green-blue eyes, grinned. She pointed her index finger and put on such an overdone reprimanding look that it made Aza giggle.

"Your memory is a sieve," she said. "Delta. I was Delta yesterday and the day before, and I shall be Delta tomorrow. Hear, now?"

"Delta. Delta. Delta," recited Aza, with firm determination.

As soon as she left, Aza looked for something to write on or with. She found nothing. But a glass of water had left moisture on the table, so she dipped her finger in it and wrote Delta on the table.

Has the illness truly taken my memory? Delta had been teasing, but what if her mind actually had become addled by the malady? The monotony of lying in a bed didn't make for many standout moments, so it was difficult to know if her memory was working or not.

Can I walk?

Today—as far as she could remember—was the first time she'd even thought about getting out of the bed. All this worry must mean she was getting better.

She rose on her elbows and, with way more difficultly than she could believe, sat crookedly, while inching her legs toward and over the edge of the bed. Her feet and ankles were grotesquely swollen. By the time she was more or less upright, one hand holding onto the bedside table and the other on the bed, her breath was coming hard.

"Whoa, Aza. What are you doing?" Vijo came in and rushed over. "Don't try to stand without help. Do you understand? We don't want you falling."

"You needn't worry," Aza said breathlessly. "I don't have the strength."

"Still," Vijo said, holding onto her by one shoulder while pulling the chair over, "it's quite an improvement that you're awake and aware enough to want to sit up." He sat across from her.

"Is it? I thought so, too. I feel different this morning. More connected. Anyway, I have to lie down." She looked at him with an apologetic smirk.

He laughed and rose to help her.

After she was situated with a plumped pillow and her legs straight and covered again, she smiled. "You are Vijo. Your sister is Eltah. I'm at the clinic in Dysand. Gerland brought me here after finding me at..." Damn. She couldn't remember that.

Vijo gave her a questioning look.

"I keep forgetting the nurse's name. She was teasing me about having no memory, so I'm testing myself. It's Delta, by the way. Is that a result of the malady?"

"Ah, I see. You're not going to remember everything that happened while you were sick, that's for sure, but in terms of the rest of your memories? No need to worry; giarmial doesn't cause permanent memory loss."

"But I can't remember where I was before Gerland brought me here."

"Rimna's."

"Oh. Yes... That's vaguely familiar. Wait a minute...I just remembered that Gerland was sick with giarmial."

"He was. See? Your memory is fine."

"He's recovered?"

"Yes. Up and about. Doing some driving, though Ness is restricting his hours. He was well enough to bring you here."

"I haven't even thanked him."

Vijo laughed. "You have. Every day, when he and Ness visit."

"Oh, for *Maripes'* sake. I'm a jacnut, for sure. Um...have I properly thanked you?"

He bent his head in a quick bow. "Yes. But there's no need. You were quite sick, but you're young and healthy otherwise, so your recovery should be complete." He looked at her through pale, lush eyelashes and said, "Unlike your departed father, for which I am very sorry and give a heartfelt apology on behalf of all Besins, especially Eltah."

"Oh. Heavens. It wasn't her fault. He waited too long. On some level," she paused for a long moment, "I think he was ready to go. I, um, have more sympathy now for someone who ignores the symptoms, since I found that quite an easy path to take."

"The mental confusion that comes with the early symptoms is a huge problem for a lot of people. Most are alerted by family members, but I guess you were staying alone?"

"You're wondering what I'm doing in this part of the city?"

He shrugged as if it was no big deal.

"It's coming back to me now. Rimna Dal let me sleep at her house while she went away to see her sister and— Oh!" She lifted her upper body. "I was supposed to take care of her cat and water her plants!"

"You can't really walk yet, remember? I'm sure Rimna's plants and cat are fine."

"Right," she said, but it was all flooding back to her now: her father's confession, her mother's things. "Vijo, I'm half-Salizan."

She couldn't believe that had popped out of her mouth.

Vijo didn't wince, look shocked, or recoil in horror. He regarded her, long and hard. *No, not hard.* His eyes—blue as blue—were soft, kind, intelligent and, most endearingly, interested. His hair, cut short in the back with tousled curls on top, was the palest buttery blond. He had a broad, open face with rosy cheeks and a smattering of small, pale freckles.

Something we share.

"I don't know why I told you that," Aza said.

"Do you want to take it back?"

"How could I? What do you mean?"

"You're recovering from a serious malady. You might still be a bit delirious?"

Her heart skipped a beat. Would he turn her in? But then she looked in his eyes again and said, "I do know why I told you. I believe I can trust you. Don't prove me wrong."

He smiled. "I was just trying—and failing—to joke with you. Of course, you can trust me. What you tell me is held in strict confidence. It explains why I didn't recognize you at first when Gerland brought you in, though."

She furrowed her brow.

"You weren't wearing Gen clothes."

"Oh. Right. You know, I haven't thought all this through. Any of it."

"That's good then. You can spend your time thinking, because that's about all you'll be good for during the next week or so. That, and learning to walk again. I'm sorry, but I have other people to see. We're hoping the epidemic is past its peak, but we're still stretched thin. I do have to go."

"Of course. Thank you. You probably need this bed."

"No. No, that bed is yours for now. It sounds as if you don't have a place to go right now, anyway. But, when you do leave us, be sure to tell me where I can find you. You have a story to tell, and I'm extremely interested." He walked to the door, turned back and said, "As well as trustworthy."

Aza's body was tired from that conversation. Her mind, however, was not; today it had reawakened to all the hard, new realities of her life. She'd just admitted to someone from another clan that she was an Undone. Was that bold? Or simply foolish?

Both.

Pre-sickness realities washed over her: sex between clans; contraceptive spells; Maleka choosing to have a baby out of clan—with Mam Sior's son, no less; the secret of her own parentage. Her mind wandered to that odd visit with Oscera.

The Tchuvari called themselves Keepers of the Magic. Aza had always thought of it in the archival sense—holding on to and keeping track of Maripesian history. But Aza's recovery gave her new clarity. The Tchuvari were keepers of more than that. Keepers of their own power. Keepers of the status quo they had instituted: the structure of Maripesa on whose joists and beams the magic hung. If the building were destroyed, the magic would once again be free. But free magic hadn't worked either. The chaos had been so extreme that the rest of the world excommunicated Maripesa, and disallowed magic for their own people.

Pulling the covers up around her, she rolled onto her side. Aza imagined having time-travelled from the old days of chaos to a new time when clans intermingled and magic was part of the peace among clans instead of being divisive.

My mother wondered about these things too.

She lay awake for a long time.

Aza would give her trust to these people who had taken her in. Them, and Reth. Oscera, she wasn't sure about yet. The other people she knew—Purples, Gen Council, Duma—she definitely couldn't trust. From them, she would disappear. But Gerland and Ness, Rimna—who knew her secret without being told—and now Vijo, she would become a new person. A new person she couldn't yet envision.

She couldn't walk around as Aza Gen in Salizan clothes. *I need a new name.* She couldn't very well waltz in and check with the registrar of names. She needed something so unusual that it was highly likely to be unique.

Arja?

That didn't feel right.

The obvious answer asserted itself. *You'll be Zaz Salizan.* Maybe forever, but at least until—as her mother had written so long ago before her own life was cut short—she could "truly live out her dreams."

What is my dream? As she floated in a semi-sleep, her mind uncensored and with a fledgling hope of some kind of independence, she began to create a vision of her future.

I will gather stories from others who have abilities akin to mine. Like Cvita and Rimna. I will discover how common they are and what is the range and the depth of these talents. Talents, perhaps, with a capital T after all. I will share who I am with these people and grow a new kind of family.

Part Two

Country

16

WOMB

The day Aza was to leave the clinic, Eltah came in with Vijo.

The women had talked several times during Aza's recovery. Eltah carried a healer's guilt for not having saved Leo, but once that sad topic was out of the way, they found each other easy to talk to, with many shared interests.

Vijo, concern in his expression, said, "Do you have a plan?"

Aza, packing up the few items she'd gathered while at the clinic, stopped and said, "Yes. It's finally settled. I will stay in the country with the relative of a friend."

"That sounds lovely for a recovery, especially this time of year," Eltah said.

"Where, exactly?" Vijo asked.

Aza wore a white, buttoned blouse, tucked and belted into a gathered, homespun skirt of blue fabric, printed with small, scattered, bright green and yellow swirls. She smiled, holding out both hands.

Eltah took one, and Vijo clasped the other.

"May I count you as friends?"

Eltah was already smiling, but she broke into what Aza thought of as her mega-smile; the one that brightened not only her deep blue eyes and her whole face, but seemingly all the surrounding space. Vijo was less demonstrative, but he was pleased.

"Certainly," he said.

"Good. I'm not going to tell you where I'm going."

"Oh, great," Eltah said, "that'll help our budding friendship grow."

Vijo gave her a look half-searching, half-resigned. He knew more than his sister did. In fact, he knew before Aza did that she was a fugitive from a Puraples' warrant. He was also the first person she'd told about her illegal provenance.

Aza squeezed their hands and let go. "The fewer people who know where I am, the better. The rule of the Purples won't last forever. They're under so much criticism for this epidemic that it shouldn't be long before I'll be able to come back and live my life without fear of them."

"Why do you fear them?" Eltah asked. "Because you stopped coming to work there? I don't understand."

Aza pushed her bag aside and sat on the bed. She patted the spot next to her, encouraging Eltah to sit.

"Just before my father died, I found out that my mother, whom I never knew, was not Gen." The color drained from Eltah's face. Aza forged on. "The particulars of my birth were discovered, though it was not common knowledge, but my father was able to make a deal with Mam Sior to spare us. I don't know what all it entailed, but part of it was my sustained servitude to the family."

"Which you have stopped doing."

Aza nodded and said, "I guess the deal is off now that father is dead. Mam Sior wants me arrested...executed, presumably. You could be questioned about my whereabouts, if it comes to that."

"We understand," Vijo said.

"I hear Mam Sior is gravely ill," Eltah said, her mood deflated.

"What's coming behind her is no better. Ferjival?" Aza visibly shuddered. "The man is not only mean; he is selfish. He can't see beyond his own goatee. We have to unseat them. I don't know how I'm going to make this happen from somewhere out where the sheep graze, but, as I said, this won't last forever."

"Keep in touch?"

"I will. Gerland will get news of me." She stood, turned to Vijo and took both his hands in hers. "Thank you for my life." She leaned in for a warm, lingering hug.

He whispered into her ear. "My honor, Aza. I will miss seeing you every day."

These words felt like the most intimate ones she had ever heard. She hugged him more tightly.

Just then, Ness walked in.

After greetings all around, Aza said, "You're sure you weren't followed?"

Ness waved her off. "Please. A mother of ten always knows everything going on around her. I'm too practiced at using the eyes in the back of my head. Anyway, they wouldn't be able to keep up with me—unless they sent a five-year-old to do the job."

"Good. You're going to help me get ready?"

Ness straightened Aza's hair with a flatiron, pulled the tresses back tightly against Aza's head into a ponytail at the base of her neck, braided it loosely and pinned it into a thick chignon, Salizan-style.

"What do you think of yourself?" Ness asked, handing her a mirror.

Aza was amazed. "Truly, Ness. I'm not sure my own father would know me without the curls." She ran a hand over her cheek and jaw bones, jutting after her weight loss. She'd never be Maleka-svelte, but she could barely be called plump anymore.

"Here," said Ness. "I brought this for you. I know you like scarves."

"Oh, it's wonderful. Thank you." She wound the blue and white scarf around the bun, knotting it to one side and over her right shoulder.

"We could put some make-up to hide those freckles, but I don't think it's necessary."

"Agreed. I'm ready. You have my instructions?"

Ness nodded. "Gerland's arranged a private coach to the strait. The driver will be outside soon. She's a trusted friend who owes him a favor. However, not a favor big enough to drive you across the bridge. You'll be boated across by another friend."

"A boat? Oh my. Why not the trolley?"

"Too risky. You're to stay off public transportation for now."

"I can't swim."

Ness laughed. "A boat that won't sink. Does that allay your fears, girl?"

Aza grinned, but it faded immediately. Her heart raced. "I can't catch up with my own life. After all that's happened, now I'm a fugitive? Going into hiding? To stay with strangers? In the country? A place I've never been? On a boat?" She sat on the bed and shook her head, staring at the rough floorboards.

"Aye, it's all quite head-spinning, isn't it? But things move more slowly in the country. You'll have time to sort things out. I hope so, anyway."

"If not, I'll just come back. I don't really feel in much danger."

"Reth's niece told Gerland otherwise. He said Ferjival seemed determined to get you. They've had Reth followed."

"I heard." Aza sighed. "Ferjival's got such a temper. He was always snapping someone's head off. I wouldn't be surprised if he started this epidemic all on his own!"

Ness patted her shoulder. "Be cautious. It's not that far away, you know. I could stand on one side of the strait, with you on the other, and we could wave at each other."

"Why Ness Salizan, that is a bald-faced lie!"

She laughed heartily. "You just won't let me make you feel better, will you?"

"Aw. You never fail to lift my mood. I'm all right. Everyone's been so kind. I'll keep my chin up, my face and real name hidden, and tell all my troubles to the pigs and sheep."

❦

Climbing into the boat felt like going into a womb. This didn't make much sense, Aza knew—wombs being made for leaving, not entering—but having been worried that a boat trip would be scary, she was immediately struck by the vessel's solidity, its depth and width and the reassuring competence of the pilot, a mature woman named Karol, who treated her with an inexplicable respect and casual affection. The boat was a steam-driven ferry with room for dozens, but Aza—she gave her name as Zaz for the first time—was the only passenger.

The night was clear, with a strong, warm breeze. The lights of Maripesa glittered on the choppy waves that smoothed out as they entered the middle of the seaway.

"Thank you, Karol," Aza said. "It seems you've made a special trip just for me."

"This is what I do," she said with a satisfied smile. "Being out here on a night like this is no chore." She paused for a moment, looked at the water, the sky, and back to Aza. "You have friends who are good people. They've vouched for you, so I'm happy to be able to help in your journey."

This statement, expressed so simply, filled Aza with deep joy. Her mouth curled into a smile as she filled her lungs with clean sea air and let it out slowly. After a contented few minutes spent in awareness of her gratitude, Aza said, "I have a strange question for you. Do you have any special talents?"

"Other than being able to land this boat where I want to on the other side?" She grinned.

Aza laughed. "That is definitely a significant talent, but I was thinking of a more magical variety. Or does that involve magic?"

Karol, still smiling, shook her head. "Just practice."

Thinking of her vision of the future, Aza explained her ability to split. *It's time to talk to each other about such things.*

"Ah, I get your drift. Women's magic."

"Yes. Is this well known that women have their own forms of magic?"

"I wouldn't say that exactly. We all know about the contraception spell, though. And there's a kind of folklore about women's abilities, right? Treated more as the mysterious aura—especially with mothers or elders. But it's not credited as actual magic."

"I've started a collection of acquaintances who have these abilities," Aza said, feeling excited. "I want to find out how common they are and the range of them. Is it only women who have these or do men as well? Do these Talents run in clans, or is it just as likely that a Salizan or a Kruik can do Splitting, for example?"

"Now that I think about it, I associate women's magic with the lower clans, Dals especially, since they have no 'proper magic'. But that's probably just what we were taught, isn't it?"

Aza remembered suddenly that she was now presenting as a Salizan. She wasn't used to the idea of being one of the "lower" clans. *You are lower than that, Zaz.* "Um..." she said, "forgive me for not knowing, but are you Salizan?" *Careful, Aza.*

"In fact, I am Karol Besin."

"No."

Her dress—sturdy shirt and men's work trousers in shades of green and brown—did not give this away.

"Yes. My father was a fisherman and my mother, the neighborhood healer. But there weren't many Puraples curses in our little enclave on the coast. The water always called to me. It was more natural to do this than learn how to cure maladies. And wearing Besin white wouldn't make sense for this dirty profession."

"Well. I'm surprised. It's nice to meet you, Karol Besin."

"And you, Zaz Salizan. How did you get interested in women's magic?"

"I always wondered if I was the only one. When I finally shared it, I heard of a different kind and, since then, another. One of my Dal friends perceives what is in the forefront of people's minds. Another one is a Kruik who can lean on others to do what she wants."

"Whoa, useful! What are you going to do with all this?"

"I plan on changing our world. Want to help?"

Karol looked at her sharply and then her face softened and she laughed again. "Count me in."

When they arrived at Luftva Landing, barely lit by a single row of gaslights running from the dock up the short distance to the road, Karol secured the boat and helped Aza to her feet.

After getting those feet on the solid boards of the dock, Aza turned back and thanked her.

"You have a ride from here?"

"My friends told me there would be someone here to meet me. I have no reason to doubt them. But I have to tell you something first. This crossing and your company has filled me with peace—so deep a peace that I don't even care what happens next. I feel reborn."

"Wow. Well, dear, it wasn't me. It's the water, and the stars. Not to mention that you seem to be on some kind of fairly profound journey. I'm happy to be a small part of it."

"I also have a confession. I lied to you about my name. I can't tell you who I am. Not right now. But I want you to know that I lied for good reasons. I don't want you to dislike me for it when you find out."

"Zaz, people don't need a solo nighttime crossing unless they have something to hide. I will not judge you." Karol winked.

"I'll be in touch when my plans to change the world are a little more defined." Aza bent down and gave the woman a hug.

"I look forward to it. Until then!"

Karol cast off and left her standing on the other side of her world.

Her ride was waiting. The elderly man tipped a shabby, woven hat and said, "Name's Eguin, Miss." He took her valise and held out a hand to help her into the seat next to his on the horse-drawn wagon. After she'd thanked him for coming out at night to fetch her, he nodded and said, "Rimna and Reva are very close. Twins, you know."

He gave the reins a shake, and they were soon rumbling down the rough road. Eguin didn't seem to have anything left to say. Even so, she didn't get a feeling that she was unwelcome, only that she was with a man who had no need for small talk.

After at least twenty minutes, he turned to the right on an even bumpier, ascending road and then took a curving right onto a rutted lane that rounded back to the left and ended at a modest two-story house flanked by tall trees. Their leaves made a mighty noise in the stiff, warm breeze.

After getting down, she stared at the sky. "By my clan! Look at the stars. I have never seen so many."

Eguin grunted and bid her to follow.

Reva met them at the door. She looked a great deal like her sister—short, rotund, with a clear, dark complexion, and white hair piled on top of her head. Her demeanor, however, was friendlier, and her gift for chatter might explain her husband's reticence. Within minutes, she'd made sure that Aza was comfortably seated with a cup of sweetened, milky tea and a plate of shortbread cookies. She'd bid Eguin goodnight and sent him off to put Aza's valise in her room. Then she sat with Aza next to a small fire.

"I understand from Rimna that you've drawn the attention of those who would harm you. The Purples are no friends of this family. You are welcome to stay as long as you need."

"That is so kind of you. I must admit that I arrive here with no plan for how to overcome this problem, even though I won't hide out forever. But I've been ill. Did they tell you that?"

Reva nodded.

"While I'm recovered, my energy level isn't back to normal and whatever ideas I had about what to do next are a bit of a muddle."

"No need to feel rushed. You'll like it here. It's a good place to get one's energy back. Do you like animals?"

"Well, yes, but I haven't been around them much. This is my first time out of the city."

"As far as what you do next, that'll come."

"I want to tell you everything."

Reva's eyebrows—still black under her all-white mane—rose.

"It's only fair that you know. My real name isn't Zaz Salizan." She started with the hardest information to say out loud. "I've only recently discovered that I'm half Salizan and half Gen."

Reva nodded as if Aza had said, "I'm fond of shortbread cookies."

"That's why the Puraples want to arrest me." She told Reva a few facts of her early life and the pertinent points of her recent one: father's death, an arrest warrant, meeting Rimna, coming down with giarmial.

"Your secrets are safe with me," Reva said. "In Luftva, yo u are Zaz, my sister's friend, who is recuperating from the malady. I'd like to see someone prove that's not the truth!" Reva's lively, green eyes sparkled in the firelight.

Aza nodded. Her back aching, her body worn out from the tension and uncertainty of the day, she took in the face of this woman who already felt like a friend. *That's two friends just tonight in my new life. Maybe I'll win over Eguin by tomorrow and make it three.* She leaned back into the soft chair and breathed a sigh of relief.

17

ENCOUNTERS

AZA STEPPED ONTO THE main street walkway in Luftva Village after visiting with Pats, the farrier, animal surgeon, and sometimes blacksmith. He was a large, gentle man she had become friendly with one long afternoon a couple of weeks before when Eguin had asked her to bring in their old mare, Ginny, to be reshod.

Her life had changed for the better in the last three months.

She had spent more time out of doors than in her whole previous life. She knew more about animals than she had previously known there was to know about them—an afternoon with a farrier could have that effect on a person. Plus, the farm had sheep, pigs and cows, ducks and chickens, two other horses besides Ginny, too many cats to count, and one wonderful old dog named Basha. More than anything else over the last month, it was being around these simple, beautiful, nonjudgmental creatures that had brought her back to health and revitalization.

But, by far, learning to ride Ginny was her biggest accomplishment. The first time Reva asked her to take the horse into the village was the first time Aza realized she was terrified of the idea. "I...I have never ridden a horse."

"That's all right, dear. It isn't hard. Eguin will teach you. Ginny is as gentle as they come."

"Um, it's...I don't know. It's that my...mother died from a fall off a horse. So I guess that's a reason to be afraid?"

"Oh dear. That *is* hard. Well...we won't push you, of course. Though it is how we get around out here. The wagon can be used, but that requires dealing with the horse. It takes more time and effort, too. Perhaps you could get up the courage to sit astride with Eguin holding Ginny. See how you feel. Maybe let him help you find out if this is a fear you can overcome?"

Reva's low-key urging, combined with Aza's wanting to be a help rather than a bother, led her to try.

Once she was on Ginny, she found it was infinitely more comforting than terrifying to be in contact with such a large, calm animal. Eguin led them around while teaching Aza the basics in as few words as possible. It seemed he had limited lifetime supply and was trying not to use them up too soon. His attitude—that of course she could do this—brooked no dispute. Of course she would. So she paid attention, calmed her rapid heartbeat when she had to, made friends with Ginny, and had even gotten comfortable with a trot, though that was as fast as she would ever take her.

Aza still wanted to change the world, but her days whiffled away, filled with simple, hard work as well as plenty of relaxation. Somehow, it felt smart as well as easy to let the troubles of Maripesa stay on the other side of the glimmering Strait of Jeka.

And then she spotted Maleka coming out of the General Store.

The last time Aza had seen her, she was a silly, slender, sparkling, playful young woman. Now she had rounded shoulders, a bit of a belly and a womanly bosom. Her once gorgeous hair lay dull and flat against her back. She wore clothing of the lower clans.

As do I.

Aza looked around. The street traffic was typically light today, and no one was paying attention to her. She watched to see if Maleka met up with anyone. No matter how serene Aza felt here, she never forgot the need to be cautious.

The last thing you need is to run into Hasip!

Maleka hefted her bag over one shoulder and set off alone northward—the opposite direction from Aza's journey home to the farm. At the next intersection, Maleka turned to the right, toward the water.

The town, only a half-dozen or so blocks square, sat a distance from the shore with a wide, long stand of tall pines and hemlocks in between. They had been conserved here, Eguin had told her, as a break from the prevailing winds.

Aza followed at a distance, stopping once to feign interest in a shop window and a second time to reposition her own parcels.

No one joined Maleka as she entered the stand of swaying evergreens on a lane that followed the coastline.

Aza sped up. When she was confident there was no one else around and close enough for her voice to carry, she called out. "Maleka!"

Her friend turned her upper body sharply. She stood, twisted, silent, her body full of tension.

"Are we alone?" Aza persisted. "You aren't meeting someone here, are you? Is it safe?"

Maleka, shocked, nodded once and then shook her head "no."

Aza closed the space between them.

"You've changed...so much," Maleka said, breathlessly.

Could it be possible that I've changed as much as she has? The circles under Maleka's eyes alone were hard to take.

A silence stretched between them. Aza felt many things—not all of them charitable. It would have been difficult to put into words even if their meeting hadn't happened so unexpectedly. So she let her body take the lead.

Aza stepped forward and hugged her. Maleka didn't reciprocate, but for some reason, that didn't matter. *She* needed to hold on to her friend after all this time and worry. Aza's solid, wordless presence won out. Maleka's stiff veneer washed away in a stream of tears as she allowed herself to merge into Aza's embrace. Her back rounded, her head tucked into the niche made by Aza's chignon and the back of her neck. Her fingers grabbed handfuls of Aza's blouse.

In a muffled voice, Maleka said, "You look different, but you smell the same."

Aza laughed.

Maleka pulled back. She found a handkerchief in her pocket, wiped at her eyes, blew her nose and said, "Let's sit down. This is too much. I didn't think I'd see you ever again in my whole life." She turned her gaze around, one way and then the other, and then tipped her head twice toward the water and started walking. "There's a spot at the edge of the trees where I like to sit. You can see the water but aren't in plain view of foot traffic either way on the shore path."

They came to a tumble of rounded boulders near the tree line. Maleka sat with her back against one of them and patted the ground next to her.

Aza sat. The rock face was warm from the sun. She took a moment to enjoy the vista. They were angled away from Maripesa proper and the view toward the northeast was of the wide, seemingly endless sea. A trio of gulls winged by and then there was only water, calm today and reflecting the blue sky.

She turned to Maleka and softly asked, "You have a child?"

"How did you know?"

"I heard. It doesn't matter from where."

"It's hard not to know who knows. We were supposed to be a complete secret...for forever. But I didn't realize that when you aren't one clan or the other, it's hard to belong anywhere. People ask questions, and even when they don't, they come up with their own answers."

"Oh, my dear friend, I know exactly what you mean. I have a similar reason for being here in the country dressed as I am. I'm living under an assumed name, as a Salizan. Do you know that Mam Sior wants to arrest me for being half-clan?"

"Hasip told me. Evidently, secrets are hard to keep in Maripesa. It's not fair! Oh, Aza, I had no idea you were here on the island. I thought of you in some crowded neighborhood in the city. You were so interested in learning about it all that I assumed you'd been able to disappear there. But instead—"

"Instead, I am living on a farm. I never suspected you were here, either. I had a hard time envisioning where you and Hasip might have gone, but—"

"Did you find my letter?"

Aza nodded. "Weeks later."

"I am so sorry."

"I wish you could have confided in me beforehand."

"Oh, but Aza, that would have been worse. It would have put you in a horrible position. I am sorry I used you. That was very unfair."

"You won't feel the need to turn me in, I hope," Aza said.

"Of course not. You could just as easily turn me in."

"And of course, I would never. What about telling Hasip you saw me?"

"No! It's our secret. To him, blood is thicker than...than sentiment. When he told me the news about you being half-Gen, it was as if he never thought about the parallels between what he had done...to...with me and what your father and mother did. I keep my mouth shut."

"That is amazingly self-indulgent and not at all surprising. Maleka, does he have any power in the family?"

She sighed and looked down at her lap, pulling at the soggy handkerchief. "He was once Mam Sior's favorite. But he kind of blew the whole power thing when he fell in love with me." The last few words were almost whispered.

"Your child?"

"A boy named Emke. And..." She glanced at Aza with a tiny remnant of the sparkle she once had so much of, "his twin sister, Capsia. They're with the nanny at our house at the far north end of the island."

"Oh! Oh, Maleka. How wonderful! But...oh my. Are you exhausted?"

"Yes. Doesn't it show?"

Aza ignored that question, instead asking, "Hasip lives there, too?" She couldn't imagine any of Mam Sior's brood choosing a simple country life over the relative glamor of the city.

Maleka stared at the water. "He comes and goes...as he pleases."

Aza sighed, reached her hand along the grassy ground and tapped Maleka's arm.

Maleka smiled wistfully and put her hand out to be held.

"Then, with both of us being older and wiser, both of us living...shall I say?...vulnerable lives, we can trust each other and *will* see each other. We must talk. A lot."

"That would improve my life more than I could hope for. It can be lonely, having babies. A lot of work and very little companionship, at least so far."

"Things have been hard for you."

"Yes. And you. I heard your father died of the malady. I'm so sorry."

"Not before telling me that I'm half-clan."

"I was so shocked. Hasip said only that his sick mother was out to get you, but that you'd given Ferjival the slip—which he couldn't help but gloat about. And...maybe it's only rumor, but he said your father kept both of you alive by letting you work for Mam Sior all those years. Is it true?"

"Leo was dying when he told me and he was a man of few words when in the best of health. But yes, he told me about a bargain. They had a—*ahem*—relationship when they were young. I guess he used that as leverage."

"But why? It makes no sense. Half-clan babies. They're the problem, aren't they? The mixing, the dilution of clan magic?" Tears threatened to spill out again. "Sorry. I'm so grateful she let you live! It's just, I think about these things. I have to...all the time now."

"I *so* understand. I don't know all the answers, other than a distinct feeling that there was something more to the bargain than just me working for her. But the real explanation is that the rules aren't *really* the rules." Aza stood up, stretched her back, looked to make sure no one was around, and started walking in a small circle. "The Uppers do what they want and who's going to tell them they shouldn't? I mean, how did you explain to yourself about the 'rules' when one of the Puraples wanted to break taboo and co-mingle the Talents by getting you pregnant?"

"I— I didn't. Stupid, I know, but we were in love. I must have been crazy. That's no explanation, but it's the answer."

Aza stopped walking and faced her friend. "Love. What a mystery. Even more to me than others, because I haven't ever felt it. I only know that the world is not neat and tidy and orderly and perfect the way I was always led to believe." She knelt down and took Maleka's hands. "I was such an ignorant *child* when we were working at the Komeh. I didn't know anything."

Maleka nodded sullenly. "We were late getting to it, but we've both had to grow up fast."

"I want to meet the babies."

"I—we—have to be careful. It's possible that I'm watched, though I just as often feel that they've forgotten all about me."

"They're probably all too distracted by the mess they've made of the city."

"We'll have to meet at my house because I can't manage with both the kids yet."

"Let's try for next week same day, same time."

"Wonderful. Is there someone you trust that I can leave a message with if I need to?"

Aza thought for a moment and then brightened up. "Yes. Pats, the farrier. He's a friend and won't ask questions...if I tell him not to."

Maleka rose and hugged Aza so hard she thought she might burst. She finally let go and said, "Aza, Aza, Aza, life is so strange. Did you even know the *word* farrier, much less *a* farrier, when you lived at the Komeh?"

Aza grinned. "I did, in fact. I'll have you know that more than once I was in the Komeh's stables cleaning renyers off the riding gear of our dear, dear first family. And I'm not Aza anymore. My name is Zaz Salizan."

"Zaz? Well, you'll have to tell that story. And me? I don't seem to have a name. I'm just the mom of those adorable twins who live on the edge of nowhere."

Sad words, but Aza saw that Maleka's eyes were sparkling again. *Hope.*

"You're all the way north and I'm way out the other direction. Also full of vast unpopulated spaces! Who knew that hiding in the open would work so well? I have so much to tell you. There's a group of women I'm getting together. I'll explain next week."

"Here," Maleka said. She reached into the side seam pocket of her Dal skirt and pulled something out. She shut her eyes while clutching it close to her face for a long moment. She chanted a few whispered words, breathed onto what she held, opened her eyes, reached out, took Aza's hand, and pressed a charm into it. "To help keep you free." She smiled.

"Thank you. I still have the butterfly you gave me. It has brought me peace many times over the months." She looked down at her hand. In it was a polished brass crane in flight. "I wish I had one for you, but you know it's never been my habit to keep charms. Except the ones you've given me."

"I know. Just a little superstition of mine. I like knowing that you have a part of me with you."

Aza, in the trees, walking back toward town, heard Maleka whistling as she went the other way.

Seeing Maleka brought back the realities of the wider world to Aza. Three weeks later, her efforts to change it started in earnest. Gathered before her were the women she could trust: Reva and Rimna; Ness and Ness's oldest daughter, Lacacia; Karol; Eltah; and Maleka. There were a half dozen others whose names Aza hadn't committed to memory yet. Trusted friends of trusted friends. There were no Kruiks or Puraples among them...yet. Or, she realized for the first time, Tchuvari.

They sat cozily in Reva's living-dining room, crowded onto the sofa—including its threadbare, overstuffed arms—on the dining room chairs and the floor, backs resting between the legs of those behind them. Each had gotten tea and sweets from the kitchen first. The atmosphere was warm, casual, and anticipatory.

Aza sat at the table, her back to the wall so she could see everyone.

"All women from all clans have the Talent to do something as fundamental and powerful as preventing pregnancy." She stopped and swallowed hard, overwhelmed for a moment by the cascade of ramifications that could stem from the statement she was about to make. She took a breath and began again. "I learned only recently about the anti-pregnancy spell." She nodded to Rimna even while thinking of Bek. "I wasn't taught it because I had no women in my life. My mother died when I was a baby. But more to the point, I learned even more recently that my mother did not use the spell even though she was of a different clan than my Gen father."

Aza saw a few mouths drop open, but that was the only visible response. It was fine. These women had the right to know that she was an Undone.

"My mother *chose* to bring forth *my life* even though it was forbidden. She could have, or according to society, should have been put to death for this choice. What kind of society does this? How many have been killed for breaking this taboo?" Aza's eyes met Maleka's briefly, but she made herself barrel on. "This capability that we all share makes me wonder why we're not more powerful in our society. It makes me wonder how many citizens approve of this rigid structure that jealously guards certain kinds of magic so that two clans always rule over the rest of us. What would happen over generations if we were all free to choose who to have babies with? What if these children could be capable of forming a society less rigid, less hierarchical, less punitive, less fearful of negative magic and ultimately, based on who we are, apart from our Talents. Perhaps it isn't mating out of clan that needs to be punishable, but instead, *the use of harmful magic.*"

A scattering of small movements traveled around the room. Of course there would be discomfort with her more radical aims and she reminded herself to get to the point: women's magic.

"If we don't like the way our society operates, we have the power to change things, because it isn't only a contraceptive spell that we have within us. We have other kinds of magic. These abilities aren't talked about as Talents with a capital T, because they don't fit within the hierarchy! They are labeled as trivial, not real—women's 'superstitions.' Why?" She paused for effect and then spoke slowly. "Because they cross clan lines. That fact undermines the rigidity that Maripesa has been living under! Valea here—" she pointed toward Eltah's friend who sat in the middle of the sofa between Eltah and Ness. "Can use her Talent to get other people to do what she wants. I have heard of a Kruik who also has this Talent. Ness Salizan, sitting next to her, can too."

Ness spoke. "Believe me, it's a handy skill to have when you choose to have as many kids as I have."

"I'll wager you use it as much on your husband as your kids!" Reva said, gently.

Everyone laughed.

"For the record, I have that skill too," said Reva.

This was news to Aza.

Reva continued, "I use it mainly on the sheep and goats."

Again, laughter rippled through the group.

"There you go. Four clans, one amazing Talent. That isn't supposed to be the 'natural order' of things, is it? How many of you have been to executions when Mam Sior recites the Law? We all know it. Have known it since we were children: 'Maripesa works because our clans are interdependent. None of us contrived to make it so. The Gods themselves determined our hierarchy. How else could one explain the exact matching, the elegant design, the genetically determined Talents that keep our society in perfect balance?' Where, I ask you, do our cross-clan talents fit in that godly scheme?"

Aza stopped for a moment, letting that sink in. She took a sip of cold tea and said, "Perfect isn't the word I'd use for it. Because of that hierarchy, I was kept in ignorance of the facts of my origin and worked as less than an indentured servant to those who oversee executions routinely. I recently lost my father to that system, as many of you have lost people you love. What would happen if that system were questioned? By a lot of us."

"We could fall in love with and have children with whoever we wanted," Eltah said quietly.

"I did that..."

Maleka. Aza's breath caught. She hadn't known that Maleka would speak and didn't know if it was a good idea.

"I," Maleka continued, "idealistically and naively fell in love with some-one outside my clan. We have brought forth not one, but two chil-dren—twins—who are mixed-clan. I refuse to use the word Undone. I was privileged in my Gen clan, and perhaps because the person I fell in love with was a person of power as well, I deluded myself into thinking that we were above the Law. And perhaps that is true, because," she held up her palms and shrugged, "I'm still alive. And so are my..." Maleka dissolved into tears. The woman next to her put an arm around Maleka's shoulders and pulled her close.

"Thank you, my friend. That was truly brave of you." Aza looked around the room. "I trust you all. I *trust* that you will keep anything we say here strictly confidential. Some of us are in real and present danger. We—those of us here today who decide to stay with this group and others we bring in—are going to explore a new kind of society. We will question the status quo. In order to do this with any hope of success, we must organize, plan, research, gather our strength, spread the word—thoughtfully, cautiously, woman-to-woman-to-woman. Let us, for the first time, see what kinds of powers we wield and figure out the best way for us to use them. I see a movement that grows steadily and moves with care and consensus, but also with as much momentum as we can muster. Because, women of Maripesa, our beloved city is at war and we have all been caught in the cross-spell."

18

CAUGHT

"Auntie Zazzie, don't go!" Capsia shouted from the open doorway. Aza laughed. She knew what the baby was saying, but it sounded more like Ah-e Az-e! Dan ga! Emke, meanwhile, ignoring her departure, was on hands and knees at Maleka's feet, watching a bug that he would likely soon pop into his mouth, if he could catch it.

The visit at Maleka's rambling, ramshackle country house was, as usual, a blur of happy chatter with Maleka while both of them tended the babies who somehow could crawl faster than they could run. Capsia was feisty, quirky, and utterly charming, while Emke was inquisitive, affectionate, and so angelic-looking that it melted her heart anew every time she saw him. The kids loved their Auntie Zaz, and she loved them back even more.

So far, they'd had no trouble finding a time for Aza to be there. Hasip sent word when he was coming and that was less and less often.

Aza, astride Ginny, got back on her way to Luftva Village.

The meandering and slightly hilly road was busier than usual because it was market day. Aza nodded at those who passed in their carts or on horseback. Steam-powered vehicles were uncommon here. When she saw one coming her way, Aza flashed to scenes of the city proper. *I'm still an outlaw.* She pulled her headscarf forward and bent the other way, as if seeing to her mount's fittings, until they were past her.

Aza planned to stop in the village to pick up whitewash powder for Eguin, and, for Reva, "as many ripe quell fruits as you can sling over Ginny's saddle."

Maleka seemed stronger today. Whatever else had happened to her expectations of a "happy life" with Hasip, she now had Aza for company, to bolster her spirits and help with the twins a least once a week. The MATRIA meetings had also helped. Strength in numbers worked. The group was becoming important to all the women.

Their new name came about several meetings back. It was Eltah's suggestion. "The first part," she explained, "stands for Matriarchally Attuned Talents. But," she pulled a face, "that doesn't exactly roll off the tongue and MAT is a less than inspiring name. I extended it to include the first six letters of matriarch. If the RIA comes to stand for something later, so be it." The group was delighted to have something to call themselves. For Aza, it made everything they did seem more solid.

No longer able to fit in the living room, they met in Reva's "house barn"—the older, smaller one that was used only for birthing animals and storage. Aza had given it a thorough cleaning, Eguin built sapling benches, and others had made pillows and cushions. *How many did we draw in last time? Close to forty.*

Lost in these thoughts, a passerby on horseback caught her eye. She turned her head to offer a polite nod and immediately turned away and spurred Ginny into a trot.

Ferjival.

Aza didn't dare look back, but she was very afraid he'd recognized her. *What's he doing here? What would he do?* He could send his minions out for her any time. He didn't have to dirty his own hands trying to catch a fugitive. But he would want to know where she was hiding, so yes, he would follow.

She heard hooves behind her, signaled the horse into a canter, then a full gallop, and held on for dear life.

There was still quite a crowd in the main street market. Slowing down, she turned to look. He was in sight! Her heart thumped hard against her sternum. *Maybe you should just talk to him. He's alone. What could he do to me? A case of giarmial, idiot. You willing to risk that again?* More likely, he'd commandeer a couple of hefty townfolk to throw her in a locked room until he could call for his own guards.

No. She would not put herself in his hands.

Aza guided Ginny off the main street and sped up.

Ferjival wanted no trace of this, his first and last visit with his stupid brother's massive mistake. Mistakes. *Twins! Blast him.* So, he traveled solo with only his trusty horse, Ric, to keep him company on this *Maripes*-forsaken road because he had to see them for himself at least once.

What ultimately happened to that Undone family wasn't his decision. His mother, though weakened by her illness, was still firmly in charge. He didn't dare broach the subject with her. Of course, *she* wanted them to stay out of sight, but Hasip was back in Maripesa, acting as if none of this had happened.

As if he thought that by living his life in public, it could make everyone forget that he'd wantonly broken society's primary rule. What a mess his family had made of everything.

When he passed the horse-riding girl dressed in homespun Dal farm clothes, it took him a good twenty paces for it to register. *Aza Gen, here. Hiding out in Luftva. It makes sense. Maleka had worked with Aza. The Gens were friends.* Had they planned this all along? Of course. Aza must have been in on Maleka's disappearance. Something about the squint in her eyes as they passed each other gave her away; guilt written all over her freckled face. *Freckles.* He hated grown-ups with freckles. *Freckles are for kids.*

His rage full-blown, he reined in his horse, turned, and started after the fugitive. Ferjival couldn't see her at first, but she came into view at the crest of a rise. For the rest of the chase, he'd catch and lose glimpses of her as they rode down the hilly lane.

He'd get her. That old nag would be no match for his racing pony.

Mother will have to give me some credit at last!

Vijo hadn't been to see Aza since she escaped across the river, but his sister had been a regular visitor, scheduling her days off when the women held their MATRIA meetings. After each one, Eltah passed along Aza's—no, he reminded himself—*Zaz's* warmest wishes. He assumed it was the same kind of gratitude that many of his patients had after having been helped to heal from a serious malady, but his sister insisted that it was more affectionate than that and encouraged him to come see her in person.

"Eltah, are you encouraging a romance between us? Has your group turned you so radical as to think that can happen between clans without ramifications?"

His sister shrugged. "No," she said after a long pause. "It hasn't. I don't see, though, why you can't have a Gen friend. You are very fond of each other, and she still isn't free to come visit you. Let's leave it at that."

So here he was.

Vijo had taken the trolley over the bridge, the first time he'd made this trip since he was a child. It had been so delightful, it made him wonder why he hadn't done this before now. His body, mind, and heart felt lighter with each step away from Maripesa's brick, stone, and steaming streets. He'd been too long immersed in the epidemic and all its misery.

Eltah had given him rough directions to Reva's farm, but he took a stroll through the village first. Happy to find that it was market day, he decided to pick up small gifts. He studied the farmers' produce up one side of the main street and down the other, then turned back, having decided to purchase a dozen quell fruits which beckoned to him from the other side of the street.

The market was busy, but compared to a city street in Maripesa on any average midday, it wasn't even a crowd. There was mostly foot traffic, the horses, wagons, and rare steam vehicles having been routed off to other streets.

Just then, he and everyone else looked up toward the sound of hoofbeats galloping in fast from the north. A woman next to Vijo was kneeling down, focused on wiping her child's face. He tapped her shoulder and warned her to get out of the way. Just then, an agile bay appeared around the curve and the rider, a Puraples dressed in the finest clothing—overdressed for the time of day, the place, and the warm weather—pulled hard on the reins.

He trampled no one, but through no fault of his own. Several people squealed at his intrusion and the child with the dirty face started coughing from the dust the horse raised.

The man sat straighter, raised his chin imperiously and, with his mount now properly slowed, meandered arrogantly through the parted market goers as if he were the King of the Realm.

Perhaps he is. The man was certainly wearing garments fit for royalty. *Ferjival?* Or one of the other myriad of Mam Sior's offspring? This one had an angular sharpness to his chin, his shoulder blades, his attitude. He would bet on it being the eldest. A pang hit Vijo in the chest. Ferjival had issued the order for Aza to be arrested. *What's he doing here? And in such a hurry.*

Aza watched from the front window of the farrier's shop as Ferjival almost plowed down a dozen or so pedestrians. He recovered just in time and was now prancing down the main street, nose in the air. But that didn't keep him from peering this way and that, looking for her, for her steed, for some clue of where she'd gotten to.

"Ye good there, girl?" Pats asked her, coming in from the back of the shop.

"I think so," she answered, not looking at him.

"Hiding from someone?"

"I am, in fact. The Puraples want to arrest me." She turned, taking a deep breath.

He chuckled, and then the noise fell off quickly. "You aren't joking."

She shook her head and looked back out the window. "Mam Sior's son Ferjival is out there. He was going the other direction until he spotted me and turned right around."

"But," Pats came over and peeked out the window, "whate'r for?"

"I used to—" No, she couldn't tell him she worked for them. Then, she would have to lie about what she did and anyway, it explained nothing. "I can't tell you right now. Please, be patient with me. It's vital, though, that you'll let me stay until he goes."

Pats held up his hands and bowed his head. "You are welcome here as long as you like. I assume Ginny's out back?"

She nodded.

"And if he dares set one foot in my establishment, I shall make certain that he's unable to set his despicable arse on that beautiful horse for the rest of the summer."

Aza beamed and turned back to the window.

Ferjival felt as if everyone on the street knew that he had lost Aza Gen and was laughing at him.

It wasn't rational. They couldn't know. But she had come down this road the same way he had and somehow managed to disappear.

He glared at those who dared make eye contact and looked back over his shoulder to see if anyone was actually bold enough to laugh. *Country flugs. All of them together with no more sense than those sheep they're so fond of.*

He made his way out of the market area, turning his horse right onto the first cross street. "Street" was more of a word than it deserved. He dismounted, tied his horse to a corner post, and started out on foot to find that woman.

Half a block down, Ferjival saw her horse's rump. It was distinctively large, piebald with puddles of black on a white and brown surface, with tangled mews. A workhorse, with no elegance to her.

The Gen had looked like a child astride it.

All he had to do was go there and wait. She would soon walk right into his itchy hands.

Vijo bought his fruit and a half-dozen pastries in case he got hungry on the walk to the farm. "I'm on my way to Reva Dal's but have never been there," he said to the baker. "Do you know it?"

"Aye, lad. Just walk south from here—with the strait on your left—down the main road. Maybe...a hundred paces after it turns from gravel to dirt, you'll see three large rocks with a smaller one on top. Take that path...to the right mind, so's you don't fall in the water." He grinned. "Eguin and Reva live up that hill at the end."

He thanked the man and started on his way, wondering if he shouldn't have sent a message that he was coming. Eltah told him it wasn't necessary, but what if they were all here at the market? He'd never met Reva or Eguin, so he wouldn't know them if they were passing right now.

He smiled, thinking of the changed Aza who had left the clinic that day months ago, her curls straightened out of all recognition. He turned back to the baker. "Excuse me, sir. Have you seen Reva or her husband in town this morning?"

"Nay, but the gal who stays with them was through here early this morning. Do you know her?"

"She is who I am visiting today."

The man rubbed his chin. "Yes...sweet gal, but I've forgotten her name."

"Zaz," Vijo said, remembering.

"That's it." The man pointed and smiled. "She told me she'd be back through here for some rolls, but maybe she forgot. I have them set aside here."

"I'll be happy to take them for her."

He paid the man, put the rolls in his pack alongside the fruit and pastries, and started walking.

Aza had seen no sign of Ferjival for at least half an hour. Pats went out the front to look for him or his horse and asking those who had seen him if he had left town. No one seemed to know what happened after his explosive entrance, but the consensus was that he'd gone on his way and was probably back in Maripesa by now, and good riddance.

"I think I'll chance it," she said when he returned. "I'm exposed here. Once I'm back at the farm, I'll feel safer."

"Would he know where you're living?"

"No," she said, "he was obviously on his way to see Maleka. Now he knows I'm on the island, too. Oh, he might ask here in town!"

"Hmm. Yes. Ordinarily people wouldn't mind sharing that information, but I doubt anyone would trust a Purple with his attitude anytime and he didn't exactly make a good impression today. But...Zaz, you'll be an open target on the road home."

She sighed deeply. "I will cut through the fields when possible."

I can't run forever. If I get caught, I get caught. Mam Sior could put her to death, but Aza didn't think she would. And Aza wasn't without leverage. Secrets could cut both ways.

Pats gave her a hug goodbye at the back door after she promised to be careful.

She slipped out the back. The three-horse stable was in shadow. It took a moment for her eyes to adjust.

Ginny nickered nervously.

What's up, girl? Only then, did she think about sending Zaz out to check the surrounding area. As Zaz split, Aza reached out, patting the horse between the eyes, rising on tiptoes in order to reach her spiky forelock.

A gloved hand covered her face from behind, fingers splayed to maximally disrupt her senses: eyes, nose and mouth, obstructed. Zaz's point of view showed her clearly what she was up against.

Aza squealed and reared backward. Ferjival's other arm came around, pinning her just under her breasts. At the same time, he clamped painfully down on her cheekbones. She could no longer move her head without risk of having her neck snapped. He pushed the pad of his other hand in and up forcefully, causing her a sharp outtake of breath. Then his hand moved to her right breast and squeezed. Wet breath coated her left ear as he spit out the words, "Gotcha, Gen!"

She went limp.

Ferjival felt her muscles go soft and didn't know what to do. All ready for a struggle, his forceful grip on her head and body seemed too much effort all of a sudden. Had she lost consciousness? Fainted? *Oh, that is irritating.*

The horse stomped nervously. Ferjival pulled away from the woman slightly. She slumped further. He hadn't really thought through what he'd do once he found her, but if he had, his version would have included a struggle, her screaming, perhaps the threat of a curse, people coming to her rescue, and his triumphant production of the writ for Aza Gen's arrest signed by Mam Sior herself; the one he'd been carrying around for all these months. Well, perhaps he had thought about it. Many times. This wasn't as he pictured it.

Bother. Never mind. I will drag her to Rik and throw her across my saddle and get home with her. Best tie her up; she'll wake at some point. Why did she faint? I didn't smother her...or smash her in the chest. Not that hard.

With both his arms around her middle, he began to drag her dead weight toward the street. His horse was half a block away and around the corner. "You couldn't be a slim thing, could you, wench?" He stopped, breathing hard. It was going to be too much effort to get her all that way.

He twisted her dead weight until he was in front of her and pushed her against the wall of the stable, as far away from that anxious horse as he could get. He slapped her. "Wake up!"

The horse neighed.

She winced and opened her eyes. "I am not asleep, Ferjival."

He slapped her again.

He could see that it hurt her, but she made no sound. Calmly, she said, "I will not go with you willingly. My large, strong friend is on the other side of that wall." She indicated the back door with a nod of her head.

Zaz, still separated, focused on his reddened hand prints on both her cheeks.

"I can curse you."

"That *is* your calling card, isn't it?"

"Shut up."

"No. Let's talk. You and your mother are fighting a losing battle. Everyone knows that you, and I don't mean the Purples in general, I mean you specifically, started the epidemic."

Ferjival's mouth went dry. "You will be executed at the earliest opportunity."

"I doubt that. But it doesn't matter. I don't matter. On that we can agree. What does matter is that your clan is hated. Rightly blamed. Your mother is on her way out. Dying, I heard. And you will never ever be ruler of Maripesa."

Her words didn't bother him that much. He was used to harsh words. No one liked him; he knew that. But even so, he felt a shiver...or, a chill...a creepy, stunning coldness slowly ascending his spine. This weird, otherworldly feeling settled in at the base of his neck. "What Gen magic is this?" he whispered.

"No Gen magic, for I am not Gen. Isn't that the whole point of this farce? Oh, well, yes. Half. But there is no 'half,' is there? Not when those in power have magic that can only hurt. Have you ever thought of yourself that way, Ferjival? Your power does harm. That's all. I find it sad."

He slapped her again. "If your strong friend is so close, why haven't you called out?"

"I don't want him hurt. Your epidemic killed my father and so many others. All because you can't hold your temper."

He didn't bother denying it. It didn't matter what she believed. *I will personally put her to death.*

But she was talking again. "I need you to let me go now. I need you to loosen your grip and let me stand. I need you to back up a step, because I can smell what you had for breakfast and it's turning my stomach."

"Where the hell did you get such impertinence?" he said, with all the privilege of his birthright. But that spot on the back of his neck was still there, and increasingly unpleasant. He was distracted by the sensation building in intensity. He took one hand off her to rub the spot.

The Gen shifted slightly. "Not feeling well? I can make it stop, but only when you've done what I say. I want to tell you something else, though, before you let me go."

His rubbing made it worse. Intense discomfort, not just physical pain but a sense of being lost, confused, disoriented. The Gen was talking and talking.

"Your mother knew from before I was born that I was half-clan. She blackmailed my father for the rest of his life. She—your old, ugly, fat, mean mother—made him pretend to care about her. Could it be any more shoddy and repulsive,?"

Ferjival winced as a tiny, involuntary moan came from his throat.

"A terrible thing to imagine. I agree. But please, continue to do so. Your mother loved him for some reason, but he did not love her. That's the sadness of it all, isn't it? Because none of you are worthy of love, much less being likable. She held my very life over his head in order to get what *she* needed. But by *Maripes*, what she, you, all your kind, need cannot be won by your dark magic. Now. Do as I say. Let me go."

The pain was sickening, but he was who he was and there was not one cell in his body who would be ordered about by this short, freckled, not-even Gen. He made a fist and hit her in the face—hard.

The horse reared and neighed loudly.

She slumped again.

The back door opened. Ferjival turned his head to look as the doorway filled with a large, muscular, angry man.

I9

✦

END GAME

Vijo decided to look around for Aza before starting to Reva's. Her unfulfilled promise to the baker that she would return was worrying, especially considering the Puraples rider's recent presence. He walked north, peering into the few shops that had windows. After two blocks, he was at the end of the village. He turned to his left and soon came to an alley only wide enough for foot or horse traffic. He started down it. There was no one about. The main street shops to his left had back doors that led here to refuse bins and storage; there were a couple of simple loading platforms.

Out of sight, somewhere down the lane, a horse neighed.

Vijo continued, now on high alert. Muffled voices rose up over the sound of his footsteps. He stopped and caught his breath, his gut roiling.

It's Aza!

He rushed even while remembering that he might run headlong into a Puraples who would not hesitate to cast a curse, if cornered. Benelek had taught him that. As he came close, he slowed down. The voices had become one voice. Hers.

Vijo shivered. *That day in the clinic when Aza came in gravely ill, barely conscious. Alone in the room with her, I felt another presence.* That presence was here now somewhere in front of him. Aza's two selves. Somehow. Something he'd read about in his studies but had discounted. Something he didn't understand other than to sense it was her magic. But her magic wasn't likely to stave off Ferjival's for long.

A deep thump and subsequent thud spurred him the rest of the way. He rounded the corner to see a three-stall stable with one large horse. A man stood in the open door of the business, his attention on something hidden to Vijo on the other side of the horse.

The man shouted, "Leave her!" and sprang forward.

A long, angry yell rang out as Vijo ran over. Aza was crumpled on the ground. The man who'd shouted was on top of the Purple trying to trap his arms and legs. Vijo rushed over, grabbed Ferjival's kicking legs, and planted himself astride them. The big man looked up in alarm at Vijo's sudden appearance.

This distraction allowed Ferjival to get a hand free, cast it toward Aza's protector, and let loose a curse.

Aza stirred, moaning. "Pats, he's struck you," she said, rubbing her head and shaking it slowly.

Vijo lunged, pinning Ferjival's arms with his hands while precariously kneeling on his legs. Vijo was a Besin and everything in him wanted to get up and help the man who would soon be suffering. But he couldn't let go of Ferjival or the rest of them would be hit, too.

Aza crawled over. "What are you doing here?" Then she looked down at Ferjival and said in a much stronger voice, "I will see you ruined."

"You are nothing! No one," Ferjival screeched. He couldn't cast another curse as long as Vijo had his hands locked against the ground.

Aza, finding her footing, rose and reached for reins hanging on a hook. She addressed the man she'd called Pats. "I know you're hurting, but we have a Besin here who'll help you as soon as we can get Ferjival's hands tied."

Pats bent down and put one beefy hand on each of Ferjival's arms. Vijo let go and repositioned so he could hold the man's legs. They rolled him over, pulled back his arms and held them as Aza wrapped the leather reins tightly.

Soon, a rope was found, and Ferjival was well and truly trussed. They were all breathless and filthy from rolling around in the dirt of the stable.

Ferjival spewed a steady stream of complaints, threats, charges, including, "You'll all be put to death before nightfall."

"Can we shut him up?" Pats asked.

"I think we must," said Aza. "His impulsive spell-casting is a danger to the public." She walked to her horse, reached into her saddlebag and brought out an apron. "Hold his head."

Once the man's mouth was full of fabric and tied with the sash around his head, Vijo took stock. Pats had spreading welts on his face and arms, and his eyelids were beginning to stick together. "I didn't bring my full apothecary, but I can get started with a treatment. Is there a local Besin healer?"

Pats, shaking his head, could barely talk, but he managed to croak, "We get few Purples here. No need."

＊

Unwilling to think past the next moment, Aza helped Vijo drag, pull, and shove the highly uncooperative Ferjival inside. Pats, as miserable as he was, couldn't tolerate their struggle, so he lifted the bound man over his shoulder and put him in a chair that Aza positioned in the middle of his tiny living quarters. While he and Vijo were binding Ferjival to the chair, Aza scribbled a sign for both doors that said, "Closed due to illness. Please do not disturb." It was true; Pats was "ill" and would need to be seen in a Besin clinic as soon as possible.

Vijo started preliminary treatments designed to reduce Pats' discomfort while Aza left to arrange transport for the two of them across the bridge. She was back in fifteen minutes, flushed, her face tight. She ushered Vijo and Pats into the business side of the farrier's space, out of earshot of their prisoner.

"We're in luck. I ran into Karol coming in on her last run of the day. She ferried me over. Remember?"

Vijo shook his head. "I had nothing to do with your journey here, Aza."

"Aza?" Pats asked.

"*Rats and bats,*" Vijo said under his breath.

"My nickname," Aza said with forced nonchalance. "Vijo and I go way back." *Two lies in one breath and to a man who just saved my life.* She breathed deeply and started again, slowly. "Karol's waiting at the main pier. She won't charge you. Once on the other side, go to—"

Vijo cut in. "I know how to get around the city, Zaz. Don't worry about us. The real question is what are you going to do with that man in Pats' bedroom. And you're hurt!"

She had never seen Vijo worked up like this. As she stared at him, Zaz slipped away and Aza saw her own face. Her freckles stood out, looking three dimensional on ashen skin. Two dark pink hand-marks showed on her lower cheeks, while her nose and left eye were bloody and turning purple from the blow Ferjival had delivered. Her eyes, however, were the same clear amber she'd seen when she was thirteen while looking through the keyhole of the chamber door. She stood immobilized, unable to think. Panic crept up from her belly. *What have I done? What choice did I have? How do we get out of this mess?*

She looked up as Vijo shuddered and looked around.

He's sensing Zaz's presence. As Bek had. And now, very successfully, as Ferjival had. Her skills had grown since the MATRIA started meeting. With that thought, Zaz slipped through the wall and Aza saw her prisoner struggling with his restraints. Zaz pinched hard on his spine near the base of his neck. He sat up abruptly, eyes wide, scared, lips parted by the wet, wadded fabric in his mouth.

I'm capable of causing pain. She blinked several times and willed Zaz to return. Looking searchingly at Vijo, she said in a voice that reflected her growing panic, "I'm going to...take things one step at a time. I suggest you do the same. I'm not going to look ahead...because I am scared out of my mind and don't know how to do what I have to. I'm so sorry you got involved. Why *are* you here, anyway?"

He smiled wistfully, briefly. "I just wanted to see you and have a day off from the epidemic."

Pats snorted. "Poor sod. Some day off this turned out to be."

"True," Vijo said. "But a healer's never truly off duty. Are you feeling better?"

"Aye, that's powerful magic. I've never had a curse before." The big man shook his head and let his breath out in a noisy whistle. "You sure I need more treatment?"

"Oh yes. I only treated your discomfort. The curse is still there. The healing won't take long, but I simply do not have the apothecaries here."

"You two, get going. Karol's waiting. By the way, Vijo, she's Besin. I trust her. Take Ginny."

"No, you might need her. You can walk, right Pats?"

He nodded, already opening the door to go.

But Vijo dithered. "This is crazy. You can't stay here alone with the de facto leader of Maripesa gagged and bound! What if—?"

"Go! Think about where I'd be if you and Pats hadn't been here. Besides, you forget, I know these people far better than most. Far better than they know I do. I'll manage. He *is* tied and gagged. He can't hurt me. I'll get help somehow."

They hugged. She held on longer than she thought he might want, but she didn't care. He came to see her for a pleasant, surprise visit and Ferjival Puraples had ruined everything. "Thank you for coming."

He whispered, "I'll be back."

She watched them, door opened just a crack, until they disappeared into the bright, ethereal, last light before sunset.

Aza didn't go in to see her prisoner. She had to regroup. Even one step at a time required one to know what the next step should be. She didn't, and despite all her bravado about knowing the Puraples better than they knew themselves, she felt no advantage. She felt alone, ill-prepared, and exhausted.

Her eyes fell on a couple of packages Vijo had retrieved from the stable after they had the prisoner under control. "He's forgotten his things," she said and then peeked inside to find rolls, pastries and fruit. "Ah. Food might help. I owe you again, friend."

She ate a few bites. It helped. Maybe a cup of tea, she thought, but to get to the kitchen, she'd have to pass Ferjival and his evil emanations. "Maybe I should just kill him, throw him over Ginny's back, cover him with a blanket, go out tonight when it's dark, and dump him in the Jeka. Wouldn't we all be better off? Wouldn't Maripesa benefit from his death? Wouldn't it be the proper revenge for all the needless deaths on his soul?"

But she hadn't a clue how to kill someone and the thought ruined her appetite. She sat, half eaten quell fruit in hand, her eyes stinging with tears that wouldn't fall.

After some unknown amount of time, Aza felt Zaz leave her. More and more, her other self did as she pleased. *She's probably going to check on our prisoner, which is good.* But that wasn't the destination. She watched through Zaz's eyes as she went through the wall to stare at Ginny's saddlebag.

The saddlebag?

Oh!

Aza sprang to her feet and went out the back door. Zaz reintegrated as Aza reached her. She undid the latch that held the bag and rummaged through it, feeling past the nilteh she always carried—just in case—and the stole she'd worn that morning when she set out for Maleka's when the air was cool. She found the small pouch that held the charms Maleka had given her over the years, her lilac leather gloves, and the soltec she'd found in Gerland's coach what seemed like a lifetime ago.

Taking what she needed, Aza reattached the bag to the saddle and spent several moments stroking and talking to Ginny, who was being woefully neglected. "I promise to get to you as soon as I can."

Then she went to have a little talk with her unexpected, unwanted guest.

Ferjival was hungry, in pain, furious, helpless. But most of all, he needed to pee.

The Gen walked in. Alone.

He worried his sore wrists against his ties and struggled to talk. The soppy mess that was in his mouth caused him to gag. As soon as she took that out, he was going to curse her with everything he had. Everything that he could do without his hands. He had had time to think, and there were some tricks he had that she wouldn't see coming.

Her hair had come loose from the Dal headscarf and was sprouting in all directions like an ivyweed in spring. Her face was badly bruised.

She leaned one shoulder against the door frame, her hands clasped behind her back, and looked at him. Her expression might best have been described as "fierce." *Where did that come from?* If he'd had an opinion about her after all those years of her cleaning his boots, he'd have called her "mousy."

"The Besin has gone off to cure my friend. Good *Maripes*, man, it feels as if most of the Besin at any one time are curing afflictions that you alone have caused. Does that seem right? Shouldn't you be doing something constructive instead of literally throwing the weight of your accursed maladies around? You must be so very proud of your 'talents.'"

Sarcasm did not touch him. He'd long ago become immune. He'd tell her that if she had the guts to take his gag out. Drool slipped from under his gag, down his chin.

They had him tied to a ratty upholstered chair. He'd already tried to loosen his binds and move the damn thing this way or that to give him some leverage, but he'd been unable to. Still, he couldn't just sit here and do nothing. He hated this woman with a passion so white hot that he felt he could curse her just by saying the words in his mind.

He tried, but of course, nothing happened.

He glared with what he hoped was an expression of hatred. *Hard to pull off when one's mouth is full of soggy linen and... Oh, what the actual hell.* He thought purposefully for a moment and then let loose his bladder. More difficult than one would think, but his rage helped and, of course, and once it started, there was no stopping. He got his only delight of the day, watching her expression change as the flood became obvious—it soaking the front of that threadbare chair onto the floor.

At first it seemed as if the realization that she'd left him tied so long that he had to pee his pants took the stiffness out of her, but it didn't last. And he, of course, was uncomfortable in new ways. Wet and smelly, soon to be chilled.

She glowered, still holding her hands behind her back. What was she hiding?

He tried to speak, but it caused him to gag again and he exaggerated the response until she approached. He continued to cough, but then felt a weird loosening of the atmosphere.

Magic. Her magic. What is it? The pressure on his neck returned. All right. So the Undone wasn't without her own tricks. He wasn't in pain now, but he was pretty sure she could apply it at any time.

She fumbled with something behind him and then untied the apron's strings and removed the saliva-soaked fabric from his mouth, dropping it to the floor. His face was wet with spit. She didn't wipe it off. She walked around in front of him again and waited, hands behind her again. *What does she have?*

Ferjival cursed her. *Drak-ji-maldifinis-...* Before it was done, he cut it short. The curse—a deeper version of the childhood drobe he and Hasip used to exchange—would be weak without the use of his hands, but still a curse. But he could feel it not working.

Never mind. After deep breathing and coughing until his throat cleared, he looked at her. "You are so dead."

"So you keep saying. It doesn't matter. You and your mother have held my life in the palms of your hands *all my life*. In fact, you hold the lives of every person in Maripesa. It's time to stop being cowed by that. If I die by your hand, I will rest easy in the sure knowledge that a movement has begun to overthrow the Puraples. One that will end the system that brought your mother to power. Perhaps it is fitting that I, your mother, and the system all die at the same time."

Aza was going to vomit if she didn't get out of here soon. Ferjival stank. Sweat, and now urine.

She needed help. But she had to move this situation along somehow. *How can I convince him to go peacefully, without revenge?* She couldn't. Revenge could have been his middle name. Even now, the first words coming from his mouth after ungagging him were the beginnings of a curse—even though his hands were tied.

He got even more frustrated, of course, and started the curse again. Aza had no idea what he might be able to throw at her.

The soltec, still hidden behind her skirt, seemed to swell and lift as the curse connected and was absorbed. It quivered in her fingers as she, too, felt uplifted. Magic accumulated in the room, as she willed Zaz to put pressure on his spine. The MATRIA had been discussing additional ways their Talents could be enhanced and used in the world—though all of it was experimental—so she was thrilled and impressed that she and Zaz were working together in this way.

"What are you doing to me?" he shouted after his curse was done.

"Any curse you utter will be turned back on you."

"You do not have that kind of power!" But his eyes rolled up until he looked like a frightened horse and he shook his head furiously as his curse settled into his body.

Vijo took Pats to the clinic closest to Holba Bridge. He had a friend there who saw the farrier right away.

As Pats was waiting for treatment to begin, Vijo handed him coins for the trolley back to Luftva.

"Oh, no, I couldn't," Pats said.

"Nonsense. It isn't as if you had time to plan this trip. Pay me back later if you like, but it isn't necessary." He wrote his contact information on his medical instruction pad and handed it to him.

"Are you going back to help Zaz?" Pats whispered, looking over his shoulder.

"As soon as I can. I am going to get help first."

They parted with promises to keep in touch. Vijo, truly unsure, about who to turn to, nevertheless, made his way to the closest Messagery. There, he dithered some more. Eltah would want to know, but what could she do? Gerland would come and might be helpful, especially if he brought his car. But was it fair to involve a man with all those children? In the end, he went with his first instinct. Instead of sending a message, he caught a trolley and worried the whole way that he was going the wrong direction.

Aza Gen/Zaz Salizan wakes in a Puraples prison. That's the way this is all going to play out. Unable to tolerate the sight, sound or smell of the prisoner, Aza sat behind the counter of Pats' business, the door to his living quarters closed. It was hours after dark now. *On the other hand, I could just be killed where I stand when they catch me.* There'd be no real benefit in Mam Sior making a public example of her and there would be considerable risk on top of what was already a groundswell of hatred for the ruling family.

Prison, it seemed, was the best she could hope for.

At twilight, she had ridden to the farm, knowing that Reva and Eguin would be worried about her. Plus, Ginny needed attention. Eguin took care of the horse while Reva was informed of what was happening. Aza had done the round trip in record time, especially considering how much Reva had pulled on her to stay, to eat something, to put a compress on her black eye. But Aza was too nervous being away.

Back at Pats, she had checked on Ferjival long enough to ensure his ties were still intact and to give him one of the quell fruits and some water. Once he'd eaten a couple of bites, she regagged him, this time tying the cloth through his mouth and around his head instead of stuffing it in his mouth.

They did not talk. Depression seemed to have overtaken both prisoner and jailer at the same time.

She sat, munching on one of Vijo's rolls, when someone banged on the front door.

She checked at the window. *Pats!* Back already! She unlocked it. There was no sign of Vijo, but she was thrilled to see that Pats had company. "Karol!" Aza gave her a hug.

"You said we could trust her," Pats said.

"*Zlo*, what'd he do to your face?" Karol asked.

Aza looked at both of them in turn, so very grateful to have accomplices. She ushered them in and closed the door. "You can trust her, Pats, but anyone involved is putting their life in danger. I don't think I could stand it if something happened to any of you because of me."

"Tosh," Karol said, "at least we have a choice. You weren't given one."

Pats, who knew very little about why Ferjival was trying to arrest Zaz, looked confused, but asked no questions. Aza made a mental note to fill him in as soon as she could. Again, she had to weigh complete honesty against too many people knowing what could get them in trouble. This thought made her grimace. Pats was up to his scalp in potential trouble and there wasn't a thing she could do about that.

"What's our next step?" he said.

"We have to get him out of the village. He's still tied and gagged, but it's become a huge mess, Pats. That chair—," she winced and shook her head, "can't be saved. Your living space is going to need a thorough cleaning and airing out. I left him long enough to go to Reva and Eguin's. They know what's happened and, being in-for-a-penny, in-for-a-pound people, have agreed to house him. There's a small barn that's almost livable, at least until it gets cold." She shivered at the thought of a long-term, ongoing situation. "Eguin's doing what he can right now to make it an adequate...prison."

"That's good. Their farm's far enough from everything that he won't have to be gagged all the time," Karol said.

"I guess so," Aza said. "I just don't foresee how this can ever end well."

Pats touched her shoulder. "I heard you tell Vijo that you weren't going to think too far ahead."

She looked at him with a grim grin. "Thanks for the reminder. Vijo went home?"

He shook his head. "He's bringing help."

20

THE TWO MOST UNBELIEVABLE THINGS

A HARD KNOCK AROUSED Bek from her stupor. She'd been slouched here for a long time on the bed at the Wardrobe, her back against the wall. She sighed, remembering the days not long ago when she was full of energy for daytime work and afterhours play. Now that she'd gotten what she wanted—a seat on the Kruik Council—she was, instead, played-out in the evenings. Life had gotten very real very quickly.

She rose and opened the door.

"Vijo? Come in! Oh my gods, it's been forever. What are you doing here?"

She tossed clothes and shoes and trash from the couch and brushed off the cushion before motioning for him to sit down.

"I remembered you saying that you had a room here, so, I asked the first person I saw when I walked in and they told me how to find you. Hope you don't ever have to go into hiding."

"Ah, my life's an open book. Sit. I'm so happy to see you. How's life treating you?" She laughed. "I guess I should ask how are you treating life, huh? Get it? I heard the epidemic's past its peak, but you'd know better than anyone else. Gods, it's good to lay eyes on you."

"It is better. In fact, I...um, took the day off. But then, something happened. Something big, and uh, scary and—"

Bek's heartbeat sped up. She waited for a moment, assuming he would start his explanation again, but instead, he shut down. His shoulders slumped.

Why is he so dirty? What the hell's going on? "So, you obviously and quite rightly came to the amazing Benelek Kruik to help you. Of course you did. Who wouldn't think of me? What do we need to fix?"

His head rose, his eyes full of pleading.

"Oh Vij, what is it?"

"It's Aza."

"What? They got her?"

He shook his head. "No. No, it's not that bad. I have so much to tell you."

"You know where she is?"

He nodded his head vigorously. "I want to take you to her right now. She didn't ask me to. I don't even know if I should, but I—"

"It's all right. You didn't know where else to turn, and you know that Aza and I are friends. But since when do you know her? Is she sick?"

"Not anymore."

"Taken prisoner?"

A small, thin wail emerged from somewhere inside him. "No. No. I'll tell you everything while we're on our way. We're going to Luftva."

Her eyes grew wide, but she began sorting through the piles of clothes. "How long will we be?"

"I don't know."

"Doesn't matter. I have a car."

"I had no idea. Splendid. We'll get there faster and can come back whenever you like."

"Right."

Bek found what she was looking for. She pulled off the loose pants she was wearing and fastened a different pair around her waist. She put one leg on the bed and began to wrap them rapidly from thigh to foot. She knotted the ends around the ankle and then did the same with the other leg. "She's not sick and she's not a prisoner. The Purples haven't caught her." Her head disappeared as she drew off her blouse and threw it into the corner. She replaced it with a simple cotton top. "Just gotta get my jacket. Is it cold out? No, but it might be over there, right? It gets windy. Do I need a change of clothes?"

"I don't know."

Bek stopped and looked at him. *He's at the end of his resources.* She went to him and lifted his chin. "I'm ready. And so-so-so happy you came to me."

Aza leaped up and hugged Eguin when he excused himself from the small, sober group in his living room. He said, "I have never stayed up this late in my life. But morning and the needs of the animals will arise at the usual time, and so must I."

"I don't have enough thank yous for what you did for me tonight."

"Tosh, lass. Enough of that. No need to gush. Things will look different, better, when the sun is up; try not to think too much till then." He kissed Reva and waved good night to Karol and Pats. Aza sat down next to Reva and said, "You should go to bed too. I'll clean up."

Reva patted her knee. "Soon. How are you doing?"

"Not great."

"It's good advice Eguin gave you," said Karol.

"We only did what we had to," added Pats, his jaw set.

"True," Reva said. "I'm proud of you all for figuring out how to handle a very sticky problem."

"Since our 'sticky problem' is...contained for now, I should go," Karol said. "Come get me if you need anything." Aza now knew that she lived two farms over, down the coast from Reva's.

It had already been decided that Pats would stay the night. His living quarters in town would have to be cleaned and aired out. Plus, Aza wanted to make sure his curse had been thoroughly healed.

"Karol," Aza said, "don't take the boat. You've got to be way too tired."

"It would be faster overland," Karol said, "but as good as I am on the water, I'm that bad with horses."

Pats stood up. "I'll take you in the wagon if that's all right with Reva."

Reva agreed, and after they left to hitch it up, she went to bed.

Aza walked outside and stood in the stiff breeze under very tall swaying trees. She listened to the clatter of the wagon wheels going down the dirt road. She wasn't sure how to get her body upstairs to bed. Even if she managed, she doubted sleep would come.

She pulled her shawl closer and leaned her tired back against rough bark. Her body hurt. Everywhere. As if, with the slaps and punch in the face, the man-handling, wrestling and lifting, tugging and pulling and the extreme, prolonged tension, her body had just decided to hurt everywhere rather than try to figure out which part should protest the most.

Wouldn't it be heaven if that were your biggest problem?

She was considering walking to the barn and sending Zaz in to spy on the prisoner when her ears picked up a new sound. Just a *whir*, but loud enough to come through the ruckus of thousands of leaves fluttering against one another.

Soon she saw lights. Her heart leapt. Vijo had no car. Gerland was the only person she knew who had access to a vehicle. Well, Duma, but...no. He was a character from a different life. She waited, hidden in the trees, still too jittery to assume the visitors would be friendly.

The car came into view. Not Gerland's coach.

What now? Her body-pain extended to the beat of her heart against the chest wall. If one more bad thing happened, she would definitely crumble into a thousand pieces.

It pulled up near the house. Vijo emerged from the passenger side. Steam, visible in the cool night air, obscured the driver as the engine shut down.

"Vijo," she said. "I'm here."

"Oh, thank *Maripes*, Aza. I wasn't even sure we had the right house, and it's so late. I'd ask what you're doing up, but I—"

"Oh my gods. Bek?"

"I'm sorry it took me so long," Vijo continued, even while Aza and Bek were greeting each other.

Bek enveloped her in an embrace. "Are you all right? Vijo filled me in on what's happened."

When she finally let go, Vijo took his turn.

Aza was crying too hard to speak.

"It's going to be fine, fine, fine," Bek said, as she wrapped her arms around Aza again. Aza reached out and took Vijo's hand.

When the sobbing let up, Aza said, "Did I know that you two know each other?"

Bek and Vijo laughed and Aza joined them, not knowing what was funny but out of an overflow of emotion. It felt so good.

"Vijo's my healer of choice. I didn't know until tonight that he had healed you of giarmial. Turns out our Besin takes confidentiality very seriously."

They had moved to the front porch, Bek and Aza sitting in wicker chairs, Vijo on the steps. Aza reveled in seeing their wonderful faces, lit by gaslight.

"I hope you don't mind that I involved Bek. She's a Kruik and has more status than the rest of us. She told me quite a while ago that you two were friends. I knew she was worried about you—about the arrest warrant. I decided we needed her help."

"It is an amazing end to a startlingly life-changing day," Aza said. "You are both so welcome that I can't put it into words. But where am I going to put you for the night?"

"Aza, the night's almost over. Look." Bek pointed east toward Maripesa. Sure enough, the sky was lightening.

"We stopped by Pats," Vijo said.

"I wanted to leave you a note," Aza said. "But things were pretty dicey at that point."

"I assumed that you came here. Luckily, I had asked for directions...before all this happened. I'm so glad you're here."

"Oh Vij, me too. I'm so lucky to have such good friends."

She filled them in on how, rolled in horse blankets, Ferjival was spirited out of the farrier's and onto the ferry. "We had to wait until the townsfolk would be sleeping. Once he was on the boat with Karol, Pats and I hightailed it down here by horse to get the wagon. I'd alerted Reva and Eguin earlier. By then, Eguin had fitted the barn with a cot and slop pot and had found a lock for the door. When we got to the closest fishing pier, Karol was waiting for us. It all worked like a charm. But—"

A silence extended between them.

Finally, Vijo said, "But you have an impossible situation on your hands."

"Aza," Bek said, "I don't know how I can help, but we'll figure it out. Maybe negotiate his release somehow?"

For reasons that she didn't stop to analyze, this alarmed Aza. "We're not there yet. Right now, I need moral support. I need to suck up some of that natural confidence you have so much of. You've already helped." She looked at Vijo. "Both of you. So much."

"I think you are at the end of your tether, Aza."

"I am. I'm hanging by one tired finger off a thin limb over the ocean." She looked up at them. "And there are pointy rocks in the water below." She grinned.

"Careful," said Vijo, "I spotted sea monsters, too."

That brought them all to laughter again.

Later, when they bullied her into going to bed, Aza noticed that her pain had lessened a little.

From a glorified stable to an actual barn. At least here Ferjival could walk around a bit, and had a jar to pee in.

They'd spirited him away in the dark of night, gagged, trussed and blind-folded. There was a short water journey. He thought four people were involved, considering how he'd been carried and handed off, though it could have been three. It is disorienting to be denied one's senses and plopped around like a piece of meat.

After the boat ride, he was put on a cart. That means at least one more accomplice. *That's up to five. Or four. How did the mouse pull this off? It's not as if she knew I was coming to Luftva today. But it almost seemed as if she had been prepared.*

Ferjival was having trouble even remembering why he'd gone to the trouble of coming alone to Luftva to see the Undone twins that his feckless little brother brought forth. Stupid. Even stupider that he hadn't told anyone where he was going.

He'd had no real plan in mind, but felt the need to see their accommodations to make sure they were far away from prying eyes. His family couldn't put the three of them to death with all this chaos. Killing his own brother didn't seem to be a workable plan, either. Though such an action would demonstrate once and for all that the Puraples were not hypocrites. But how terribly unpleasant would that be? He had no stomach for it.

The worse the epidemic had grown, the more deaths that occurred and—really more importantly—the more economic chaos that had come about from so many people being sick, the more the Puraples were demonized. Timing was everything. Once the epidemic—waning now, by all accounts—was over and the city on an economic upswing...maybe then. Until then, he had simply needed to see how well they were hidden. Perhaps it was curiosity as well, and the need to impart a stern warning to the weak and silly—though yes, physically appealing—Maleka. A thousand curses on Aza Gen that she had been on the road at that moment.

They have to let you go, he thought for the thousandth time. Kill the soon-to-be Ruler of Maripesa? Unthinkable. Keep him prisoner? Even more ridiculous. But for now, he had to be smart. No more curses. No losing his temper. He would act the ruler he was. *Implacable. Imperious. Indefeatable. Is that a word? Undefeatable, then.* They would see that he wasn't scared by their dirty barn that smelled of animals.

There *was* a little window near the top of the roof that let in light. That was pleasing. Sunlight slashing across the floor this morning gave a bit of warmth. He was able to work his stiff legs and appreciated not having to sit in his own pee. They'd given him clean trousers, so that was good, though they were made of harsh, rough fabric. Do the Lowers go about in such discomfort all the time? He thought not. They probably gave him these to increase his discomfort. Never mind. He would be strong.

"Call off the search for me," Aza said. Ferjival had been in the barn three days and it was taking a toll on everyone. Aza couldn't yet envision an end game that would work.

"Why would I do that for the person who's holding me prisoner?"

"*Because* I am holding you prisoner."

Ferjival shrugged and peered at her from his bench—the one that Eguin had made for her MATRIA meetings. *How unappealingly ironic.*

"You have to give *me* something if you want something *from* me. Anyway, how am I to call off a search when I've disappeared off the map?"

"I'm prepared to let you go."

He couldn't help it; his face gave away hope. Then his usual expression of disdain and ennui returned. "I don't believe you."

"Something we have in common, not believing each other. It's just that I've decided not to murder you, so this is already a huge concession on my part. I *could*, or my friends could. No one knows where you are. If they did, Luftva would already be overrun with guards." She paced back and forth near the barn door, soltec in one hand, hand in her pocket. They'd untied him except for a metal chain around one ankle attached to the bed—thanks to Pats' handiwork. "But I know from living in your house all those years that you have a habit of falling 'off the map' from time to time. Some brothel in outer Maripesa or a room at the Wardrobe where you sleep off whatever pleasures you've used up? I don't know. I do know that no one misses you. Not really. They might be angry at you for not showing up to a meeting, or more likely, a sporting event. But, surprised? Or, even less, concerned enough to look for you? No.

"We, frankly, don't want the burden of you. So, we've discussed doing away with you. Dumping you in the strait where you'd be taken far downstream to the Tchoperes where no one knows you and even if they did wouldn't recognize you because your face would be eaten off by the fishes by then."

"You talk such a big game, Gen. But you're a nothing. Not fit to clean my boots."

"Ah, how apt an insult. I was very worthy to clean your boots when you were dependent upon me to get it done."

All this mocking chatter exhausted her. She hated talking lightly about murder, which was all bluff. And the thought of having cleaned this man's things all those years made her want to vomit. She gripped the soltec more tightly. "Think about it, Lord Ferjival. Isn't it rather lovely to live a clean life where you aren't constantly needing your boots purged of Kruik retaliation?"

Ferjival made a disdainful noise that emanated from the back of his throat.

"Let me know when you're ready to negotiate your release."

"Wait. Don't go. I'm ready."

Aza, at the reinforced barn door, looked back over her shoulder. "Hmm, no, I don't think you are."

She walked out into the sunshine of a perfect fall day.

The farm sat a distance from the strait on a high ridge. The breeze smelled of open water and the grasses, crops, and wildflowers that grew between here and there. Aza paused to appreciate it all. She took several deep, slow breaths and managed a few worry-free heartbeats before her troubles returned. A few heartbeats and then: *What the hell am I going to do with him?*

"Are you ready? It's time," Bek said, looking for all the world like a farm girl—strapping, strong, thick black hair escaping from a knot at the base of her neck. Aza smiled. Bek always provided her with a little more confidence than she naturally possessed. Was this magic?

"I'm ready."

It was a MATRIA day. Since their 'sticky problem' was housed in the barn they usually used, they'd moved the meeting to Karol's farm. It was getting to be quite a journey for those who lived north of Luftva, like Maleka, and of course anyone who came from Maripesa proper, but it was secluded and Karol had been thrilled to offer it. They'd outgrown the house barn, anyway.

Vijo had returned to Maripesa the day after the crisis began, feeling the necessity of getting back to work and the need to maintain normalcy in the face of what was about as abnormal as anyone of them could imagine. Bek had sent word to her family that she was taking a holiday in the country.

On the way to the meeting in Bek's car, they chatted effortlessly. Aza marveled that this woman was not only her friend, but cared enough that she'd go this far out of the city to be with her when she needed it most. She had never felt so many divergent highs and lows in the same day, much less moment to moment.

Aza counted sixty-two.

It took forever for the meeting to get underway, because people kept showing up. She had thought Karol's porch would be big enough for all, but instead it looked like a fair now with a full porch and people scattered on the lawn, sitting on blankets, shawls, and aprons.

Karol got more energized with each new arrival while Aza grew wearier and more insecure. Every time she opened the meeting, another group would walk over the grassy hill from the roadway below. Finally, her adrenaline spent, she sat down and let everyone visit and settle while she fretted about how to proceed.

Now, half an hour later, things were moving along quite well. *I shouldn't have worried*. Benelek, even though this was her first meeting and she had only learned about the MATRIA in the last three days, held the lot of them, enthralled. *As she does...* She stood on the grass in the shadow of the porch overhang, giving them her reaction to learning about the group.

On the way to the meeting, they'd talked nonstop about this group's potential, Bek's new position on the Kruik council, even Maleka's situation. They hadn't seen each other since that night at the Wardrobe. Aza's heart filled as she remembered again that Bek had been worrying about her since then. Also, that Bek wasn't just an interesting person Aza met and then re-met one of the craziest nights of her life—well, now, *two* of the craziest nights of her life. She was a true friend. Of all the unbelievable things that had happened recently, this felt the most amazing.

Aza sat up straighter and refocused on the meeting after a Besin woman with a baby on her hip said, "It's all very well to talk about magic and strategic doubling or tripling the usefulness of our Talents. Like using teams of Patterning and Forcing, or Splitting and Moving, to get those in power to make better decisions, but what are we left with once those decisions have been made?" She looked around and then said, "I'll tell you. It all rapidly goes back to the way it is now: broken. If they made bad decisions for the rest of us once, they'll make them again. We have to gain access to—"

"The clan councils," Eltah said, "like Bek here."

"And the Synod!" someone from the grass yelled.

Enthusiastic murmurs erupted. This had been discussed at every meeting, but there were so many new people here this time and, Aza had to admit, the idea of gaining access to seats of power was always an aside for her, something for down the road. She had been more interested in the magical and hereditary part and less about the politics of it. Maybe she needed to change that position. Or maybe it was reasonable or even beneficial for someone else to take that part on.

Aza rose and touched Bek on the forearm. The two nodded at each other and Bek asked for quiet and sat down on the steps.

Aza cleared her throat, stood as tall as possible and pitched her voice loud enough to be heard. "In considering clan councils and the Synod, we should not leave out the Tchuvari."

A few gasps and at least one exclamation of glee were heard, followed by a hush. Aza smiled. "It's a lofty goal. But not that long ago, I had a most interesting conversation with one of them; a woman named Oscera. I was unprepared for it and, to be honest, they might have been so open and forthcoming with me because of my inexperience. What I now have the context to understand is that it isn't just us and those like us who want change. The Tchuvari, some of them anyway, recognize that this system their ancestors devised no longer works. At the same time, being steeped in the history of Maripesa, they fear the kind of chaos that reigned before we had a Hierarchy of Talents, so they won't assist in bringing it down if there's nothing better to put in its place."

Rimna spoke up. "But surely none of us could actually enter the Tchuvari."

Bek repeated what the older woman had said so that everyone could hear, and then added her own comment. "I was under the impression that membership was fixed, as in any clan."

"Not true. They are generally celibate, remember? They'd have died out generations ago if it were fixed. But their procedures for gaining members are esoteric and the process selective, so their numbers have diminished. Oscera said they need new blood. I was so green behind the ears when I heard this that it passed through my mind that they wanted actual blood!"

Laughter spread through the group.

"Oscera explained that the original members of the Clan Tchuvari were those with multiple kinds of Talents."

"Were they Undones?" someone asked.

"Ah, see? There *were* no Undones then. The clan structures weren't in place yet. There were families with specialties—a tendency toward one of the Talents. But the taboo against genetically mixed offspring came later."

"What's their position on our Talents?"

"I don't know. But I'll find out. Oscera asked me to come back when I was ready."

Aza stopped, remembering that odd, confusing day. She looked up at all the eager faces and couldn't, in that moment, trace the events that had brought her to this point. She lost her train of thought. And then, suddenly, without knowing she was going to, she said, "Oscera told me: 'You are more than you know.'"

"What did she mean?" Karol asked.

"Unclear at the time. They were talking about how some Tchuvari are open to change. And then they said, quite pointedly, 'You are more than you know. When that statement makes sense, come back and see me.'" In retrospect, I believe she was imprinting that message by use of magic, by using a matriarchal Talent on me."

Aza looked around at the MATRIA. Her MATRIA. "I have a context now for her words. I have a natural power of Splitting and—because I've been exploring women's magic with all of you—now know that I have some abilities of Patterning, Forcing, and Moving. Oscera saw that in me. And now, I know that there are many of us who embody more Talents than we originally knew. Have you found some of these abilities growing in you now that we talk about them and give them value?" She saw nodding heads and heard murmurs of assent. "And we haven't even begun to reach out to the Undones."

Several voices rose up and soon there was lively discussion—and a few arguments—about the Undones. Even good-minded women had prejudices fostered over a lifetime. Aza made eye contact with Bek. She rapped a gavel on the porch railing. "Let's come to order."

"Yes, the Undones," said Aza. "Reject them and you reject me. *All* of our society must work together if we're to achieve fundamental change. We don't know yet what it will look like. We must begin even before we have a unified vision of the future.

"We must organize according to our abilities, both magical and practical. Some must recruit. Some explore the magical possibilities. Some strategize to gain political clout. I want to speak with those who are interested in that last task after this meeting. We should adjourn soon, but my parting advice is to be open, but careful. Do not give us away to those who would try to crush us, but also don't be fearful, for we are bigger and broader now than a few people meeting in a parlor or barn. Be optimistic. We're a movement now. We'll make mistakes and we'll disagree, but beware of falling into tribal thinking. Don't let anyone from inside or out deter us from our most immediate goal: to have women's magic be integral to our society. "

A deep calm followed. Even the children present had settled down and were lying in their mothers' arms or resting on the grass, listening.

When the silence broke, Aza sat down and stared into the distance, the sea breeze reaching her face. Chatter and movement swirled around her. Her mention of the barn where they last met reminded her of Ferjival's imprisonment. A massive secret none of these women could know, though it could easily be the downfall of this movement. She was responsible. She had to solve the unsolvable.

Part Three

Cathedral

21

TURNING AND RETURNING

FERJIVAL TRIED TO KEEP track of time, but he suspected himself of making marks in the wooden doorway twice some days. He did not believe that he had ever neglected to make a mark. He counted them again.

Thirty-seven. So, maybe it was thirty-five or as low as thirty. A month might as well be a year, or forever.

He'd been forgotten. Given up for dead. Unmissed. Life moved on without him. He would never be ruler of Maripesa or anything else. He no longer thought he'd literally rot here, because they were caring for him, but what difference did it make if he had no life—here or there?

He walked to the rough bench that served as the only furniture other than his bed—a simple iron bedstead with a mattress filled with *Maripes* knew what. Horsehair? Wool? Probably wool. He did stay warm at night and there was no heat in the place, so maybe wool. Speaking of warmth, it would soon be winter. His jailers would have to deal with that.

He sat, head down, looking at his hands, which showed signs of aging. He thought of Eguin and Reva's old hands. They were the people he saw the most—though he never knew who might undo the lock, slide the barn door open and enter with *his* soltec hanging from a chain around their necks.

His precious soltec—so cleverly swiped from the old uncle when he was young. *I had some smarts. Always thinking ahead. Planning for the future. My future as ruler of Maripesa. Why did Mother never cease telling me that I was only good for gaming, gambling, and partying? It wasn't true. She never gave me any praise or credit.*

He tried to imagine what was going on in the city. Whether the epidemic had waned. Whether his mother had recovered enough to re-take the reins of power. Or whether someone else had. Inexplicably, these thoughts imparted a strange sense of calm.

I have nothing to strive for anymore. Not even getting out of the barn, though of course he still wanted that. Wanted his freedom, at the least. But he now knew that he had no life to go back to. When he went back to his city, it would no longer be his. He would be laughed at, mocked, or most likely, disregarded.

The lock squeaked. He sat up straight but did not face the door. He had learned that the morning sun would stream in and blind him momentarily.

Someone entered.

The barn door closed and was locked.

He looked up.

Reva. Short, plump, white-haired, her eyes were pale olive green and almost disappeared under all the wrinkles. Her small nose was lumpy, her skin deep brown with darker circles under her eyes. She didn't smile often. When she did, he couldn't help but feel that he'd somehow earned it.

"Good morning, sir," she said. "I've brought your breakfast and another book. Eguin said you'd finished the last one. I'll also empty your pot. How are you this morning?"

He slumped a little, his elbows on his knees. "I am tired of this."

She walked to him and pushed the breakfast tray forward until he raised his hands and took it. It smelled and looked delicious, as he knew it would be. Three times a day, she delivered the best food he'd ever eaten. Nothing fancy, but always hot and as fresh as it would be possible to find. Today she'd made him three eggs, a delicious corn mush—salted and buttered, a couple of tiny pan-fried fish, buttered toast with homemade quell fruit preserves, and a pot of tea covered in a gingham cozy.

"How do you have bread made so early in the day?" he asked. In his life at the Komeh, he'd never once wondered about the process of making food before.

"Oh child, that's yesterday's bread. Today's is still rising."

He bit into the thick slice. "Do you churn the butter?"

"Of course. Who else?"

"I don't know. Could I...maybe—" He stopped.

"What?"

"Learn how?" Ferjival had no warning this question would come out of his mouth. "You asked me how I am and I must tell you I'm feeling very odd." He looked up at her and words, previously unformed in his mind, spilled out. "As if I've crossed a threshold. I don't feel...good. Or happy. But also, not upset or angry. I was very, very angry at first. Who wouldn't be? Who wants to be trussed like an animal and put in a barn? Yes, just like an animal." He took a bit of toast, paused, not really thinking anything except that it tasted perfect. After swallowing, he said, "But you and your husband have treated me very well. Your food—which I've only just considered that you have to make for me and bring to me out of your busy day—is wonderful. How I am today is...t hankful. Thankful, not for all of this—" he lifted his arm, indicating his prison, "but for this." He touched the tray. "Thank you, Reva."

"Well," she said with a small smirk, "I'm glad I asked. You are welcome. We wouldn't starve ye, now would we? I am only giving ye what I feed my husband. Well, a little less, mind you, because he's out working hard and we wouldn't want you to get fat on our watch either, now would we?"

This, he knew, was a joke. He was and always would be rail thin. But humor wasn't available to him. He regarded her dispassionately, feeling disconnected from himself.

"Go on then," she said. "Eguin caught the *tal*—them, fish—this morning. Eat before it gets cold. I'll be going now."

She picked up the key hanging from her neck on a long chain and started to put it in the lock. But first she turned back and said, "Would you churn butter if you knew how?"

"I would be happy to have something to do. Is it hard to learn?"

She chuckled. "I couldn't tell you, since I've been doing it all my life. But I shouldn't think you'd have too much trouble getting the hang of it. I'll discuss it with Eguin. Enjoy your breakfast and your book, Ferjival."

She left, and he tucked into his meal.

With the view of sun-kissed ochre fields and indigo water splayed before her, Aza sat alone on Karol's front porch, trying to decide what to do with her day. She had slept in Karol's spare bedroom, as she often did now.

A gooey pool of guilt sat in her belly, along with the milk-laced mug of tea she'd just drunk. Guilt plagued her because first, she'd leaned on Reva and Eguin for help, second, she'd taken Ferjival prisoner and left him in their barn and, third, she wasn't there half the time to take care of the nasty-tempered scoundrel as well as no longer helping them with the farm. This, after all their kindness to her.

And yet, she *was* working. There were so many things to do that she often, like this morning, couldn't decide which was more pressing. The MATRIA had accomplished amazing inroads into the councils in less than a month—due in no small part to Bek's charm and access to Maripesians of all clans.

"Timing," Bek kept repeating, "is everything."

The timing for getting their people into the administration of the clans was perfect because so many old-timers had died of giarmial. Even some of the middle-aged ones had to take positions in family businesses due to vacancies. Some were still recovering from the debilitating malady.

Bek encouraged those with Forcing skills to work with those who had an interest in being on the councils and sub-councils, in order to move their acceptances along more quickly.

The woman would arrive at the prearranged council meeting with one of these talented friends and express interest in sitting on the council. The leadership would suddenly find themselves without objection to the placement of a woman on the team, even though they traditionally would have presented a lengthy list of reasons why it might not be the right time.

Sure, it was cheating, but the Uppers had always used magic to their advantage; why shouldn't they?

Bek reported yesterday that they'd achieved sixteen total: three on head councils and the rest on sub-councils. One position had gone to Eltah and Vijo's cousin. That meant representatives of the MATRIA were on Besin, Salizan and Kruik councils already.

Aza would bet her soltec that Bek would be Kruik Leader before too long. *She could be running Maripesa some day.* This thought made her grin widely. She took a moment to be grateful for the time to think, the beauty and solitude of the spot, and the breeze on her face. *Guilt be damned.*

The sound of a steam-powered engine reached her ears. Her heart leapt. Bek? Back so soon? She rose, started to go inside—a habit of hiding herself that she developed over these long months in Luftva—and then stopped. Aza was sick of hiding.

She stood at the end of the porch in her cross-clan clothes—part Salizan prints, part Gen pastels, part Dal practicality. She was a new breed of Maripesian for sure. Soon, up over the last rise and around the bend, came a familiar coach.

"Gerland!" she shouted, dashing down the steps.

Aza got to the coach as he turned off the engine and climbed out. She threw herself into him and he laughed, giving her a bear hug.

"Are you alone?" she asked.

"I am, Aza. Oh. Should I call you Zaz?"

"Nay, I'm Aza again. I couldn't keep up the lie. And now with, you know, our 'guest,' what's the point? They will arrest me or they won't. What brings you here this gorgeous morning?"

He asked if he might have a cup of tea. Aza ushered him into the most comfortable chair on the veranda and went to make a fresh pot.

She was soon back with a tray that included a few finger sandwiches and sweet biscuits as well as tea, milk, and honey.

"It's so good to see you," she said, preparing his cup. "Though I'm thinking of the fares you're missing and wondering why you've come all this way on a workday."

"It is good to see you, too. You are the picture of health, my dear. "

Aza could not say the same. He hadn't gained back the weight he'd lost from giarmial.

Gerland took his teacup and gazed for a moment at the skyline of the city. Aza turned to it, as well. The cathedral spire from the Tapinak rose high above it all, shining a pale glowing coral where it caught the sun.

Gerland sipped the hot drink, seemingly gathering his thoughts.

Aza waited, unease growing.

When she couldn't take the suspense any longer, she said, "You have bad news for me. I can tell. Are they still searching for me? Do they know where I am? Is my arrest imminent? Or is it Ferjival? Whatever it is, I can take it. Just tell me. Please."

He smiled wistfully and turned, setting his cup on the table between them. He then rose slightly, lifted and swiveled his chair to face her, and sat down again. "It is bad news, but not about that. Not directly, anyway. It's your clan." He cleared his throat. "Uh, your first clan. The Gen."

"What is it?"

"They've named a successor to your father."

Aza needed that moment to take this in. Of course, there would be a replacement. It simply hadn't crossed her mind in all that had happened over the last six or seven months since Leo died.

"It's Duma," Gerland said.

Her head jerked up. "What? No. He wasn't even on the council. What about his father or one of the other elders? That makes no sense."

"I knew you would want as much information as possible, so I went to see Reth."

"Oh, how is he?"

Gerland chuckled. "How could one tell?"

Aza smiled. "True. Maybe *I* could, but only because he was my nursemaid from an early age and only companion—such as he was."

"He *is* unsettled about all this. There's more. Duma's family is taking the Villa as their own."

Aza's mouth went dry. "Holy Talents," she whispered. "I— I guess it *was* the headquarters for the leadership of the clan, so—no one is living there. Well, Reth. Reth is still there, isn't he?"

Gerland put his large hand over hers. "I think, not so much. My impression is that he moved back to his own clan sometime after you went away. He arranged for and has supervised the cleaning and upkeep of the Villa. Except for a watchman at night, however, no one's been living there for a while."

"I see." She didn't seem to be capable of forming another sentence.

Gerland filled the gap. "I wanted to be the one to tell you. Personal items, belonging to you and your father, are still there. Duma hasn't moved in yet. Reth has delayed what he believes is inevitable. He told them the place needs a deep cleaning and—" he smiled— "treatment for evidence that small animals had made their way into the building. I think this was a fib, or maybe an exaggeration, but a believable one. Reth wants you to know that he will oversee the move, and the early part of this transaction. I do believe that's the right word for it."

"The house? The estate? But...it's mine, isn't it? Or—" Aza realized she had no idea if the house actually belonged to Leo. Perhaps it *was* owned by the clan.

"This is why I came. I could have messaged you if it had just been about Duma being named leader. No, I came because— Aza, it's time you returned to the city."

The blood seemed to leave her head. She squeezed her eyes shut and focused on breathing until the feeling passed.

"It is?" she asked.

He nodded.

"You seem certain."

"I am not sure what will happen. Of course, I don't want you to be arrested. But Maripesa is different now, in many ways. The epidemic changed us. People are scrambling to make sense of things. Everyone is angry at the ruling family. There are rumors that Mam Sior is too ill to govern. Your MATRIA is known, talked about. Yes, maybe in whispers and only in people's sitting rooms. But it has taken hold. Don't you see? All of this changes you. Changes who you are in the city. You were a weakened, recovering fugitive with no family when you left. You will return with some status across clans and a few allies in high positions. You have more friends, more visibility, more recognition, and a lot more support."

"And I have to confront Duma."

"That's my Aza."

Aza gathered her things, hugged Karol goodbye, and was soon on her way with Gerland back to the farm.

"Are you scared to go back to Maripesa?" he asked.

"I don't know. My heart is beating really fast. Is that fear?"

His eyes didn't leave the rutted dirt road. He shrugged. "You tell me."

"I'm feeling everything at once. Suddenly, I'm missing my father more than I have since he died. I am angry about Duma. He's completely wrong for that job! He has no ethical underpinning!"

Gerlands eyebrows rose. "I had no idea. Isn't his father—"

"Palter, yes. *He* would have made sense. Why did they skip over—oh *Maripes*, maybe he died of giarmial, too. Did you ask?"

Gerland shook his head. "What else?"

"Anger at Ferjival. Guilt about Reva and Eguin. I can't just leave them to take care of *my* prisoner. It was bad enough that I was spending so much time at Karol's."

"This is all hitting you at once, Aza, but you can't *deal* with it all at once. And not by yourself. Talk to Reva. See how she feels about taking care of *our* prisoner. You have other friends. Karol can help them, and what about Pats? And Maleka?"

"Pfft!" The noise escaped her mouth involuntarily.

"What?"

"Oh, Maleka. She's dropped off the edge of the world as far as I can tell."

"She is raising twins."

"I know. But she could send a message now and again, couldn't she? It hasn't been that long, I suppose, since I saw her, but—oh!" Aza slapped herself on the forehead. "I'm such a dunce. She *had* to distance herself because of Ferjival. He's her brother-in-law."

"She's not exactly close to the Puraples family."

"No, but that's no help. She's at risk of execution and has to protect her kids, as well. I've just been so busy, distracted, that I hadn't taken the time to think that she stopped coming to meetings soon after Ferjival became our 'guest.'"

"Speaking of execution. Is that worry on your list?"

Aza laughed. "Seems like it should be. But it's way at the bottom."

On the driveway to the farm, the looming trees swayed before them as if in welcome. Aza thought back to the night of her arrival, and how much stronger she felt now. She could never repay these two selfless people.

Just then, Reva and Eguin came out of the house to greet them.

Soon they sat at the table with small plates of bread—still warm from the oven—potted meat, cheese, and a variety of fruits and raw vegetables.

The atmosphere was lighthearted as they laughed at Eguin's story of a lamb that had gone missing. After much worry and to-do, he found it safe and sound, in the smokehouse. "Have no clue how she got in there," he said, shaking his head. "Mayhap, it was the neighbor, playing one over on me. But I can't prove it."

"More likely the sprites comin' to visit," Reva said, winking at Aza.

After finishing, Aza leaned back and rubbed her belly. "Oh my. I didn't know how much I needed that. Thank you." She paused, growing sober with what she had to say. What came out was as simple as it was inadequate. "Thank you. Thank you." Tears welled up, and she saw Reva's face grow solemn. Concern deepened the wrinkles around her eyes.

"Why, child, what's the matter?"

"I have to go back to Maripesa."

Eguin leaned on the table, causing teacups to rattle on their saucers. "Is it safe?"

Gerland explained the main reason for Aza's decision to go back.

"Well," Reva said, rising to replenish the teapot, "then you must. Aye, but we'll be ever so sorry and lonesome for you. Will you stay there?"

"I only just learned of all this an hour ago. I've no idea. But I have to see to my father's estate, his legacy. And mine."

"Of course you do," Eguin said.

"And we'll see to—" Reva said, jerking her head twice toward the house barn, "our sticky problem."

"We need to talk about that," Aza said. "I was already feeling guilty about him."

"Ach," said Eguin dismissively.

"It is actually all right for now," said Reva. "We're making some progress with the boy."

Aza's eyes widened, and she glanced at Gerland.

"What does that mean?" Gerland asked.

"Yes, do tell," added Aza. "What does progress look like in such a person?"

"If you go over there now, ye'll likely see him churning our butter."

Silence followed this unlikely statement.

Aza started to giggle. Gerland joined in with a deep chuckle. The older folks smiled, but didn't seem to find it all that funny.

"I mean it."

"How did you get him to do actual work?" Aza asked.

"He wanted to learn." Reva stood and began clearing the dishes. "So, I showed him. That was about a week ago, I'd say. He was clumsy at first. Right foul-tempered about it, too, but I was patient. You know what I think?"

"What?"

"He's seen very little of that kind of patience. I think he may have been without it all his life."

"Are we talking about Ferjival? The supposed heir to the ruler of Maripesa?" Gerland asked.

"No, she's right," Aza said. "His mother treated him as a whipping boy. Not literally, though she may have whipped him as a child. I wouldn't put it past her. But with words. I can't actually remember ever hearing her say a neutral word to him, much less kind. She wasn't much better with her other sons, though her daughters were treated a little better. But Ferjival was constantly criticized and undermined."

"So you've cured him with kindness, have you, Reva?" Gerland asked, amused.

Reva wiped her hands on her apron, and reached for a cake sitting on the sideboard. "Mr. Gerland, I don't say that at all. I think he's got some rot at the center of 'im, but he's not raging anymore. I don't fear that he'll curse me when I walk in. He's been changed by his circumstances. Don't you guess that you might be changed in some way if your freedom was suddenly taken from you?"

Gerland nodded. "Point well taken, Madam."

Eguin said, "Listen to this. One night, he said, 'I know you're taking care of me without thought of payment or return of any kind.' And something like, 'Though I've had servants at my call all my life, I never thought about them. They were just there, in my house. I suppose they get paid, don't they? I don't even know.'" Eguin paused for a moment and took a noisy slurp of his milky tea.

Reva sent a kitchen knife deep into her cake and lifted the first slice. She placed it on a saucer. "Brandied pear cake," she whispered, so as not to interrupt Eguin.

"He even spoke of you, Miss Zaz. Oh, I know that's not your real name, but you'll always be that to me, if you don't mind. He said, 'The Gen was there cleaning our Kruik curses from the time I was...fourteen or fifteen. Before her, we had someone else. They were interchangeable to me, as were all the servants. Of course, the Gen had more status, but what did that mean to me? Nothing. I just called, and they appeared, and did whatever I needed them to do and then they disappeared.'

"So I says, 'What's different about what we're doing then? We bring you food, wash your clothes, take away your slop pot, and bring it back clean. Aren't we the same as your servants?' And do you know what he said?"

"I can't wait to hear," said Aza.

"'*You* don't have to.'"

"Oh."

"'*You* don't work for me. You don't care about my status or who my family is. You had nothing to do—and believe me, I know this—,' he said, 'you had nothing to do with taking me prisoner. That was all my own doing.'"

"No!" said Aza. "He said that?"

"By my curses and cures," Eguin said, holding up his right hand. "And then he says, 'My mother wanted to catch the Gen; I didn't care or even know what her story was. I was just trying to gain my mother's approval. How stupid can a person be?' he asks. 'That was never going to happen! And I know that the Gen, or you, or any of the people who've looked after my needs while I've been here, did not have to do it. You all did it because—' and there he stopped, Miss Zaz. He just stopped and stared into space and I finally said, 'Do ye know why?' And he looked at me and his scrawny, mean face looked even scrawnier in spite of all the food he's been putting away and it looked like he might cry but didn't really know how to make that happen. So I said, 'They did it because it's the human thing to do. And because they have a dear friend you've been terrorizing for no good reason that any of us can conjure up and we all want to help her. So we're taking care of you to help her.' And one other thing, I told him, 'Even if we're all guilty of keeping you under lock and key, we aren't going to forget that you're a human being just like we are, one who needs food and clothing and a bit of a smile here and there.' That's what I told him."

"*Spellfire,*" Aza whispered, awestruck.

"My dear Reva and Eguin. You have changed him. It's remarkable," said Gerland. "And extremely unexpected."

Aza rose from the table, her cake untouched. She felt unsteady on her feet and paused, holding on to her chair for a moment. She closed her eyes and shook her head slightly. When she opened them, she saw these three wonderful people—her friends. People who had helped her first, as naturally as they now helped Ferjival. Had *she* been as appreciative as Ferjival was now? Or had she always taken peoples' service for granted, as he had? Reth, for example. Reth, who was always at hand. Didn't he have needs? Who took care of him after Leo's death? Not her. She had not a thought for him as she ran off with no forwarding address.

"I—" she said, still feeling shaky. "I must talk to him. You shouldn't trust him too much." But those words sounded patronizing. These people had been alive much longer than she. Maybe they were better judges of character than she was. What did she know about anything?

"You all right?" Gerland asked.

"I will be. I'm so touched by what you've told us. You continue to amaze me with your grasp of *everything*. I can't thank you enough, but I will keep trying. Let me go see our prisoner. Then I'll be ready to go."

It had been many days since Ferjival had seen the Gen, and his anger bubbled up. His soltec hung from a chain around her neck, along with the key to his prison and a necklace she always wore. He'd only noticed the necklace because of the other hateful things hanging around her neck, but it kindled a memory—though vague as to when or where—of a glowing stone caged inside a filigreed, tear-drop shaped pendant.

As I am caged, though not so prettily.

So here again was the unlikely woman who had bested him.

But as she turned and locked the door behind her, his ire dissipated—like bubbles do. All except one last bitter thought: *I could overpower her, take the key and soltec and escape before the old folks ever knew I was gone.*

The old folks. The thought of them washed him in shame. He nudged aside the churn, finished now. He'd been ready for Eguin or Reva to come and be proud of him. Ready to show that he'd done a good job. And then *she* pops up. Even a prisoner should have the right to see only those people he wants to see. But this thought, too, was a revelation. He'd never considered prisoners as persons, much less persons with rights.

Aza Gen stood, her arms behind her, back against the door. Sunlight came through in bright, thin strips and the haze of dust thrown up by the sliding door made a halo around her curls. She wore an unholy mish-mosh of clan clothing—Gen blouses, Kruik pants, Dal apron, Salizan stole.

"I am sitting here wondering why I haven't tried to escape."

A crease appeared between her eyebrows.

"I'm a man, bigger than you, younger than Reva or Eguin—though even at his age, I'll admit, he's probably stronger than I am. So it wouldn't have been much good—me trying it with him. But Reva? I could have taken the key...and *my* soltec from her, and left. How long have I been here?"

Aza lifted her left shoulder and twisted her mouth a little.

"You are just going to let me talk, are you? Well then, all right. I... I'm changing because of all this. I needed to. But I still hate what you've done to me. I hate that I had to leave my life. That I *have* no life back in Maripesa. But I admit to you now that it—" He stopped. *I have changed. But I can't say to this person that it was more my fault than hers. I should shut up. Be more careful.* "Reva and Eguin seem to have the Talent of softening a person," he said. "You don't have the same effect on me."

Aza laughed, softly. She moved now, for the first time, coming closer to him, perching herself at the edge of the bench across from the bed where he sat.

"I'm sure I don't. But I have to disagree that Reva and Eguin are practicing some kind of Talent on you, though the results may be magical."

"Simple kindness, eh?"

She nodded, and Ferjival found himself mirroring her movement. They looked each other in the eyes for a moment.

"So what's the plan, Miss Gen?"

She looked down and wiped some insignificant dirt off the bench, before saying, "You were talking about having no life in Maripesa anymore. I understand that feeling. I had to leave my life too, you know. It wasn't a choice I would have made if you and your mother and your clan hadn't been trying to arrest me. We have both been victims of that arrest order, haven't we?"

"I know, I know. I had a choice. You didn't."

"I wasn't going to say that, though I can't deny it. But Reva—who has the same effect on me as she has on you—reminded me that your mother has mistreated you terribly. I lived in your house." Aza whispered this last sentence with intensity. "I observed the way she undermined your every effort to gain her approval."

Ferjival rose, and the woman reacted with fear, holding up the soltec.

He felt a surge of pleasure that he could scare her, but the goodness of that feeling dissipated quickly. He paced toward the door and back again, noticing, as he did, the sour, acid smell of his pee in the slop pot. *This is intolerable. Her being here.* He cleared his throat and said, "This is my space. It is small and not what I would choose, but it is mine for now and I'm finding that your presence is taking away what peace I've found. Would you please leave?"

Aza Gen's mouth dropped open slightly. She lowered her gaze and said, "Yes. Please sit on the bed. I will go once you're out of my way."

He couldn't help but enjoy this tiny bit of power that he'd happened on, quite by accident. He stalked over and plopped down on the thin mattress.

She rose and walked to the door, turning quickly to keep her eye on him.

"I don't have a plan for you," she said. "I wish to *Maripes* that I did. I won't see you here again. I'll send in whoever is available if there's something you need to know." She sighed deeply, looking to the side toward the corner of the barn. "We can't keep you here forever," she whispered. Then, in a normal voice, "Please continue to be at peace with Reva and Eguin. They are the innocents here and should always and forever be treated as such. Can we agree on that?"

"Of course," Ferjival said. "I'm not a monster."

She regarded him sharply, eyes remaining on him as she unlocked the door, slid it open only as far as necessary and left, bolting the door behind her.

22

HOT WATER

"GERLAND, WOULD YOU MIND if I sat in the back? I need to think."

Of course, he readily agreed.

Aza instinctively curled herself into the bench corner behind the driver's seat, where she had always tried to sit when she was traveling from the Komeh to home and back again. That had been her life. All she knew. And now... *Now I have neither.*

Not Gen work nor home nor family.

And yet, I have much more.

At the bridge, she kept her eyes on the glistening water instead of looking ahead at the buildings in the city. When Gerland had asked this morning if she was afraid to come back, she hadn't been sure. Now she was sure.

She was.

A memory came of that day she rode home in the coach with Duma. The first time she'd seen him since he was a boy. His dove grey gloves, impeccable clothing, ready smile, and charm. She looked down at her hands, now roughened from farm work. She had always had servants to put their hands in hot water for her, just as Ferjival had. Garnia had intimated once that she was spoiled.

"It's good, Aza," she whispered to herself. "You have the power to change your life now. So do it."

Into what, though?

She thought of the arrest warrant and how all that had been turned on its head when Ferjival became her prisoner. *Odd, these similarities between us.* Once the differences in personality were stripped away and she looked at the emotional facts of their lives, it was similar: both lost, adrift, missing one parent while growing up and—according to Gerland's reports of Mam Sior's health—soon both parents, without any of the surety their past lives afforded them. *Do all adults feel this way at this time of life?*

All too soon, they arrived in Maripesa. The noise of the city felt like an assault. Screeching streetcars. Honking horns. Whistles of traffic wardens, wheels on the roads. Steam exhausting from dozens of vehicles and buildings. And so many people.

She wished now that she had sat up front. She wanted to ask Gerland whether the city was recovering. Whether people had stopped dying from the epidemic malady. She tapped on the glass between them.

He opened it and said, "I'll pull over the first chance I get."

He soon did so at a coach stand on the edge of the cathedral grounds. Aza scooted across the seat and got out on the right side. The area was green, shady, and lush. She felt a little spark of optimism.

Gerland leaned over and opened the door. "Want to hop in?"

She stretched the door wider and bent her torso into the cab. "Don't you need to get back to your life?"

He laughed in that gentle way he had—making light of life as his first instinct. "I have set aside my whole day to you, dear Aza."

"I do not deserve this gift," she said, laughing too. "You may have inadvertently delivered me to where I need to be, though." She turned back to the Tapinak's turrets and spires showing above the tall trees.

"The cathedral? You have a plan?"

"I wish. No, but I only just realized that I'm not dressed for the city. I'm going to cause a stir in these countrified, unclanned clothes I've taken to wearing."

"Hmm. True. It might not do to call attention to yourself on your first day back."

"Right. And I can't just waltz over to the Villa and confront Duma without some preparation and further knowledge about what's gone on. I should see Reth first. Do you know where he is?"

"I do, in fact." He reached into his breast pocket and pulled out a calling card, handing it to her. "He gave me this."

"Wonderful. What I am thinking is that I know someone here. They told me to come see them when I needed to. I think this is the time. And then, after," she flapped the card he'd just given her, "I'll find Reth. And then—" She looked up at Gerland's concerned face, not knowing what else to say. "And then, once it's all done perfectly and in the proper order, I'll show up on your and Ness's doorstep one day and invite myself to dinner with you. I bet the kids have grown since I've seen them! Is everyone healthy?"

"As healthy as a houseful of kids could ever be," he said softly. "The main thing I need to know is how to find you. Ness would kill me if lost track of you again."

"Well, we can't have that." She thought for a moment. "Let me go in and see if I can find Oscera. I don't know how long it will take. Can you wait for me here?"

He nodded, but looked unhappy.

"Would you like to come?"

He brightened up.

They left the coach where it was parked and walked down a well-tended, lush, and calming wooded path.

I couldn't possibly have a more pleasant reintroduction back to city life.

They emerged into a side garden of the cathedral, this one, a formal geometry of beds holding tiers of flowering shrubs, fading now. The post-flowering aroma verged on overwhelming. At the towering, pale pink edifice, they walked the loose-pebbled path around to the imposing front steps. Gerland now seemed hesitant, but she grabbed his hand and they started up. At the top, he stopped and looked back at the view.

Aza turned, glanced at his face, and followed his gaze. Gerland seemed overcome. She put her hand against his back. "Nice, huh?"

"'Tis a beautiful city. From afar."

She didn't speak for a moment. They were both survivors of giarmial. So much needless suffering.

"We're working to make it better."

He nodded and turned.

She pulled on the huge door and marveled again at how easily it opened compared to its mass. "There's magic in this place," she whispered.

"I should hope so."

Aza was still laughing when Freja, her guide from the last time, appeared.

They were shown to a waiting room. It wasn't long before Oscera arrived and greeted Aza with a somewhat formal hug. They turned, introduced themselves to Gerland and then back to Aza. "We are very happy to see you again and so sorry about your father's death. Are you well?"

"Thank you. Yes. Though, I had the malady as well. As did Gerland. We were well taken care of by the Besin."

Oscera sighed. It was an unexpected gesture from one so self-contained. "We also heard of the arrest warrant. But you're fine. We are so relieved. Now, to what do we owe this visit?"

It was Aza's turn to sigh. *How to sum up what had happened? How much to tell? What to leave out? Oh* Maripes, *just start talking.* She swallowed hard and said, "I need your help to sort out how to move forward, not only with my life, but with what has become my mission. I've—somewhat inadvertently—started a movement of women. We call ourselves the MATRIA. We're attempting to value and utilize our naturally occurring cross-clan Talents to help our city and citizens. You need to know this and, I hope, be part of it and help us and I have so very much to tell you and I don't even really know where to start or why I trust you. But I do." She had been looking Oscera in the eyes as this barrage of words spilled out and now, still looking at them, she began to tear up. "I need a temporary place to call home. Is there any, any possibility that I could stay here?"

Oscera brightened. "Why...yes. Of course. Can you tell me—?" They stopped, peered intensely into Aza's eyes and then said, "Never mind. What kind of accommodation? A room? A suite? Or perhaps—" They thought for a moment. "There are three cottages on the grounds. We will need to inquire."

Aza, amazed that her impulsive idea was met with such ready acceptance, looked back at Gerland who, standing now, was looking at Oscera and nodding in silent approval. He looked down at her and said, "A cottage sounds lovely, doesn't it?"

"Oh yes," Aza said, turning back to Oscera. "If it is at all possible. It does sound perfect. I can pay for it."

Oscera nodded, but said, "Details later. Let's talk to Freja. They know the facilities better than anyone."

Within the hour, they'd settled the deal and Aza was the proud recipient of the simple wordspell for the front door to the most charming home she could never have imagined.

The two-hundred-years old, thatched-roof house was round. Aza walked through the front door into an area defined by a small table for calling cards, and a wrought-iron coat tree. A round chimney took up the middle of the house. It was encircled by a staircase made from cleverly pieced wood of a honey-gold color. Aza walked left into a receiving room with two settees and end tables. Beyond that stood a small dining table and chairs.

Still going clockwise, the dining area gave way to a simple but well-equipped kitchen with an open hearth in the fireplace. From there, a mudroom, no more than three paces wide, held the back door. Continuing in the same direction, Aza—speechless—walked into an ample parlor filled with comfortable-looking furniture that took up the last third of the downstairs space. And there she was, around and back again to the front entry. She turned back to the parlor, noticing the curved mantel, and a raised hearth fitted with cushions to allow one to sit on either side with feet near the fire. It all looked perfectly dusted and plumped and ready for occupancy.

With Gerland in tow, she explored her new accommodations more closely, turning in circles, taking it all in, wandering through each room over and over, looking into cupboards, empty corners, the upstairs closet.

"The fireplace is so clever," Gerland said.

"Isn't it? Thank *Maripes* Reva and Eguin taught me how to build a fire. And, oh! My own kitchen? Whatever will I make for myself? Perhaps Ness could share with me some basics? Do you think?" She didn't give Gerland time to respond. "I'm pretty helpless at taking care of myself. I never had the— Meals were always— Oh, never mind. It's very exciting. Ooh, look out the back," she said, housekeeping worries gone as she leaned over the sink on tiptoes and looked out the kitchen window. "It's lovely. Come with me and see." She fairly leapt to the back door. The house sat in a clearing a three-minute walk from the Tapinak.

Even though it was near the towering pink cathedral, the house felt utterly secluded. The trees were three or four times taller than the thatched roof. A groomed path through the woods led right to the house, but at the entrance to the yard proper, a bronze sign read, "Private Residence." While surrounded by trees, the clearing it sat in gave enough space for the mid-day sun to shine down on it.

"It's perfect, Aza. How did you know?"

"Know what?"

"That you needed to come to the cathedral."

"I never thought of it until you pulled up nearby and I saw the spire."

"When are you going to give yourself a little credit for having some talents other than Splitting?"

Aza walked over to him. "I don't know what you mean, 'give myself credit.' What good could that do anyone for me to give myself credit? We are who we are, Gerland. Do you give yourself credit for your easy, good-natured personality? Is that not magic enough for anyone? Never wanting what you can't have, but always appreciating what you've been given? And treating everyone with respect and kindness? So while, yes, in MATRIA we have been exploring the possibilities of our skills, as well as the idea that we may all have tendencies to magic that have atrophied due to disuse, I'm not sure that's the same as 'giving myself credit.' If I do have some premonition skills, then I shall use them appropriately, I hope. But it's no more to my credit than is your exceedingly pleasing personality to yours."

Gerland's face gave little away. He was smiling, but he didn't say anything immediately.

"I'm sorry," she said.

Gerland's smile vanished. "For what?"

"You complimented me. My response was too blunt. I didn't mean to be rude."

"I was not offended. I was only thinking how much you've changed, how much you've learned. Being out of the city was good for you."

Aza let her breath out noisily. "Whew. Tell me if I ever get too full of myself, will you? And yes, being in Luftva broadened me in every way." She put her hands on her hips and looked around. "Now, I have to think about what comes next."

"I shall get your valise out of the coach and then see about getting you enough provisions to feed yourself for the next day or so."

"Oh gods. Thank you. Could you do one more thing? Send a note to Reth? Tell him where I am and ask him to come by tomorrow?"

When Gerland was gone, Aza allowed Zaz to split and have her own look around. Around a round, she thought, feeling silly and playful. "A round house for us, Zaz. We shall chase each other round the hearth until we figure out what to do with all the problems we have gathered."

Reth arrived the next morning looking both the same as always and very different. Trim, impeccably groomed as she would have expected, but with dark circles under his eyes and a slightly sagging jawline; he had aged, even though she'd been gone months, not years. She hugged him as she never did when he was a servant in their home and ushered him into the parlor near the curved window overlooking the back garden. The sun had warmed this spot and Aza took pleasure in asking him to wait while she made tea. She came back with a tray and went through the formal motions of serving him—for the first time in her life.

He, never one to make someone else feel self-conscious, took all this with aplomb. Soon, he asked, "Gerland must have told you about the council's decision."

"Yes. It's why I've returned. Reth, what right does Duma have to take my home?"

He put down his almost empty cup not so gently and said, "Technically, the Villa belongs to the clan; at least that's what they tell me. I've delayed the transfer, but Duma is pushing me. Plus, no one knew where you were, much less when or if you were coming back. The council plans to meet there even before Duma moves in. They're eager to put things to right. It wasn't just Leo who died of the malady. So did Retika and Garshon and old Lekt."

Aza's eyes filled with tears. "Old Lekt?"

"He'd lived through many things that might have taken his life, but it was an unnecessary malady that took him. I haven't gotten over it, Miss Aza. I don't know that I ever will."

"So the ranks of the council were thinned and Duma pushed himself forward."

"Exactly. The others, it seemed, were mainly pleased that someone wanted the job, especially with the mess that's been made of everything."

"For all I know, he could be a good leader. But he's..."

"Young?"

She hesitated.

"Unproven?" he ventured.

"I was going to say 'untrustworthy.'"

"Do you know something? I presumed the two of you had a falling out, but it was hard to know what with all that happened. I couldn't ask, of course."

"I found out months ago that he knew the circumstances of Maleka's disappearance but didn't tell me."

"Is she all right?"

"Oh, rats and bats, I'm sorry. Of course, you wouldn't know. She is. We found each other by accident and had many visits for a while." The subject of Maleka brought home again just how difficult integrating back into Maripesian society would be. She looked at Reth and made a decision about something she'd been considering.

"You know better than anyone that I never really had a family. Father was ...incapable. I am building a new kind of family and consider you part of it. If you'll have me, I...would you—? Could you be my pretend father?"

His eyebrows, usually so perfectly still, shot upward. His face, usually so impassive, moved about, wrinkling here and there.

"I know. It's presumptuous, I just—"

"Aza," he said, very gently, "it's all right. I'm deeply touched. Yes."

She teared up. No more "Miss Aza."

They talked through lunch and into the early afternoon.

Reth told her of his meeting with Ferjival and how he'd been followed by Puraples security. "They may check in on my whereabouts now, but I think their attention is elsewhere at this point."

Aza filled him in on her illness, who had helped her escape, who was "family" and who wasn't, all about Maleka, and the biggest secret of all: that she had Ferjival Puraples churning butter in a barn on a farm in Luftva.

Reth smirked and then broke out into a deep belly laugh.

Aza delighted at seeing him laugh. He was being so casual and real with her. So unguarded.

"Reth," she said quietly after his laughter had softened, "I find myself looking at my past life with so much more perspective. I want you to know how much I've changed. My eyes are open about what it means to be in service to other people—people like me who never ever questioned why you were there or if you wanted to be."

He nodded. "You're releasing me from my role. I understood that when you asked me to be your new father." He grinned again and said, "You were in service every bit as much as I was, with less choice than me, actually. I could have found work elsewhere in one of my clan's businesses, though that would have meant a step down in status and pay."

"You were paid for your service."

"Of course."

"Do you know who was paid for mine?"

"Well...I—" He looked at her sharply and then down, shaking his head slightly. "Your father must have been, since you were a child when you started. But you told me the day you left that you thought Mam Sior was blackmailing Leo."

She nodded. "So she wouldn't put both of us to death."

His lips pursed as he inhaled sharply. "You've been through your mother's things?"

"I have, but there wasn't much."

His shoulders slumped slightly, and he let out his breath, slowly and deliberately.

"Anyway, the ancient history will get sorted out. I'll have to go through my father's accounts soon."

"Yes, about that...I have taken the liberty of starting the process of sorting and consolidating his papers. Dividing personal documents from clan business...though to be sure, most of it is clan-related. I will have to move his personal effects out at some point if Duma insists on taking possession of the Villa."

Aza frowned. "Yes. I know I have to deal with all that, but I feel we have more pressing business. Reth, are you working for someone new?"

"No. I continued to draw my wages, as you requested, from your father's—ah, excuse me—*your* estate. Duma has asked me to stay on, but..."

"Will you work with me? With me, not for me, though we'll keep the pay structure as is."

"Yes. Yes. What do you need me to do?"

"Everything! I don't know! There is so much to be organized and communicated. I need allies. I need someone to introduce me to parts of society that will be important in what the new Maripesa will look like."

"A new Maripesa?" He beamed. "You're reminding me of your father." He paused for a moment, rubbing his jawline, and then went on, more energetically, "Sounds like you need me to be your man about town. To deliver messages and set up meetings. To find how who the sympathetic ones in each clan might be. I can handle your financial matters. Shall I set up the rental payments on this lovely cottage?"

Aza could feel her spirit lifting. "Could you?"

"I shall be delighted to try, Miss—no. I am delighted, *Aza*."

23

UNGUARDED

The woman who came in the wee hours had been of average height and weight. The barn was dark, and she held her dim lantern so that it shone more on him than her. Ferjival had a fair memory for voices. Hers was unfamiliar.

Her coming woke him from a deep sleep.

She stood, back to the barn door, but without locking it. Her voice rang out strong and bold. "It has been determined by a vote of the M____, that you shall be released."

Oddly, his heart hadn't leapt at the news. Perhaps because he had been asleep? After the woman left, he had sat on the side of his cot, his head in his hands, and tried to make sense of this news. *What was that word she'd used? Started with an m.* Some—who?—group had voted on his release? What could it mean?

He had walked to the door and opened it. A blast of cool air hit him in the face and his eyes closed involuntarily. When he opened them, he saw the night sky, clear, almost cloudless, and a bright, almost full moon illuminating the landscape he'd been living in, but had not laid eyes on until now.

Reva and Eguin's small house sat to his right across a tidy yard. A barn, larger than the house, sat behind it. A calico cat walked directly to him, slowly, deliberately. She rubbed against his bare leg. This touch—so soft, so rare—sent a pleasant shiver through him. After that, he felt calmer.

His eyes moved from the house up to its backdrop of swaying trees and down to the winding roadway that quickly curved out of sight as the land sloped toward the Strait of Jeka. A harvested field took up the level land directly in front of his cell. Beyond that—far away, but the next thing he could see—was the water, its choppy white caps lit up, twinkling in the moonlight.

"You are free to go," she had said. "Reva asked me to tell you that you are free to stay as long as you might like."

Free to go.

It was as if the words didn't come together to make a complete thought; as if they were part of a dream that seemed to make sense while asleep but fell apart on conscious examination.

Free to stay.

Leaving the door open after his exploration of the surroundings, he had crawled back under Reva's quilts and slept soundly.

Now, close to midday, no breakfast had come. Likely there'd be no lunch. He was free to find his own food, presumably. He wanted to walk to the house, knock on the door, and ask Reva what he should do. But he also wanted not to do that.

He was troubled for the first time in weeks. While a prisoner, he hadn't had to worry about the world and his place in it, or whether he was doing the right thing or not, or what people thought of his actions, how they judged him. And people out in the world did judge him. People in his own clan most of all.

He sat in his rough cloth pants and undershirt listening to his stomach rumble.

Later, he got up, put on his boots and walked to the big barn accompanied by two cats. Eguin looked up at him without surprise.

"Good afternoon. I am wondering if there might be a need for butter to be churned? I am hungry, and I'd like to do something to earn a meal, if I might."

Eguin turned his head away, so Ferjival didn't know what kind of response his inquiry elicited. Perhaps the man was laughing at him. Perhaps he was moved in some deeper way.

Now that he was free, he had to consider such things again.

But when the old man turned around, his face gave nothing away as he said, "The horses need hay. Take this." He handed him a pitchfork. "I'll show you how much to give them. While you're doing that, I'll ask Reva to make you up a plate."

Aza opened the door to Oscera. "Good morning! To what do I owe this pleasure?" Then she noticed the strained look on the woman's face. "What is it? Come in."

She ushered Oscera to the dining table. Aza had just gotten a fire going in the hearth. It had taken a bit of the damp chill from the room already.

"We doubt that you've heard," Oscera said. "Mam Sior has passed away."

"Oh, my." Aza sat down.

"Natural causes. Not giarmial. The Tchuvari got word overnight. At dawn, a Puraples official informed us that a cathedral funeral is to be held in three days.

We've all been in a state of frenzy since. It's been a long while since we've put on such an event."

Aza thought of Ferjival. Guilt arose at the stark realization that he never saw his mother alive after that fatal day in Luftva Village.

Oscera stared at her.

"I'm sorry," Aza said, shaking her head. "My mind was on—"

"Ferjival," Oscera said. "We as well have him on our mind."

"Should I send a message?"

"I think not. The news will travel quickly."

"Do the Puraples have their succession plans in order? She's been ill for some time."

"We're worried. The last time this degree of chaos coincided with a ruler's death, there was war. Ultimately, the Kruiks were defeated, their leadership ranks so depleted that they never recovered to the power they once had."

Aza's mind went to Bek. She had tried without luck to contact her. Messages went unanswered.

Oscera continued. "Our separation of magical powers was supposed to keep the city out of chaos, not ensure it."

"But it used to be far worse, right?"

"Back two centuries, before the Hierarchy of Talents? Yes. No stability of government, economy, or community. Neighbor against neighbor, each person for themselves. That's where the expression 'sleep on your own shoulder' comes from. Take care of yourself because no one else is going to. I'm worried that the Kruiks are going to make their move."

"To take over top position in the city?"

"Yes."

"This is the problem in a nutshell, Oscera. What about a system of power sharing instead of the only outcome being one of victory and defeat? Why should those who hold negative powers be the only ones with a voice? Isn't that a basic flaw in the system you Tchuvaris fostered?"

"We are part of the sect who want massive, fundamental change, remember?"

Aza smiled. "I remember. *Some* of you, not most. Have you eaten?"

"A piece of fruit earlier. We would love some breakfast."

As Aza got busy, Oscera said, "It's going to be a crazy few days with Puraples crawling all over the Tapinak. You must be cautious. Beyond that, we shall wait and see." They looked up at Aza. "The best outcome for you would be having the Kruiks in charge of the city."

Aza had feelings about that, about what the next Maripesian government should look like, but she wasn't ready to discuss it, and this was all too much

so early in the morning anyway. She knew only one thing: Mam Sior was dead
and things would change.

"I vote for tea," Aza said, "before designing a new form of government."

Outside, purple smoke poured from the Komeh's chimney, announcing
Mam Sior's death. Every neighborhood's journal would put out a special edi-
tion. The news spread rapidly in the city, but it would take longer to reach a
small farm in Luftva. Purple smoke didn't carry that far.

During the week his mother died, Ferjival had learned to muck out a stall, milk
a cow (though even he could easily admit he had no talent for this chore), and
where and how to store the grain for winter. He fell asleep every night as soon
as his body hit the cot, amazed at how exhausted a working body could get.
Reva and Eguin, true to their word, accepted his continued presence without
the slightest hint of impatience.

Each day brought more rather than less confusion about where he should be
and what he was supposed to do with the rest of his life. All this, in the midst
of learning what it meant to work for his bed and board.

This alone felt unambiguous. It was purely good, while everything else was
trouble and turmoil. One minute he was contentedly caring for large animals
and cherishing the awkward, uninformed steps that had led him here, and the
next, his mind swam with outrage and venom that he'd been imprisoned in a
barn.

While he did not want to walk back into life at the Komeh, his brain still
fantasized about it. Him in fine country clothes. Soft leather britches. Boots in
black, a shirt of cotton so finely spun that the fabric looked polished. A cravat
in rich colors. A long jacket in lush wool—a fine purple, grey, and black tweed,
perhaps. A new hat and gloves. Dressed so, he would arrive unannounced
during the council meeting, striding in, a changed person. All faces would turn,
all eyes on Ferjival Puraples—strong, tanned, shoulders and mind broadened
by his time in the real world. And then...

Nothing.

His brain had nowhere to go after that. What? His mother's face would show
delight at his homecoming? She would bolt up, toppling her chair and rush to
him with tears in her eyes at finally seeing her eldest again after all these weeks?
No. Those hefty chairs did not topple. His brothers and sisters? Would even
one of them clap him on the back or embrace him at his resurrection? No.

There were no good outcomes in Maripesa, so he worked on his cow-milking
technique, forearm muscles singing with pain.

Out of habit, Vijo walked to the clinic early in the morning. If the epidemic had been a nonstop nightmare of confronting one life-threatened individual after another for months on end, the lull of activity following it presented its own challenges. Vijo had been like a skittish cat at first, expecting to turn around and find another rolling, growing wave of illness forcing its way into the door. When that didn't happen, he felt adrift, even while being grateful that it was over.

Since he had become a full-time healer—albeit not that many years ago—there had always been a slow but steady stream of maladies to treat. Some were accidental, others cast impulsively in anger, spite, from a broken heart or jealousy. The human condition on display every day, with enough breaks from the action to keep it from being overwhelming. And then, the epidemic. A constant stream of potentially deadly giarmial.

And now, almost nothing. It was as if the Puraples had lost their Talent. Maybe they'd learned their lesson? That was definitely too much to hope for. But the quiet, the lack of dis-ease was palpable, and, he thought, a portent of change. The question foremost in his mind: *What would I want to do with the rest of my life if there were not enough maladies to keep me busy?*

On entering the clinic, Vijo noticed the sound of anxious chatter.

"Did you hear, Vij?" Eltah said. "Mam Sior died."

The Kruik Council had been in session since the news of Mam Sior's death reached them. Bek sat with perfect posture and composure in her fresh seat at the table. So did another woman, Havah, who had been admitted onto council at the same time as Bek.

She'd met Havah through the MATRIA. The woman had a powerful Leaning Talent.

While Benelek Kruik would have had no qualms about getting assistance from matriarchal magic, she hadn't needed it. She had her looks, height, bearing, confidence, charisma, and connections. Nonetheless, she and Havah had an understanding. They were a combined force and would use whatever they needed to in order to help the council make the right decisions.

The council had long been preparing for Mam Sior's death. The giarmial epidemic had the whole city not only outright hostile to the Purples but also in enough chaos that most would welcome a change in leadership.

Old Frag was speaking. "We should not use the weapon. At least give them a chance to capitulate. Let them know that we have it and are willing to use it. But we should not further damage the city we want to rule. Show the people that we have their interests at heart."

Bek sighed inwardly. The old fellow was sweet and well-meaning, and she basically agreed with him, but he would not prevail. This debate could go on endlessly, but after all these months, everyone in the room knew that the weapon would be used.

"We already have a strategy," Leader Rodjo said, "to be put in place upon Mam Sior's death. Now that has happened and it's no time to be planting doubts about decisions already agreed to. With all due respect to our elder council member," he nodded to Frag. "We proceed as outlined."

The strategy had been written up long before Bek and Havah had attained a seat at the table. Though Havah had the stunningly useful ability to change the mind of any person, she could only muddle their minds long enough to bend them to her immediate will. She couldn't give them new brains. And it didn't work on a roomful of people. They'd tried that early on. Five of them got headaches and excused themselves, and Havah wound up in bed for a day and a half.

All magic has its time and place.

Havah's personality was not bold. She would always wait for Bek's cue. That was the good news, Bek supposed, but she chafed at the limits of her power. It had been more fun during the early days of the MATRIA when so many of the women were hungry for guidance. Leadership was her thing. She shouldn't be at the low end of twelve, sitting at the end of a long table in this stuffy room. They needed a fresh breeze in here.

No time like the present.

"Leader Rodjo, if I may…We must alert the Gen. Give them a little time to prepare," she said.

Several of the councilors objected, either outright or under their breath. Even though they would never dare do this to the other men in the room, they weren't called on their bad behavior by Rodjo. That did not improve Bek's mood one bit. She rose, placing her right fist on her hip and making eye contact with Havah. The hand placement was a sign.

Bek walked to the front of the room and stood next to the Leader. He looked at her, mouth open, eyebrows raised. "See here. This is highly irregular."

"We are about to declare war on the things that make this city function. It will affect not only the Puraples but every clan—as giarmial affected everyone."

"That's not true." The voice came from the end of the table. "Giarmial struck the Puraples as well, but—"

Bek felt the shimmer of magic as Havah leaned on the man.

In a commanding voice, Bek continued. "We are no less susceptible than anyone else to the stagnating results of the weapon we've decided to use. Will we be able to take a trolley if its engine is gummed? No. Will we suffer as everyone else if our supply of...say...pipe tobacco is cut off because the assembly line at the tobacco plant can't produce another jarful until the Gen come and clean it up?"

"Targeted attacks. We aren't spewing curses over the whole city willy-nilly."

"Gen aren't our allies. They work with the Purples!" This came from the middle of the table. Wilklo, she thought.

"Old school thinking, boys," Bek said. "I will go along with your strategy, but I was not here when it was planned. Neither was Havah. We, as full members of this council, must have input."

"That's not the way it works."

"Havah? What do you think?" Bek asked, unable to keep a slight smirk from pulling at her lips.

"Councilor Wilklo, this shall be the way it works from this point forward." Havah could lean on someone without saying a word, but her Talent was much more effective with the force of her voice.

Wilklo looked confused, rubbed his eyebrows fiercely, and then said, "I, uh, I do see your point..."

"Exactly," Bek pounced. "Since the plan has yet to be carried out, it can always be improved. A work in progress, as we see what needs modifying along the way. If we're to be the ruling clan of Maripesa, we must have as many allies as possible...perhaps even, in time, the Puraples."

Even matriarchal magic couldn't control the snorted objections to this, but Bek didn't care. She was in her element at last.

The afternoon of Mam Sior's death, Aza was at home planning an agenda for the MATRIA meeting to be held at the cathedral that evening. Reth was out, messaging the first ten on their list. Once received, those ten would spread it to ten each and so on until all registered members were notified. Their membership had grown to several hundred. Aza didn't even know the exact total.

Her doorbell rang, and she opened it to see a uniformed Messagery boy. He craned his skinny neck to look around at the house, his feet fidgety, as if he were incapable of holding still for even a moment.

"Message for Aza Gen," he said in a high voice.

"That would be me," she said automatically, even though she rarely thought of herself as a Gen anymore. She took the message from him. "Thank you. Would you like to warm up for a moment? I have a fire going."

"Oh no, Miss. I have five other messages that are marked "Important." But thank you for your offer." He touched the brim of his cap and bowed slightly. He started to leave but turned back and said, "Yours was marked Urgent, so I delivered it first."

"Oh! Well done, then. I'd better read it."

Aza closed her door and broke the seal as she walked into the parlor. The fire crackled pleasingly. She read, "Urgent: Inform Gen Council that a major display of a new, combined Kruik curse will be forthcoming. Muster your people; the city of Maripesa will need you in record numbers."

The message was unsigned, but she knew it was from Bek. Aza's heart skipped a beat. Bek had simply been extremely busy. That's why she wasn't answering her messages.

Aza lowered herself to the couch. Her day just got busier. She would deliver this warning in person. That meant doing something she'd been putting off since she'd returned: facing Duma.

24

.⊱⋅⊰.

THE BEST TIME FOR ROMANCE

AZA KNEW THAT RETH had years of practice at getting messages to the Gen Council, so when he heard that would be his next assignment, he fairly glowed. "But shouldn't Leader Duma be the one to call the meeting, or at least be notified first?"

"Of course he should," Aza said, bitingly. "Sorry. Don't mean to take your head off. But this is a true emergency. Duma hasn't even held one meeting yet. Evidently, he's too busy thinking about how to redecorate my home! When I explain what this is about, I will be forgiven for not following protocol. I can handle Duma's hurt feelings or anger or whatever his reaction brings."

Four hours later, she was let into her own home by a houseman who did not recognize her. Once in the oh-so-familiar courtyard, she—wearing traditional Gen clothing for the first time in months—clasped her gloved hands in front of her sash and said, "I am Aza Gen, daughter of former Leader Leo. I'll go to the council room."

"Let me—" he started.

She cut him off with a breezy, "I know the way."

None of this was his fault, but she couldn't help having an attitude, considering the circumstances. She was early, but reached the doorway to find a full room. The buzz of conversation stopped. Everyone turned. Duma was not present. Willa was the only other woman in the room. They immediately made eye contact and Willa gave her a friendly nod. *I need to seek her out when I get time. She might have Talents, and would be valuable to the MATRIA regardless.*

The councilors rose to greet her. Her acidic mood softened. She felt their sympathies, respect and, from those she knew well, affection. None had seen her since Leo's funeral. Some spoke about their confusion regarding the arrest warrant and their fear that she might never be able to return. Miervaldis, Leo's closest advisor, gave her a warm greeting and told her how much he missed

Leo. And then, before her was Maleka's father, Jea, his face full of emotion. He hugged her tightly.

Aza filled up with guilt that she hadn't gone to see him and his wife immediately upon entering the city to tell them that Maleka was alive and that they had grandchildren. But how difficult and tricky would that conversation be? She found herself in tears. Jea let her go and then embraced her again. The rest of the room had broken into twos and threes and there was a noisy drone of conversation. Aza whispered in his ear, "Maleka is alive. She lives in the country and I've seen her over the last months. I will come to your home soon and tell you what I can."

Jea pulled away, holding her by the upper arms, his face wet. He looked at her searchingly and something approaching a smile came to his face. He mouthed the words *thank you*, and then let her go, facing the wall as he reached for his handkerchief.

Aza turned to see Duma standing at the head of the table, unnoticed by the others. She strode toward him and extended a gloved hand—her favorite, lavender ones. "Duma," she said, "thank you for your cooperation." The handshake was perfunctory. Aza couldn't help but remember their first one in the coach. His touch had been very different. Perhaps Duma was similarly preoccupied with memories because he said nothing.

Perhaps he would have come up with something, but Aza turned and said as loudly as she could, "Attention, please! Thank you for coming." The group grew quiet. "I've been warned of an imminent emergency that will require all of the Gen Clan's energy and cleverness. The Kruiks are positioning themselves to make a bid for power by attacking the Puraples and the city with a new combination curse."

Behind her, Duma cleared his throat and said, "We, ah...I should call the meeting to order."

Aza couldn't have imagined this moment. Now that it had happened, she couldn't help but enjoy it. He was, in effect, asking her permission to call *his* meeting to order.

"If you like," she said, "but since I'm not officially a member of the council, perhaps it would be all right for me to provide the information I've been given and then let you start your meeting, so that the council can sort out in a more formal way what's to be done about it. I can't stay long as I have other commitments. Please. Sit."

Duma, dressed in his signature grays, seemed adrift. His skin was grey toned too, except for his cheeks, which had grown rosy. Without taking his eyes from her face, he reached back, found the arm of his chair, and sat down.

Aza concisely delivered the news of the crisis that was about to put their clan under a strain like nothing had before.

When a barrage of questions came at her, Duma's awkwardness disappeared. Standing up, he called for order and used Leo's gavel to properly open the meeting. He asked Jea to find a chair for Aza. When she was seated and the room was quiet, he turned to her. "The information on this new Kruik 'weapon' is credible?"

"Yes. It comes from a Kruik friend who is well-connected and involved. Additionally, weeks ago, I heard from a Besin friend that this person had told him the Kruiks were developing ways to combine curses for maximum impact. Likely the epidemic and Mam Sior's illness sped up this new flux curse."

"It will be directed at the Puraples, right? But how will we know for sure we can clean it, if it's new?" These questions came from Miervaldis.

Why wasn't he considered for Leader? On the other hand, she had to admit, he had aged when she wasn't looking. Perhaps he simply stepped aside for the younger man.

A buzz of talking arose again. Duma, warming to his role, cut in. "Gentlemen, and my ladies, let us not devolve into overlapping jabber. As I see it, we would be smart to assign these functions: Fact-gathering, Planning, Organization and Communication. There will be others, I'm sure. Altrek," he turned to the Secretary. "Did you get that?" When the man nodded, Duma said, "Please keep us on track when we veer off, as I'm sure we will. So, first, information."

He looked intently at Aza, who withered a bit under his glare. She had already said what she knew, and he had now taken charge quite effectively. "Is there a question on the table?" she asked.

"Can you find out more? Get corroboration? Tell us the source. Can we find out what this curse is? Do we know when the casting of this curse will happen?"

Aza cleared her throat. "I've told you what I know. However, I can attempt to see my source—who I will not name—today. But surely I'm not the only one of us with a Kruik contact. As far as the curse, we should go on the assumption that it involves growing vermin like the common renyer, since that would keep it spreading, combined with some version of dahke that makes it gummy and more difficult to clean."

"Confound them," Jea said.

Miervaldis said, "There's one of their curses I haven't seen in many years. It's like a renyer, but grows much faster. I can't bring up the name at the moment..."

"Well, if we remember it, the Kruks certainly will have," said Duma in a strong voice that silenced side conversations. "Let's proceed with a guess that it's a combination of the fastest growing and the most mucilaginous fluxes we've cleaned. Any kind of head start we can get on researching the possibilities will be invaluable. When we are adjourned, I will alert the head of Gen archives to get his people on this. By the time we hear of the first instance of this curse being set, there will hopefully be a plan in place for cleaning it. Then we can test out our techniques and what we must do to improve it. What's next?"

Aza sat back and watched the interactions of the council members with Duma. She hated to admit it, but he was doing a good job. *Well, we need someone competent in charge right now. Maybe he is the one.*

"What do you think about that, Aza?"

Her cheeks flushed. "I'm sorry, my mind wandered. What's the question?"

"What's the likelihood that the Kruiks could actually wrest control from the Puraples?"

"I'm no expert on politics."

"You worked in the home of the ruling family for most of your life," Duma said gently. "We know that you can't tell the future. Just give us your opinion."

"The Puraples are weakened, but in truth they have been weak for some time if Mam Sior's offspring are any indication of the state of the rest of the clan. Perhaps being at the top of the heap is destined to breed sloth, selfishness, pettiness."

"Tell us what you really think," said Miervaldis.

Everyone laughed.

"I—I really must go soon, but I have something rather astounding to share with you." Aza was unsure if this was the right thing, but she had been looking at the faces and was reminded that she knew most of these people. They could be trusted—at least with this news. "I am responsible for having held Ferjival Puraples prisoner in a barn in Luftva for the past few weeks."

No one uttered a word.

"I assume you all know about the arrest warrant for me."

"We are unclear on the details, Aza," Palter said. "There are...rumors."

She bit her bottom lip and said, "Yes, of course. The details are mine to tell, but not now. You should know the details surrounding Ferjival, however." She told the story quickly, leaving out Maleka, and not mentioning the names of those who had helped her.

"Living in a barn," Willa said. "That is rich."

"But I hasten to add, no longer under lock and key. It might have been better if Ferjival had been imprisoned during this upcoming crisis, but he has been free to leave for over a week. I don't know his status at the moment, but he's been in no hurry to get back to this side of the strait. The family he's staying with noticed rather drastic changes in his attitude during the time he's been incarcerated. He calmed down and became so reasonable and, I guess, bored, that he asked for work. He took over the chore of churning butter."

Laughter and hoots sprang up around the room.

Duma asked, "Aza, aren't you in danger? He will come after you."

"I am, I suppose. Well, it seems we *all* may be in danger. I believe, though, that enough has changed since I went into hiding that I won't be anyone's focus, especially now that Mam Sior is no longer with us. The state of Maripesa is my focus. Not only getting through this coming emergency and a possible change of power, but what it is possible to do as clans and individuals to foster fundamental changes so that it works better for all of us. The Besin Clan is still recovering from the strain of treating a whole city from a malady that should never have been released!"

"Ferjival's personal work, too. That's what everyone believes," said Duma.

"I have no inside information about that," Aza responded, "but he was spell-happy and full of resentment toward the world." She was silent for a moment, pondering the irony that such a privileged individual should be resentful of the society he held power over. "I just thought of something we haven't talked about," she said. "The cleaners in Puraples' households. We should recall them."

"Why?" Duma asked. "They'll be needed more than ever."

"But stop and consider: is it to our advantage to help the Puraples fight the Kruiks?"

"Don't fool yourself, girl," Miervaldis said. "The ruling clans are two sides of the same coin. The Kruiks will be no more magnanimous to us lowers than the Purples have been."

"More than that, it is our job," Duma said. "And being helpers to the Ruling party gives our clan status over the Besins. We'll lose that advantage if the Kruiks win."

Aza turned to face him fully. *There he is. The Duma I know him to be.* She stared, and when someone else started to speak, she raised a gloved hand without turning her head. The voice faded.

"What constitutes status, Duma Gen?" she said, looking him in the eyes. "Is it an advantage over my friend Garnia Dal who mopped the floors in the Komeh? Or little Doret, who got up before the crack of dawn to set fires in all the hearths? Do you have any idea how many hearths there are in the Komeh? No. I wouldn't have either except that I asked. Twenty-seven. Doret, of course, had to have help with that job. One small child couldn't have done it. How does cleaning curses raise me higher than her?

"I was sent away from home at eight years old to work in the the premier household in this city. If you think that role, that duty, to work for the highest of the high was a privilege, then you should not be leader of this clan. I assure you, cleaning renyers off the family's boots did not *feel* like a position of status. We are in service to people who throw about spells and curses as if they are playthings. We literally clean up their messes. What you fail to grasp is that the Besin and the Gen are equals in this 'advantage.'

"If *you* had acquired giarmial as I did, or had loved ones who died of it, and if your status had been such that you were treated in a clinic instead of having healers come to your home, you would have unending *respect and admiration* for the Besin. Instead, you dare to raise yourself above them. And you do this not because of your own prowess or dedication in cleaning the current ruling clan's curses, but that of your clansmen and clanswomen. Leo would *not* approve."

Aza rose. The council sat in stunned silence. She cleared her throat and said to the assembled, "I have overstayed my welcome. I have this one request. You are still low in numbers on this council. Invite new blood into this room. Specifically, women. Change is afoot. If you are to be *high in status* in that new world, you'll need fresh, innovative points of view. I will provide Altrek with a list of recommendations for your consideration.

"Pertaining to the current crisis, I will report back soon. I hope that I may continue to be a part of the organizational strategy that we've come up with tonight. If you need anything from me, let Reth know. I will do everything in my power to help you, my friends, my clan, my family, and our city. Good evening."

Duma stayed behind, but many of the council members followed her into the courtyard to give her a personal goodbye. By the time Aza climbed into Gerland's coach and asked him to take her home, she was utterly depleted.

"I have to miss the MATRIA meeting," she said to him. "Please ask Ness to take the lead and give her my apologies. Also—" She dug through her satchel, looking for Bek's warning message, while shaking her head at how quickly things were heating up. She found the note and handed it to Gerland. "It's not private anymore. You can read it. You'll see how important it is. Please give it to Ness and ask her to tell the others. The MATRIA must have a strong presence at the funeral. I'll be in touch with her tomorrow. For now, and I'm not sure where I will find the energy for it, but I have to track down Bek."

Bek paced in her room at the Wardrobe. It wasn't easy considering her long legs in the small, crowded space. But her nervous energy was almost painful. She'd gotten a message from Aza stating only that she would show up here tonight.

She missed Aza. The days Bek had spent with her in Luftva were among the best she'd ever had. Like a different life altogether, to be in such a beautiful place with people she cared about while imagining a new kind of future. But she hadn't seen her or even returned Aza's messages since she came back to Maripesa. She had plenty of excuses lined up, but they'd all dissipate when faced with...well...with that face.

Mam Sior's funeral was the day after tomorrow and would likely be a disaster. She'd done everything she could to get cooler heads to prevail while being fully conscious of the irony—what with her having been so aggressive in her hatred of the Purples for so long. But now, having achieved an avenue for fostering positive change, she had no more need for spell-casting. Of course she wanted to wrest power from the Purples, but that didn't mean throwing the whole city into chaos again. But as it stood, the Kruik Council was dead set on proceeding with their new weapon.

Bek hadn't even considered attending the MATRIA meeting. She was, whether she liked it or not, a representative of the clan that was about to unleash misery on everyone.

War. Bah.

A rap on the door.

She yanked it open.

That face was flushed, as if she'd been rushing, running. It seemed to glow from the inside. With what? Purpose, commitment, excitement, cold? Yes, likely all those things, and maybe fear, too.

Aza's curls escaped from a scarf of deep blues and greens. She wore Kruik slacks, several layers of Gen blouses, a felted jacket in rich blue made from the wool of Reva's sheep. Bek had been there when Reva was sewing it.

"Come in. You look wonderful. I've missed you so!" Bek reached out to pull Aza into the room, but her arms just kept going and enveloped her in an embrace. Aza was warm and cold all at the same time.

Aza hugged her back. That was all warmth.

Thank Maripes, *she doesn't hate me after all.*

This thought allowed Bek a release of the tension she'd been feeling all night and filled her up with instant joy. She lifted Aza off the floor and turned to get her inside. Once there, she mashed the door shut by backing into it. Aza, her toes only brushing the floor, grinned widely, filling the room with her spirit.

"Bek..."

"I'm so happy to see you. You look amazing."

Aza's soft brown eyes opened wide.

Bek didn't want to let her go. She took a step forward and stumbled over something. The back of Aza's thighs went up against the fat arm of the couch and she fell backwards. Still holding on, Bek fell on top of her.

A soft "oh" escaped Aza's mouth.

That was all that was said for a long while.

They kissed. Sweetly at first, then deeply, hungrily.

Bek reminded herself that Aza was inexperienced sexually, unless that had changed in the last few months. But even if so, she shouldn't take things too far too fast. There was absolutely no doubt in her mind, however, that she and Aza were feeling the same need for each other.

When it was time to take a breath, Bek laughed lightly as she leaned back and pulled off Aza's scarf.

"Don't stop," said Aza, huskily. "I do not want this to stop...ever." She tugged Bek to her, the two of them lying more or less side by side now, but with one of Bek's legs over Aza's hip and the other one mostly on the floor.

"Yes, yes," Bek said, "but on the bed. It's not that far."

They burst into giggles.

"Nooo, it's too far. We'll never make it," Aza said. "You should kiss me first in case we get separated."

Bek obliged.

When they climbed onto the bed, things slowed down. Bek kicked some items off so they could stretch out. They lay on their sides, face to face, with Bek's arm under Aza's head. With her other hand, she stroked Aza's hair, playing with a curl, taking in the smell of this person she'd admired all these months. "Since the day I opened the door and saw you on the stoop of my parents' house, I have wanted to kiss you."

"No."

"Oh yes. I pushed that desire down. Accepted the fact that we were friends only. But now...oh Aza." She whispered this.

"Now's not exactly a great time for a romance," Aza whispered back.

"Aw, anytime is the best time for that." She ran fingers over Aza's cheek, her ear, her neck and down, lightly stroking her left breast. "Oh girl, it's time for you to roll over so that I can get these endless layers of Gen blouses off. It's going to take hours."

It didn't.

Bek drove her to the footbridge across the street from the Tapinak. After one last, long, passionate kiss, Aza got out and waited until Bek drove away before walking home.

She wasn't used to being out on her own in the middle of the night. But she wasn't fearful. Tonight, this city belonged to her, as if she easily held it and all its problems in the palm of her hand.

Bek loved her. Bek had wanted her at first sight, even when she was a scrumbling, bumbling, know-nothing girl who had not one clue what she was doing. Something desirable showed through from inside her too short, too plump, too freckled, too curly-haired self; something that could appeal to someone as magnificent as Benelek Kruik.

She floated down the path through the woods to her magical, circular, hidden, safe home in the shadow of the pink cathedral. *This city is good. It is all good and it will always be good.*

Even when she got into her house and saw that Reth had left multiple messages, it didn't burst the bubble she was suspended in. She could deal with anything that came at her. This bubble was unpoppable.

She undressed, each layer associated with a specific memory of her time with Bek. She climbed into bed naked and fell asleep immediately.

Despite her late night, Aza woke early, momentarily unsettled about where she was. *The Round Cottage. Bek. Bubble. Life is good.* She moved her body sensuously between the sheets, rolled onto her belly and touched herself while her breasts rubbed against the mattress. She came almost immediately. A long, slow, deeply felt orgasm...and there she lay, face down, arm spread out over the expanse of the bed, grateful for it, for clean sheets, for sheets at all. For Oscera. For whoever built this house. For all the people who built, made, crafted, laundered. For another day and being alive to all this gratitude.

"Thank you," she said softly. "Aza!" she said loudly, rolling over. "You are happy. You have never been happy ever before because you have never felt this way." She not only loved Bek and her friends and her life, but she loved herself as well. Because if someone as amazing as Bek could love her, then she was a far, far superior person to what she had previously believed.

She got up, made her bed, took a bath, and dressed for the day—simply, in the Dal skirt she'd gotten in that used clothing store the day after her father's funeral when she left home for she-knew-not-where. As she looked in the mirror, while tying a scarf around her head, her mind passed over the many ways she'd matured since that day. She spun around, twirling her skirt, laughing at her foolishness. "Some adult you are."

She went into the sunny kitchen but didn't bother to make a fire. She lit the stove, heated water and had cheese and fruit, humming all the while. She had work to do. Responsibilities. Somehow, soon, she must focus, to get back to the harsh realities of current events. She'd gotten none of the answers from Bek that she'd gone there for. But she couldn't find it in herself to care.

All will be well.

After eating, Aza retrieved the messages and took them to the dining table. *Can I do what I need to do feeling this way? It's not a good time for romance, Bek, whatever you say.* But Aza wouldn't have changed one second of what had happened.

Yesterday had been an exhausting, intense, worrisome day. Her alienated but fierce feelings as she entered the Villa as a stranger. The uncensored reprimand she'd delivered to Duma for his snobbery and pride in what was an unearned, privileged status. It was hard to imagine that had been her speaking when she compared herself to how she felt now. *Like two different mes.* A pleasing shiver went through her. Zaz had split when she and Bek were making love, hovering outside her body, showing Aza another view of her lover, both of them admiring Bek, drinking her in.

She stared at the stack of messages.

This beautiful city that I, just last night, held in the palm of my hand, is in deep trouble. Focus! You are full of love-energy. Use it!

The top message was from Reth: *I will be at your service all day tomorrow. Arriving at Round Cottage around nine o'clock unless I hear from you to the contrary.* Aza checked her watch. Not eight yet. Good.

Tomorrow's the funeral.

Did Ferjival even know his mother had died? Surely, by now. He would come back. No matter.

Aza would not be attending.

There were messages from four Gen councilors discussing various points that had been brought up in the meeting, including suggestions about ways to proceed, questions about details of the warned Kruik attack, and—from Maleka's father—one expressing how delightful it was to have her back and hoping she'd consider a permanent position on the council. It brought tears to her eyes. Then again, it wouldn't take much in her highly charged emotional state. She wrote a note to herself to find time for a long visit with both Maleka's parents. There was a message from Eltah with a report on the MATRIA meeting. She set that one aside for a closer look.

The last message was addressed to Zaz Salizan. "Oh!" she exclaimed, delighted. *Who could this be from?* She undid the seal. The paper was full to the margins, covered in a neat, but eccentric handwriting. "Dearest Aza, I hope and trust that this message finds you well. Gerland told me where to direct this letter. It is truly thrilling to have you back in the city again, though it's a major concern that you might still be in danger. I want to see you when you have the time. I know from Eltah that you are expecting trouble from the Kruiks, something along the lines of what we talked about a while ago. It may get dicey for all of us, especially the Gen, eh? Just, please, don't forget about me. Things keep moving along at such a rapid pace—doesn't it seem? I keep thinking that I will have a moment alone with you. A time when we can relax and get to know each other better. I guess I'm missing that day I imagined having when I took the trolley over the bridge to Luftva—that day all hell broke loose. I am looking forward to having that time with you, when this turmoil we're living through is behind us. Or, maybe, before, if possible. I hope you will let me be of service to you, the MATRIA, or in whatever way I might be able to help. I think about you every day. Hoping to see you very soon. — your friend, Vijo."

"Oh," Aza said. *Vijo*. She loved Vijo. Loved him...like a brother. Or she thought she did. On the other hand, she had no reason to think that their relationship would or could ever be anything more than that. He had kept her alive and nursed her back to health, helped her escape, and saved her from being arrested by Ferjival. He had done so much for her, and she hadn't repaid him at all. Not that he would want payment. He liked her. Or maybe he didn't know for sure. Maybe he just—as he said—wanted to get to know her better. But maybe to see if he liked her...as more than just a friend.

The note sat in her lap, her hands limp, her bubble gone. She'd get it back. But life was complicated, and she was already feeling overwhelmed on a day that might prove to become even more difficult.

25

THE CONNECTION

BEK WALKED WITH A hundred other people up the steps of the Tapinak wondering where Aza's cottage was. She hadn't talked to her since...night before last. Things had been too crazy. Aza had sent her a message. All sunshine and hearts. Bek smiled at the thought and wondered if, in acting on impulse and passion, she'd gotten in over her head. Aza was young and inexperienced. Bek loved her dearly, but...well, time for that later. Right now, she had to focus on the crisis about to erupt.

Today, it would all be set in motion. Bek and Havah had leaned on the councilors until Havah had almost dropped from exhaustion, but the real problem was that the councilors weren't the ones who would spread the curses. They weren't even giving the orders. They'd long ago farmed out the authority, so they could passively step aside with a nod to those hungry for revenge.

Bek knew those people. She had been one of them. Part of what had kept her so busy over the last few weeks was her efforts to calm them down. She'd taken out one by sending in a MATRIA member to seduce him. It wasn't quite as sleazy as it sounded, even in her own head. The two knew and liked each other. It was more a showing-up-at-the-right-time, and being-really-persuasive situation. But for all she knew, this fellow had passed along his targets to someone else. It was all truly out of her control.

She hated that.

Bek caught the eyes of MATRIA members here and there in the crowd.

Aza would not be here. Bek wondered about Ferjival. She had sent a message to Reva. The response was that Ferjival had left before they heard about Mam Sior's death. Ferjival hinted to Eguin that he was going to take his time getting back to Maripesa. Bek sighed. Another thing that Aza wouldn't be forgiven for. Though, maybe Ferjival wasn't important anymore. That was a rare happy thought.

She nodded at Carmista, a Salizan woman with a powerful talent for Patterning. She had done some amazing demonstrations of her abilities when they were all still meeting at Karol's. There'd been a long discussion about an as-yet untested theory of chaining their Talents for a more powerful effect.

Bek finally got into the nave. The huge space was filled with rows of occupied chairs facing the inside of the temple, toward the elaborate gold and rich wood altar. The front rows to halfway down were a mass of purple. The Puraples Clan out in full force with all their finery on display. The Kruiks filled rows behind them, but they weren't *en masse,* and as people worked their way in there were smatterings of all clan clothing.

That's the kind of Maripesa I like. All of us mixed together.

She found a seat just as the music, which had been processioning them forward, stopped. Without it swelling, the crowd noises made it seem like a city street rather than a sacrosanct space. Everyone must have thought so because the drone of voices softened. Now Bek could see the casket, ostentatious even by Puraples' standards.

Of course, Mam Sior. Even after death.

The Tchuvari—one on each side of the platform—began, even before everyone had found a seat. There would not be enough chairs. The crowd, coming in from behind, moved up the side aisles until they were even with the Puraples' rows, but came no closer. When they stopped, the people near the doors continued to press in.

People are pressed too tightly. She spotted Carmista again. The woman looked about halfway to panic.

The music started up again. They were meant to be silent while the casket lowered to the altar, but just then, the massive, two-story doors they'd all come through closed, with a slow but powerful whoosh of air.

Those nearest the doors squealed as they were almost caught in the push. The space darkened and the Tchuvari who'd been conducting the service looked up and toward the back. Soon, the diffused glow that always seemed to emanate from the walls of the building intensified, lighting the space.

One of Mam Sior's relatives—Bek, distracted by what was going on behind her, hadn't heard who—began a eulogy.

One of many, likely.

Where Bek was seated, people could barely hear. There was a drone of noise from the unseated people behind her. When the first woman finished, another clan member got up and droned on about the great woman that the city had lost. Conversations started up nearby. Then, during the pause between speakers, a woman stood in the row just behind the gathered Puraples Clan.

Dressed in all black, she climbed onto her chair, raised her fist, and shouted, "Sior killed my daughter!" A collective gasp arose.

"Sior killed my daughter. Sior killed my daughter."

A Puraples man pulled at the woman's legs, but she seemed to be rooted in a solid state. *Through force of will,* Bek thought. *Passion and desperation and grief, not magic.* Then, two men grabbed her from behind and toppled her. That didn't stop her voice, however. Though now muffled, "Sior killed my daughter," was still being heard.

She was silenced, by what means Bek couldn't know.

Another voice rose up. Bek turned to see a woman in black on the shoulders of a similarly dressed tall man standing near the back. She shouted, "You cannot silence everyone who had relatives executed by this vile woman. We thank *Maripes* that Sior Puraples is dead! Death to the Purples! Death to those who condone summary executions! Death to the Purples!"

A contingent of Puraples security rose from chairs near the front and roughly shouldered their way through the packed aisle. When they met resistance, they openly threatened people with a curse.

At that, most let them pass, but fear spread faster than magic and by the time they reached the row Bek sat in, the screaming woman told the man whose shoulders she was on to get them out of harm's way. He backed up against the doors. Normally they swung easily in either direction, opening at the slightest touch despite their size and bulk. But that did not happen. The man shoved with his shoulder while the woman reached forward with both hands, pushing against them. Nothing happened. Others joined in. The doors didn't budge.

Bek, standing now, could see and hear the panic spread: ripples of shrill voices, swiveling heads, rising bodies, reaching arms.

One of the Tchuvari spoke from behind Mam Sior's suspended coffin, their words extending to the farthest reaches of the nave. "People of Maripesa! Do not fear. We are safe here. The cathedral is warded. No curses can be cast within these walls. Do not panic."

Bek wondered if the Puraples' security knew that. Probably. They would be counting on the fact that those they wanted to intimidate didn't know or would forget in the heat of the moment. Three security men reached those trying to open the huge doors. The protesting man lowered the woman from his shoulders, stood in front of her, and punched the first Puraples to reach him in the face, knocking him to the ground. Everyone near them stood, stunned for a second, before the other two security men moved in, wrenching the man's arms behind him and cursing him with words, if not magic. The woman started shouting, "Killers, killers, killers all!"

Someone closer to the front yelled to the Tchuvari, "Keepers, why won't the doors open?"

"We will have them opened soon. Do not panic. Do not worry." Music swelled around them and Bek watched helplessly, while the Puraples Clan were herded out of the nave by a side door near the altar.

Vijo arrived late. He'd been undecided about whether to come to the funeral. When he finally chose to, everything that could have delayed him, did. He might as well have stayed away. But he was curious, not about what would be said about the woman, but who would come and what kind of mood would dominate.

One of his delays had been a sweet note from Aza. He had it now in the breast pocket of his jacket, a rectangle of warmth emanating from it. Perhaps she'd blessed it; perhaps it was his fertile imagination. She hadn't said anything that personal, but it was simply good to be in touch with her again. She'd told him where her house was. That had pushed him to get out of the house and to the cathedral grounds.

There, crowds of people converged, walking on the pathways, in the gardens, and—he saw as he emerged from the wooded trail he'd walked in on—streaming up the wide steps. He joined them.

Almost immediately, he heard a shout and then two, or maybe three, voices raised in what seemed like a cheer. A young man ran up past him and when he neared the double doors, yelled, "A Kruik curse on the soul of Sior Puraples!" His declaration was followed by several others.

Vijo ran, but by the time he could gather speed and reach the top step, the curse had been delivered and was already spreading. Fast. Abnormally fast. Not that he'd had direct contact with that many growing flux attacks. But he had made it his business to study all magic and...this wasn't normal.

Bek's warnings. A Kruik weapon.

A sickly green-grey moving flux spread half-way up the crack between the two doors. It was also multiplying up the sides as if to seal them. Vijo stood transfixed, along with most of the other people, and watched as the renyers—or whatever vermin this was—spread, coating the outer doors of the Tapinak.

Pulling himself from the mesmerizing sight, he looked around. The Kruik who cursed the building had fled. *But where? Maybe they went into the cathedral by another entrance.* It would be easy to disappear in the huge building and eventually find a way out on the other side. Vijo said to no one in particular, "Let's look for another way in!"

He turned to the left of the massive doors, staying clear of the grainy ooze that now almost covered them. A walkway stretched along the perimeter of the building.

Someone behind him said, "You go this way. I'm going to see what's on the other side."

Another voice said, "Let's find those bastards."

Vijo continued and soon found a recessed alcove at the back of which was a normal-sized door. He ran to it, realizing that there were several other men behind him. He pulled on the handle.

Locked.

"Damn!"

The man behind him said, "Let me have a look at that."

Another added, "At least it's not cursed, bud."

The first one voiced agreement and said, "I'll have it opened in no time."

As the man worked, Vijo went back toward the cathedral entry. Now that he'd had time to think about it, it wasn't likely the Kruiks had gone into the Tapinak. The door was locked. On the other hand, they could have locked it after entering, ensuring that they wouldn't be followed. But he was more worried about what might be happening inside the nave. *Did the funeral-goers inside have any idea what had occurred?*

Outside, the crowd had doubled. They stood, taking in the growing horror that now completely covered the doors and was inching its way over the polished pink stone of the cathedral itself.

It was nauseating.

Vijo heard a shout and ran back to the door. The fellow had picked the lock. He and his compatriot were already running down the narrow corridor. Vijo followed at a slower pace. Soon, the other two were out of sight.

He had some familiarity with the cathedral, though he'd never been in this section. The central nave, where he wanted to go, was to his right. The first chance he got, he took a corner going that direction.

Good. This hallway was wider. Up ahead, he saw a Tchuvari. He said, "Excuse me? Hello?" but the person ducked into a doorway. Either they hadn't heard or seen him or they didn't want to. He found a room labeled *Vestments. Getting closer.* He came to a three-way intersection and halted, trying to decide.

Stopping for that moment allowed him to hear...something. Not sounds he would have expected of a state funeral, but many voices, shouting, crying out. He went straight. At the end, he chose right and suddenly there he was, behind the podium; stage left to the funeral of Mam Sior. Her massive casket hung in mid-air, half-lowered, hovering over its clearly intended position on a raised platform surrounded by dramatic arrangements of plants and flowers—most of them shades of purple. He looked around the corner and saw pandemonium.

Half the people were struggling down the aisles away from the doors and half were pushed up against them, trying to get them open. He spotted Benelek standing amid the chaos.

Running up the ornate wooden steps onto the stage where the Tchuvari Keepers would ordinarily stand, he said as loud as he dared, "Benelek!"

She turned, trying to locate where the voice had come from.

He waved his hands. When she finally saw him, she smiled, looking relieved. She started his way through the now-empty chairs. Vijo hopped off the stage next to the dais that was to have held the coffin and met up with her.

"Where did you come from?"

"I was late. Bek, the doors—"

"Oh, we know. That's part of what caused the riot. Not part of the plan, I was told, but they seem to be locked. Or stuck or—"

Vijo shook his head vigorously. "You don't know?"

"What?"

"Cursed. And in a dramatic way. I've never seen anything like it."

Bek's usually glistening skin greyed.

"In minutes, it took over the doors and is spreading rapidly over the building."

Bek put her hand to her forehead and rubbed. She staggered slightly, and Vijo took her arm.

"It's all right," he said.

"No," she whispered. "It really isn't."

Aza sat on the stone patio near the front door, sketching for the first time since she'd been back from Luftva. She was trying to capture the view of the Tapinak spire behind the thick stands of trees between her cottage and the cathedral building when she looked up and saw Reth coming down the path. She had asked him to go to the funeral to be her eyes and ears, so she was surprised to see him here long before she would have expected the service to be over. Then she realized he was practically running.

She went to meet him. "What is it?"

"Come. We need you. The sanctuary doors are closed and locked. Most of the Purples have gone, led out through other exits by the Tchuvari, but before that...Aza...people rose up and called them out on their executions. Puraples security started after them. It's chaos."

Aza looked down at the simple clothes she had put on this morning—not suitable for going into the cathedral—but no matter. She grasped Reth's arm. "Let's go."

The nearest entry was on a lower level than the Grand Nave. Aza followed, letting Reth retrace his recent steps. He soon had them going up a double set of stairs and into the choir entrance. It was deserted, but from here she saw the nave floor, filled with disarray, chairs overturned, and people wild with fear, panic, and rage. Puraples' security was still here in force—and force they were using against anyone who got in their way—as if punishing others for the death of their leader.

Aza descended the winding steps to the podium. Her heart leapt at seeing Bek near the stage just below her. And Vijo! She knew from one of Oscera's tours that the acoustics were designed to make one's voice carry from this spot. She cried out, softly, "Bek, Vijo," and they turned at once. Looking relieved, they started toward the steps.

Before they could get there, Aza shouted, "MATRIA!" Her voice carried to the corners. Many looked up, but only a fraction knew what she meant, so it was soon obvious who her people were.

Some stood on their chairs. Others walked to open spaces, set apart where they could be seen.

Vijo and then Bek reached her. She looked at them, not knowing what to think or feel, but at the same time, knowing exactly what to do. Whether it would make a difference or not, remained to be seen. With her eyes on the women standing tall, she shouted, "Work your connections!"

Vijo whispered, "Aza, security has spotted you. You must leave."

Her heart jumped, but she looked away from him and gave her orders. "Focus on Puraples security! You can do this."

In the passage of those brief moments, her women, her friends, the MA-TRIA, spread themselves so that a rough pattern emerged with no more than a body length separating any of them. None of them knew if the attempt to chain their Talents would work. They had been talking about it since the days at Karol's, but it was no more than a theory.

Aza spotted Eltah, Karol, and Rimna! And where Rimna was, Ness couldn't be far behind. *There, there she is.* On a chair toward the back corner on the last row. Ness was a powerful Leaner. Maybe the most powerful. Practically glowing, she—even with her small frame—stood as firm and solid as a statue of a goddess. From her—Aza could feel it—the connection began to flow from one woman to the next.

Aza sensed the links happening and spreading out from either side of Ness. She found faces she knew even if the names hadn't been committed to memory.

"Bek, do you see?" But when Aza turned around, Bek had vanished.

Vijo, his cheeks pink, skin pale, looked surprised as well. "Where did she go?"

"I don't know, but she...she's missed...this." It was working. She turned back to the sanctuary. Calm radiated from the MATRIA grid. Some women had their eyes closed, others stood as naturally as if on a street corner, looking around, with pleased expressions. Some held their arms out as if to feel and extend the magic.

The violence paused. Some guards walked up the side aisles, filing out slowly, no emotion on their faces. A handful of others must have been the target of some close range, pointed Leaning because their expressions showed utter disorientation. Those people who had been manhandled were also stunned, but since no one was bothering them, and the panic had dissipated, they stood, straightened their clothes, whispered to their neighbors and checked themselves for injuries.

"Come on," Vijo said. "Let's show people the way out."

"Yes," Aza said, tears in her eyes. "Our first MATRIA magic in public. I need to join it."

By the end of the day, the devastation was apparent to all Maripesians.

There had been many more targets than the symbolic one, the Tapinak. It was now common knowledge that, while the cathedral was warded against curses inside, it was most definitely not on the outside. Encircling it was a widening grey-green ring of what the populace was already calling The Spread.

Aza tucked away new knowledge that Tchuvari wards did not hold sway over MATRIA magic. She would explore that later. For now, the city was at a standstill.

Aza and Oscera were at the Round House trying to figure out next steps.

"How can they expect to gain the trust of the citizens by befouling the city this way?" Aza asked.

Oscera scoffed. "They don't care about the citizenry."

The nearby Council of Clans building where the Synod met was covered roof to basement in the scourge—unusable until an entrance could be cleaned. It was likely that the curse was growing inside too, through door and window cracks.

But this and other building targets weren't even on the priority list for clean-up because Kruiks had, in coordinated attacks, struck most of the trolleys in the downtown core, including the one across the Strait of Jeka. Coaches and Messagery bicycles were targeted as well. In less than a day, the Kruiks had immobilized the city.

After helping get people out of the Tapinak, Aza had worked her non-magic connections to set up two separate headquarters in the cathedral—one for the MATRIA, and the other for the Gen, who needed a command center to operate from. She felt proud of how much preliminary work they'd done to be ready, even though no one had imagined it would be this extreme.

Oscera paced. "The very idea that one gains control by engendering trust would be foreign to them. They are trying to bring down the Puraples by ruining *them*. The rest of us are inconsequential. Bystanders, nothing more."

"Then they're only showing themselves as anachronisms—as bad as the Purples. Those women who stood in the sanctuary, exposing themselves to the power and cruelty of the ruling family, and protesting the sanctioned murder of their family members, they are the future. Maripesa is changed. Have you ever heard of such public behavior?"

"No. Well, yes...but not in generations."

"We're going to be seeing a lot of it. Have you heard what's happening with the Puraples?" She was worried about another outbreak of giarmial.

Oscera shook their head. "So far, we hear only of personal attacks on Kruiks. Vijo reported in from the Noptva clinic. He's been working non-stop, but no giarmial yet."

"Duma reports similar personal Kruik attacks on Puraples. How charming. Our city has devolved into hand-to-hand combat."

"How are the Gen going to tackle the broader problems?"

Aza sighed. "One doorway, engine, gear, or spoke at a time. Our plans seem to change hourly. There's a meeting soon. I should go." She looked up at Oscera, whose expression showed sad compassion.

"Do I look that bad?" Aza asked with an unfelt smile.

Oscera laughed softly. "Not at all. I just know how beset you are by people needing your counsel."

"It does seem that way. I don't know when—or how—that happened. As I told you at our first meeting, I am not important."

"Stop that."

"I'm serious. I'm—oh hells, it doesn't matter. All this would be so much worse if I didn't know what was happening. I would hate that. That's always been my thing, you know?"

"What?"

"Being a snoop. I 'sat in' on Gen Council meetings without actually being in the room. I eavesdropped on the Purples the whole time I lived in their house.

Oh. I just thought of something. Has anyone checked on the Komeh? Seems like that would be a major target."

"*We* can do a little snooping as well."

"Great. On the other hand, who really cares, right?"

As she gathered up the papers she needed, said goodbye to Oscera, and took the short walk to the cathedral room where the Gen had their working group, Aza thought of those she had worked with at the Komeh. What would happen to them if the Purples were no longer the ruling family? Would they still have jobs? She couldn't imagine that household without Mam Sior's firm hand. Or without Ferjival's limp ones. As useless as he always had been, he was more capable than the other siblings. Not that it had to be someone from Mam Sior's direct line to head up the clan. *That's probably what will happen; some other branch of the family will be waiting in the wings to pounce on the head position...rather like*—she walked into the Gen Room—*Duma had been.*

He sat toward the end of the long table facing the doorway, papers, maps and messages and councilmen in a messy swirl around him. He had taken off his jacket, his sleeves rolled up, though he still wore his gloves. Aza looked down at her own hands, uncovered. The Gen had a complicated relationship with their gloves.

She sighed. *We are all going to be up to our elbows in vermin soon, so gloves it will be.* She took a pale coral pair out of her apron pocket, put them on while she walked in, and went to work.

Ferjival walked in the front door of his home.

It was late afternoon of a cold, dreary day, but the lamps were unlit and no fire glowed in the hearths on either side of the massive room. His booted footsteps echoed.

He was filthy and exhausted, for he'd come all the way from Luftva Village where he'd retrieved his horse from that Pats fellow. That had been an awkward, though ultimately peaceful, exchange. The man showed a lot of decency, if not forgiveness, toward him. It was the farrier who informed him that his mother was dead.

It was good to be reunited with his horse. Ferjival rode him up the coast and across the older, smaller bridge to the north of the village. The last thing he wanted was to run into someone he knew on a public trolley or coach, and it had been healing to ride Rik again. Rik, who had never crossed his mind in all those weeks Ferjival was imprisoned. He would have to go back to reimburse Pats when he got things straightened out here.

But he was *here* now. The Komeh felt abandoned. The flowers on the central table were not only funereal lilies; they were actually dead. *What in* Maripes *has happened?* He started to shout for the maid, who normally would have arrived the moment he set foot in the house, but he couldn't remember her name.

He ran up the steps to the third floor where the family bedrooms were. He needed to change clothes. At the closed door of his room, he hesitated. What if they had thought he was dead? Or never coming back. What if they'd cleaned it out? Or someone else had taken it over?

Instead, he walked down the hall and knocked on Hasip's door. No answer. He went to Dusia's, Leona's. No answer, no answer. *No one here.*

Something kept him from ringing for the servants. He thought of Reva, of Eguin, and said under his breath, "I'll make my own damned butter."

Ferjival took the steps to the mezzanine level and down the long hallway to the council chamber.

He hesitated again. He did not want to act out his fantasy and walk in on a room full of clan members.

Zlo, this was hard. So much harder than any part of his imprisonment. And yet, his mother had died. He couldn't just ignore that fact. He had to face this, to see who was to take her place. He knew it wouldn't be him, and he didn't mind. He didn't know what he'd do with his life, but ruling the city of Maripesa didn't interest him anymore. That's one of the few things he did know.

He cracked the heavy door and peeked in.

Ferjival cried out, the sound bouncing off the high ceiling and coming back at him. A gasping sound gargled at the back of his throat. Eyes wide, mouth contorted, he reared back, shutting the door as quickly as possible. He pulled on the latch firmly, needlessly, and then let go, bending down, hands on his knees, trying to understand what he'd just seen. The room—the seat of government of the City of Maripesa—wallpapered in embossed purple, paneled with the finest carved mulhao wood and filled with ornate furniture, was now covered in a slimy, oozing, moving Kruik curse.

"Where is everyone?" he screamed.

"Sir?"

He turned toward the voice behind him. "Who is it?" The growing twilight and lack of lit wall lamps made it almost impossible to see down the passageway. He walked, feeling somewhat comforted that it had to be a servant and not a family member. No member of his family would call him "sir." He could just make out a woman standing next to a table. Then she held up a lantern and walked toward him.

"Why, as I live and breathe, is it Lord Ferjival?"

"Yes," he said. "I've forgotten your name."

"Garnia, sir."

"Of course. Garnia. I apologize. It's been a rather trying day."

"Sir...where have you been? We had no word from you for so very long. Do you know that—?"

"I heard of my mother's death. But I was in the country, so the news didn't get to me before the funeral. Where is everyone? What has happened to" —he slumped slightly, placing a hand over his belly at the thought of the cursed room and pointed his arm back toward it— "the chambers?"

Garnia shook her head back and forth slowly. "*Bosh*. No one should have to see such a thing. Well now, I'll fill you in as far as I can, which won't take long. The Kruiks have cursed the city, full on. It started the day of your mother's funeral. What was that? Three days ago? No, I think it was only two. But..." Her voice trailed away and so did her eyes. They traveled to the floor and stayed there.

"The Kruiks are making their play for power. I see." Garnia's lantern cast an elongated, eerie light as the rest of the space filled with dark. "But...where are our Gen? Why has that" —he pointed again— "been allowed to grow unchallenged?"

"Sir, most of the household help are with their families. It's difficult to get around, what with the trolleys out of commission. I came back at great difficulty today and only through the kindness of a coach driver who charged me very little. I wanted to see to a few things in the kitchen so that a bad situation wouldn't be even worse when this is all over. But, the Gen...sir."

"What?"

"The Gen are full-out working to clean the mess that the Kruiks have made of the city. Your house, I would assume, is not at the top of their list."

26

HAND AND GLOVE

"I CONVINCED THE GEN to stop cleaning anything that directly helps the Puraples," said Aza. She'd invited a core group of the MATRIA, plus Vijo, Gerland, and Oscera over so that they could all compare notes and keep up to date with everyone else. These were the people she trusted the most, not counting Reva and Eguin, who would not have been able to travel into the city.

All my trusted friends, except Bek.

The thought made Aza tear up, so she ruthlessly ordered her mind not to go there. She managed this only because there were so many pressing issues. As bad as things were, she was grateful to be distracted from the pain in her heart.

"We've recalled all the household cleaners and put them to work on larger problems: machines, anything with moving parts or essential to the messaging system, gets the highest priority."

"Are you getting on top of it?" Ness asked.

Aza sighed. "We can't tell yet."

"But," Vijo asked, "does the Gen cure work?"

It had been a huge problem. Bek's warning had come way too late and wasn't specific enough for the Gen to know ahead of time if they had a solution for The Spread, so they had to fight it the old-fashioned way: by trial and error.

"We don't call it a 'cure,' Besin," she said, teasing him. "Our *cleaning* works—now. But initial attempts weren't successful. We knew simple renyer removal spells wouldn't work, so we combined those with the one for dahke and that was better; it took out a lot of smaller infestations. There are at least two layers to the problem. The first is to make sure the wiping treatment is one-hundred percent effective. We certainly don't have the luxury of time to go back and re-clean what's already been done. The second is that not every material reacts in the same way to the curse. Now we know to tailor our efforts to what we're cleaning. We have an extensive set of firsthand reports from our hardworking Gens and can make better guesses based on that. But it's been slow, and for the huge tasks, we're coming up against the third major layer to be figured out. How to clean with something other than—" She held up her forefinger. "Mops and brushes are being manufactured and imbued, but that's a work in progress."

Vijo visibly shuddered. "My greatest sympathies to the Gen. If I can help, let me know how."

"The coaches—all the ones I know anyway," said Gerland, "are back on the road."

"And they are working night and day on the trolleys."

Aza nodded her head vigorously. "That's their priority. But what of the Kruiks?" she said, abruptly changing the subject. "Bek has abandoned us." This came out with more force and bitterness than she intended to reveal, but the general murmurs of agreement that followed must have meant that they felt the same.

"No word?" Vijo asked.

"Not since she disappeared in the cathedral the day of the funeral."

"I will try to find her," he said.

"Oh, don't bother. I understand you have your hands full with the Purples' counter-offensive."

He shrugged. "It's crumbs compared to the epidemic. I have time and want to do more than just routine cures."

"I'm surprised to hear you talk that way," Ness said. "You've always seemed so content with your role."

Aza watched him as he answered Ness, the two of them interacting affectionately. The sun shone on his soft-blond curls—proper, large, loopy curls, not the wiry squiggles that came out of her head. He was an attractive person, no doubt about it. On a level that existed parallel with her outward practical daily functions, she was checking herself, her feelings. It was still no time for romance, but with Bek having left them all, and most especially Aza, she would be stupid not to consider whether she had feelings for Vijo that went beyond friendship.

She admired him. She loved him.

She sighed. That would have to be good enough.

During this conjecture, she missed hearing Vijo's response and now everyone was quiet, waiting for Aza. She took a deep breath and said, "What can our MATRIA do? That's my big unknown. The connection we made in the nave was so much more successful than any of us could have predicted that I want to focus on that. But there's no time."

Karol said, "There's great enthusiasm in the membership. Those who were there and part of the first real MATRIA patterned connection, have spread the word, and it's not only brought in new members but also renewed interest in exploring other options for combining individual talents for newer, wider purposes."

Oscera spoke. "Might we be a part of those meetings?"

Aza and Karol looked at each other. Aza answered, "Of course."

"Now that we've seen your women working in concert, connecting and intensifying their individual talents by linking them to others with similar ones, we can't wait to see where this goes."

Gerland asked, "Am I the only one here who didn't get to experience it?"

They looked around. "I guess so," said Karol. "Even Vijo was in the room."

"Even Vijo?" the healer said, putting on a hurt look. "Yes, even a nobody like Vijo could see that those women took control of that melee. They established a...grid of power. I mean, you couldn't see anything happening—other than women standing tall and very, very focused—but if you knew, like I did, that they were in command of Talents and were working together, you could sense it. I get a tingle remembering the magic in the room. It was easy to see the results. The security men, who were intimidating and roughing people up, just stopped. They stood up and looked around like they'd lost themselves, or lost time, or simply didn't know where they were. The panic dissipated. People started talking softly and looking for misplaced belongings. Someone—was it you, Aza? Someone said, 'Come toward the stage and we'll show you another way out. Everyone is safe.' And they did. End of riot. End of chaos. Done."

"Gerland," Aza said, "Ness was our locus. The absolute source of our connection. She looked amazing and strong and solid and bold, and you would have been so very proud of her."

Ness lowered her head, obviously embarrassed at the praise, but Gerland, glowing with pride, lifted her chin and said, "I've seen that strength every day since I met her. Doesn't surprise me at all."

After the meeting broke up, Aza approached Oscera and said, "Do you have some time? I have a crazy idea I'd like to discuss with you."

"Of course."

"Remember the day we met?"

Oscera nodded, cheeks coloring.

"What if I'd never met you? I've lain awake thinking of all the things that have fallen into place since that day."

"We're sure you could say that of many people. Besides, meeting you was always on our agenda."

Aza wanted to know why. Something about her father. But that would have to wait.

"You took me to the Archives. Could we go there now? I'd like to talk privately, and I think it's the place to do it."

There wasn't a lot of talk on the way, which was fine with Aza, who felt nervous about how Oscera would react to what she had to propose. When they arrived, Aza said, "The soltec display?"

Oscera turned and began walking. Aza caught up and said, "How long has the Tapinak been warded against curses?"

"Oh, since they were devised, we imagine. Why?"

"Who else uses wards?"

Oscera didn't answer. They rounded one more curve and said, "Here we are."

Aza moved forward, looking at the collection: seven soltecs in varying designs and sizes, plus a space for the missing one.

"Do you remember how interested I was in these?"

"Yes. We assumed you had seen one used, perhaps by your father?"

Aza spun around. "You think Leo was the thief?"

"Don't be offended. Someone took it. We could only hope it was someone who used it for the best possible reasons. Leo would have been that kind of person."

Aza shook her head. "I don't know what to say to that. Why he, of all people, would be a suspect? No. The soltec was in the hands of Ferjival Puraples before all this happened."

Oscera said, "The Puraples? We're surprised, only because they seem quite happy to fight fire with fire, so to speak. We thought it would fall into the hands of a citizen who needed the means to ward off an attack of negative magic."

"It was, I believe, a kind of power ploy for him. He nipped it from an elderly relative when he was quite young."

"How do you know?"

"He left it behind in a coach after a spellbattle with a Kruik. I found it—this was before I met you—but I didn't know what it was. Not until you brought me on a tour."

"You had it then? Why didn't you tell us?"

Knowing this question would be asked, Aza had thought through her answer beforehand. "I was too aware of how much I didn't know. I wasn't ready to divulge the fact to anyone. As it turned out, I was right to keep it."

"Not that we doubt it, but why?"

"We used it on Ferjival in the early days of his captivity when he threatened to curse anyone who came within striking distance. The first time I brought it out, he exclaimed, 'Where did you get my soltec?'"

"Oh, ho. An easy confession, eh?"

"Not the most careful of individuals."

"Where is it?"

"I left it with Reva and Eguin."

"The Tchuvari Archivists will be eager to get their hands on it."

"This is what I want to talk to you about."

"What?"

"Wards, soltecs. The average citizen knows almost nothing of them, right?"

"The Tchuvari kept this Talent as their own. We can give you a rundown of the history of why."

Aza waved her hand. "I have the gist of it. Order out of chaos, with the ultimate ability to protect oneself, in the hands of those who created the orderly system. But you brought me in here with the radical notion that the system is broken, right?"

"We did." A tiny smile played on their lips and then disappeared.

"That we must devise a different kind of order. I've been thinking that the MATRIA, magic that cuts across clan lines, was that new way. And it is part of the answer. But we also need to add wards to our plan."

"Not following you."

"Ward power for the citizenry."

"And that means—?"

"You said it: those who have negative magic will always hold power. They've taken our city back into chaos for the second time *this year* because we can't stop them. We only have the power to clean up their messes, not prevent them."

"Oh, Aza dear, it's a closely guarded Talent. You must see that." They stopped, clearly struggling with the idea. "The Keepers of Magic have always protected wards as...as the cure for what can go wrong."

"Clearly, the Tchuvari have not cured what has gone wrong in the last year. The power is in the hands of too few, Oscera."

"We can't ward everything."

"No, but we've had the schooling now, haven't we? First, protect those things that are essential to the working of the city. Trolleys, ships, coaches, printing presses, timepieces. I propose those be warded as a matter of course and be put on a schedule to make sure the protection doesn't erode."

"That's a 'first'? Of how many? Aza, that would take dozens of people working all the time. There are too few of us. We can barely take care of this building!"

Aza could feel her jaw set, thinking of the hundreds of Gen now working all over the city, and the months that the Besin Clan had devoted night and day to healing citizens from giarmial. *Oscera is protected from the realities of life here in their pink stone tower. It is they who are naive.*

Aza willed her face to soften, breathed in gently and let it out, saying, "I've sprung this on you and it's too much too soon. I have no power over the Tchuvari. But you must see how helpful it would have been, when we got warning of this attack a week ago, if we could have called on teams of warders to protect certain essential buildings and transportation hubs. We could have prevented much of this disruption."

"And," Oscera said, softly, staring at the display of soltecs, "*we* are mission-bound to keep Maripesa from falling into chaos." They paused and then angrily said, "We knew we were on the road to ruin! We preached it over and over and nobody here would listen!" Aza touched their forearm and Oscera finally looked her in the eyes, and said, "Of course you're right. It doesn't help with this crisis, but going forward, we must have a plan. We must, somehow, bolster our numbers."

"There's more." Aza gestured toward the display of soltecs. "My second proposal: make more. Give them to the middle and lower clans. We must have the ability to protect ourselves. Don't you see? If we had the ability to stop a spell or a curse, then we could live our lives doing what we wish, what we are good at, instead of cleaning up the curses and spells of the ruling families! They couldn't lord their punishments over us!"

Oscera held Aza's eyes, but slowly began to shake their head back and forth. "It won't work. We can't make one of these for everyone. We can't have a society where people wear these around their necks like jewelry. We...we—" The word caught in their throat. Oscera cleared it, and said, "We would be a society of suppressed magic."

For a long moment, Aza regarded this person she admired for so many reasons, and then she turned away. It *was* an emptying thought. A society whose very structure rests on interdependent magical abilities suddenly turns into a society like the rest of those in the world. A world without magic.

She walked a few steps and then turned. In spite of this stark vision of the future, she would proceed. Looking at Oscera in the dim glow of the walls of the Tapinak, she still believed that this could work if the Tchuvari were on board. That wouldn't be easy. More than anyone in this society, they lived their mission of keeping Maripesa magical. It was not what they did, but who they were. And of course the Puraples and the Kruiks would fight this. The most powerful would be against it. This change she envisioned wouldn't be quick. Perhaps it needed to proceed beneath the surface. She took a deep breath and let it out.

"Is the process by which soltecs were made still known?"

"Someone knows it. Not me."

"Who?"

"Aza..."

"*You invited me in.* I want what you want. To make Maripesa better. I'm not going to push you on a 'soltec in every hand.' I see that's too much too soon. But at the least, while we are in crisis, the Tchuvari must work with the Gen to ward what we have struggled so hard to clean. Can you help me with that?"

Oscera stood up taller, regaining their composure with a change of posture. "It's the least we can do. We apologize that we didn't think of it. Truly, we need you more than we knew...to help us change in positive ways. We will meet with the appropriate persons today."

"Good. And perhaps you should let them think it was your idea."

Oscera laughed, but Aza heard the strain in their voice when they said, "We worry about your drive to make change happen fast, Aza, but...we're patient with you and that impulse, maybe because—" The woman grimaced, struggling to hold back emotions. Once under control, Oscera said, "Because we didn't always make the best decisions in our younger years." They looked at her with transparent anxiety.

I am about to find out the real reason I was always on Oscera's "agenda."

"Is there something you need to tell me?"

"Yes. We don't know how. We— *I*...have a lot of...shame about...all this. Did Leo give you things that belonged to your mother?"

Aza eyed her warily. "I got them after he died."

"There was a journal?"

Aza's heart sped up. "Yes."

"We hope you can find it in your heart to forgive us, but that journal was written by us, not by your mother."

Aza winced and turned away.

Oscera spoke rapidly. "Your father asked us to write something that would be good for you to read after you grew up. Something that would inspire you and give you confidence that you had a mother you could be proud of. His attempt to give you something honorable to hold onto as you continued through life while in the dark about the rest of this."

Aza's mouth dropped open. *An honorable lie?* Another one of so many. She shook her head as if to clear it, but that did nothing to sort the jumble of half-truths and emerging tidbits about her early days. "You must have found it a very strange request," Aza finally said, her mouth dry. "Who is Arja Salizan?"

"Where did you hear that name?"

"It was written in the journal."

Oscera shook their head and said, "We forgot about that. Arja is our given name."

"You said you were Gen!"

Oscera paled except for pink rising up their neck. "We are. Writing our given name in the journal was a clumsy attempt to make a future link with you. We told you we were foolish. But even then, we feared the chaos this beginning would mean for you. Salizan was our best guess of your mother's clan. Without evidence, by the way. Your father wouldn't talk about her."

"You never met my mother?"

"No! We knew only that she was not Gen. But...there's more." Oscera took a deep breath and said, "Put yourself there, Aza. He couldn't marry and live with your mother, right? He also couldn't suddenly have a child with no wife. You would have been immediately identified as Undone. So Leo promised to get us into the Tchuvari Clan if we pretended, for a time, to be his wife and the mother of his child."

"I asked if you were my mother!"

"We are not."

"That would have been an extremely good time to tell me all of this!"

"You had no idea that you were half-clan at our first meeting. How could that be our story to tell? No. That was your father's responsibility. We don't apologize for that, but this deal with Leo was a choice we made. It was our way out of an impoverished existence. And...and we *helped* you and Leo. We may have kept you both alive. We're sorry not to have been honest with you, but *he* had to be honest with you first."

"This all explains my impulsive question about whether you are my mother. On some primal level, I remembered you. Is it possible?"

"You were so little."

"I need some order to all this. Did I live with my mother first before she died? Did Leo take me after her accident?"

Oscera gave her a pleading look and shook their head slowly. "We do not know exactly when your mother died, but we assumed it was in childbirth."

"What? No."

Oscera ignored her and said, "Our 'marriage' lasted almost three years. You were close to newborn when we all moved into the Villa. It was a new neighborhood for Leo. He hired nannies and wet nurses. Aza, we were only a friend to, and conspirator with, your father, not a lover. Soon after Reth was added to the staff, we faked our death in a horse-riding accident, entered the Tchuvari Clan and changed our name." Oscera paused. When Aza didn't speak, they said, "The city, my dear Aza, is full of such charades."

Reeling and bitterly angry, Aza stared at the thoughtful, strong, intelligent person in front of her and wished that Oscera/Arja could have been her mother. It would be good to have a living relative to vent her fury on.

So many lies.

Cause of death: a horse-riding accident—a quick, simple phrase. One a small child could understand, latch onto, tell other people, hold as truth. One that no one could or would question. An essential part—perhaps the easiest part of all—of a well-planned, well-executed charade. It all fit, like hand to glove.

Aza touched the stone wall to steady herself as Leo's deathbed ramblings became newly important. She remembered little else than being told she wasn't Gen. But he talked of Sior. Several times. Leo feared her absolute power with his dying breaths. Leo's bargain gave him his life, the life of his child, and a lifetime of being under Sior's thumb.

So that's it then: Sior executed my mother.

27

HELPERS

Vijo spotted Bek emerging from the Kruik Clan headquarters. He walked toward her.

"Is this a coincidence?" she asked, giving him a hug.

"No. I've been waiting for you."

"You're brilliant, darling. What's up?"

"Aza's worried about you. For starters."

"Worried? About what?" Her hand went into her jacket pocket and began fidgeting with something.

"You disappeared rather precipitously during the funeral chaos, and no one's heard from you since. Aza called a meeting at the cottage this morning. We could have used you there as our only link to the Kruiks. Could you at least have written to decline? Politeness, you know."

Her green eyes squinted at him. "Do not scold me. I am, as you all would know if you thought about it for two seconds, busy. The council is meeting almost nonstop. As far as Aza...well, she's in charge of the MATRIA, but not the rest of us. I have my own responsibilities. You were at the meeting? I thought it was just her...group."

"Did you and Aza have a falling out?"

Bek laughed dismissively.

"Why is that funny?"

"Why am I in trouble with you? I have an existential crisis on my hands and you're here treating me like a wayward schoolgirl. I— I don't know what to say. Here's the deal: dear, sheltered Aza—who *is* like a schoolgirl—and I had the opposite of a falling out a night or two before that disaster of a funeral. We made love. It was great. Wonderful. We both needed it in the worst way."

This news was not exactly a surprise to Vijo. Aza hadn't told him any details, but it was obvious something had happened between them. Nonetheless, the fact that it was sex and not just a gradual, growing intimacy took him aback.

He immediately began to self-correct. *You are an idiot if you didn't see this. It isn't as if Bek is known for her caution or excellent impulse control.*

Bek looked away from him, took a breath and started talking again, more slowly. "I assume, considering all the messages she's sent since, that she had the impression I was going to spend the rest of my days as her—I don't know—shadow? I am doing what I was doing before that happened between us. Right? You can see that, can't you? Not like we were in close contact before. I'm trying to take control of the Kruik Council—for the good of all, frankly.

"Only now, because of the disaster we've made of this coup, I have to do it quickly instead of gradually. So. I'm busy. Consumed. Please deliver that message to Aza. I'll be in touch when this all settles out, but likely not before. In fact, here..." She reached inside her leather bag strapped over one shoulder and pulled out a message card. "Turn around so I can write on your back."

Vijo didn't move fast enough, so she twisted him by the shoulders, placed the card on his upper back and wrote on it. "There. Want to read it? No? I don't care. Sorry to treat you like a Messagery boy, but really, Vijo, you're all tripping over each other to act like her servants. Who made her boss? What has she ever done? She almost died, she...she put together this idea of the MATRIA and that's great. Good for her. Full marks. But it doesn't mean we all work for her! Find *your* life, Vijo, and stop mooning over her."

What's happening to her?

Sure, Bek was opinionated, brash, uncaring of what other people thought of her. But not uncaring. She'd always spoken of Aza in glowing, affectionate terms and her speech, in general, had an element of humor. *That's what softens her. What makes her overwhelming personality tolerable.* This sarcasm and disdain for both of them was worrying.

Bek said, "For the record—and please pass this on to *our* friends—I'm going to turn this whole crisis around. I'm going to get the rogues under control. I'm going to have them join a 'sub-committee' so I can keep a thumb on them. No more transportation woes. No more citizens' lives being disrupted by Kruiks. We target Puraples until they are as aware as the rest of us that they are no longer in charge of this city. Once the Kruiks are in charge, then...then—" She held up the message to Aza and foisted it into Vijo's hand. "Then maybe it'll be a good time for romance."

Vijo looked down at the card. When he looked up, she was walking away.

She glanced back over her shoulder and said, "Or maybe just a good time. I love ya, Besini."

❦

Bek flicked the corner of the card in her jacket pocket as she paced the council chambers. It was an old message from Aza. She kept it there as a distraction. Right now, she had to do what she could to refrain from screaming at the old men on the council who would not listen to reason. Screaming would not help. Answering Aza would not help. She felt like a caged wildcat.

And they always snap at some point, don't they?

She had a plan, but they weren't listening. And Havah, her MATRIA partner, wasn't here today. She and half the other members hadn't shown up.

"We won't take any action," Rodjo said, in a tremulous voice that ran up and down Bek's spine like cold fingers. "Until the majority of the council can arrive."

"Leader," Bek said, her voice tight, but not loud or disrespectful. She looked at the recording secretary and got a nod from her in return. Bek wanted this recorded, even if—especially if—the rest of the council members weren't here. "Inaction isn't an option. Kruiks are out there throwing about curses as if they were candy. We must condemn this and get them under control. Do you agree?" She ended the sentence with a huge smile and a positive tone; it had worked in the past.

"Oh, I totally agree that the youngsters have made things worse."

"We don't know how to control them," said Metin, one of the other two councilmen there. Evidently, his vocabulary was mainly made up of: *I don't know, we can't, it won't, they shouldn't.*

She nodded at him, still smiling, and said, "We know the dilemma. We can't take official action because people can't get here because our own people screwed up the transportation and messaging system. We must get those things working again. I know some Gen. I can get them to help us."

"Gen work for the Puraples."

Maddening. "In this case," she said, "they must work for us since our people went overboard and have hurt our ability to move about the city—as well as everyone else's."

Bek thought about the Talent to Lean that Havah wielded so well. She knew MATRIA talents could sometimes be honed with practice, and she had been working on it. She just didn't believe it yet—not in herself. It was worth a try though, just in case, because she needed this more than she'd ever needed anything.

"From all my accounts," said Councilman Wilklo, the last of the five people in the room, "the Puraples are shut down as well. The Komeh's abandoned and their council hasn't even met. It was a stroke of genius befouling their chamber."

"We can all agree on that," Rodjo said.

Havah had told Bek that she went into a different "space" when she Leaned, that it was magic, not confidence, but that they felt similar. Bek fantasized that different space—a space within—and conjured up as much confidence as she could, which was considerable, of course. She was, after all, still Benelek Kruik.

"Yes!" she said, brightly. "I simply need a nod of approval, Leader Rodjo, Councilors Wilklo and Metin."

She slowed her speech and pointed all of her will at Rodjo. "The decision will be temporary until the full council meets." She nodded slowly. Rodjo moved his head slightly, following her movements. She felt a little...sparkle radiating through her. "Put me in charge of getting this crisis under control. Temporarily." Something was...building. Turning to Wilklo, she said, "Help me help you. It's temporary." To Metin, she said, "I will have the backing of the council to intervene in the disaster we've been left holding. It will help all of us."

Bek literally leaned on the table as she focused on each councilor in turn, making eye contact, doing her best to slip into and stay in that "different space." They said nothing. All watched her. "I want control of this council for the next week. Nod your heads if you agree."

She straightened up to give the recording secretary full view of the three of them nodding.

"Got that, hon?"

"Yeah. How'd you do that?"

Bek spread her arms palms up, gave a little shrug and said simply, "Magic."

Fifteen showed up.

Bek knew where to find the ringleaders of the little suckers...the young people who had gone on a cursing spree since the funeral: The Wardrobe, where, fortuitously, she was practically a legend. Earlier, she had told every under-aged kid she could find to spread the word to anyone in their crowd who'd been a part of the "lesson" they'd delivered to the Purples to "Meet me at the Wardrobe tonight around midnight."

She bought them all drinks as they grouped tables together to form a mismatched whole. A few other people might be coming in and out, but the word needed to spread, so if anyone happened to eavesdrop, that wouldn't bother Bek at all.

"We have to finish what we started. I am officially a Kruik Council member now. But, boys and girls, let me tell you that doesn't mean that I'm like the rest of them. They are old school; I am new. Shiny and new. That's why I wanted to meet with you. The Kruiks have, in less than a week, brought Maripesa to its knees."

A cheer rose from them.

Waiting for them to calm down, she noted that she'd have to shear off the six girl-types later to see if they had any matriarchal Talents. Either way, they might have more sense than the rest of these hoodlums.

"The Gens are working flat-out to clean up our messes, but that does not mean you and your friends should re-curse what's been cleaned. Do you hear me on this one?" she asked, eyebrows fully arched.

"But why?" a fellow with a shock of bright red hair sticking out from under his cap asked. "If it's worked so well, then why not more?"

"Glad you asked." She stood, leaned her hands on the table, and made eye contact with as many as possible. "What's our end game?" When no one answered immediately, she said, "Well?"

"To take control from the Purples," one of her girls said.

"To be the ruling clan," said another.

"Exactly. The purpose, please note, is not to piss off every other clan. Is it?"

"No," said red hair, "but we want them to know that we have power over them, don't we?"

"Of course, but you have to think about where we want to get to as soon as possible! We've already accomplished what you are thinking of as 'the end.' But it's not the end, it's the middle. We've gotten to the middle thanks to all of you! And as soon as we're done here, it'll be another round of drinks for you all because every person in this big wide city now knows that we have power over them. You shut down the city!"

Bek threw up her hands in a victory pose. They all cheered. Others in the bar were paying attention now. She leaned in again and in a loud but conspiratorial voice said, "*We* must act as one to accomplish the rest. Are you all with me?" She got nods all around. They were in the palm of her hand, and she hadn't even attempted to use magic. But maybe it was coming more easily. Maybe she was. "*We* are going to leave off the cursing of *all* the broad targets. No more buildings used by the public. No more transportation. No more Messagery bikes or coaches. Got it? I know that's fun, but we're not playing, are we? We are serious. What's the end goal?"

"To be in power!" one gal said, and then the others joined in.

When they settled down, another one said, "Do you mean we can't do curses anymore?"

"Who do we want to defeat?"

"The Purples."

"Then, target the Purples." She nodded at each one as she made eye contact. "That's your motto. No collateral damage. You may use your imagination within that assignment, but be careful with businesses. This will take some finesse. In fact, are any of you good at research? Like analyzing things? How about you?" She turned to the girl on her left who hadn't said much but seemed to be simmering with passion. "What's your name?"

"Leti."

"You are in charge of this. No one curses a business unless Leti approves it. Leti, you have your work cut out for you, because you have to determine what Puraples businesses we can disrupt without disrupting the rest of the citizens. Find out what services are duplicated. Both the Purples and the Kruiks have distilleries, for example. She held up her drink as if to toast. "Getting rid of the Purples' product would just mean that people might have to change brands, but they wouldn't go thirsty, would they?"

Leti nodded vigorously. "I get it. Target only businesses that will hurt the Puraples, not anyone else."

Bek gave her a beaming smile. "How did I know you'd be a natural?" She turned to the rest of them and said, "In the meantime, while Leti is doing her research, the rest of you lay off Puraples' businesses and just target the Purples themselves. Their homes, maybe a private car here and there, and their bodies. And remember: the Gen are not our enemies. Only the Purples. Got it?"

They got it.

28

A FANTASY COME TRUE

FERJIVAL MADE HIS RETURN known. It had been a rough week, with each step humiliating and painful. But he was beginning to understand that pain can be borne more easily if one expects and accepts it as inevitable.

People reacted in individual ways, but not one person treated him with the kindness that Reva and Eguin had shown him every day. His family, whom he now could see with an outside perspective, were cut from the same cloth as he was. None came by kindness naturally.

He had clarity about one thing: he wanted kindness in his life again. It was, in fact, his only goal for his future.

The good news for him was the deluge of bad news in Maripesa. Because of this, his return was not even close to being the center of anyone's attention, so he escaped detailed interrogations about what had happened to him in the weeks he'd been missing.

The Kruiks struck fast and hard after his mother died, and there had been no letup. The city was crippled. The Gens had all but abandoned them. He'd lost count of the number of rants he'd heard in council—temporarily head-quartered in the Council of Clans building since the Komeh continued to be overrun by the Spread—about the "crumbling of the hierarchy" and the Gens' reneging on the age-old agreement that "kept the society working the way it was supposed to."

The Gens didn't refuse to come. They simply responded that their priority was to get the transportation system and the essential businesses of the city running again; that no personal cleaning could be done for the foreseeable future. No matter how many rants there were, no one could say the Gen were derelict in their responsibility. Garnia had summed it up perfectly: "Your home is not a priority."

Ferjival had been admitted back to the council table without question. The rest was up for grabs.

Mam Sior had not left an heir-apparent and even if she had, there was no agreed-upon rule of succession. That was usually fought out over a period of time, with the interim council leader being the most senior member. Most succession periods, however, were not characterized by the utter and complete chaos they were in now—with the Kruiks actively trying to wrest control of the city away from them.

He sat in the last seat on the left-hand side of a very long table, as far away from the Council Leader Droht as one could be. At the moment, Hasip had the floor. He had—in the space left by his mother's death and his eldest brother's unexplained disappearance—come to think of himself as the next natural leader of the Puraples Clan.

I was captured and held prisoner because you, Hasip, had the stupidity to get a Gen girl pregnant. With twins, no less. And that caused you to supersede me.

Thank the stars.

His serenity in the face of all the upheaval had been noted by a few, but it was assumed to be grief—a reaction to losing his mother. He had not one shred of grief, however. He could breathe now. Gratitude was his primary emotion. He would not fight to be ruler of this clan or this city. Let Hasip, or whoever, have it. He was above the fray, and it felt great.

If anyone had asked his opinion, he would tell them that Hasip was not fit because he had broken the rules so boldly. Everyone here knew, of course. How many of these men... hmm, they were all men, come to think of it. He didn't think that his mother would like that very much. Not that she'd ever lifted a finger to foster leadership in the women around her. How many of these men had done the same as Hasip?

"We have the power to take back the control we've lost, but we must act decisively, broadly, and without mercy," Hasip said.

Oh my. He's full of passion all of a sudden. Threatened loss of power will do that to a person. Ferjival thought of himself on that fateful night at Pats'. He would have killed them all where they stood if he could have.

"A weak response from us is worse than none at all. We must use the most effective and powerful weapon we have."

Ferjival couldn't help himself. "Surely not giarmial, brother. That's what got us into this mess."

Hasip looked as irritated as Ferjival could have wished for. As if his eldest brother was a biting insect too far away to squash. *Maybe that should be my role.*

"Giarmial is not our most powerful deterrent, though I suggest we use it as necessary. No, our most awesome power lies in what we as the current ruling clan have used repeatedly: execution."

Ferjival sat up.

A rumble of voices came from the others.

Hasip didn't let it grow. He continued, "Every member of the Kruik Council executed by week's end. Do you hear me? Every one of them."

"See here, my good man," said Droht, "executions can't be done just because you don't like someone. They're for breaking the laws by which this society functions."

Hasip didn't let this information slow him down. "Using unauthorized magic to stage a coup against the ruling clan *is* breaking the law. It can't be allowed to work, don't you see? Because if it does, then no one is ever safe."

Ferjival shook his head at this bit of illogic. *Unauthorized magic? He is a brat of a boy who wants to do exactly what he wants without any checks. He's never had magic directed at him in this way. He doesn't get it.*

But he kept quiet. Another councilor said, "The Puraples are extremely unpopular at the moment. The epidemic is all too fresh. Executions will not help that. If we push people too far—"

"What?" Hasip all but shouted. "What will they do? They've never liked executions. Of course not. That's the point. We must demonstrate our power. Otherwise, power is meaningless, a construct of convenience with nothing behind it. It is exactly what we need at this point precisely because we are not in favor with the citizens *and* because a threat to our survival is practically on our doorstep. How would you suggest we keep the Kruiks from taking over?" He paused, but only for a moment. "Don't even try to answer that question. There is no option that will work. We must execute those who won't hesitate to take our position. I call a vote for myself to be Leader."

"What? No," said Droht. "We aren't ready. Hasip. Please."

A call for a leadership vote was binding.

Stupid of him. Ferjival was alarmed. That the situation was crucial, he agreed. That some might need to be punished, sure. But a wholesale execution of a clan council? Just for doing what the Kruiks and the Puraples had always done? No. That was an overreaction by a long shot and everyone else in the room knew it.

Ferjival stood, getting everyone's attention. "A leadership vote must have at least two options. Otherwise, councilors wouldn't know who would become leader if they vote against the one who is standing. Having been out of the loop for a while, I'd like to know who else is in the running."

Hasip shot him a look that could kill.

The chair said, "Quite right. Look here, Hasip, I'm going to postpone this vote for—wait, wait, calm down. We'll take it today. I just need a break. Permit an old man a chance to relieve himself, would you? And when I return, I intend to lead a discussion about our alternatives. Not in terms of actions to be taken, but in terms of leadership options." He gave Hasip a steely-eyed stare and then rose to leave the chamber. As he walked by Ferjival, he nodded, looking toward him with much softer eyes.

Several of the others rose from their seats and gathered in small groups or went outside for a smoke.

Speaking of smoke. Hasip looks as if he might burst into flames. His brother glared for a moment and then came to his side.

"You weasel."

"Yes?" Ferjival said, not about to rise to the bait.

"Are you drugged? Are you crazy? Why'd you bother to come back at all if you aren't going to support your side of the family? Oh. Oh, I get it. You're trying to sit back and let us all fight it out, so you'll be the last man standing. I didn't know you had it in you, brother."

"I do not have it in me. I don't want the job. And before your little speech, I would have assumed that you were going to be the leader. But...I didn't like your speech or your strategy. It's wrong."

"Luckily, no one cares what you think."

"Opinions don't travel well from person to person, do they? But facts. Facts are a different matter."

Hasip scoffed. "What are you babbling about? I stated the facts. This is war. Don't you get that? Doesn't anyone get that?" His voice grew louder and shriller with each word.

Good lord, he reminds me of...me. How horrible.

"Do your worst, brother." Ferjival stood up, dipped his head and said, "If you'll excuse me. I also need to empty my bladder. I will see you soon."

Hasip turned on his heel and started over to the largest grouping of councilors to plead his case.

Ferjival, his jaw set, walked from the room and found Droht.

"I have compelling and undeniable evidence that my brother is in no way even marginally fit to be ruler of this clan, much less this city. I am going to retrieve it now. It will take a few hours, though. Would you be able to postpone the vote until I return?"

"I think we must," the man said. "I'm glad to have your support. I don't take well to being bullied in my own clan council. Can you be back by eventide?"

"I can and will. Thank you, sir."

He turned to leave, and the old man called out, "It's good to have you back, Ferjival. Whatever happened during your time away, it has matured you quite nicely."

Ferjival wanted to be appreciated, but couldn't find a place inside him to put this praise. As he rushed to complete his errand in time, he remembered that it was the Gen mouse's actions that had made him into a better person.

This, too, was hard to live with.

Maleka's house was more of a country manor than the practical farmhouse of Reva and Eguin's, though it showed many more signs of neglect. Ferjival arrived with his bodyguard, Rand, and three others. As he robustly knocked on the door, his heart leapt at what he was about to do. *What would Reva say?* But this overlay of guilt was unwarranted. He was trying to save lives, not take them. After Hasip was literally faced with the undeniable truth of his unfitness and once the council could no longer pretend they didn't know, his brother would be properly sidelined and cooler heads would prevail.

The servant who answered the knock questioned who they were and what they wanted. "Trained to be discreet, I see," he said before elbowing his way in, his men following.

"She's not 'ere!" the girl shouted.

But of course that's what she'd say. Her scream was obviously meant to warn the lady of the house. He tromped through the empty downstairs rooms, then posted men at both doors and went upstairs with two others. Maleka was huddled in bed with her twins. How old were they? *A year at least, I should think. And of course, they are crying. Of course.*

"Ferjival. What's the meaning of this?" Maleka said with self-composed outrage. "Has something happened to Hasip?"

"Not yet, Madam. But we are here to take you and the babies to him."

"Where?"

"I'll tell you once we're on the road. We'll be on horseback, so wear something appropriate and tell the nurse to wrap them up well. She'll come too, I suppose."

This was getting overly complicated already. They had four horses, so the women would each have to take a baby and ride in front of the bodyguards.

"Hasip and I have a code word. What is it?"

"I have no idea. He doesn't know you're coming, but it's necessary and I have no intention of leaving here without you, so get ready."

"I won't. I am your sister-in-law and you will treat me with respect. How did you escape, anyway?"

He sighed. "Maleka, I am not your enemy. But you aren't in a position to demand respect. You and my brother broke the law in a most egregious manner.

I am not in favor of executions, and, in any case, I wouldn't put my brother to death. However, he's on the verge of doing harm to our clan and city. You will help me stop him. How much do you know about what's going on in Maripesa?"

"I know Mam Sior died and heard the funeral was some kind of disaster. Did they let you out because of her death?"

"Doesn't matter. Something like that. Listen. Things are falling apart. Because of that, no one really cares about what you did. I need you to calm Hasip down. He wants to execute the entire Kruik council before the end of the week! And, we have to vote on whether or not he's going to be council leader before the end of the day. Will you help me?"

"I don't know why I should."

"Because people will die if you don't."

"Why do the babies need to come? I don't want to bring them."

Good. She's softening. He truly did not want to force her; that would be ugly.

"Oh. Well, all right, then. The girl can take care of them? Sure, that works. If you'll cooperate, then I promise to bring you back soon. Depends on what's happening and if this works, but it shouldn't be long. She'll be all right with them?"

"I've left her overnight with them before. But...I'm scared. I've been hiding here so long."

"You wouldn't believe how much I understand that feeling, Maleka." He sighed again. "Here's the thing that might help you believe it: Aza Gen—or whatever name she is going by now—is walking around the city a free woman. She's pushing her weight around in charge of some new group. I have no idea what they do, but Aza showed up at my mother's funeral when everything was in chaos after the Kruiks had cursed the Tapinak. She and her group did something...I don't yet understand what, but they magicked everyone into calming down. The important point is: She's a free woman and no one's going after her."

"Mam Sior's dead," Maleka said, thinking out loud. "She's the one who wanted Aza executed."

"And she was my mother, so watch what you say. I won't hear her bad-mouthed. Quickly, get ready. Bring a change of clothes, and dress warmly."

In the end, she came willingly, so he could have done without all the muscle, but maybe it helped convince her. He left one behind to watch the house and make sure the nurse stayed put. The kids would have been a nice touch, but it was quicker this way.

At the Council of Clans building, Maleka, pale and tense, walked with him, though he kept a hand on her upper arm. When they got to the council door, he left her with Rand and went inside.

They were still there, debating the leadership position. Droht looked up and grinned. "Ah, Ferjival, were you able to get your business done?"

"Is that what we've been waiting for?" Hasip said. "We're in crisis and can't call a vote until Ferjival does his errands?"

Ferjival strode forward. "I ask permission to address the council."

"Granted."

"I have evidence as to why Hasip Puraples is unfit to lead the Clan Puraples."

"What!?" Hasip said.

"Quiet..." said the Chair.

"You will not survive this betrayal."

"I wouldn't care, Hasip, except that a leader must listen to reason. Your plan to execute the entire Kruik council is lunacy. Council, I present to you..." He opened the door and stood aside.

Maleka walked in like someone being led into a dragon's lair. Her face relaxed slightly when she saw Hasip. His face did the opposite.

"I introduce to you, Maleka Gen. Maleka worked at the Komeh as a cleaner of curses right up until she was mysteriously abducted by three men dressed in black. The kidnapping was a sham. She is the wife of Hasip and the mother of his two children. Twins."

Maleka's gaze hadn't strayed from her husband. "Hasip? What's going on?"

"Madam, do you have children by Hasip Puraples?" asked Droht.

She nodded, looking as if she might collapse.

"This woman is the flesh and blood evidence that my brother shouldn't be leader. I expect this council to do the right thing."

"The right thing," spat Hasip. "You wouldn't know the right thing if it kissed you on the lips!"

"An apt expression, considering you took this very young lady from her job, her clan, her city, and hid her in the country and left her there. And in a shockingly disheveled house, I might add."

Hasip smashed his fist on the table. "We're going to be destroyed and you're worried about past indiscretions?"

"Yes. I am. If you're threatening to put to death so many others, I want you to face the fact that you are, according to Maripesian covenant, more guilty and more deserving of death by execution than they are!"

"Hasip?" Maleka said, very quietly. "May I go?"

Ferjival squeezed the back of the arm and said, "Not yet. What say you, Council? Do we have another candidate who's thrown his hat into the ring? Or shall I proceed with articles of execution for cross-clan breeding?"

Maleka gasped.

An uneasy silence settled over the room. Hasip sat with his head in his hands, his face red and contorted.

"We discussed this while you were out," Droht said, finally. "We—and I know that I represent all the councilors except Hasip—when I tell you that we would vote for you, sir, if you would agree to stand for the position."

Ferjival's mouth gaped.

Hasip stood up so quickly that his chair tumbled over.

The noise drew everyone's attention.

In the silence that followed, Ferjival stared at it.

My homecoming daydream. The acceptance. The accolades. The overturned chair.

A sickeningly twisted fantasy come true.

29

CONSEQUENCES

"THANK YOU FOR TRACKING Bek down," Aza said as she paced. "She's extremely busy, then. So, what was her...mood?"

Vijo sat on the patio at the Round Cottage watching her.

Even though the day was chilly, Aza needed to be outside. She felt emotionally itchy, as if she would benefit from a hard scrubbing, or...a dive into salty water followed by a roll in sand. None of these things, though, would help. This sensation resided under the surface, untouchable.

She would live with it. Use it.

Vijo didn't answer at first. Clearly, something was weighing on him.

Aza sat down. His blue eyes met hers and he said, "Bek told me something she shouldn't have. I'm going to tell you, even though you won't like it, because, in the long run, there should be no secrets between us."

Aza's stomach roiled.

He reached over and put a hand lightly over hers. "She said that you two had a special night together."

Her "itchiness" became painful. She pulled her hand away and grimaced as she lowered her head. Shame flooded her.

Vijo touched her again. When she didn't pull away, he looped his fingers around hers and pulled her hand until it was on the table between them.

The instinctive touch of a healer? Was there more bad news to come?

"Aza, you've done nothing wrong. Nothing. To answer your question, her mood was all over the place. It was a short exchange. She seemed really happy to see me, but was irritated that I 'scolded' her for not answering messages. Her need to take care of important Kruik business is her priority. She feels you should understand."

"So, my constant messages were part of her...irritation?"

Vijo squeezed her hand. "I think so. Can you hold off for a while? Or will that be too difficult?"

Aza smirked despite her intense misery. "Yes, to both. I can stop messaging, and it will be hard." She breathed in raggedly, pleased only by the fact that she wasn't crying. "Thank you," she said in a whisper. "You are a" —she was going to say "good friend" but thought better of it— "an amazing person. I never forget that I owe my life to you, but what I'm second most grateful for is that you have stayed a part of this life that you saved. I know that all your healthy patients aren't that lucky."

His cheeks colored slightly—which she liked. He let go of her hand, looked down and then back at her more boldly and said, "Thank you."

She took a deep breath and found that it didn't actually hurt. Her chest still felt as if a boulder was resting on it, but it functioned. She looked at the leafless trees swaying heavily in the gusty wind.

Use your misery.

"Vijo," she said, "changing the subject...oh yes, *Maripes*, please, let's change the subject! I have the need of something, but don't know how to make it happen and I'm wondering if you might be the person to help me. I know you've made a study of the magic of Maripesa."

He sat up. "That's an intriguing opening. I don't know if I can help or not, but I'd bet my apothecary that I know more about the full range of Maripesian magic than anyone in this city. Well, anyone who isn't Tchuvari."

"It has to do with the soltec. Do you know what that is?"

His eyes widened. "Yes. But I'm surprised you do."

"Right. Well, I found one on the floor of Gerland's coach months ago. I picked it up and put in my apron pocket, not knowing what it was. Maybe that was stealing, but I knew it was something special and I wasn't about to let it go without knowing more about it."

"I don't blame you at all. You had no idea of its function?"

"Not until I met Oscera. That happened some weeks later. I came to the Tapinak and as part of a tour, they showed me the soltec display. That's when I learned about personal wards."

"Right. Used a long time before the Tchuvari wrote the covenant that brought Maripesa out of chaos."

"Exactly," she said. "Have you seen the display?"

"As a schoolboy."

"Do you remember the missing soltec?"

"I do. Though it was only my burgeoning obsession with other people's magic, I suspect, that made that jump out at me. Oh! You found the missing one!"

Aza nodded. "Our own Ferjival Puraples dropped it in Gerland's coach. Imagine his surprise when I pulled it out at Pats' that night you captured him."

"I captured him?" He laughed uneasily. "You are trying to win me over with flattery, my dear. If anything was ever a joint effort—and I stress the word 'effort'—it was capturing Ferjival."

They shared a laugh over what was one of the hardest nights of each of their lives.

"Where is your soltec?" Vijo asked. "And does Oscera know?"

"It's still with Reva. I left it so that anyone looking after Ferjival would be safe if he tried to put a spell on them. They needed it at first. But he...calmed down pretty quickly."

"Once he knew that his curses wouldn't work."

"Right. Though, she and Eguin feel he truly went through some kind of transformative experience while there."

Vijo grunted in disbelief and said, "What do you want me to do?"

"Figure out how it works."

His eyes grew wide. "Is *that* all?"

"I know."

"The Tchuvari must know. They're the keepers of the wards."

"I want to change that. That's the point. I have a vision that puts the ability to ward in the hands of the citizens. All of them."

"Whoa." His head started bobbing up and down. "Yes. I can see that. I mean, what harm would it do? And it would..." His voice faded out as he took a long moment to think of the consequences.

Aza couldn't wait. "The Tchuvari, as things stand now, aren't going to go for this idea. Oscera is the most forward thinking and they recoiled when I told them my idea."

"You came out and said that to them?"

"Yes. I didn't think they would react the way they did. I mean, Oscera will probably come around, given time. But the hardcore of Tchuvari? No. They'll have to die off before we'll get any real change. The other thing that will be changing, though, is that they *are* dying off as a clan. 'Seeding' recruits who are open to our ideas could help. But that will take years. We don't have years. We need the ability to ward as soon as possible.

"Oscera agreed to push Keepers to use warding spells liberally in the city to help the Gen clean up this mess. The trolleys, the essential buildings, the bridge. But they shut me down hard on the manufacture of more soltecs. That's where you come in."

Aza watched as Vijo's eyes unfocused, his mind drilling down on...what? The situation, the potential, the risks? His head started moving back and forth very slowly.

"What?" Aza said. "You can't help me? What is it?"

He snapped out of his reverie, took her hands in his, and said, "Oh no, I'm in. I am all in."

Ferjival moved into his mother's office to conduct day-to-day business. The Komeh was unclean, but the curse hadn't traveled this far and Ferjival intended to strong-arm Gen help long before it came anywhere near. He'd convinced Garnia and some staff to come back so that he, at least, had meals prepared and clothes cleaned daily. So while the mansion was otherwise empty—his siblings refused to come near it as long as the Spread remained—he was better here. It was hard enough for him to fathom sliding into his mother's role without being in some generic building. Being in the literal seat of government helped.

So what if the house was cursed? He'd once lived quite happily in a barn.

Duma Gen had come yesterday, and always the dandy, was dressed to the hilt. They knew each other well from the polo fields and the Wardrobe. In another kind of society, they would have been friends. So it was with no little irony that they faced each other—each of them now leaders of their clans. But Duma had put him off. "The Gen will, of course, clean the Komeh. However, we have a strategic plan and must proceed as it outlines," he said.

"How can you begin to think that the seat of government isn't a priority?"

"With all due respect, Ferjival, we prioritize what most affects the functioning of our city. You could, if you wanted, move the 'seat' of government to another building that is unaffected by the Spread. It is" —he bowed slightly— "your choice."

Ferjival shook his head. He needed to put that exchange behind him. He rose from his mother's massive desk and went to the ceiling-to-floor window. The bare trees were bleak and so was he at the prospect of winter.

He thought back to the calm he'd felt at Reva's. *Being treated with kindness even when he'd done nothing to deserve it.* It was becoming harder to hang onto. His mother was dead, but he was still being disrespected despite being voted her successor. No one, it seemed, gave him the unquestioned authority to rule that they had Mam Sior.

Mother, did you have to earn the respect, the fear, that people treated you with? Were your early days as Ruler fraught with insults? He could barely imagine his mother as a younger ruler. She had been...how old when she took over from her uncle? Close to thirty, he thought. Maybe a little older.

But younger than you, Ferjival. And a woman to boot. Most men must have wanted to undermine her authority. "That could explain a lot," he said out loud. "She had to be tough all the time." *She certainly warmed to that role.* He tried to think of one thing that had gone right since the council voted him Leader. After a moment, he gave up. It wasn't helping.

A knock at the door.

"Enter."

Jetal walked in. The youngest, newest member of the Puraples Council, Ferjival chose him as his ombudsman. This would be a new position and he informed the council that no staff or adviser would be more important to him. The ombudsman would act as the liaison between the Ruler and city.

One might think that such a job description would be so broad as to overwhelm anyone, but Jetal had smiled, accepted the position gladly and taken to it like a charm to a blessing. *There it is.* The one thing that had gone right.

"Good morning, Jetal. Would you like tea?"

"No, sir. Thank you."

"What do you have to tell me this morning?" He sat down, not behind the desk but in a chair near the windows. He motioned to Jetal to sit. Ferjival's was the larger and taller of the two and the more comfortable. Mam Sior definitely knew what she was doing.

"Sir, I want to apologize for the negativity in today's report. Believe me, I know the power of positive news and I looked for some. But anything positive that I could come up with was only positive because nothing worse had happened yet. Do you understand what I'm saying?"

Ferjival was conscious of his own breathing—too shallow and fast. He thought of the process of churning and his breathing slowed slightly. He nodded. "I believe you're trying to tell me that our power position in the city isn't lost as of yet, but that our struggle against the Kruiks isn't going as well as we would like?"

"Exactly. They seem to have stopped cursing the larger venues. As I told you yesterday, most of the trolleys and coaches are running. Messageries are working again. Most people can get where they want to go, so the city seems to be working."

"That sounds like good news."

Jetal gave him an apologetic look. "Yes, but technically, that is yesterday's news, and it is due to the Kruik's actions, not ours."

"The Gens though, they're doing their job to clean up the Spread?"

He nodded. "Great numbers of them are working literally night and day, sir."

"Good. So now, hit me with the bad news."

Jetal leaned forward, his elbows on his thighs. "Sir, the information about Hasip has...gotten out."

"That he wasn't named leader?"

"That he has had children with a Gen woman."

"Right..."

"I am told that it was a badly held secret before Mam Sior's death. Perhaps some Kruiks knew, but didn't speak of it. Perhaps someone from the Gen clan? It could be that the servants had overheard talk. The problem now is that it seems to have spilled out of many places at once so that it is, I'm afraid, the talk of the city."

"That is very bad news."

"Yes, sir. Add this to the protests that caused the melee at your mother's funeral and the simmering rage at lives lost due to giarmial, and we must face the fact that the population's hatred for us has reached heights hitherto unknown. I fear that if the gossip continues unbated we may have a hard decision to make."

"*I* would have a hard decision, you mean," Ferjival snapped, his voice sharp and hard. It had been a long time since he'd felt sudden, intense anger. He let himself feel it. It encompassed many things. Hasip, his mother, whoever had loose lips, and Maleka Gen for allowing his brother to impregnate her. Hell, she probably tricked *him* into it! Duma Gen, for his insubordination. Aza Gen. Yes. Always, her. And himself, of course. He'd started the epidemic that brought out the underlying hatred of his clan. "What else?" he spat.

"The Kruiks are targeting Puraples as individuals. It's...not pretty."

Ferjival paled. No Gen to clean up personal curses.

"We'll have to confront this Hasip issue head on," Ferjival said. "Call a council meeting this afternoon. We'll meet here. Before you go, inform the staff and see that someone is sent up to move furniture. And refreshments. We'll need that too."

Jetal gave him a complicated look, nodded, and left.

He's probably upset that I'm ordering him around like a footman. He's a council member, not a servant.

Ferjival rushed to the door to apologize, but the man had already disappeared.

Vijo was at a meeting of what they had started calling "Aza's Council" with tongues firmly in cheeks. As usual, Bek was not in attendance. Aza seemed to have found her bearings, though Vijo thought it likely that she'd only pushed her feelings down. If that were the case, there'd be a future reckoning, but for now, Aza was on her game. The news of the day was that Hasip had been put under house arrest.

"So far, I haven't heard Maleka's name mentioned," Vijo said.

"I'll go to Luftva as soon as we adjourn," Aza said. "We must safeguard her and the kids."

Karol said, "Please let me take you. I can port us in closer to her home than Luftva Village. It'll save time and avoid attention."

This suggestion was met with great approval, but Vijo said, "I'd like to go with Karol instead of you going, Aza. The mood in the city is ramped up. With all these calls for Hasip's execution, it isn't safe for you—with an outstanding warrant on your own life—to be caught out in public."

Karol immediately backed Vijo up.

Aza pursed her lips in a pout that made her look like a nine-year-old, but agreed to their plan.

Less than an hour later, Karol and Vijo were hurtling through the city in the back of Gerland's coach. Not half an hour after that, Karol cast off into the choppy strait. It was overcast and cold. So far, it hadn't rained, but the wind was fretful.

Vijo admitted to being nauseated.

"What? You're a healer. Have you nothing to use for seasickness?" Karol teased from her post at the stern.

He shook his head with a grimace. "There's a nausea cure for side effects of maladies, but Besin treatments have never been geared for the total range of human suffering." It was one of the things he wanted to change about their clan's specialty.

"Here." Karol tossed him her leather tote. "You'll find a remedy in there. Marked as 'baystele.' Put a leaf under your tongue and keep it there as long as you're able. Then spit it into the water with a curse."

"What?" Vijo asked, rummaging through the bag. "Curse the strait?"

She threw back her head and laughed loudly. "Not a real curse. But isn't that what you'd like to do right now? I think it helps with the treatment."

He grinned in spite of his nausea as he finally located the herbal remedy. "You have a healer's instincts for certain, Karol."

"Besin born and bred," she said, her eyes on the horizon.

By the time she pulled the ferry alongside a small dock with the word Hogling painted in faded yellow on the pier post, Vijo was feeling better.

Just as Karol had predicted, the place was deserted. Even though neither of them had been to Maleka's before, Karol was familiar with the community and Aza had drawn them a precise map. Karol shoved it into her shirt.

After a brisk fifteen-minute walk, they reached the overgrown garden gate, which, as Aza had said, "Isn't a real gate, but only a space between two garden walls that once sported a gate." They instinctively slowed down, pausing behind a profuse rose bush full of dead leaves. Karol tugged Vijo away from its thorns as they leaned forward to peek at the front of the house.

They both pulled back abruptly and looked at each other.

"Is that a guard?" Vijo whispered.

"Looks like it."

A rough-looking fellow sat in a chair not far from the front door. The chair tipped back against the trunk of a large tree. Vijo looked again. "His eyes are closed."

Karol motioned him away from the gate. Once they were out of hearing distance, she said, "Why would there be a guard?"

"Maybe Hasip kept one here for Maleka's safety? But something tells me that's not what's going on here. What should we do?"

"Well...if there's a guard on the inside too, we're going to need help."

"Where are we going to find help?"

She shrugged. "We'd have to go back to the boat, down to the village, see if Pats is available, and come back again."

"That'll take too long. What if we decide that there isn't another guard?"

"Sneak in 'round the back?"

"I like that idea a lot better."

They entered the overgrown fields of the property, choosing a wide enough berth that they couldn't see the house for a good five-minute walk. Then they veered toward the right and spotted its copper chimney spouts, green with age. They walked up to the backyard, hid behind a row of the ubiquitous wild roses, and inspected the area.

Small vegetable garden gone to seed. Chair swing hanging from a huge oak limb twisting in the gusty breeze. Small, rough stone patio. Back door. No signs of life.

With a nod to each other, they set off, practically tiptoeing across the unkempt lawn.

Vijo peeked in the back windows while Karol went around to see if the guard was still in his chair.

She came back quickly, nodding. "He's snoring."

"Let's do this."

He tried the back door. Unlocked. He looked at Karol gratefully. She had told him that country folk didn't keep locks on their doors. They entered a small room that led into a simple, messy kitchen.

They split up, and it didn't take long to meet back in the middle, at the front of the house near the stairwell. No one was on the first floor.

A single wail split the silence.

"One of the babies," Vijo whispered. He peeked out the window and nodded to Karol. She started up the stairs. He kept an eye on the sleeping guard.

Once on the upper floor, Karol softly called, "Maleka? It's Karol and Vijo."

Vijo didn't know what he'd do if the guard came in. Maybe he should think about that. He heard a door open upstairs and then he heard it close. His nausea came back. The fellow outside was large, though more fat than muscle. Vijo had neither. He'd never struck anyone in his life unless you counted what he'd done to help capture Ferjival. He didn't count that. He'd mainly sat on the guy's feet while Pats did the capturing—poor Pats. Hopefully, there'd be no such dramatics today. What was it about Aza that got him into these situations? He looked out the window, startled to see that the man's chair now rested on four legs. The guard was still seated, but awake.

Should he go up and tell Karol? What was taking so long? The guard was rubbing his face. How often might he check on the people in the house? Likely never. He was probably just ordered to stand guard outside. Make sure nothing bad happened. Make sure they didn't escape. Either way, they had to hurry.

Escape, quietly and quickly, with babies. That's easy.

He went upstairs and as he got to the top, Karol came out with a toddler in her arms. Following her was a young woman holding the other child. "Vijo, meet Jula, the nurse. She's concerned about Maleka, who left days ago. How many was it?"

"Five, I think," the girl said in a wispy voice. She looked exhausted, with deep circles under her eyes, her skin ashen.

"Are you all right?" Vijo asked.

Karol looked back at her. "See? I told you he's a healer. She's tired and worried because Maleka didn't come back. I've told her that Maleka sent us to fetch the twins, but she's a little confused and, of course, wants reassurance that she's doing the right thing by letting us take them." Karol was talking fast to get him up to date.

Vijo needed to slow everything down to calm the girl. "Ah, yes. I understand," he said in his gentlest, Besin voice. "It's a tricky situation. If we had thought of it, we should have asked her to write a note."

"Weren't do no good," said the young woman. "I can't read. Maleka would know that."

"Well then, that's why she didn't suggest it. We didn't even consider that you might think we were anything other than her good friends doing her a favor. Aza—uh, Zaz. Zaz Salizan would have come but—"

"Oh sure, I know Zaz. Haven't seen her in ages. Well. Then, how long a journey do you have? They're fresh changed and not hungry now, but it won't be long."

"We won't be going that far," Karol said, obviously trying to keep things vague.

"If you have some...food, or milk, we could take..." Vijo said, trailing off. He didn't even know what kids ate at their age.

"Sure," she said.

The children were awake and contented for now. Karol held the girl, Capsia. She was listening to them talk. The boy had a piece of hard biscuit in his mouth, drool coating his chin, neck, and shirt. "Take Emke here and I'll get a pack together for them." Jula started downstairs. "What about the guy outside? Does he know you're here?"

"Uh..." said Vijo.

"Let's go to the kitchen," Karol said. "If you'll get things together, I'll level with you."

Vijo's eyes widened.

The girl took this in stride evidently because as soon as they reached the kitchen she began pulling glass bottles off the counter.

Vijo gave her his backpack.

"Maleka's in a bit of trouble," Karol said. "And that guard out there is not on her side. So we don't want him to know that we've taken the children."

The nurse didn't even look up. She continued preparing bottles and nodded.

"So if it's all right with you, we'll go out the back so that he doesn't know we've left."

"That's a good idea. He's a bad lot, that one."

"What do you mean?" asked Vijo.

"Aw, he's been trying to get at me since they left. I held my own and reminded him that he'd be punished by that Puraples if he touched me. He backed off, but it's only a matter of time. That's one reason I'm so tired. Slept with one eye open. I'm going with you. I mean until we get away from the house. From there, I'll go home if it's all the same to you. I wouldn't stay here one more minute than I had to. Don't even know why they left him except the Purple fellow was gonna take the babies with him and then Maleka says why don't they just stay here. He promised her she'd only be gone overnight. That was days ago."

She held out the pack full of the provisions. "I know she's in trouble. I got eyes to see. She's got Undone babies, that's what. I don't suppose you'd be able to provide me with some compensation for my time and trouble."

Karol said, "We don't know how much she pays you, but we'll give you what we can."

"Good. We'll settle up once we're away."

Vijo opened the door, and they slipped out across the lawn and through the fields. After parting company with Jula, they headed straight to the shore.

"It's too far gone," Jetal said.

"If you don't do this, Hasip will take the rest of us down with him."

"Here, here. Cut him loose or we all sink."

Ferjival couldn't change their minds. He had tried. Had been arguing all morning, to the point that they had convinced him rather than the other way around. But he simply didn't know how to order the death of his own brother.

"I— I have no experience with setting up an execution. Perhaps someone—an elder member of the council who had some, ah, interaction with Mam Sior when these, um, events have been held..."

Silence.

Ferjival hated every one of them and their heavy breathing.

"I see. You've made me Leader when I told you I didn't seek or want the position. Now you expect me to order my brother's death when it isn't something I support. It is unfair."

The chorus started again, sure and unrelenting: "You accepted the leadership." "You must have seen this coming, knowing as you have for a long time about your brother's perfidy." "What did you expect when you brought his concubine into the council chambers?"

"I expected to keep my brother from putting to death dozens of Kruiks!" Ferjival shouted. "I did not expect the news of his indiscretions to leave this room!"

His words were undermined by the fact that they were in a different room. Not for the first time, he wondered at his decision to meet here in the once-grand Komeh, now being slowly coated by Kruik filth. At night in bed, he could almost hear the vermin crawling closer. Duma Gen had stopped answering his daily messages. Did his mother ever once have as bad a time as he had every day?

"The Puraples have put their own to death before. Despite what the journals are writing," said the archivist on the council. "I've looked it up. There are several."

"Several?" Ferjival said, dryly.

"Three, sir."

"Out of how many executions?"

"Ah, I—" He started ruffling through papers. "As you know, they've become less frequent as people learned to stay in their places. He shrugged his shoulders. "I could give you an educated guess. It's more than three hundred, less than five."

"Five?"

"Five hundred, Leader Ferjival."

"Good lord. And out of that...five Puraples."

"Uh, three, sir. According to my research, sir."

"Good. Great. No wonder they hate us. You win. The execution will be held tomorrow at dawn. Got that Jetal? Meeting adjourned. Go away."

"Sir, what about the Gen?"

His mind, preoccupied with the creeping curse overtaking his seat of power, thought of Duma first. Then he realized what no one had talked about during all this time: Maleka had to die as well. "Her too, of course," he said, as if he hadn't forgotten her completely. Gods, this day just kept getting worse. He sat upright. "The children. Send Rand to fetch them immediately."

30

TOLLED

BEK ARRIVED AT THE Execution Grounds before dawn.

She leaned against a leafless tree, watching as people arrived. There weren't many. Jetal told her it had been scheduled this early to keep down the interest.

The wind was bitterly cold, and she hadn't dressed warmly enough, but she would stay.

I won't die today—not of the cold or anything else. But I know people who will. Damn this winter wind and everything and everyone else.

She would bear this wind as she bore witness.

The knowledge of Maleka's death invaded Aza's bedroom through a steadily ringing bell in the cathedral tower next door: the tolling as mournful as a moan but more insistent. Aza knew the misery in her ears, in her heart, in her gut, as a coating over her skin—all before there were words.

She rose, walked to the bedroom's terrace doors and went out.

The day, nodding to the deed, was grey, but also bitter cold where it had been only hinting at winter before.

Aza needed to take care of many things. But first, she needed to stand here and shiver. She needed hot tears to spill down cold cheeks and fall off her chin like summer raindrops onto her nightgown. She needed to feel the needle-pricks jumping and quivering in her chest as she breathed as shallowly as possible. She needed to let her body rule ruthlessly over her mind, which was not her friend right now because it had the ability to generate words which she did not need to hear, to remember, to know. No words. No words. She willed herself to focus only on her frozen feet, her nose—cold, too, and dripping—and the goose-pimpled flesh of her upper arms numbed to her gouging fingernails.

Sometime later, first one and then both of the twins cried and she joined her voice with theirs, wailing at the steely sky.

The execution warrant had been read by Jetal, though signed by Ferjival Puraples, Leader of the Puraples Clan, Ruling Family of Maripesa. Then the nameless Tchuvarian took over. The once—though fleetingly—happy couple had not looked at one another, did not reach out, hold hands, or acknowledge each other in any way. Maleka's face was reddened. Hasip's ghostly pale.

Ferjival, in the Komeh, had seen all this and more through the limbs of barren trees from his mother's office window.

The council members who bothered to show up were upset that the babies weren't there to be killed as well.

Ferjival had literally thumbed his nose at them. He counted it a victory of sorts against the meanness, the unfairness of these men who made him Leader to make him kill his own brother. A minor victory, perhaps, but he was grateful to have it tucked away in his aching heart.

Brava, Aza Gen. You pulled that one off, too.

Now, unable to stop shivering, he looked toward the execution grounds and wondered how many his mother had overseen. She had read the order at the last one. How long ago? Two years? No. Less. He had ridden up late after a polo match and was attracted to a pretty young Gen. Only at a second glance had he realized she worked for the family. He'd exchanged a few words with her before she...she fainted when the spell was cast.

He started to shake all over. He tried to breathe deeply but couldn't seem to draw in air. He panicked, his breaths shallower and faster, as his fingers and toes sang with a thousand pinpricks. He grabbed the frame of the window, reliving the moment his brother's head went limp. Seconds later, Maleka Gen, undone victim of nothing more than a young woman's romantic hopes and dreams, died too.

The mourning bell, tolling at his command, would continue until he ordered it silenced.

That weasel Ferjival couldn't even do the deed himself.

Bek, sick to her stomach, would not mourn Hasip who had done this to himself in full measure. But she couldn't help wishing it had been Ferjival. Everyone hated Ferjival enough to kill him, whereas Hasip was a nothing.

Her fists were tight bundles. It wasn't the cold, though her body had been completely overtaken with it. It was rage.

The rank abuse of power by the Puraples family was on full display. *I will personally defeat them.* The Kruik Clan was far from perfect, but anything would be better than what Maripesa had been subjected to over her lifetime. No one group should hold power for so long.

She also blamed the Tchuvari. She blamed herself for not being stronger. And she suddenly, achingly, missed Aza. Aza, who had come to her, showed up unannounced on her doorstep one day, seeking clues to the disappearance of her close friend Maleka.

The babies... Where are the babies?

The bell, at some point during the day, became a comfort rather than a horror. It kept Aza going on to the next step, sometimes the next breath. Everyone came. Reth, Vijo, Oscera, Karol, Eltah and, no, not everyone. Not Bek, but she wouldn't have been welcome today, anyway.

Once back from the country, Vijo had messaged to ask where they should take Maleka's children. She asked him to bring them here. But at that point, they didn't know Maleka would be executed. Now it was obvious that they had to be hidden more carefully.

They sat in the parlor, chairs pulled up close to a roaring fire. Aza sat at one end of the couch with Capsia, uncharacteristically listless today, draped across her lap watching the flames.

Reth had just volunteered to take the babies to his sister's house. He recited a glowing list of her qualifications when Aza held up a hand to stop him. "I appreciate the offer, but my objection is this: The Purples know that you and I are close. They had you followed for months. It's too risky for the twins and your sister."

He dipped his head to her and went off for more tea.

"Where can they go that they won't be obvious to neighbors?" Vijo asked.

Oscera spoke up firmly. "They should stay in the cathedral. Taking in foundlings is part of our mission. We showed you our dorms and school, Aza, remember? It's the perfect, the only, solution. They would be near you."

"I won't be staying here forever," Aza said, before she had consciously made that decision.

Oscera's eyes widened.

A knock at the door interrupted the conversation, but before Reth could answer, Gerland entered, bringing cold air with him. He took off his hat and began shedding his outer wear. "Sad day, everyone," he said. Reth brought him tea, which he received gratefully after sitting down.

"Thank you for coming. And for your help with the rescue," Aza said, as usual, glad to see him.

"It was my pleasure. I needed to come as soon as possible this morning, not only to express our deepest condolences, but also because Ness and I have a proposal."

And before he could say it, Aza guessed.

"We want Maleka's children. They can be raised by all of us. We won't be greedy; we'll share them with our friends. But they'll be safe with us, because who are we? No one. And there are so many of us already that two more won't even show up on the chart. What say? Can they become part of the Gerland and Ness Salizan's family?"

Aza took a deep breath as everyone waited for her reaction. Tears, at the ready, started. "You are hardly 'no one.'"

He grinned. "Well, no. But to the Purples."

And then there was someone else at the door. Reth excused himself and before Aza knew what was happening, Bek appeared, steam rising from her body.

After everyone greeted her, Vijo suggested that it might be a good time to prepare a meal. Karol rose, saying, "Yes, and the twins need a proper nap." She took Capsia from Aza. Eltah grabbed Emke from his toys and they took them upstairs.

Aza and Bek were left alone by the fire.

Bek didn't move. The warming of her body felt simultaneously pleasant and unpleasant.

Aza regarded her neutrally.

The overly hot room worked on Bek from the inside. She began to sweat even while her toes were still numb. She could hear a pleasant buzz of noise from the kitchen, and that finally released enough tension for her to be able to speak. "I— I went this morning. I needed to be a witness. I wanted to tell you..." She started to cry.

Aza teared up, but combined it with a look of pure, righteous anger—chin high, eyes wide.

"I'm so sorry. I needed to know if the babies were safe. That's why I came. I will leave if that's what you want."

Aza's back rounded, her face dipped into her hands, suddenly crying so hard that she couldn't respond.

Vijo poked his head around the curved staircase. He evidently thought there was no immediate crisis because he went away. Bek moved forward. She took off her not nearly warm enough coat and folded it on her lap as she sat in a chair next to Aza.

"May I touch you?" she asked. She didn't think Aza would answer, but she wanted to at least voice what she was about to do. "I don't want to upset you more and if you want me to leave or to just sit here and do nothing and be quiet, I will. But I want to touch you, so that's what I'm going to do now. Just tell me when you want me to stop and I will." She moved her chair closer, leaned over, and gently, loosely, encircled her arms around Aza. It was awkward, as the chair's arm kept her from a proper hug, but Bek immediately felt better. Aza relapsed into a fresh wave of hard sobs.

After some time, with no letup of the misery, Bek, still touching Aza, got up and sat next to her on the couch. She wrapped an arm around her shoulders and nudged Aza's cheek to lie against her upper chest. Aza didn't resist.

Bek murmured noises—the kind a mother might make. Soothing nonsense for when words won't work because life has lost the meaning of meaning. She lightly stroked Aza's upper back while her wool blouse became sodden with tears. Feeling returned to her fingers slowly, and the physical warmth between her and Aza became the only important thing in the world.

Simultaneously, they raised their heads when the cathedral bell went silent.

"Oh," said Aza, her voice thick.

"Yes," said Bek, whispering.

Aza pulled away, wiping her face on her apron.

"You're wearing a Gen apron," said Bek. "I haven't seen that in a while."

Aza gave her a withering look.

Bek, too late, knew what she'd said wrong. She'd been absent and wouldn't know a lot of what was going on in Aza's life.

"Do you want me to leave?"

Again, Aza said nothing. Fresh tears fell.

Eltah came in. "Our meal is ready. Come and eat with us."

Aza let Bek help her up. They walked into the dining area together, while Bek chattered about the Round Cottage and how unusual and charming it was.

The mood remained somber, but after having eaten a bowl of soup and some bread, Aza seemed to find some equilibrium. "Bek, Vijo and Karol rescued the babies. They won't stay here. We aren't sure yet where they'll go."

"I'm so grateful they're safe."

"Yes. So. How goes the takeover of the city?"

Bek winced at the barb in the question. She looked around. She was on the outside of this circle. These good people all knew that she could soon be a member of the ruling clan and as such, would have power over them. She lowered her eyes and thought about what she wanted to say. Finally she spoke, looking at anyone but Aza. "I shall defeat the Purples. I don't know how long it will take, but it's coming—I feel it. This city has been subject to their deadly whims and peevish cruelty for too many years." She paused. After clearing her throat, she said, "I should tell you. I have risen to the rank of Leader of Kruik Clan Council."

Karol whistled softly.

Vijo said, "That was quick work."

Bek shrugged. "I'm practicing some of our MATRIA techniques. They have aided me, but I'm also helped by the pitiful lack of leadership that the Kruik Council represented over the last decade. We've just about stopped the Spread. Well, new curses."

"How?" asked Oscera.

"Young people were doing a lot of it, so I told them to stop and enlisted their help. I'm keeping them busy, finding them eager and able to take orders. My new army."

Silence followed this—what she thought of as a joke. "I— I'm sorry. I didn't think before I spoke. You should realize that they are fighting the Purples, not you."

Aza said, "Not now, maybe, but for how long?"

Bek looked at her at last and whispered forcefully. "I am not your enemy. I will never be your enemy."

Aza did not make eye contact.

Bek looked at the others—sitting at the table or leaning against the cabinets, meal over, arms folded, waiting. Perhaps not judging, but leery, unsure of her, of her motives, of her clan.

A long silence stretched before Aza stood and said, "I need...to lie down. Bek, thank you for coming. In fact, thank you for being our eyes this morning, for bearing witness. Someone needed to and I am grateful to you for that. Please keep the memories of this morning tucked away in your heart. You are on track for becoming the Ruler of this city and if you are to be true to your word and not set yourself up as my enemy, then the murder of my dear friend Maleka Gen for cross-clan breeding will be the last one ever held in the city of Maripesa. And, if it isn't—" She leaned down, her face inches from Bek's. "If it isn't, I will personally defeat you—whatever that means and by whatever means."

She walked out of the room. The rest stayed quiet for a few moments and then slowly started gathering dishes and cleaning up the mess.

Bek rose and said, "Goodbye, everyone. Take care of yourselves."

Only Vijo answered. "Be well. Be safe."

She retrieved her coat and went into the cold.

31

·ঔ৬·

THE LOCKBOX

AZA ENTERED THE BUILDING the way she always had, through the servant's door in the basement. When Garnia, in the kitchen with two young helpers, spotted her, Aza winked at her and gestured for her to follow. The housekeeper joined her in the hallway. They hugged tightly.

"Is there anyone in my old room?"

"Tosh, girl. There's no one in any of the rooms. We all hightail it home afterhours."

"Why?"

Garnia made a ticking noise with her tongue and said, "It is only Lord Ferjival here. The place is overrun with the Spread. It won't be long before the house is unlivable."

"No." Aza's eyes widened in horror. She hadn't been to a Gen meeting in weeks.

"They cursed the council chamber is all, but with no Gen to clean it, it spreads a little more every day. The master sends messages to Duma Gen, but as near as I can tell, he stopped responding."

Aza felt neither a sense of victory nor compassion.

"And," Garnia said, "you know about dear Maleka, I guess."

About this, Aza felt everything at once. She enveloped Garnia in another hug. She'd forgotten that Garnia would be someone else who grieved Maleka. "We have her babies," she whispered in the woman's ear. "They are safe. I'll see to it that you meet them before long." She leaned back and looked at the woman's dear red face. "Did you know there were twins?"

Fresh tears started. Garnia smiled through them and shook her head. "Someone should just shoot him."

"True. But he's in his own private hell, isn't he?"

"Aye, by *Maripes*, he is. Just living here in the footsteps of his mother with the Spread growing over it all." She shuddered, paused for a moment and said,

"Please don't be angry with me for still working for him. I happened to be here when he showed up after being gone so long. This was after Mam Sior died. It weren't a pretty death, but then, they often aren't, are they? She was more than ready. Anyway, Ferjival arrived one day when I'd dropped by. He assumed I'd be staying on, so I got the two girls to help me and...well, that was before the...the execution." She dropped her head and swung it back and forth.

"No need to apologize for your kind soul. You are faithful to the place, not the family. If the Spread gets close to the kitchen, send word. I'll tell Duma to get some Gens to clean *your* part of the house."

Garnia grinned widely. "Oh, it's good to see you. What brings you here?"

"It won't surprise you that I want to do some snooping. Is Ferjival around?"

"He's to be gone all day. Said he was going all the way to Luftva."

Aza's mind went to the twins and then she remembered they were safe. Maybe he was going to the farm.

She walked into the Komeh's massive entry. Barely daring to breathe, she turned in a circle mid-way between the front doors and the octagonal table. It had always been graced with huge bouquets, but the vase was half full of brown stems with dead leaves and petals strewn about. The unlit chandelier seemed to sag with cobwebs. Her eyes went to the majestic windows at the far end, and she gasped to see vermin spreading at one side along the frame, with tendrils reaching out along the small windowpanes.

"How can you live here, Ferjival?" And, not for the first time, she felt sadness toward him, rather than anger. She hated him for that, and moreover would always and forever hate him for taking Maleka from the world.

Steeling herself, she started toward the council chambers, pulling gloves from her apron pocket and putting them on.

Aza had spent her life cleaning Kruik vermin, but the sight of the befouled chamber still took her breath away. The Spread was so thick at this end that walking through it would be impossible. She backed up, closed the door, and went down the servants' hallway to the anteroom.

She surveyed this tiny space where she'd first experienced Zaz. The Gen cleaning tray stood in the corner. She hadn't laid eyes on one of those in a long time. A bit of vermin was just beginning to grow up one leg. *Now, that won't do.* She had a compulsion to clean it. Some standards had to be maintained even in the direst of circumstances. Perhaps, though, she should just take it with her when she left. She had, beforehand, arranged for Gerland to pick her up here in an hour's time. Best to get on with her business, which was to find any ammunition she could to use against this family, so she could exact revenge for Maleka's death. And her mother's.

She opened the door to the infested room. The Spread was less evident at this end and the floor was not yet slippery. She went in. Zaz left her, and Aza felt her viewpoint split. A second later, she was in Mam Sior's secret room. It was messy with letters and papers strewn about, just as it had been the first time Aza had seen it. *She likely never came back here after that day.*

Aza put gloved hands on the wall next to the fireplace, fingering the paneling, following the seams, pushing here and there, digging into the cracks and crevices, looking for the mechanism by which a secret panel would open.

Why didn't I ask Garnia? She must know! Someone had to clean these rooms. She'd go back and ask if she had to, but she pressed on, sure she could figure it out. Several times, she had Zaz pass back through the wall, so she knew she was in the right vicinity, but there didn't seem to be any trigger. She reached the wall and looked back to the fireplace thinking how tall it was. *Mam Sior was short. Shorter even than me.* Whatever controlled the entrance needed to be within easy reach.

She stood, frustrated at not being clever enough to find what had to be there. Zaz came back to her with a swoosh and Aza wondered for the first time if her ability to think was diminished when she was using her Talent. It was well known that the use of magic tired or could deplete a person in other ways, but mental capacity? Perhaps.

Taking a deep breath, Aza walked, being careful with each footstep, to the far side of the fireplace. The Spread was worse here, but not as bad as near the main entrance. She looked around. Everything seemed to be in place, but she'd never spent time in here. Her work had been done in the margins of this fine house—in corners, niches, and nooks, like the anteroom.

Aza turned and was just about to head off to get Garnia, when something not quite normal caught her eye. A servant's call bell on the wall next to the door to the anteroom. She walked to it. The call bells she was familiar with were round ceramic fittings with a pull knob in the center. This contraption, fastened to the wall near the corner and slightly above waist high, looked to be an older design—smaller, more ornate, with an extension, a decorative metal arm of sorts. *A servants' bell that isn't a servants' bell.* She reached out her dirty, gloved hand and pushed the arm down.

The wall panel slid open, and she stared into Mam Sior's private room.

She plucked a match from the metal holder on the wall and lit the sconce filament. There was the small chaise where Sior sat the day Zaz discovered this room. Aza flinched at the memory: Sior's face in intense pain. Not stern, or angry, or mocking, but pained. Like a struck match, empathy flickered to life. She hated that. Aza wanted to be led by the blind rage she felt toward this family.

It must be returning to this place where I grew up that's making me indecisive and soft. It's all right, match flames don't last long.

So far, the room was unaffected by the curse. Aza worked rapidly to clear the space of all personal items. She gathered the letters, documents, and sketches that were lying about. The contents of two drawers were dumped into her satchel. One was obviously where most of the papers, sketches, and notes had been. The other was a mess of ordinary detritus that gathers in all homes: message cards, wicks, hair pins, nets and combs, keys, a brooch, coins, more than one letter opener, pens. But Aza didn't know what might be helpful, so she would take it all. Under the chaise, where Sior had kicked it, was the heavy metal lockbox. She hefted it with a grunt. Aza wouldn't want to walk a long way with it, but it was manageable to the front entrance where Gerland would be waiting.

Aza escaped the room, the chambers, the anteroom, leaving all doors open as she went. Whispering as she went, a silent apology to the cursed cleaning table—her compulsion gone. *I do not clean for you anymore.*

With her heavy load, she happily walked out the front door of the forsaken crumble of a formerly grand home.

Gerland worried out loud the whole way back to the Round House. *Stealing a locked box from the ruling family? Unthinkable.* Nevertheless, he carried it for Aza and put it upstairs. He even volunteered to help her pick the lock, but she refused and sent him on his way. She lockspelled both doors, drew all the downstairs curtains, and went to her bedroom.

The box sat on a table that she used as a desk. It faced the terrace doors. She sat down and looked out the glass panes for a while. She could see treetops and sky, but knew that if she stood, there would also be a bit of the skyline of the city and a glimmer of water. There were so many things she needed to do. See Reva and Eguin. Connect with at least a half dozen or so MATRIA organizers. Go through and remove all their belongings at the Villa. Pay her respects to Maleka's family. *I have to go see the twins!* Gerland had reassured her that they were settling in happily. They loved being around all the children and vice versa. But Aza couldn't let them forget their Auntie Zaz.

"Aza," she said out loud, "you are procrastinating. Let's get this open."

The lock opening was on top, in the center. It was rounded on one end, splayed at the other, with a large keyhole like a door key.

She found a blanket, spread it on the bed and dumped the contents of her satchel onto it. She had seen several keys. She found four.

"Hmm, and why would someone keep a key in the drawer over a cabinet that held the locked box?" *Maybe a person with a secret room.* It was worth a try.

Two were obviously too small. One looked like a door key. She tried, but it didn't work. The fourth looked promising. Her heart raced as it fit and turned part way. It did not open the lock. She sat, looking at the thing, feeling stupid that she hadn't taken Gerland up on his offer.

Bosh, why didn't I search Mam Sior's office or bedroom for a key? Because I wanted to be rid of that abandoned shrine to power as quickly as possible! The thought of going back into that house made her want to throw up. *I will lug this thing to Luftva and ask Pats to take it apart before I'll go back there!*

A vague memory nagged at her. She could almost conjure up a picture of a key in a pile of other things very much like those she'd taken from Sior's drawer. But she couldn't pinpoint where or when. Because she couldn't think of what else to do, she went downstairs and looked through all the drawers. The longer she looked, the more obviously useless this seemed. Why would a key in a house she randomly moved to fit a lockbox she'd just stolen from a house she'd worked in? Then again, it was in the realm of possible because very old keys were made more simply and could open a variety of locks from the same time period. It was a miniscule possibility that soon became a moot question. She found no key.

Besides, her nagging memory wasn't *that* recent. *Maybe from Reva's house? Could be. But anything from there would be even less likely to open Mam Sior's box.* A memory from when she worked at the Komeh? Aza fervently hoped not. She thought of Pats. *What is needed is his brute force.*

She gathered everything she could find in the house that could possibly be helpful in picking a lock or dismantling a metal box. As she was looking around for other tools, Zaz drifted away.

Soon, her other eyes showed a carpetbag on the floor of her closet.

As Zaz reintegrated, Aza sprinted, dropping a fish knife on the stairs but not bothering to retrieve it. She opened the closet and reached for the bag Gerland had brought over after she moved here. He and Ness kept it for her all those months since she'd fallen ill at Rimna's house.

Her mother's things. *Or Oscera's things. Or Arja's. Both, all mixed up.* Maripes, *what a jumble.*

Putting it on the bed with the rest of the mess, Aza fingered the necklace she'd worn constantly since she found it that night. "I've been too busy to get back to all this," she said, in defense of herself to herself. Aza had strange feelings about that night at Rimna's. She had been delirious, after all.

Life had pelted on. Aza had important things on her plate and Oscera's confession had made Aza even less likely to dig into it. That the journal was a phony ploy of Leo's to keep her in the dark forever? *Ugh.* It was all ultimately unimportant. Aza no longer had time or patience for a little girl's dreams of her lost mother.

She opened the bag. The journal sat on top. She ran a finger down its spine and tossed it aside. She dug under sketches and cards, set aside a perfume bottle, a bone brush with matching broken mirror, and dug into the corners of the bag.

There. She plucked out a key, pleased that her memory had been accurate, but knowing it was no more likely to open Mam Sior's locked box than any other key in Maripesa. It looked the proper size, though, so she walked to the table and pushed the key into the hole. A shiver went down her spine. It seemed to fit, but then so had one of the others. She twisted her hand and turned the key. It clicked.

She pulled up. The box opened. Inside was a deep, orderly stack of letters and papers. Aza's knees buckled. Luckily, there was a chair to catch her.

Long into the night, Aza examined the correspondence of a lifetime. She had four piles: Of no interest to anyone. Of no interest to her. Possibly interesting. Interesting.

Most in the Interesting pile were letters from Leo to Sior. Aza had only read about a third of them, but had sorted them by date. The earliest ones were actual love letters, or more accurately, lust letters. The two of them couldn't wait to find the time and place to "be together" again—over and over and over. It turned her stomach, but there was no doubt that they'd had a love affair when they were in their late teens. So much for her and Bek's disbelief that any older generation would have done such crossed-clan activities. Her father had said as much, though so vaguely that there was no way she could have comprehended it at the time.

The correspondence stopped for a time when Sior married, but cropped up again years later and, though she saw no references to Leo's marriage or a half-clan baby or any kind of contract, Aza knew from the dates that Mam Sior must have begun to require this written...adherence from him around the time Aza was born. Part of her payment for not having the both of them executed, along with her mother. *How could anything be more pitiful?* From what she'd read so far, the later correspondences had nothing sexual in them, but they were kind and always signed, *With Love, Leo.*

All this diluted Aza's anger, if not her incredulity, at her father. He was so shamed and desperate for forgiveness at the end, and now she at least partially understood why he waited so long to tell her.

I have to get some sleep. Why am I doing this to myself? This is about bringing down the Puraples, not about my personal family history. But she was obsessed. These people were dead. She had to keep reading to see if there was an explanation of how Sior found out about Leo's Undone child. Perhaps Sior had always kept tabs on his life. If she still loved him despite her subsequent marriages, she could have been jealous enough to do that. So...maybe she confronted him with his transgression. He parried with her own—their own—affair, of which there *was* written proof.

Zlo! I have to go through all Leo's personal papers. He must have letters from Sior. Again, why hadn't she thought of it before now? *Because you have been busy trying to make this whole society better! You don't have time or energy for all this! What difference does it make now? These people are all dead. Your mother, Sior, Leo! I survived. Like Capsia and Emke will survive. It happens. This ancient history is not important anymore!*

Except this: Written proof of Sior's affairs and blackmail could be a part of Aza's revenge. Ultimately, it just might be that woman's cruel, self-serving hypocrisy that would permanently ruin Ferjival and the rest of his clan. She certainly didn't believe Leo had continued to love the person who held him and Aza hostage. He had to continue the charade, including finding a Gen woman to pretend to be her mother after Sior killed her real mother in secret.

Did he love her? Grieve her?

Exhausted, Aza sat on the floor, numbed by it all. She could feel no grief for a nameless mother lost so long ago. Or for a father so compromised. There was only rage—her normal state of being these days, since Maleka's murder. But she couldn't feel that *every* moment. For now, she was beyond tired, her back hurt, and she'd had nothing to eat for hours. She stood and stretched, groaning with the effort.

Looking down on the empty lockbox, she noticed that the bottom was a different color than the box itself. She leaned over for a closer look. A piece of greyed paper lay flat, fitting tightly to the contours of the box. She dug under the sides of it and lifted out a large, once-sealed envelope. There was a neat slit along the top edge. Aza pressed the sides open and saw a sheet of paper inside. With two fingers, she fished it out. She let out a long slow breath, her eyes scanning down to the bottom, seeing two signatures: Sior Puraples and Leo Gen. A legal document.

The contract.

Aza crumpled to the floor.

Here it was: her father's promise to indenture his daughter Aza to Sior's household in exchange for her pledge not to put her to death for being half-clan. Seeing it in stark black and white was completely different from knowing it. *How had he lived with it?*

She lay on her side for a long time, not crying, not feeling much at all, but tired, so tired. She wanted only to sleep, but knew she couldn't. She needed to pee, was dirty and hungry, and her bed was covered with junk. But she had to take care of herself, or she'd get sick again and then she wouldn't be strong enough to take down the house of Puraples.

Aza lifted herself on one elbow and sat up, still holding the envelope in her left hand. There was something else inside. She turned it upside down and shook. A yellowed card of heavy stock drifted to the floor, face up. Without touching it, Aza read.

State of Maripesa
<u>Official Name Registration</u>
Date: April 3, 1867
Given name: Aza
Gender: Girl
Clan: Puraples
Born to: Sior

Vijo arrived early to the Round House dressed in several layers with hat, gloves, and scarf. It had been five days since anyone had seen or talked to Aza other than to hear, "Go away!" from inside the Round House, but Vijo had a plan. He would camp out on her doorstep, using to his advantage the frigid weather that had taken hold of the city the day Maleka was killed. If Aza knew she was hurting someone else with her actions, she'd reconsider her behavior.

He pounded on the door relentlessly until he heard her screaming: "Go away!"

"It's Vijo! I will wait in the cold until you let me in."

No response.

"It's below freezing!"

"Then go home, you fool!"

"I am staying!"

He sat in a chair he'd put in front of the door, tucked a blanket around him, and pulled out his reading material: an old tome on methods of imbuing objects with magic. Every so often, he banged on the door. When he got cold just sitting, he walked around the house and banged on the back door and every downstairs window.

His hands and feet had long gone numb when Oscera arrived with hot tea and egg pies. He managed to burn his tongue on the first one, adding to his misery, and any warmth he got from the snack dissipated rapidly, but at least his belly was full. To keep from freezing, he paced back and forth on the short stone patio, banging on the door every time he passed.

You're just going to have to break in. Shouldn't Oscera have a key? No, it's a spelllock. Freja might know. Unless Aza spelled it when she moved in. Never mind. He wanted Aza to let him in. He rewrapped his face with his scarf and kept walking, angry now. *What is wrong with you, Aza? If you don't want to see anyone, fine, but tell us to our faces. Don't make us worry about you needlessly. How can we know what to do if you just disappear? That's another thing—Bam!—why did you stay here with your misery? You could have told us that you needed some time away and wanted to—Bam!—be alone and we would have all respected that. If you didn't want to actually see anyone, then send a message. I think...I think—Bam!—you wanted someone to force you to come out, to be seen. Otherwise...why stay here? It is just—*

His fist was raised for another hit on the door when it opened.

Aza glared at him.

He glared back.

Vijo had enough perspective to know that this would have appeared funny to someone else. But not him. Not now. And it was clear, not to her either. He counted to himself at a normal speed and got to fifty-five before he saw a tiny change in her scowl.

"My house is getting cold," she growled

"You must let me in. I am...frozen."

She turned away and started toward the kitchen, saying, "You really are the most irritating person. So very—" She turned around at the counter, leaned on it and folded her arms—"stubborn."

He closed the door behind him and followed her, his face alive with pin pricks—and not in a good way. He could feel the cold radiating off him.

"You fool," she said. "I'll make a fire."

"Why hasn't the fire been going all morning? What is wrong with you?"

She ignored him until the fire roared to life.

Suddenly, he couldn't wait to rid himself of the coat. He finally got it off after wrestling with numbed fingers. He gratefully sat in the kitchen chair she pulled up for him in front of what had settled into a middling fire.

"I guess I'll have to stoke that thing. What with all the cold air you've let in." As she worked on it, she said, "This is the most irritating thing a so-called 'friend' has ever done to me. I have a perfect right to not take visitors, curse you. By my clan, who do you think you are, invading my privacy this way?"

It went on and on.

He said nothing. Just accepted the warmth of her fire, the tea she brewed, and the sound of her angry, bitter voice.

This is love. I love her. It doesn't matter if she can or can't love me. It doesn't matter if she even knows. It only matters that I know. It may hurt as time goes on, but for right now, it feels fine. Good, even. It feels good to not be nobly standing aside to make room for Bek, who is great, but all wrong for Aza. I may not be good for her either, but I do know her. I knew she wouldn't let me suffer out there for too long. Not because it's me. She would do the same for any friend. Really, anyone. And maybe that's the problem. Maybe Aza will never be just for one person. It doesn't matter. I love her. Even her outrage.

"Vijo!"

He had stopped listening to her rant some time ago.

"Yes?"

"Are your feet warming up?"

He sighed and wiggled his toes. He'd taken off his boots earlier and still wore socks. "They are a bit painful, but no permanent damage."

"I wouldn't think so."

"Aza?"

"Yes?"

"Tell me what's going on."

"No."

"Tell me what isn't going on."

"Stop it."

"Now that you've let me in, I won't leave until you confide in me."

"You will leave when I tell you to."

"You look...dirty. Have you given up bathing?"

She literally growled at him. "Who the hell do you think you are?"

"You know who I am. I am a healer."

"You have too much time on your hands, then. Go back to proper Besin work and leave me alone."

"About that!" he said. "You asked me to do some work for you. Remember?"

She sighed. "Of course I remember. But I don't care anymore."

"You'll care about this. I am so impressed with myself that I've started thinking of myself as more than a healer. I'm becoming a mage."

She laughed.

It was more scoff than amusement. A snort, really, but he'd caught her off guard. She had been amused. And distracted. Progress.

"A rather old-fashioned term, don't you think?" She brought over a large plate—filled with bread, dried figs, and cheeses—sat at the table, selected a hunk of cheddar, and started munching.

He pulled his chair over and took a slab of bread. "That's why it's good. I'm convinced I know as much about the...*science* of magic in our fair city as anyone. More even than the Tchuvari. Not that I've actually tested that theory. It doesn't matter. It's not a contest. But I've made progress in figuring out how those soltecs work. I've even started making one. That, as it turns out, may not be my forte. But I could tell someone how. Or I could learn metallurgy and blacksmithing."

"Maybe Pats would help."

"What a great idea!"

"So, no more simple healing?"

Vijo shrugged. "I can't not be a healer. It's pretty much in my makeup, you know?"

Her face clouded, and there was a sudden change of subject. "I won't be able to tell you what has happened in my life that makes me not want to talk to anyone. But I will tell you that everything is different now and that it's going to take me a long time to deal with it and that I may never deal with it or be the same ever again. So don't expect me to be the same."

"Sure," he said softly. "No problem." Her face was set in a scowl, but she looked up at him out of the corner of her eye. "Tell me this, though," Vijo said. "Does this new Aza bathe? Wash her hair? Because that is one tangled, filthy mess you've got on your head."

"Gods, you're irritating! How did I never notice this before?"

He reached over and put his hand over hers. Thankfully, the touch seemed to calm her, and he wondered for the umpteenth time how much unconscious magic he had in him. He whispered, "I do not know what to say to the new Aza. I'm feeling my way. It's like trying to treat a case of giarmial when the first three treatments haven't done what they're supposed to. I did it with you once. You wouldn't remember, but I do. My magic hadn't worked. You were better, but not well. So I...felt my way. I used a little of this and more of that and figured it out."

The scowl dropped away and left only sadness on her face.

Maybe I do have some untold magic in me. "This is me, Aza. *I* have not changed. I don't give up on someone I think I can help. You are hurting. I don't know why. I'm pretty sure it's not from a curse or spell. It's probably a real life hurt heaped on you in a completely natural way by some human. But it's a puzzle I am going to solve. Count on it."

She got up and walked toward the stairs. Before leaving the room, she said, "The fire will have heated the water, but would you pump the cistern? I have to bathe."

An hour later, she called, "Vijo? You still here?"

He walked to the bottom of the stairs. "You know it."

"Want to come up?"

He did. And he did.

He worked at not showing any shock at the utter chaos of her bedroom. She'd invited him here, so something had loosened inside her and he didn't want her to tighten up again.

She wore a heavy robe over a winter nightgown. Her hair was wet. She hung her head and said so softly that he almost missed it, "I'm too exhausted to clean off my bed."

His heart pumped one extra hard beat at the misery in her voice. "Let me. Sit down. Here." He took some papers off the only chair in the room and put them on the floor. He crossed to the bed, gathered up the corners of the small blanket, lifted the jumbled mess off, and placed it on the floor of the closet. He went back to the bed, straightened the coverlet and wiped off dust and such.

A bitter laugh made him turn around. "Now, Aza," she said, still looking hurt and miserable, "was that so hard?"

He went over and gently took her forearm. "Come on. Get in bed."

She came willingly. He pulled down the top bedding, and she took off the robe and crawled in. "I've been sleeping downstairs."

"It's going to be fine. You've got your bed now. What else do you need?"

She started to cry.

"Oh, Aza. What is it? No. Never mind. Just let it out. Cry as much as you need to."

"It's all I've been doing for days!"

He handed her his handkerchief. "No wonder you're so tired. It's going to be all right. Is it Maleka? You were so angry that I thought that would carry you for a while, but it seems to have hit you all at once. Just feel what you feel and keep letting the tears come. It won't last forever."

At this, she wailed, the tears coming harder.

He sat next to her, saying nothing, until the fresh wave waned. She burrowed down into the pillow, lying on her side facing him. "It won't get better. I know that's what people say, but it won't. I am warning you. Do not say that to me again."

"Sure."

"Vijo?"

"Yes?"

"Will you—? Would you—?"

"Anything."

"Would you consider lying down with me?"

She fell asleep in his arms. He had never been happier, which made him feel ashamed because she was so very troubled. When his arm went to sleep, he carefully rolled Aza over and slid it out from under her. He thought about getting up and doing some snooping to see what all these papers and letters and documents and that heavy old lockbox were all about.

Her father's things? Zlo, she's been through a lot. Her father's death, her loss of clan, her illness, the arrest warrant, the stress of having Ferjival as prisoner, a broken heart from Bek's dismissiveness, and Maleka's execution on top of it all.

But he guessed there was something more. *What could be worse than all that?*

He didn't get up. He lay with her and thought about what he might be able to do to help, but that proved to be a circle of unknowing, so he thought about the puzzle of wards and soltecs and magicking objects. He'd read much but had to fill in what wasn't written down by extrapolating from silly, simple charms to something as profound as a ward against curses. And when he grew tired of magic, he thought about how wonderful it felt to be warm, in a bed with clean sheets, with a woman he loved. And, eventually, he fell asleep too.

32

ADAPTING TO CHANGE

AZA WOKE FIRST—BLEAK, BEDRAGGLED, but somewhat rested and grateful to have Vijo sharing her bed. A strange calm—or was it resignation?—had, at this moment, replaced misery and rage. It wouldn't last. In this relative serenity, she started talking softly—in a whisper at first.

"I have to rethink every single thing about myself, Vijo. I'm not Gen. I'm not even Salizan. I am Puraples, and the worst kind of Purple. Sior was my mother, gods help me. I am hateful to myself. I want this fact to go away. I won't ever be happy again."

She paused as a few tears escaped, but they didn't start a deluge.

"I keep thinking, *this is the worst part of it*. And then I think of some new worst thing. And then another. There's no end to the nightmarish ramifications. I'm not only an Undone, I'm the product of two horrible human beings. Their actions are incomprehensible. My father's memory is false and sickening. He lied to me my entire life. My mother didn't die when I was a baby, more's the pity. And I, who never had a cousin much less a sibling, with no one other than my father to call 'family,' have—guess what?—a huge family! A family I loathe. A family everyone loathes. Eight half-siblings? Oh gods! Only seven since my half-brother Ferjival—*Maripes*, I gag on it—put *our* brother Hasip to death."

She thought of Maleka, and a few more tears rolled down her cheeks.

"I want to...I don't know. I was going to say I want to go to the country and live out my days milking cows and taking over chores that Reva and Eguin are too old to do. Would that be so wrong? Then maybe I wouldn't have to think about all this. It's as far away as I can imagine being. But maybe I should go farther. What's beyond the farms and the fields? There's more, right? I mean, there's a whole world out there, so I should maybe just go away. I wonder how much money I have. I should find out. I should..."

More tears. This time a lot more. "Spells, they're never going to stop."

Once the flood passed, she looked at Vijo. His eyes were open.

"How long have you been awake?"

"Long enough."

"You got the picture, then?"

"I know Ferjival is your half-brother."

He said this calmly. *He isn't so appalled that he's jumped out of bed shouting in horror. That is good. Bless him.*

"All right," she said with a sigh. "Thanks for everything."

"It's my pleasure."

She took a few minutes to wipe her face and blow her nose, and then turned to him. "We should have sex. I know the spell. Not that I've used it before. Is it immediate? I mean...do you have to wait for it to take effect? I guess not."

"Stop."

"What?"

"We are not going to have sex right now."

"Oh. Shouldn't we? We're in bed together. I'm so thankful you're here and I care about you so much and you're so good to me—better than anyone, really. And I—Well, it's about time for me, I think. Past time. And—"

"And it is the absolute wrong time, even if we do happen to be in bed together." He rolled over and motioned for her to come into his arms.

She hesitated and then did so, resting her head on his chest, snuggling into him. "It seems like the right time. You don't want to have sex with me?"

He sighed loudly. "Oh, yes. I do. Very much. But Aza, you're having a major crisis. I don't want to have sex with you when you're so emotionally drained and worried about this huge secret you've uncovered. When and if we do have sex, I want it to be about us. I want it to be at a happy time, or at least a time where we can both be focused on just us. I think that won't be for a while."

"Hmm. Well, we'll see about that. But I understand. I'm very inexperienced, Vijo. I want to change that about myself."

"But...why? What difference does it make?"

Now it was her time to sigh. "I—" She had to stop because she was crying again. "Damn these tears!" She rolled over and wiped her face on the pillow, already damp. "I want to be a woman, but I still feel like a little girl. I didn't even know about the anti-pregnancy spell until this year." She stopped and gulped back tears. "And then I fell for Bek. We were together one time and, and...I just thought—well, I thought many things. It felt so good to be touched." This last word was whispered. "Oh gods, I'm sorry. I shouldn't be talking to you about her, but I just wanted to answer your question and I can't not talk about Bek, because she's my only sexual experience and it was great, but is that because I love her or is it because it was my first time?"

Vijo smiled. "Everyone loves Bek, Aza. Or wants to. She's easy to fall in love with. Don't beat yourself up about that."

"But I guess it wasn't...real."

"Whew," he said. "'Real' is a very solid word for something as ephemeral as love...or sexual attraction."

"Is it? What about Ness and Gerland? Or Reva and Eguin? Is their love not real?"

He smiled again, but this time a full-on grin. "Are you always so talkative and philosophical first thing in the morning? Because...me? I'm not. I just wake up, pee, maybe bathe and then have my breakfast. Maybe then I'm ready to figure out answers to life's deepest mysteries. But that's just me."

She laughed, amazed that any kind of expression of happiness could come out of her after what had just happened. "Ah, Vijo. Thank you. Go, relieve your bladder. Thanks to you, I'll get up with a teeny-tiny glimmer of hope that I can continue with life—such as it is."

Three days later, there was a knock at the Round House door. Aza was still shaky, but knew she had to face the world—at least *her* world. She opened it, expecting to see Reth or Oscera or perhaps a Messagery boy. But her heart leaped in her chest at the sight of the familiar, yet terrifyingly powerful, old man on her doorstep.

"Council Leader Droht?"

The Puraples elder gave a small bow. "I wish you no harm, Miss Aza."

"What are you doing here? How did you find me?"

He looked around as if worried that someone might hear, but of course, no one was nearby. "I won't intrude on your life, but I wanted you to know that your arrest warrant is no more. You probably assumed that after Mam Sior passed away, but I felt you deserved some personal assurance. However, my primary mission is," he reached into his coat and pulled out a sealed letter, "delivering this."

"What is it?" Aza asked, unwilling to reach for it.

"Shortly before Mam Sior passed away, she wrote it and asked that I hand deliver it to you as soon as possible after her death. It took a while to find you."

"Yes," she breathed out. "That was the idea."

"I know, but to be honest, we weren't trying all that hard. Most of us were extremely busy just trying to keep up with each day's crisis."

She gave him a side glance. "Like everyone else in the city."

"I guess so."

She took the letter from him not because she wanted it, but because she didn't know how else to get rid of him. "Forgive me if I cannot offer my thanks."

"Understood. I wish you well." He turned to leave.

"Droht?"

"Yes?"

"What's happening with the Puraples?"

He didn't answer for a few moments. He stood, rubbing his mouth between two fingers. Finally, he said, "We may fall."

"What?"

"There are...ongoing negotiations. It does not look good for us. Mam Sior, I'm afraid, despite her commanding presence and all her many offspring, did not build a...um, stable bridge to the next Leader. We have been in chaos since she passed."

"While the Kruiks have been preparing for some time to take over?"

"Correct."

"We all must adapt to change."

He nodded to her, turned, and walked away.

Aza closed the door, leaned against it for a few moments, thinking about adapting to change. Then she went to sit by the fire next to Vijo. "Did you hear?"

"No, but I saw it was a Purple."

"Mam Sior's closest advisor."

"Wow. And...?"

"Officially, I am no longer a fugitive. Not from the Puraples, anyway."

"Who else would want you arrested?"

She shrugged. "Whoever is in charge of enforcing the rules? From what Droht said, likely the Kruik soon."

"*Zlo*," he said softly. "That's...hard to imagine."

"And this." Aza held up the note. "It's from my *mother*." The word came out with such bitterness that she felt a spasm in her throat as if she might bring up bile.

"Oh my *Maripes*, Aza. That's..." He shook his head slowly. "I don't even know what to say."

"Yeah. I understand that."

"Are you going to read it?"

"I have to."

Neither of them spoke for a while, as Aza fingered the heavy paper and deep purple seal. Finally, she ripped it open and unfolded it. Her breath caught in her throat. Vijo put his hand on her arm. She read out loud.

"Aza,

I would not have executed you.

The way you looked at me at Leo's funeral convinced me that he had told you our secret before he died. With everything in such turmoil, I could not risk that you might spread to all of Maripesa that I had a half-clan child. But I only wanted you close by. Arrested, under my control, but not dead.

I had plenty of opportunities to have you executed, but I always wanted you alive. I wanted that while I was pregnant and constantly worried that my then husband—Ferjival and Hasip's father—who himself was near death, would be suspicious and tell others. I wanted you alive when Leo and I negotiated whose child you would be. Leo won that one, which was fortuitous because no one would have believed you were pure Puraples with all those freckles you developed. (Everyone was told that my pregnancy ended in a stillbirth.) I wanted you alive even when it was clear Leo had come to detest me. I wanted you alive as a reminder that we had loved each other when we were young, and that once, a long time later, had relations that brought about you. I told him, by the way, that I'd done the contraception spell. He had no responsibility for bringing you into the world. It was my decision alone.

Now, at the end, I look at all my children and see nothing of myself. There's not one of you who is even ambitious, much less a leader or visionary. You least of all. I watched you be nothing but subservient, uncomplaining, satisfied with your lot. I have learned, ironically, that clan traits are an unreliable thing to base one's society on.

But I was your mother, and I loved your father for most of my life. — Sior Puraples"

Aza let the paper fall into her lap.

"*Maripes,*" Vijo said.

"I know." Aza looked into Vijo's blue eyes. "It's the best thing she could have done for me."

He looked incredulous. "What do you mean? It's horrible."

"My constant worry since I found out has been: What if I am like my mother? But she said that I'm definitely not—in any way. She's dead. Thank *Maripes* I didn't have to tolerate her as a parent all these years, and now I'm free of her."

When the grip of their short winter passed, the Puraples flag—a gold-feathered raptor on a field of purple and black—came down from the Council of Clans building.

Tapinak bells—different ones from Maleka's—chimed to announce to the citizens of Maripesa that the hierarchy had shifted for the first time in most people's lives. Slowly, the Kruik flag, of midnight and royal blue with pale blue ripples, rose over the city.

Vijo and Aza watched from her balcony.

Oscera had come to tell them the news after it had been decided early that morning. The leaders of all clans met in the inner sanctum with the Tchuvari Keepers—the highest of the high—and the consensus had been that the Puraples were sufficiently weakened—economically, politically, physically, and morally—that they no longer held the power position in Maripesa.

Benelek Kruik, Leader of the Kruik Council, was named Ruler of Maripesa.

"What a stunning rise," Vijo said. "I also happen to believe she'll do a stunning job."

"I'm not so sure," Aza said. "Power corrupts, doesn't it? I feel somewhat responsible for Bek gaining her lofty position."

"Is that a delusion of grandeur, Aza?"

"Maybe. No. She used matriarchal magic to become leader of her council. That wouldn't have happened without me introducing her to the MATRIA."

"She isn't evil. Besides, I'm the one who brought her out to the country. You might as well say it's my fault. Speaking of the country, could we go today to retrieve the soltec?"

They'd spent the morning talking about Vijo's progress with the wards and soltecs. He had so much enthusiasm for what he'd learned, and she needed his expertise more than ever now. If she could put some protections in place for the citizens of Maripesa who had gone so long without any, then she just might be able to get through the ugly realities of her life that could never be warded.

Aza had made progress on this as well, even though there was no possibility of forgetting her hard new reality for more than a few minutes at a time. She likened it to what she knew of childbirth. Ness had explained the brilliant way the body had evolved labor pains that lasted for no longer than one to three minutes and then went away completely for twice that long. "That way," Ness said, "we can stand what would otherwise be unbearable." So Aza coped by attempting to lengthen the time she maintained focus on something else. She had to live in the time between the pain.

"So what do you say? A trip to Luftva?"

Aza smiled. "I would love to go see Reva and Eguin, but not today. Won't there be heavy traffic? Celebrations?" She shrugged. "I guess we don't know how this is supposed to work, since most of us have never been through a change of ruling families. Let's plan a spring picnic at the farm with all our friends."

"Right, then I'll take the day to do more study."

"Vijo...you know there are soltecs much nearer to us than Luftva."

"Well, sure. But—"
"Ask no questions, my good man. I know the way."

33

ACCOUNTABLE

THIS WAS AZA'S FOURTH time in the seedy lobby of the Wardrobe—such an unlikely spot for so much learning.

The night Duma brought her here, over a year ago, she knew nothing about the mixing of clans, the social "scene" that some people in the city played with, or the anti-pregnancy spell. That night, she found out Duma had been keeping secret the rumors about Maleka.

She could think the name "Maleka" now without having physical pain, but it filled her chest with what felt like emptiness, even though that made no sense.

The second time was right after Leo died. The day she'd walked away from her old life and saw Bek in the arms of a woman.

The third time was *her* night to lie in that messy bed and be transported by the lovely Benelek. That it turned out to be sexual pleasure instead of love wasn't the worst lesson she'd ever had.

And now.

This time, she would provide the education to others.

Aza had scheduled this meeting in the wee hours to avoid having any-one else around. She arrived early and took the elevator to the roof. A crisp, promise-of-spring breeze stroke her face as she emerged. The gaslights were still burning. Good. She wanted to see their faces.

She sent Zaz out to watch for them.

First came Ferjival. Zaz stayed with him. He stopped on the third floor to knock back two drinks. Aza went to the far corner of the rooftop and waited in deep shadow. He arrived, a third drink in his hands, and stood at the half-wall looking out at the city.

Zaz missed Bek, who suddenly burst forth from the stairwell door.

Ah yes, I forgot. She likes to take the stairs. It keeps her options open.

Bek saw Ferjival and let out a low groan.

He turned around, startled.

"You?" he said. "You put Aza Gen's name on the message? Or made her write it under duress?"

"Shut up. I did no such thing. Obviously, Aza asked us both to come."

Neither said anything for a long moment, but Aza thought there might be more between them. She waited.

"So," Ferjival said, his voice gruff, "you did it. You'll pardon me if I don't congratulate you. You used some underhanded tactics, even for Kruiks."

Bek laughed lightly, genuinely. "The capacity for self-delusion and hypocrisy is strong in your clan. Underhanded? You put your own brother to death in an attempt to hold on to power." Her tone went from chatty to venomous in two sentences.

"We followed the law."

"Oh, really? We both know your clan used the law when and if it suited your purposes. Spare me your propaganda. We won fair and square."

"You persuaded the Gen to stop working for us!"

"Oh no. I did not." She sounded genuinely affronted that she'd been accused of something she actually had no part in, but then said, "I should have. I thought of that tactic long ago. But no. The Gen made that choice. I was busy with other strategic planning."

"Attacking our livelihoods!"

She grinned and bowed regally. "That, I take credit for. Me and a sharp little teen who's now on my staff. She really got it right, didn't she? Pinpointed attacks that brought you down in days after months of skirmishes. Yep, I impressed even myself on that one."

"I'm leaving."

Aza stepped into the light.

"You've been here all along?" Bek asked.

"Uh-huh."

Ferjival rolled his eyes at her. "Grow up."

"Oh, I have. Both of you had a big hand in that, I must say, but yes, I've come a long way in a year."

"You and me both, sister," said Bek.

Aza winced internally. She was a sister to one of them, but it wasn't Bek. "I asked you here to put you on notice."

"Of what?" said Ferjival, scornfully.

"Bek, you first. We're friends. I hope that continues. I admire you, as most people do, but power can twist a personality. I won't hesitate to call you out when I see it happening."

Bek's face went hard, but she said, "Feel free. I can take it."

Aza turned to Ferjival. "We have much unfinished business between us. We could never be friendly, much less friends, but I don't consider you my enemy."

"Aw, how heartwarming...after you held me prisoner for weeks."

"If I hadn't, you would have put me to death. Besides, while I don't expect a thank you, we both know you benefited from that time away."

"You two," he said, shaking his head. "It's so convenient that your arms are long enough to pat yourselves on the back. It's no credit to you, Gen, if I made the best possible use of my imprisonment."

Aza felt bitterly amused that he continued to call her "Gen."

"The three of us have very little to bind us and yet we are bound by our influence over segments of the populace."

Bek, it seemed, had lost her voice, but Ferjival's emotions were on full display. "You? You are nothing. An Undone, half-breed or double-breed? A mongrel. Oh, I see...you're talking about that little women's group you got together? Ooh, Bek, Queen of the City will be quaking on her throne over a few old crones who know how to—what? Predict what color outfit the next person who walks into the room will wear?"

"Of course you underestimate the MATRIA. Good. Continue to believe that our Talents are small and unimportant. You will learn. And this is one of the warnings I serve notice of—" Aza paused, and when she spoke again, her voice was deeper, slower, stronger. "The MATRIA stretch across all the clans, including the Tchuvari. We subvert the status quo."

"Good. Lately, the status quo hasn't pleased me so well."

"In addition to the MATRIA, my plan is to organize *my* people, *my clan*: the Undone of this city. Do you have any idea of the numbers we represent? You wouldn't, because no one does. But it is my mission going forward to find out. And, don't forget: The Undones will encompass the full span of Talents."

Bek finally found her voice. "That remains to be seen. Plus, numbers mean nothing. There have always been more Salizans and Dals than Puraples and Kruiks. I don't mean to be rude, but so what?"

"She's right. There is no power in the city except the two ruling clans."

"It's clear that neither of you has the imagination to take in what I'm giving you notice of. Everything changed while your clans were warring. Ignore that fact at your peril. Now, we have the traditional clans but also the MATRIA which crosses all clans, and we will soon have organized Undones, new name yet to be decided. And there's more! Last is the group that had grown so devastatingly passive under Mam Sior's rule: the Tchuvari. They are awake now and I will not let them sleep again. I am on their council."

"Doesn't matter," Ferjival said. "They have no teeth."

Bek said, "As leader of the city, I will be happy to work with the Tchuvari to improve relations between all the clans."

Aza gazed at her. The breezy, unthoughtful way Bek let these words float from her mouth, convinced Aza that she would rule as she pleased—given the chance.

Aza said, "Ferjival, maybe you are so far out of the loop that you don't know this, but Bek knows. The Tchuvari are setting up a system to ward essential services in the city. Never again will the Kruiks have the ability to do what they did the day of Mam Sior's funeral.

"And there's more. I am heading up negotiations for a Gen-Besin coalition. Before responding to any crisis initiated by the casting of curses by either of the once-called 'ruling clans,' the leaders of the two helping clans will confer and coordinate their responses. We will no longer be working in a vacuum. We are natural allies who somehow forgot that over the decades. We will use a combined stop-work action whenever necessary to *hold you in check*."

Ferjival sat down and looked around as if in boredom, but fidgety hands gave away underlying agitation. Bek's shoulders and chin kept rising higher and higher.

Aza took a deep breath. "One last thing. I have in my possession and safe-keeping all the soltecs that once lay as artifacts in our Archives. I took eight of them to complete the set along with the one you stole, Ferjival."

"It was given to me," he spat. "And you stole that one from me. How can you stand there so holy and innocent while lecturing to us as if we were the wayward children?"

"Why? What significance do the soltecs have?" asked Bek.

"I shall keep my own counsel on that one."

"Planning to take our magic away?" Ferjival laughed, but it came out as more of a snarl.

"Excuse me if I don't start worrying about that one anytime soon," said Bek lightly. "Besides, the Kruiks will be very different rulers than the Purples have been, so there will be peace between clans."

Ferjival snorted.

"Peace? Perhaps," Aza said. "All citizens should welcome that. But even peace will not give you the same conditions that the Puraples took advantage of. I know it's a lot to take in, but you'll have all the time in the world to process what it means for the ruling families to have to contend with—" she held up her hand and counted them off—"an independent, helping class made up of Besins and Gens working together to decide when and where they clean up your messes, a cohesive clan of Undones with their own accumulations of Talents, a cross-clan matriarchal subset who will be expanding their own awareness and practice of their unique and very practical magic, a newly activist and growing Tchuvari ready to change society in fundamental ways, and my pet soltec project." Aza pinned Bek with a stare.

Bek said, "Aza, I know things have been rough for you lately, but you seem to have taken your grief and built it into delusions of grandeur. You'd think that you'd been made Leader of the Ruling Family instead of me."

Aza shook her head slowly. "I'm only giving you fair notice that Maripesa is not the same place it was—for better or worse. I'm sure there will be both."

Bek started toward the elevator. Ferjival turned to do the same.

"Please wait, Ferjival. I have something I need to say to you after Bek is gone."

He looked as if he were going to ignore her, but Bek brushed in front of him and whispered viciously, "You owe her!" She swooped around him, disappearing into the stairwell door.

Ferjival, shoulders drooping, slightly drunk, turned to face her.

Aza came closer and said, "I am your half-sister."

An extended silence stretched between them.

"I found out a few weeks ago after our mother's death. I haven't been able to deal with the details of it all to determine where I fall in line amongst you and your siblings, but it is true nonetheless."

He sniffed. Turned, and then turned back. He opened his mouth and shut it. He opened it again, and said, "A vicious lie."

"Oh, please. Why I would make this up? I have proof."

"My mother wanted you dead."

"No, she wanted me...found. She always wanted me under her thumb. I think you can relate to that, no? And anyway, whether she would have executed me doesn't matter. People do these things to family members, don't they?"

"I—*Spellfire!* I didn't want to! I was overruled. Cornered! Besides, that's—" He stopped, his head and shoulders sloping even more. He teetered, and Aza thought he was going to collapse, but he didn't. He got very still and nothing on the rooftop moved for a long while except the flickering flames of the gaslights. "My mother and your father? I don't believe it. Why do you?"

Aza sighed. "I have the official registration of my birth. I have some of their correspondence. If that's not enough for you, she wrote a letter to me shortly before her death telling me that she was my mother. She also said that she tricked my father into impregnating her."

He looked like he might throw up. "Why?!"

"She loved him, and our society forbade that love. She was obviously ambitious, but also wanted to hold on to the past. That's as sweet as it gets, because she used their child...me...to keep him under her thumb as well."

He sighed. "That rings true. What could he have had that made it worth her trouble?"

"An illusion of being loved? I guess it might be complicated. As you have time to consider all this, I think you'll find, as I have, that some pieces fall into place. It is a hard truth for me, you know."

"You hate the Puraples."

"I do."

"You are one of us." He said this slowly, as if impressing the words into mud.

"Registered at birth as a Puraples, yes. But according to the law, I am what I have known since my dying father told me my mother was not Gen. I am Undone. I can...I swear I will wear that label proudly."

He straightened his back and said, "Bully for you. Glad you're doing so well with your life. Mine is shit, as always."

"You can build a better clan, Ferjival."

"Me? You must be joking. You know what I'm fit for? Sitting on my arse in a barn churning butter. Thanks for leading me to that happy conclusion."

"I wanted to tell you how much I hate you for killing Maleka, but there's no pleasure in kicking a man when he's so far down."

"Again, I didn't want to. I brought Maleka back as a last-ditch effort to keep even more people from dying, but immediately became the council's patsy and then their scapegoat. The end. I *am* sorry about Maleka. I should have tried harder to save her. My brother got what he deserved."

"*Our* brother," Aza said, softly.

His head shot up, and they looked each other in the eyes for the first time tonight. He shook his head in continued disbelief. "You got her kids, though, right?"

"They are safe."

"Good. I'm going."

"I think it would be best for both of us if you kept this a secret."

Ferjival stared at her, considering, and then nodded. He walked to the elevator, and while waiting, said, "If you are half Puraples, can you cast a malady?"

The question shocked Aza into silence.

"Something to consider," he said, disappearing into the elevator.

Aza pressed her forehead against the wrought iron gate and peered into the sun-dappled courtyard of the Villa. Having finally found the time to move Leo's papers and personal items, she arranged to meet Reth here. Duma, what with the city's upheavals, had yet to move in, so a handful of new staff kept the place from being abandoned.

She swung the heavy gate open and slipped in. Everything seemed familiar. The bright shiny tiles. The same lush plants and flowering vines. The tiered fountain splashing, as always.

All the same, except the place smells different.

"Ah, Aza," Reth said, emerging from Leo's office to her right. He held several black folios in one arm.

"Good morning," she said, walking toward him.

"I got things sorted, so hopefully our chore won't take all day."

"Thank you," Aza said. "Obviously, I am not looking forward to this. I've put it off so long."

"Anyone could understand that. I started going through your father's documents way back when you were in Luftva. I was concerned that Duma would want to use his office, so those are the files I moved first. I was just in there checking the drawers and cabinets one last time. And a good thing, because I found these."

"What's in them?"

He held out the short stack and said, "I'm not sure. The one I looked at was notes from recent council meetings."

Aza took the top one and opened it. A familiar scent wafted up, causing her to let out a small gasp.

"What is it?"

Aza shook her head slightly. It took a moment for her to speak. "The first thing I noticed when I arrived is that the courtyard smelled different, but I didn't know until this minute what the difference was." She looked up at him, tears in her eyes. "His pipe smoke. The paper reeks of it." She lifted the folio to her face, inhaled deeply, and handed it back to Reth.

He smelled it, his face lingering near the likely unimportant top document. "Yes," he said, "*his* scent."

"Powerful, right?" Aza said, remembering the pipe ritual, the pauses her father took to tamp, light, smoke, relight. It was part of him. Inseparable from his being. All of that, and the rich smell of his tobacco.

Reth's eyes had gone red. She reached over and put her arm around his. "Are you all right?"

"Yes. Yes, very powerful. Let's go. With these, everything from Leo's office is in the library."

"Good. My favorite room after this one."

They walked in together arm in arm. On the right side was a formidable wooden library table on which Reth had neatly arranged staggered stacks of books with folders of papers in-between. "I tried to sort personal papers from Gen business so that we can get through them as quickly as possible. And then, here," he went to one end, "the personal files are also sorted into broad categories. Financial, here. You'll need to look at them closely, so I suggest taking all of these," he gestured over a section of the table, "to the Round House."

Aza sighed. "Yes. Thank you, Reth. It's...overwhelming. What would I do without you?"

He smiled. "I am so happy that I can help. I'm also happy that you're here at last. When I was putting all this here, I had no idea if I would ever see you again!"

"Oh *Maripes*." She walked over, put an arm around his back and rested her temple against his coarse linen jacket. We've both been through a lot." After a moment, she let go and said, "Right. Are there crates available to pack these in?"

He nodded, and after showing her where Leo's personal correspondence was, went to fetch what they would need to transfer files to Aza's home.

Aza's trepidation went deep. She did not want to uncover any more secrets in her father's life. "It's all right. Your mother's identity is the worst thing you could have uncovered. You will deal with it all over time. As you are ready."

She might find some more depth of information about Oscera—Arja's—time with her and Leo. That might be interesting. Or disturbing. And of course, further correspondence from Sior that could be useful, and even more disturbing. Her need for revenge was dissipating, but it could return. All of it still felt odd and unreal.

She caught sight of something in the middle of the table behind a stack of books. It was almost invisible in the dark room on the dark table. She stood on her tiptoes and reached over with some difficulty to touch it.

"*Zlo*, it's a lockbox."

Reth came back in, awkwardly carrying several crates.

"Reth."

"Yes?"

"Could you reach this for me?"

He walked over and said, "Oh, that. I had never seen it before. It was on the lower shelf of the bureau behind his desk, back in the corner. Hard to even see it back there." He picked it up and put it under one arm. "Where do you want it? I don't know if there's a key. Perhaps in the things I took out of the top drawer of his desk."

"Put it in a crate, please." Aza felt slightly dizzy at the *déjà vu* of it all. "I know where the key is."

"You do?"

"I never showed you Mam Sior's lockbox, but it looks just like this one. And, the key...well, it was the least of my worries when I found out that she was my mother, but it's nagged at me. Why would a key kept in the attic of this house open a lockbox that belonged to her? But I see now that they had identical boxes. It seems likely that the locks and keys were identical as well. Sior's key must still be somewhere in the Komeh."

Reth shook his head, trying to catch up. "The key in your keepsake boxes opened...?"

Aza nodded. "A lockbox just like this one that I took from Mam Sior's hidden room."

Reth put the box in a crate, pulled out one of the chairs, and sat down. "What do you think might be in this one?"

"Leo would have kept his copy of their contract."

"Oh, yes. He would have."

"The planning that went into this whole charade! Part of it was to acquire two lockboxes where each could keep their copy hidden away."

Aza walked to the window overlooking the back garden. "Sior even had a hidden room for hers."

After some time, Reth said, "Are you all right?"

"I will be."

Aza walked back to the lockbox and said, "Could you take this to your place? I don't want it in my house yet. We think we already know Leo's deepest, darkest secret, but after all that's happened, I wouldn't put money on it. Secrets, though—" Tears welled up, threatening to spill over. Her eyes stung, her nose hurt. *No.* She squeezed her nostrils between thumb and index finger. *Too many tears already.* She swallowed hard and waited until it passed.

"Secrets have...power. It's almost like magic, the way they undo the careful, multiple layers we've hidden them under."

"And the lesson of that?" Reth asked.

"Don't keep any?" Aza said.

He laughed softly. "Good luck with that, my dear. Let's pack up and leave these secrets in the past."

They did, but Aza now believed the past was, in many ways, in front of her yet.

EPILOGUE

THE FIRST WARM DAY of March, Vijo, Aza, and Reth arrived at the farm around lunchtime. They were immediately swept up in the boisterous vortex that was Ness and Gerland's family. Eguin was right in it, playing games with the kids. Rimna had come with Gerland's clan and she waved to Aza from the porch where she and Reva were visiting. Karol, Eltah, and Pats would all be joining the picnic.

Maleka's spirit hovered over Luftva like a rain cloud, but today Aza was comforted by the fact that if Maleka could look down on this gathering, she would see her beautiful children, safe and healthy in such a large, happy family.

Gerland, carrying both Capsia and Emke, came to them with greetings, putting the children down on the grass.

Aza reached into her pocket and knelt down. "I brought you something special."

The children's reactions showed their divergent personalities; Emke stood in place, wide-eyed, open, but holding back, while Capsia bounded over, boldly eager.

"For you, Caps, a butterfly." Aza brought it to her mouth and breathed a blessing: *may you float through life collecting all good things*. The charms were fastened to tiny chain bracelets. She put it on Capsia's wrist.

Aza turned to Emke, opened her hand and said, "For you, I have a—"

"A bird," he said, fascinated.

"Yes, a special bird called a crane." She blessed his: *may you fly high and safe over all life's troubles*. She put it on him. Both children fingered and beamed at their bracelets. The blessings were really too large for a charm to hold, but Aza could only give what was in her heart. She fervently hoped the kids would sense their mother's presence in the charms she had given to Aza.

Vijo soon lured Capsia away, showing her how to lie on her side and roll down the gently sloping hill. Aza picked up Emke and laughed, watching them. He laughed too. She looked into his huge hazel eyes, so like Maleka's.

"Hey," she said, "you remember me, right? I'm your Auntie Aza."

She felt her mind catch for a moment; a catch that was both a snag and a comprehension.

Aza squeezed Emke tightly to her chest—an action she felt was imperative in order to keep her heart from bursting. She pulled back, looked him in the eyes again and said, "I am actually, really, literally your aunt! We're *family*. I'm your Aunt Aza. Can you say that?"

"Zaz," he said, except it came out more like *Zaza*.

Aza's heart almost stopped. He remembered her from the visits to the country house when his mother was still alive! "Yes, yes, yes," she whispered. "I am Auntie Zaz. Or Zaza, even better. Would you like to roll down the hill like Capsia and Vijo?"

He grinned and struggled to get down. "Zaza roll, too." She nuzzled his neck—a rushed affection which he did not return. But that was all right; he'd already given her more that she could have asked for, certainly more than she'd expected. She lowered him to the grass, and he ran off yelling, "Roll down! Zaza roll, too."

Vijo scooped Emke up and spun him. He arched back and laughed so infectiously that everyone within hearing distance joined in.

Aza took a moment to grasp what had just happened. At last, something good, something pure and wonderful, had arisen out of the nightmare of finding out her mother was Sior Puraples. Emke and Capsia were her niece and nephew, and she was their aunt for forever and always, and nothing and nobody could take that away from her. She had a real family to love.

Squealing, she threw herself onto the grass and rolled down the spring green hill. Each time her body circled around, Aza saw the shimmering skyline of Maripesa, its pink cathedral spire catching sunlight again and again and again.

ACKNOWLEDGEMENTS

I have a three-quarters of a century of people to thank, but it isn't my job to bore people, so I'll try to edit.

Thank you to writer and editor, Charles Coleman Finlay, for a timely and insightful developmental edit of this manuscript and for his subsequent coaching. His advice, support, and enthusiasm for the story helped move it out of my computer and into the world, and got me over a very large mental/emotional roadblock. My thanks, also, to Hilary Turner for her editing assistance. I am indebted to my niece, Diana Shepard Stephens, for a late, great, eagle-eyed edit so thorough that it still amazes me. She not only cleaned up my chronically confused commas, but also pointed out spelling and word errors, typos, and extra or missing words that had escaped multiple previous edits and proofreads. I also value her occasional offered opinions on the style and/or readability of certain passages, as well as her hearts and smiley faces. To my cadre of Advance Copy Readers, thank you from the bottom of my heart for your willingness to help, your feedback, and your keen eyes.

Thank you to:

- my 4K creativity partners Suze Corte and Quinn Corte for knowing, supporting, and believing in me.

- my sons Carson Metzger and Tyler Metzger for always being interested and interesting, offering both wisdom and practical advice and for always being there for me.

- my step-kids Tara Eden, Karissa Fyrrar, and Coral Feigin for letting me grow on you. It's mutual.

- my brother Robbie for lifting me with sincere praise, and my broader family: nieces and nephew, cousins, and all my in-laws for your love, support, and for being readers.

- Group: Pat Ritter Ritchie, Lisa Black Auerbach, and Suze Corte. You know what we are to each other. Without us, I couldn't have done anything as well as I have.

- my writing friends and groups who have kept me writing and improving at it for over twenty-five years. Sherry D. Ramsey, Julie A. Serroul, The Story Forge Writing Group, Genre Writers of Atlantic Canada, 7th Prime Viable Paradise people, Codex, and the early Nanowrimo community.

- my friends Kathy Griffith and Barb Donovan for their ever-present support and encouragement.

- my husband Barry, who doesn't love any written fiction (though he lives in hope for a movie version of my work), but who loves me more and better than I have any right to expect.

- my parents, Edwina and Corey, who were intelligent, creative people, forward thinking, open to new ideas, and imbued with a strong sense of justice and compassion. No matter what kind of crazy plot and wacky characters I set out to write, my stories always echo your values, your souls. I consider that a very good thing.

ABOUT THE AUTHOR

Nancy SM Waldman ended up in the woods of Cape Breton, Nova Scotia, Canada after growing up in Texas, enjoying lengthy stays in Connecticut, and a short one in London, England. She lives with her husband Barry in a house built in 1900, which they, in a fit of newlywed enthusiasm, painted in five bright colors in the early 2000s. The paint is peeling, but their love is adhering nicely.

Nancy's short stories have been published online in AE: the Canadian Review of Science Fiction (Editor's Choice Winner), Perihelion, Fantasy Scroll, and others; in anthologies, including Tesseracts Twenty, Futuristica, Vol 1, Lazurus Rising, and all the outstanding Third Person Press books. Her two volumes of collected short stories, *As Far As* and *Rooster's Dawn* were published in 2021. Readers have described these stories as "fascinating and strange, with brilliant beauty," "layered," "funny," and "consistently excellent." She is a member of the Science Fiction & Fantasy Writers Association and SF Canada.

She has two sons, three step-daughters, and four amazing grandkids. In addition to writing, Nancy enjoys cooking, growing plants, all kinds of creative arts, and helping with Barry's educational charity, EPIC.

Find Nancy online:

- Website: https://nancysmwaldman.com

- Newsletter: https://nancysmwaldman.eo.page

- Social, etc: https://linktr.ee/nancysmwaldman

- EPIC: https://epiccharity.com

Maidenform

An alternate history, science fiction, road trip!

In 1956, socialite Monique Rodney is caught in a web of eerie intrigue after she embarks on a road trip to deliver a mysterious package for her old acquaintance and fugitive from the FBI, Robert "Oppie" Oppenheimer. Traveling in ever-widening circles from Virginia to New Mexico in a series of fabulous fifties cars, Monique must protect her innocent companions—nephew, Tommy and book buddy, Sandy (who may not be as innocent as she appears)—while staying ahead of various interested, sometimes violent parties, and coping with the unexpected presence of other-worldly technology. The journey exposes her closely-held secrets, returns her to a past she had long ago disavowed, and accelerates her into a future she never could have imagined.

Coming later in 2025

The Kindest Chaos

Book Two: The Last Magic City

Our four main characters from *Every Rule Undone* are back—making trouble, making progress, making love, making magic, and maybe even churning butter—in this second book set on the islands of Maripesa!

This story focuses on healer Vijo Besin, whose scholarly interest in all kinds of magic has turned into a full-time endeavor—or is it an obsession? Aza Gen finds that organizing a new kind of society while dealing with an increasingly complicated personal life is challenging. Bek struggles to reconcile her very important position with her still-youthful proclivities. The angsty antagonist Ferjival Puraples searches for his sliver of happiness by making fundamental changes in his life. But how will these people and the city-state of Maripesa react when a true antagonist arises from the last place any of them expect?

Coming as soon as possible!